DEDICATION

This novel is dedicated with love to my wife, Ann. I am forever grateful for her love and support. It is also dedicated in loving memory of my grandparents, Alice "Kitty" Tobin, Edward Raymond Tobin, Heath Skinner Seapy, and Ophelia "Bunny" Seapy.

ACKNOWLEDGMENTS

Special thanks to my friend, Chris Becker, who suggested I revisit a series of short stories I wrote back in 1989-1990.

Special thanks also to my friend, Chris Berry, for his support and suggestions while writing this book.

CHAPTER 1

Friday 21 November, 2008. Buena Park, California. Just after 9:30 p.m.

Traffic on Beach Boulevard is heavy this evening, and many of the drivers are getting irritated with it. Victor Trent sits behind the wheel of his Sentra, waiting for the light to change so he can turn into the parking lot of the Orange Curtain night club. In the passenger seat is his younger brother, Arnold, ogling the women walking by.

After the light changes, Victor scowls and makes the turn into the parking lot. As he pulls into a space, he looks over at his brother. "What time is it?"

Arnold whips out his cell phone. "Nine thirty-five p.m., big brother. We should hurry up and get inside to get a good table. Katrina is DJ tonight for the karaoke." He chuckles. "I so love watching people make fools of themselves, and you know, Katrina enjoys having us here. It's good for her morale."

Victor smirks and laughs as he and Arnold exit the car and head toward the club. "Kat could care less about me. Oh yes, she is polite to me, but that is only because she does not want to offend you. She thinks I'm way too cerebral, far too jaded, and too stubborn and fussy for my own good." Pausing and noting Arnold's rather quizzical look, Victor continues. "Look, she is your fiancée. I am happy for you both, unlike Mom and Dad. I brought you here tonight because your car broke down again, and it was an excuse to get out of the house for a while. You know that I detest these techno dance clubs."

Arnold sighs. "I know that, Victor. I really think Kat likes you though. At least you give her the benefit of the doubt. Mom and Dad, I don't think they ever will."

Victor nods, keeping a poker face.

After a brief wait in line, the bouncer checks their IDs, and they go in. Loud techno music blares from speakers strategically placed around the club. The dance floor is packed. Victor and Arnold make their way to the upper level in the back, where Katrina is setting up the karaoke equipment. Arnold waves to her, and she waves back, beaming. She then takes a quick glance over at Victor and nods.

"Yes, that woman is really into me," Victor mutters sarcastically.

Arnold pretends not to hear him.

Arnold finds a table right near the karaoke stage and watches Katrina go through her sound checks. Victor looks back out at the main room and watches the people dance. "Hey, Arn. I think I will go sit in the main room for a while and sneer at the rabble."

Arnold nods. "Whatever makes you happy." He sees a rather sinister look cross Victor's face. "Not too happy. I mean, you can't be throwing the lemmings off the cliff. It's way too unsanitary."

Victor finds himself a small table with a good view of the dance floor. He orders a Cuba libre from the cocktail waitress and observes. He sees several attractive women, none of whom, he is certain, are up to his intellectual standards. At twenty-eight, Victor is a haughty, jaded intellectual. His mind is keen. He enjoys spirited debate and discussion, and he is convinced of his ethical and mental superiority over humanity at large. He proudly calls himself a misfit among misfits. He smirks.

The only thinking going on in this place is about sex and drugs and lousy techno music.

He watches the crowd intently, observing and judging all of them ultimately unworthy of his august presence. *Arnold needs to get that car of his fixed once and for all. I'm tired of bailing him out so he can hang out with Kat.* He sighs heavily and shakes his head. *I guess it beats spending the evening at home. Dad is being particularly obnoxious these days.*

Shortly after ten o'clock, Brenda Rennert pulls into the parking lot in her silver Honda Civic. She comes to this club frequently when she is in Orange County. Dancing, for her, is a release as well as a celebration of being. A bit short, she is considered handsome. She has long, auburn hair and piercing green eyes, classic Dutch features. Brenda is looking sharp tonight, her little black dress hugging her slender body. She is wearing small ruby earrings, a necklace with a cross that has a small ruby in its center, and a stylish ruby ring on her right hand. Checking herself in the rearview mirror, she nods in approval.

What a week, she thinks. *I just want to lose myself on that dance floor for a few hours.*

Brenda looks like she is twenty-two, but that is off by over two hundred years.

She was born on May 16, 1753, in Rensselaer, New York. Brenda is 255 years old, because she became a vampire on June 1, 1775 at age of twenty-two.

She isn't at the club to feed, having already bled someone on Katella Avenue, near the House of Mouse. She is going to the Orange Curtain with just dancing on her agenda.

Brenda reaches the front door of the club and waves to the bouncers. "Hi, Chad! Hi, Alvin! How's it going?"

They both look at her and smile.

Chad unclips the rope and makes a theatrical bow. "It's going well, Bren. First decent night here in weeks. Blasted recession is hurting everyone. Go on in."

She gives both of them a beaming smile as she enters the club. As usual, when she walks past them, she feels Chad ogling her and thinking of what he'd like to do with her. *Always the same,* she thought. *Chad wants to do me. No chance, boyo. You're not my type.*

As soon as she pays the cover charge and enters the club proper, Brenda's preternatural senses notice that the atmosphere is considerably different on a psychic level. There are always a few dims, some latents, but tonight, there is a bright—actually, two brights. But one is loud and clear over the general hum of the uninteresting thought patterns of most of the club's patrons.

Such depth. That is most unusual for this club. One she identifies rather quickly, having felt that presence before. *Ah. Arnold Trent is here tonight, doubtless with Karaoke Girl. I don't know what he sees in her. No depth, that woman.* She then finds the one who is, on a telepathic level, broadcasting like a radio beacon. She observes him while the cocktail waitress takes his order for another Cuba libre. *Ah. That is Arnold's eldest brother, Victor. He resents being here.*

Watching the cocktail waitress go to another table, Brenda decides to have a little fun at Victor's expense. She looks at the waitress and thinks, *Forget.* As usual with the general population, the waitress does exactly what Brenda suggests; she promptly forgets about Victor's order.

They are so easy to play mind games with.

Brenda then goes out and dances for about fifteen minutes. She notes that Victor's snide commentary drops off, a bit confused that he has not yet received his drink order. She looks at the cocktail waitress; thinks, *Remember*; and walks off the dance floor.

The cocktail waitress jumps, rushes to the bar, and gets Victor's Cuba libre to him in haste. "I am so sorry, sir!" the waitress says, shaken.

Victor looks up, smiles, and hands her a tip. "No problem. It's so loud in here I can't blame you for losing track of my order."

Brenda notes the polite behavior. *Very well then. Ticked off and being petty though he is, he is not a snobby jerk like so many of the local intelligentsia are.* She then sits down at a table and observes Victor for a few minutes. *Keen mind. Very inquisitive. Feels like a misfit among misfits. A lot of what he does, he feels like he does "for the good of the order," like being here tonight to help Arnold out.. Lives at home. Twenty-eight years old. Still a virgin.* She continues reading Victor's surface thoughts. *This one could be interesting to my natra; he shows all the signs of being an old soul.* She looks over at Victor again. *Is he special enough though? I must ponder this for a while.* She stands and returns to the dance floor.

At about eleven o'clock, Victor lets out with a very caustic thought: *This place is filled with losers. How vain, how shallow they all are. What a waste of food and air!*

This struck something of a raw nerve with Brenda. Scowling, she looks right at Victor and thinks, *If this place is filled with vain, shallow, worthless losers, and you are here, what must that make you?*

Victor's reaction is instantaneous. He jumps as if stabbed. His mind, which had basically been an open beacon all that evening, was suddenly shut off to all. The only sign one could read was by looking into his piercing hazel eyes. She watches as he starts a very methodical scan of the room, seeking the source of that thought.

Now Brenda is impressed. *Such speed! Being able to lock his mind up that tight against outside intrusions! I have never witnessed a mortal able to accomplish that before.* She leaves the dance floor, pulls out her cell phone, takes a quick picture of Victor, finds a private table, and speed dials her natra.

"Yes, Brenda?" a low, husky female voice says over the cell speaker. "What do you have for me?"

Brenda answers in the special tongue of the Plaz Seschni. "Aurea, I have witnessed a mortal at this club throwing up a mental field of protection instantly, blocking all outside thoughts and basically terminating all outgoing thoughts. It was extraordinary! I am sending up his picture."

Aurea responds momentarily. "I see. Pray, what did you do that provoked him into this defensive measure? I am certain he did not take that step just for laughs. I see, shall we say, shock and outrage on his face. A casual observer might see that face as emotionless, but I do not."

Brenda then explains the events of the evening in exact detail while Aurea listens intently.

"That's not sporting, dear, but it is fascinating in its own right. Does your phone have video capability?"

"It does, for about a couple of minutes. What do you have in mind?"

"If this Trent fellow is not too agitated now, perhaps you can stream me some video? I would like to be able to study him with something more substantial than that still photo."

Brenda looks over at Victor. He looks calmer, still in defensive mode psychically, but the agitation is passing. "I can do it. Give me a few minutes, and I will upload it to you and call back."

She moves carefully, blending in with the crowd so Victor will not take notice of her. When she has a clear line of sight, she carefully uses her cell and activates the digital video for about ninety seconds. She then walks over to a quiet table and uploads the packet to Aurea's computer.

When she is about to call, Aurea calls her back instead. "You have found not just an old soul, my foara; you have located an ancient soul. I shall have to find out more about this Victor Trent so he can be evaluated appropriately."

"Do you need me to do anything else? Sadly, he just isn't my type. He's definitely too melancholy and too cerebral to spark my interest. For you, though…"

Aurea chuckles. "No need to put yourself out further, Brenda. At least not tonight. I'll have Zachary troll the various databases and find out what I need to know before I take any action regarding this fellow. I have seen mortals do what he did before, but it is very rare.

In the end, he could prove to be a rather valuable find, and if so, you will be rewarded."

"That sounds grand indeed." She watches Victor as he walks back into the karaoke room. "It looks like he is getting ready to leave. I really shook him up. Well, back to the dance. A fine evening to you, Aurea."

Aurea bids Brenda a good night and ends the call. Swaying to the beat, Brenda bops back onto the dance floor. She catches the surface thoughts of a tall, blond man with piercing blue eyes. She smiles at him, thinking, *You want to do what to me? Make me beg for it and do it all night long? Honey, you couldn't even keep up with me if you tried! If you only knew how foolish I could make you look…*

It was 2:30 a.m. on Saturday, November 22 on Staten Island, Greater New York, where Aurea resides. A rather nondescript two-story house in a quiet neighborhood, Aurea shares the house with her longtime friend Carol Ann Vincent. She looks like she is in her early thirties—medium height, slight build, and long, black hair with piercing brown eyes that look like they could see into your soul. She has very patrician, classic Mediterranean features. Tonight, she is dressed in a tank top and shorts, staring intently into her computer screen, studying the video of Victor Trent that Brenda sent her. It has been many years since she has found a mortal to be this intriguing. She toys with the large ruby ring on her right hand, thoughts racing through her head. It is a real find, after all these decades!

When Aurea Octavia Bodellini was born, the Roman Republic was still a going concern. Raised in Pompeii, she became a vampire at the age of thirty-one. An elder of Order Ruby, she is now 2120 years old. Aurea has seen a lot, done a lot, and tends to be a bit jaded. Tonight, though, she is excited.

I must learn more about this man.

She makes a call through her computer to the recognized supreme computer geek of greater New York, a mortal named Zachary. Zack accepts the connection, and his face fills Aurea's computer screen. She smirks, noting the several cans of energy drinks scattered around Zack's workstations. He always has at least six computers going at any one time.

Zack looks up into his web cam and smiles. "Madame Aurea! How have you been? What's up? You definitely have something on your mind."

Aurea favors Zack with a smile. "Yes, my friend. I do need your services, your expertise. I need you to check the databases and find out everything there is to know about Victor Trent of Orange, California. I have sent you the information we have in an attachment to the secure e-mail."

Zack takes a long draw from his energy drink, punches a couple buttons. "I got it. I'm sending my bot out. Give me about fifteen or twenty minutes and I should be able to send you enough information to know this Trent character better than his mother."

"Call me back when you have the data."

Zack nods and breaks the connection.

Aurea sighs. "Such a keen mind, such a great talent, and he has decided to go with Order Emerald once he is ready to cross over. Oh well. At least Sapphire won't get him." She then meditates and awaits Zack's return call. *I need to relax. This Trent needs to be handled carefully.*

A few minutes later, Carol Ann comes into the office, breaking Aurea's reverie. She notices right away that her housemate is blood drunk, her elegant green dress torn in several places, with several prominent blood stains.

"What the blazes happened to you? Who did you kill?"

Carol Ann regains her composure. "I was just walking through the park a few blocks away, when some stupid punk put a knife in my back and said he was going to rape me. So, I whirled on him, took the knife and castrated him, and then I drank all his blood and tore his body to shreds." She looks down at her dress. "Of course, I also ruined this lovely dress. What a jerk!"

Aurea smiles benignly. "Go get cleaned up and sleep it off. You downed enough blood for a couple weeks. If there is no body left to be found, the cops aren't likely to care. It's just another missing person in the big city."

In a flash, Carol Ann tore off the dress. She admires her own svelte form. "I think he was high on crack or something. His blood tasted off. He ruined the underwear too. Geez! What a night I'm having!"

Aurea watches her leave the office. *That one seems to find trouble. Fourth time this year she has killed. Justified, granted, but for a Ruby at five hundred and thirty years, that can be troubling.* She sighs and ponders. *Impetuous, but she is a fine and loyal friend.* Her computer beeps, and Zack's face comes back on her screen.

Zack chugs another energy drink and then looks up. "Well, the nets don't have a lot of information about this Victor Trent. No criminal records. A couple of the alphabet agencies have minor files on him because he has written articles critical of the American imperium. They basically don't care about him. He was born in Van Nuys on May seventeenth, nineteen eighty, firstborn child of Robert and Susan Trent. Victor graduated with a master's degree from California State University, Fullerton this year. Double major: criminal justice and philosophy. He has roughly thirty-five K worth of student loans outstanding. Has a sister, Zoe Magdalene, born in Northridge on September twenty-fourth, nineteen eighty-three. Finally, his youngest brother, Arnold Richard, was born on April fifteenth, nineteen eighty-six in Brea. Anyway, I have sent you the files with the links where available. Hope it helps you with your project."

Aurea starts scanning the files. "Yes, Zack, as always, you have been most helpful." She presses a few buttons. "You will note that what I just sent you is substantially larger than your normal fee." She watches him blink in surprise and nod accordingly. "You may regard that as hush money, Zack. I must have your word that this entire matter and any future involvement you might have with me regarding Victor Robert Trent of Orange, California, will remain strictly confidential until I tell you otherwise. Do we understand each other, Zachary?"

Looking a bit shocked, he nods vigorously. "Yes, Madame Aurea. We never had this conversation."

Aurea smiles benignly. "I knew I could count on you. Have a pleasant night, Zack." With that, she breaks the connection. She starts reading and pondering all the material she has received with intense interest. *Let's see if you are what I think you might be, Victor.*

Victor woke up to the sound of his alarm clock at nine o'clock. He had a fitful sleep, dwelling on that odd telepathic incident at that blasted club.

I have heard, if you will, random thoughts before, but that was directed right at me! I really wonder who did it and why!

He goes down the hall and enters the bathroom, where he showers and shaves quickly. He has to be at the store by ten thirty to open up. Due to the bad economy, the only job Victor had managed to find was as a sales clerk at Dasher's, a secondhand bookstore and DVD outlet.

I didn't go to school to be a clerk, no matter what Dad says.

He then goes back to his room, gets dressed, and then walks downstairs. As usual, his mother is up, but his father is still in bed.

As he pours himself a bowl of cereal, his mother puts down her newspaper and smiles at him. "Did you have a good time at the club last night, dear?"

Victor grabs a cup of coffee and then sits at the dining room table. "What do you think, Mom? Arnold needed a ride because his car was in the shop. That club plays techno. I hate techno. That place is filled with boring, trendy wannabes. I'm not into karaoke, which is what Kat does there at the club. So, do you think I had a good time?"

Susan Trent scowls a bit. "No need to be so bitter, darling. I'm sure Arnold appreciated you taking him there. How was dear Katrina?"

Victor chuckles. "You accuse me of being bitter. Now you are being sarcastic, mother. Still, on the off chance that you really do care, Kat seemed her normal self. I did not spend much time in the karaoke lounge. I had a couple drinks and sat and watched the people dance. I got irritated. No big deal."

Susan lets that subject drop. "Are you going to be home for Thanksgiving? Do you know if your sister and brother will be here? I'm just trying to plan this out. It would be nice if all you kids could be here. Grandma Azalea and Grandpa Fred will be here. I know that they would love to see you."

"Well, the store is closed that day, so I will be here. I don't know what Zoe's plans are, and as for Arnold, I'm sure that he and Kat will be here. It's free food for them after all. Are you inviting Uncle Reggie this year?"

Susan sniffs a bit, seeming flustered. "Now, honey, you know your dad doesn't get along well with his brothers. I know that Reggie, unlike Clyde, lives close by, but I doubt he would want to come."

Victor just rolls his eyes at that. Before he can respond, his cell phone rings. "Well, Mom, guess who is calling me? Uncle Reggie! Imagine that." He gets up from the table and walks into the living room, leaving his mother to tsk in disapproval in solitude. "Hi, Reggie! What's up?"

"Hi, Vic! Got any plans for tonight? Hope you don't because that wicked cool blues band I was telling you about will be performing at Chez Bing in Burbank tonight. Worth the drive! I kid you not!"

"Wow! You mean Midnight Silk will be performing tonight? I'll be there for sure! I get off work at seven. What time will the band start their set?"

"They'll start at about nine. The club is on Glenoaks, a couple blocks north of Olive on the right hand side of the street. It isn't very big, so pay attention. If you get to Magnolia, you went too far."

"Sounds excellent, Reggie. I have so wanted to see this band since you lent me that CD. I will see you there at about eight thirty, traffic gods willing."

"Zoe and I will save you a seat at a table. Oh yeah. Forgot to tell you that Zoe will be there. She's coming down from Santa Barbara. She will be staying with your grandparents a few days. You can tell Sue that Zoe will be there for Thanksgiving."

"Sounds great, Reggie. I'll see you and Zoe tonight." Victor clicks the end button and then goes back and sits down with his mother. "Well, Mom, Uncle Reggie said to let you know that Zoe will be here for Thanksgiving. I will be seeing them tonight in Burbank. I'm going to see a truly excellent blues performance. So much better than that blasted techno crap."

Susan nods. "So you won't be home for dinner tonight. Well, I hope you kids have fun. Say hi to Uncle Reggie for me."

After cleaning off the table, Victor heads out to work, beaming. Spending time with his uncle is always mentally stimulating. Zoe, well, she always makes Victor feel important and wanted.

At last, I'll have an evening with intelligent people.

Victor leaves the store promptly at 7:00 p.m. He changes his clothes and then takes the 91 freeway to the 5 freeway and heads up to Burbank. Traffic is light, so he reaches the club just before 8:00 p.m. He arrives just as Zoe pulls into the lot in her silver Toyota Corolla. Victor stands by his car while Zoe gets out of hers.

She's beautiful, as always.

She sees him, and her face lights up. Victor walks over to her, and they embrace.

"It's great to see you, little sister."

They look into each other's eyes and smile. Anyone who did not know they were brother and sister would likely presume they were lovers.

"It's great seeing you too, big brother. I've just been so busy up there at the university! It has been hard to get any time off!"

As they start walking toward the door of the club, they see their Uncle Reggie pull up in his old, green Ford Pinto.

"So, how are Mom and Dad doing these days?"

"About the same as usual," Victor replies as their uncle gets out of his car and starts walking toward them.

Zoe puts her arm around Victor's waist. "They're really that bad, huh? Geez. I was hoping they might have calmed down a bit since you graduated and all. I guess Dad is still pissed off that you didn't knuckle under and get an MBA. That's rude and petty and venal of him."

Reggie gives Victor and Zoe a hug, and then they head to the door. Victor is pleased to see how intelligent the crowd looks, unlike the folks at the Orange Curtain last night. He is a bit bothered, though, by the vibe he is picking up from one of the bouncers. This guy definitely has a chip on his shoulder, and he is being unnecessarily rude, in Victor's mind, toward some of the female patrons. When he sees the man eye Zoe and scowl, well, that is intolerable.

After his uncle goes in, Victor shows the bouncer his ID, locks eyes with him, and says in a very low voice, "Stop being so rude to the women. It is disrespectful and lacks honor. Just do your job or go babble in the corner for a while and grow up. I will not let you spoil my sister's evening."

The burly man's jaw drops. He nods and mumbles, "Sorry," and walks away.

The other bouncer shrugs and checks Zoe's ID without incident.

After they find a table, the bouncer goes back to the door and treats all the incoming patrons respectfully.

Zoe looks at her brother. "What did you say to him, Vic? His attitude just completely changed. He was being such a jerk!"

Victor shrugs. "I simply told the man to do his job and stop treating the women so rudely. I was not going to allow him to be rude to you. I am here tonight to enjoy some great music and great conversation with my two favorite people in the world. Nobody here deserves to be hassled by a jerk with a chip on his shoulder."

Reginald Trent nods, and Zoe gives Victor a peck on the cheek. "My brother is always looking out for me."

Victor chuckles at that, but then he nods, knowing that the statement is true.

None of the patrons of the club might have taken note of what Victor did to the bouncer, but two of the members of the band did: Midnight Silk and Vernon Scott. Walter Scott, the other band member, had been doing some equipment checks when the incident took place, thus missing it.

You did just see what that mortal did, Vernon? Silk asks telepathically.

Not only saw, *Silkie,* Vernon thinks back, *I* heard *it, loud and clear. Never seen a mortal do anything like that. How about y'all?*

Drat, Walter thinks as he finishes the sound checks. *I miss out on all the interesting stuff.*

Silk points at the table where the Trents are seated. *Three brights at the same table, and they are all related. The oldest one is Reginald Trent. I recognize him. He has been to some of our gigs before. The guy who mentally thrashed the bouncer, he is Victor Trent, and the woman is Zoe Trent, his sister.*

Vernon frowns. *They're brother and sister? What a shame! They make such a nice couple! Look at them! Their faces are beaming, they look into each other's eyes, and they pay attention and actually* listen *to each other! The chemistry is just striking!*

Silk nods. *Indeed. I shall chat with them after our first set. They might be persons of interest to one of our elders.* They then resume getting ready for their gig.

What might not be obvious is that Midnight Silk, along with Vernon and Walter Scott, are Ruby Order vampires who happen to be highly talented blues musicians and are much in demand. Their tales are interesting ones. Midnight Silk was born on the Adler Plantation in South Carolina on March 1, 1830. Her given name is Sallie Jean Adler. Her delicate features, light skin (an octoroon or high yellow in the slavery era) earned her a spot as a hostess at the manor house. She escaped in the spring of 1861 and became a vampire in March of 1862. She has a voice that rivals the famous Lady Day, Billie Holiday. While she is tall, her two male companions, Vernon and Walter Scott, tower over her. Unlike her, they are pure African, born in West Africa in the summer of 1809. They are twins. They were sold into slavery in 1827 and shipped to America, where they were sold at the Charleston slave auction and worked the cotton fields at a large plantation in northern Alabama. They escaped together in September of 1834 and became vampires on the same night on October 13, 1834. They have incredible bass voices and make the perfect backup for Midnight. They have been performing in this ensemble since the early 1980s.

At precisely 9:00 p.m., the house lights dim, and the band comes out. The audience applauds, as does Victor, with quite some enthusiasm. These folks had been there and done that.

Toward the end of their first set, Silk points at Reggie. "Sir? Do you have a request tonight? I'd like to sing a song by Lady Day, and I can tell you have one on your mind. What would you like to hear?"

A stunned Reggie takes a moment to respond. "Anything would be great, but if I have to choose one for tonight, it would be 'Don't Explain.'"

"That's a fine choice, sir. Thank you. I will dedicate it to you and your charming companions."

She then proceeds to sing the song while Victor and Zoe sit, awestruck. Vernon just smiles.

Silkie sure knows how to wow an audience, especially when she has ulterior motives.

They finish the set with another song of their own. "We'll be taking a twenty-minute break, friends," Vernon says, "but stick around for the second set. We'll be doing some classic jazz and more righteous blues!"

As the audience applauds, Vernon makes eye contact with Silk. "I'll give Dave a call, let him know what we saw happen here, and see what he thinks ought to be done."

Silk nods. "I will go and chat with the Trents, get a feel for them." She looks over at Walter. "I suspect you have found an audience member you can get a pint from? I sense you thirst tonight." Walter nods in the affirmative.

With that, Vernon takes out his cell phone and walks off to make his call in private, Walter walks into the audience to get a pint of blood to slake his thirst (from a sweet young lady who was just beaming to see him approach), and Silk walks over to the table where the Trents are seated. Reggie and Victor both stand while she approaches.

Chivalry isn't dead, she thinks approvingly. Telepathically suggesting to the rest of the audience to ignore them so they can have some level of privacy, she smiles at the Trents. "May I join you fine folks?"

Reggie smiles. "Of course, Miss Silk."

He pulls out a chair, and Silk sits down.

"It is such a pleasure to actually talk to you! I have been a fan of your band for several years now."

She makes eye contact with all three of them, taking their measure. *They are all special,* she thinks. *They are all old souls. Zoe is very old, and Victor is positively ancient. He is very special.* Breaking off, she smiles. "Please, call me Silk. All my friends do." She looks over at Victor. "Are you enjoying the music? I sense that it resonates with you, speaks to your soul."

"Interesting that you would put it that way, ma'am, I mean, Silk. You're right. A lot of your original songs seem to transport me back. They show me images of a time past that I likely experienced." He looks straight into her eyes, fascinated by the depth he perceives. "I know that this is a really odd question, but do you believe in reincarnation?"

The boldness with which the question is asked surprises Silk. "Actually, Victor, I am certain that reincarnation is a fact. I have seen karma in action. It just makes sense, really. I mean, just one lifetime and that's it? That, to me, is the belief that makes no sense."

Zoe smiles. "You know, Victor and I are sure that we have been together in many past lives. We know that we are twin flames."

Silk nods in assent.

Silk then receives a telepathic message from Vernon. *Dave says to call Aurea after the show. This is more her area of expertise.* She thinks back an affirmative reply. She looks over at Victor. "What kind of images are you seeing when you listen to our songs?"

"I see groups of slaves working in fields on indigo and rice plantations. I see an auction. I see slaves working in warehouses on a wharf, filled with cotton. It is so vivid, just like I was there."

Silk smiles knowingly. "The ways of the Weave can be difficult to discern, Victor. I recommend you continue your studies. Be especially aware of your karmic ties and your cohort group." She looks over at Zoe. "I am not an expert on this subject, but I am certain that you and your brother have been together in many past lives. I am familiar with the twin flames concept, and I am certain you are correct."

Zoe reaches over and gently squeezes Victor's hand. "I know it is so."

Victor's face lit up with a rare smile. "It is refreshing to be able to talk about this and be taken seriously. All of my objectivist associates would think I was a raving, irrational lunatic to assert that reincarnation is valid. I keep hoping to find tangible proof that I could wave in their faces, make them see."

"I think it is fair to say that Ayn Rand was an excellent philosopher when it comes to the fields of epistemology, metaphysics, and especially ethics. Her esthetics, what she found pleasing in art? To each their own, says I. I can certainly understand her disdain for organized religion. To deny even the possibility of the divine spark, well, that was an error." She chuckles. "Well, she knows better now."

All around the table nod.

With five minutes before the next set, Silk shakes Reggie's hand. "It has been a pleasure to meet you, Reggie. I trust we will be seeing you again at another show soon."

Reggie nods enthusiastically. "Rely on it, Silk."

She then shakes hands with Zoe. "I hope to see you at another show soon. You are very blessed to have a brother like Victor. You are very strong as well, Zoe. Don't sell yourself short."

"Thank you, Silk. We will stay until you are done with the third set. It was great to meet you!"

She saves Victor for last on purpose. She looks into his eyes, seeing strength, power, purpose. "It's a pleasure to meet you, Victor. I am certain that you will have a most interesting life. Live each life to the fullest, and learn all you can. Have fun while you do it though. That is essential."

Victor shakes her hand and does not break eye contact, very unusual for a mortal. "Thank you, Silk. I will definitely come see your band perform again, maybe even bring some friends." After that, Silk takes her leave and returns to the stage to start the second set.

Victor looks over at Zoe, perplexed. "Did she infer that I have a difficult time having fun?"

"Infer nothing, brother dear. You do have issues with having fun and relaxing. Lighten up!"

The second set concludes at ten fifteen. Some people leave at that time, but most remain, including the Trents, who are talking animatedly about the music and watching the crowd. Midnight looks at her cell phone and sees a text message. It is from Aurea, urging her to call between sets if at all possible. She heads into the small dressing room and makes the call.

"A fine evening to you, Aurea."

"Good evening, my friend. Dave West told me that you and Vernon experienced a fascinating psychic event at the club tonight. He mentioned a name that became familiar to me last night: Victor Trent."

A picture then appears on Midnight's cell screen.

"Is this the man we are speaking of?"

"Yes, my friend. He is here tonight with his sister, Zoe, and his uncle, Reginald Trent. They are fascinating people. I talked to them between the first and second sets. Victor reminds me of someone I knew back in my mortal days. I can't quite place him, but the feeling is strong."

"I trust your intuition, Silk. What did you discuss with the Trents? What are your impressions of them?"

"They are all brights, no question," Silk states. "I used no glamours, no form of mind control. I am quite certain Victor and Zoe would have seen through them and become suspicious if I had. Reggie might have fallen for them; he was in awe of me. We talked about the music, reincarnation, and objectivism. Strange mix, granted, but you know, the conversation just flowed so naturally. They have many karmic ties between each other, no question. Victor is the oldest soul, but not by much. Zoe is only marginally younger. In fact, I am certain that the two of them are twin flames. Reggie is also a very old soul. I sense the touch of the Plaz on Victor and Zoe but not on Reggie. Aurea, it is such a rare pleasure to speak with truly intelligent people. I like them."

Aurea considers this for a moment. "So, Silk, you think that Victor and Zoe were vampires in a previous life? If you are right, this would make them both persons of interest."

"I know you are concentrating on Victor, and I can understand why. Unless I am seriously mistaken, he has had important roles to play in the past and will likely have such in the future. That said, let me make clear that he and Zoe are very tight. If they were not brother and sister, they would be in a committed relationship. If Victor is brought into our circles, we would do well to do likewise with Zoe. She cannot be ignored as a force in Victor's life. She would not allow it. Neither would he."

"Thank you for your insight and your initiative, my friend. I know that you have another set to play in a few minutes, and I will let you get back to your band. I see that I have some decisions to make sooner rather than later. To think, a few days ago, I was complaining to Carol Ann about how dull things had become. Well, no more of that. I guess my wish for some excitement has been granted."

"I tell you, Aurea, when I touched him, I could just feel the years, feel the energy. I had very similar impressions from Zoe. Indeed, whatever you have in mind, put it into play. Glad I could help."

Thusly, the phone call ends. Silk goes back out to the club, where Vernon and Walter are getting the equipment ready for the final set. They look at her questioningly.

All is well, she thinks to them.

They nod and go back to their tasks.

What a night.

Back at the house on Staten Island, Aurea is pacing in her office, considering what the next step ought to be. Emotions race across her face. So vexed is she that her fangs are protruding slightly from her upper lip, a clear sign that she is in deep thought.

This is a rare opportunity. I must act. Time is of the essence. However, it also needs to be done properly, by the protocols, by the numbers. This could have a major impact on Order Ruby. She paces some more and then mutters, "Actually, this could impact all three orders. Or, it could turn out to be a flash in the pan. What ought I do?" Carol Ann walks into the office, having heard Aurea mumbling and muttering and pacing. Her face shows an air of concern.

"What is troubling you, my dear? I haven't seen you fretting like this since shortly after the incident in Avignon. You are usually the calm, rational one, and I am the crazy, emotional one. Tonight, I feel like those roles have been reversed."

Simply hearing the word *Avignon* mentioned breaks Aurea out of her reverie. Her fangs retreat back into their sockets, no longer visible. She looks at her friend. "I see you have stayed out of trouble tonight. You look marvelous. It's sad that your dress was so trashed that you had to burn it."

Carol Ann scowls. "You knew I would be staying in tonight. Besides, you are just trying to distract me and change the subject. That won't work. I know you too well. You can tell me that this is none of my business, and I will respect that and go back down to the library room and read. Or you can tell me what has you so worked up and I will try and be helpful. It's your call."

Aurea sighs and sits down. Then she tells Carol Ann all she knows about Victor Trent. She shares the information that Zack had sent to her the night before. With the telling, emotions start racing across Carol Ann's face. Once Aurea is finished, Carol Ann goes over to her desktop and does some research on Zoe and Reginald Trent. Satisfied, she turns around and looks at Aurea in admiration.

"I don't think you are on the wrong track here. I agree that we should be keeping a close eye on Victor. He needs to be taken out of his comfort zone. His psychic powers will intensify in an unfamiliar environment. Then, possibly, he will do one of the things that would make it imperative for us to put him to the test and either bring him into our circles or terminate him."

Aurea nods solemnly. "Truly cold, my friend, but you are absolutely correct. He may or may not enjoy life in metropolitan Los Angeles, but it is home, and he is comfortable there, just as I once was in Pompeii." She scowls. "Just as I once was in Avignon." She pauses and stares into Carol Ann's eyes. "I know only too well that if Victor is an ancient soul and shows signs of having been an ancient vampire in the past, Maurana will have to be consulted, which will, inevitably, bring me back to the attention of Pa Anovas. I admit that that gave me pause in considering what to do. Brenda's call gave me a lot to think about. Silk's call tonight, though, really pushed me. That is why you found me so agitated."

"Well, not to add to your agitation, but, given what I see here, I have to agree with Silkie. Zoe is also a force to be reckoned with. We can't ignore her if we want Victor, especially if they really are twin flames. Granted, for a few weeks, we can separate them, but in the end, we will have to deal with her as well. Theirs is definitely not a normal brother-sister relationship. I'm sure that they can read each other's thoughts. He won't keep secrets from her for very long. She is one of about three people Victor actually trusts. Reginald Trent is another one. Reginald is bright, well read, and knows that there are ghosts and studies the paranormal. However, he presents no threat factor."

"I agree with you. Silk is right. Meanwhile, where should we move Victor so that we can keep tabs on him and see if he should be tested or if, in fact, he is just an ancient soul passing through that we really need not deal with?"

Carol Ann leans back in her chair and ponders this. "Okay. Let me see if I have this clear. What must a mortal do to make being put to the test necessary and desirable?"

Aurea replies thusly, "Generally, it boils down to 'hearing' the thoughts of a vampire when that thought is not specifically directed at you, also, coming up to a vampire and saying you know what the ring stands for. Setting someone or something on fire telepathically would also be grounds for testing." She sighs. "It tends to work best when it is simply a telepathic event. Usually, the vampire it happens to won't just kill the mortal on sight for that, unless a tangible threat is perceived."

Carol Ann nods. "Very well. That makes sense. Now, the question is, where do we want him to move, and how do we get him to go there in the shortest time feasible without tipping our hands and making him suspicious and without arousing undue attention in our own circles? That is also imperative."

Aurea considers this. "I know where we should get him to move to. Did you read his master's thesis, *An Examination of Ethics and Honorable Behavior in 21st Century Government and Political Systems*? If not, it is quite the read and most revealing."

"I will read it. However, having read some of his articles and blogs, I know that he is a firm believer in self-responsibility, self-ownership, private property, individual freedom, and so forth." Carol Ann pauses and then looks at Aurea in disbelief. "No! You can't possibly mean *that* city!" When Aurea nods, Carol Ann just stares in disbelief. "He'll *hate* it there! It stands for everything he is against! That place is the belly of the beast to him. Besides, how could we make him *want* to go there?"

Aurea smiles again, positively beaming. "Make him want to go there? No, that is not likely. Make it worth his while to suck it up and go ahead and take the job we will have offered to him? That I think we can do. Consider, Victor has a master's degree, and the only job he has found thus far in this shaky economy is as a store clerk. He is twenty-eight and still lives with his parents, with no prospect of getting out anytime soon. Plus, he has roughly thirty-five thousand dollars worth of outstanding student loans. Indeed, no, he won't *want* to go there, but I am certain we can have an offer made to him that would be against his rational self-interest to refuse. Then he will be close by, and we will be able to act, should the situation merit such."

Carol Ann shakes her head and sighs. "You are so cruel, my friend. I see your point though. Tell me how we are going to get Victor to accept a job offer in the Imperial City, Washington, DC? Who will we get to offer the job? It can't be one of us or anyone directly affiliated with any of the orders. I suspect you have some politician in mind. Now, share your plan with me, as I sense that you have this figured out."

Aurea sits down and starts working on her computer. Keying at lightning speed, she enters into the secure website for Order Ruby. "I don't so much have a politician in mind, as I think I have a connection in Los Angeles who deals with that circle of thieves." She scrolls into the metropolitan Los Angeles index and smiles when she sees the name she is looking for. "Ah yes. Cliff Nash. He can make this happen for us. He has the connections and the stomach for it. What luck! The directory says that he happens to be online now." She punches the code in for a private connection and waits.

A few seconds later, a face fills Aurea's computer screen. This man is dressed in a brown smoking jacket. He could pass for thirty-five, but Cliff is actually eighty-three years old, having been a vampire now for nearly fifty years.

He smiles and says, "Aurea, my dear. Such a rare pleasure! I haven't seen you since that Redemptionist fiasco back in two thousand five. I sense this isn't a social call. No such luck. What can I do for you?"

"I'm here with Carol Ann, who you also know. Are you alone tonight? If not, is there anyone nearby who could overhear our conversation? This is a very delicate matter. Privacy and discretion is vital."

Looking a bit stunned, Cliff says, "I am alone now. Anneliese left a couple hours ago. I'm not expecting anyone else until tomorrow afternoon." Looking a bit perplexed, he continues, "So now, what is this all about? It has to involve someone or something here in Los Angeles for you to contact me."

Carol Ann snickers a bit at the mention of Anneliese. Aurea shoots her a withering glance and then returns her attention to Cliff. She presses a few buttons.

"I am sending you some confidential files. Please look them over, and then I will tell you what I need you to do."

Cliff nods in acknowledgement. He openes the file and looks it over. A bemused look crosses his face. He looks back up. "You know,

I have heard of this Victor Trent fellow. He's an interesting writer, definitely brilliant if socially inept. No, I have never met him, but I can tell by looking at him that he fits that intellectual mold. So, what do you want me to do to him, or do you need something done for him?"

"I need you to convince a representative to give Mr. Trent a position on his staff in Washington, DC, a position that would require him to attend embassy parties and also travel to New York City on occasion for UN functions. It's probably best that this be one that has a district at least partly in Orange County."

Cliff's jaw drops in surprise. "Are you serious, Aurea? I have read enough of Trent's blogs and online articles to know that he has no use for politicians whatsoever. He doesn't believe in meaningful change via the ballot box. He thinks the current system is rigged, and he has a point. He would probably turn the job offer down flat!"

"Victor is bored and is looking for a big change in his life, one that would take him far away from his parents. This is a man with a master's degree who is working as a clerk at a secondhand bookstore. No, he won't *want* to take the job, but I am ninety percent certain that he will. That part, however, is not your concern. Is there a representative who you could convince to make Victor such an offer?"

"Without a doubt, Bob Moore from Newport Beach would be the easiest one. That guy is so malleable, if I suggested he should leap from a skyscraper in downtown LA, he would do it. I can contact him right after Thanksgiving and get him to make the offer. Will that be soon enough for you?"

Aurea smirks. "That will do nicely, Cliff. "Make sure, when the job gets offered, that Victor is told that a third of his student loans will be written off after having been on the staff for six months. It helps to have a hook like that when one is making an offer to a hostile recipient. Now, as to your fee, I will give you ten ounces of gold once I am informed the offer has been made to Victor. Is that acceptable?"

"This Trent fellow must be really something for you to be this generous, madam. Yes, that is most acceptable. I would love to know how you figure he will accept the offer once made, but, as you say, that is not my issue. It's a pleasure doing business with you."

Cliff and Aurea then sign off. Aurea turns to Carol Ann and smiles.

"Now the wheels have truly started to turn. Victor will be in the Imperial City by early January, and then we will be able to discern just how psychically powerful he really is."

"Indeed. Now, though, we have to wait and be patient, which is more one of your virtues than it is mine. I'm glad he is *your* project!"

CHAPTER 2

Tuesday, December 2, 2008, a blustery, late autumn day in the city of Orange. It's just about one o'clock, and Victor Trent is winding up his lunch break. Dasher's, being a secondhand store, is doing a rather brisk business in spite of the bad economy. Victor puts down the Philip K. Dick novel he is reading.

"Got to get back on the sales floor," he says to himself with a sigh.

As he starts to get out of his chair, his cell phone rings. He takes the phone out of his pocket. Not recognizing the number, he adopts a very formal demeanor.

"Victor Trent speaking."

Immediately, his ear is assaulted by what he regards as an insanely cheerful female voice.

"Good afternoon, Mr. Trent. I'm Mathilda Cross, administrative assistant for Representative Bob Moore. He would like to make an appointment to talk to you about an employment opportunity for a staff position at his Washington, DC office. When would be a good time for you?"

Victor stifles his irritation. "Okay. Who are you really? Did Arnold put you up to this? If he did, this is lamer than most of his jokes."

The voice becomes querulous. "Arnold? Joke? I assure you, Mr. Trent, that this is a legitimate call. The representative is eager to discuss this job opportunity with you."

"I don't have time to play games. Tell Arnold to try a more convincing line next time."

Not fifteen seconds after pressing the end button, his cell phone rings again. Seeing the same number come up, he lets the call go into his voicemail. He then goes into the employee washroom to clean up and calm down. Just as he is about to go back out on the sales floor, his voicemail chimes. He punches in his code and listens.

"I can understand you being skeptical about this, Mr. Trent. I was surprised to learn that there was an opening at the DC office myself. Look. Just do a reverse phone number lookup on this number. You can see for yourself that this is really Representative Moore's Newport Beach office. Then please call back and ask for me. Good afternoon, Mr. Trent."

Scowling, Victor walks over to one of the store terminals and does as Mathilda had suggested. Sure enough, the number actually was that of Representative Moore's office. He then goes a step further and checks out Moore's congressional website. Sure enough, a Mathilda Cross is listed as the administrative assistant for the Newport Beach office.

"This doesn't make any sense. Why would a politician want to offer me a job?"

When Victor takes his next break at about two thirty, he steps outside and calls the number. He asks to be connected to Mathilda Cross, which was done promptly. Sure enough, the same insanely cheerful voice came back on the line.

"I'm so glad you called back, Mr. Trent. Bob is really eager to meet you. He says he thinks you just might be exactly what his staff in the Capitol needs. When could you come down here for an interview?"

"I'm off on Wednesdays, so tomorrow would work, unless that is too soon."

"Actually, that would be perfect. He will be in all day tomorrow. How about I put you in for a 10:00 a.m. appointment. Is that okay?"

"That will be fine, Ms. Cross. I already looked up the office address, so I know where you folks are and how to get there."

Mathilda bubbles over with what Victor regards as excessive mirth. "That's perfect indeed! I will let the representative know that you will be here tomorrow. Have a great day!"

Victor puts his cell phone back in his shirt pocket. After staring at the traffic going through the intersection of Tustin and Katella, he walks back into the store, shaking his head.

"What the heck? I've got nothing better to do. Still bet this turns out to be some stupid joke."

Pulling into the garage at his parents' house later that evening, Victor sees Arnold pulling up right behind him. Still perplexed by the unexpected phone call at work, he glares as he steps out of the car. "Pretty lame joke this afternoon, Arnie."

Arnold simply stares at his brother. "Joke? What joke? I was at work all afternoon. Want to call my boss?"

Victor sighs as he and Arnold walk into the house. Susan is putting dishes away. Robert, as usual, is sitting in his recliner chair, watching some science fiction show on his big-screen TV.

"I got this call from someone claiming to be from Representative Moore's office. Says he wants to talk to me about a job opportunity on his staff in DC. Figured it had to be a joke, but then I checked online and saw the number really did belong to his office in Newport Beach."

Arnold shakes his head. "No wonder you thought it was a joke. Why would a politician want you to work for them? Anyone who bothered to read your master's thesis would certainly know where you stand."

Robert Trent looks over at his sons. "Yeah, Victor. Who would want to give you a real job anyhow? You majored in criminal justice and philosophy. What did you figure to do with that degree, read Nietzsche to inmates on death row?"

Victor rolls his eyes and ignores his father. "Anyway, I have an appointment for ten o'clock tomorrow. So, I guess I will find out then if this job offer is legitimate."

Robert lets out with a derisive snort. "It has to be a mistake. They probably think you are somebody else, someone who went to college and earned a degree that mattered. Maybe Moore is losing his marbles."

"Dad, I'm not going to argue with you tonight. I have no idea why Representative Moore would think I have any interest in working for him or going to Washington. I will find all that out tomorrow. How are you doing, Mom?"

Susan came out of the kitchen and gave Victor and Arnold a hug. "All right, honey. Making plans to get the whole family together for Christmas, even Uncle Reggie and Clyde. All of your grandparents will be coming. You *will* be here, won't you, Victor? Even if you do get that job with Moore, surely it won't start until January. Arnold, Katrina is certainly invited if she isn't busy."

"Don't forget to invite your sister Cyndi, Susie. If I have to endure having my brothers under my roof, then you have to have your sister come too. Besides, you know your mom would be upset if you didn't invite her."

Susan sighs. "Yes, dear. When I said I wanted to try and get the whole family together while we still can, I meant it. I invited Cyndi Lou and Glenn. They plan on being here for Christmas dinner."

Arnold and Victor assure their mother that they will be home for Christmas dinner. They then retire to Victor's room, where they continue their discussion of the day's events.

"Essentially, Arnold, I think that this is some kind of mistake. I never sent them my resume. Sure, they could have downloaded it from one of the employment search sites, but why? Almost seems like someone's idea of a *Twilight Zone* episode. I mean, me, working for a politician, in Washington, DC, of all places. Can you imagine?"

"I agree. I mean, I haven't read all of your master's thesis, but I don't have to to know what you think of the present state of politics in this country. For the most part, I agree with you. So what will you do if this is on the level and Moore actually does offer you a position on his staff? Will you take it?"

"I will cross that bridge *if* it becomes necessary. Until then, I will just deal with what I do know to be the case. I have an interview tomorrow. We both know that most interviews simply end in getting a note or an e-mail saying, 'Thanks, but we gave the job to someone else.' I refuse to speculate, because really, I just don't know how I will react to such an offer until it is made. I will say that I find the very notion of working for a politician, working for a government that I hold in more contempt than I do organized crime to really be quite nauseating."

"Everyone has their price though, Victor. I wonder just what yours might be."

In the early morning hours of December 3, in Avignon, France, Ruby Order vampire Phillipe La Mer is putting the finishing touches on what is to be his last will and testament. After 250 years, the guilt of the crime he had committed with his long-passed friend Jacques Vachon weighs too heavily on his soul to continue on. The dreams are so vivid now that he is afraid he is losing his mind. He checks his desk, making sure all is in place: a farewell note to his porfo, Jean-Jacques Mondair; his written confession; a DVD in which he explains it all; and a will. Satisfied, he steps outside and watches the eastern horizon brighten. He wants to go out with the dawn's first rays, however, having been a vampire for over five hundred years, it would take at least an hour for the sun to destroy him. Not wanting to go through that agony, he douses himself in gasoline and gets a lighter out of his pocket and waits.

As the sun breaks the horizon, La Mer ignites the lighter and then explodes in a ball of flame. His final thought: *You were a fool to believe us, Kristano. She was innocent. We killed your sister. You will know that soon enough. Time to go…*

Victor pulls into the office complex at about nine forty-five in the morning. Representative Moore's office is in a rather plain-looking building on Newport Boulevard, just a few blocks away from the Pacific Coast Highway. To its credit, the building was painted recently, but it has seen better days. Victor checks his tie in the mirror gets out of his car and smooths out his black slacks. He takes a look at the office door and shrugs. The moment of truth has arrived.

He enters and heads over to the reception desk. Chatting animatedly on the phone is a short, blonde woman wearing a red blouse and a rather short skirt. When she looks up and notices Victor, she puts her call on hold.

"Can I help you, sir?"

"Yes. I have an interview with Representative Moore at ten o'clock. I spoke to Mathilda Cross yesterday."

Her face brightens. "You must be Victor Trent. I heard a lot about you yesterday." She presses a button on her intercom. "Mattie? Victor Trent has arrived. I'll get him started on the paperwork." She takes out some forms and attaches them to a clipboard and hands it to Victor. "Mattie will be with you soon. Just go ahead and start filling out these forms."

Victor takes the clipboard and sits down. The top one he expected: a standard employment application. The consent to a background check was also no surprise, as was the ubiquitous drug test form. Looking further, he found federal tax forms and a form for DC withholding. This struck him as rather odd, as those forms only came into play once a job offer was made and accepted. He is about to remark to the receptionist about this when a woman comes into the reception area. Tall, brunette, brown eyes, wearing a smart, tailored business suit, she walks over to Victor and extends her hand.

"Victor Trent? I'm Mathilda Cross. It is a pleasure to make your acquaintance."

Victor shakes her hand, admiring her firm grip. "It's a pleasure to meet you as well, Ms. Cross. I'm very sorry about the mix-up yesterday. I just never expected that a representative would actually want to interview me for any position at all. I am still very surprised that this is really happening."

Mathilda smiles benignly. "Call me Mattie, please. Bob warned me that you might react that way, given your background. He has read a summary of your master's thesis, and, frankly, that is why he has taken an interest in you." She leads Victor out of the reception area and takes him into a rather austere office. "Why don't you go ahead and finish filling out the paperwork? I'll let Bob know that you are here."

Victor sits down at the desk. "Do you folks really want me to fill out tax forms before the interview? Kind of seems like putting the cart before the horse. I'm sure you will be interviewing other candidates for this position."

"Actually, Victor, you are the only candidate we are interviewing for this position. Bob seemed rather intensely insistent that you were perfect for the job. He is an outstanding judge of character. However, no, if you don't feel comfortable filling out the tax forms before an actual job offer is made, you don't need to. It's completely up to you."

Mathilda leaves the office, and Victor ponders what she had said.

"This has gone into the land of the truly bizarre. I'm the *only* candidate for this position? I'm *perfect* for the job?" He starts looking around for hidden cameras, becoming certain that this has to be a setup for some bizarre reality show. *I swear, if this turns out to be a joke or a ploy for some insipid TV show, I will flog the perpetrator.*

After a few minutes, Mathilda comes back into the office. "Bob is ready to see you now. Please follow me."

Victor stands up and follows her down the hall. Before opening the door to the representative's office, she takes the clipboard.

"You won't need these. He has your résumé. The application is simply for the files." She then opens the door.

The office is spacious. Representative Moore is seated behind a large, tiger oak desk, a beautiful antique. An ornate nameplate on the desk reads, "Honorable Robert Moore, US Representative, Congressional District 48." Along the wall are photos of Moore with the more recent US Presidents. Moore looks exactly like the pictures Victor had seen on television and online: tall, ramrod straight, steel-gray hair, piercing hazel eyes. The man looks like a predator. He rises from his chair and extends his hand as Victor enters the room. Mathilda takes her leave and shuts the door. Victor and Moore shake hands, and then they both sit down.

For a few seconds, neither man speaks. Victor still feels like he is being set up for some joke so bizarre that a member of Congress would actually take part. Moore then smiles and clears his throat.

"It is a rare privilege to meet a man of principles like yourself, Mr. Trent, all too rare indeed. Inside the Beltway, most folks I deal with change alleged principles like they change shoes. They stand for what they determine to be politically expedient. Not you, though. Clearly, not you. You are part of a very rare breed. You say what you mean. You stand by your principles no matter what anyone else thinks. That is very admirable."

"I do the best I can, Congressman. What would the point be of my saying I believe in something if I didn't practice what I preach? That is what I find contemptible about the vast majority of politicians; they promise the electorate whatever it takes to get into office and then act in ways completely contrary to those words."

Bob Moore smiles and nods. "Well said, sir. I see you have no fear of speaking your mind, even to someone like me. In your mind, I am part of the problem. Well, frankly, you could be right. Answer me this: Do you think the republic can be saved? Or have we gone too far down the road of empire?"

"What is there to save, Congressman? The republic was fatally flawed from its inception. The so-called American Revolution was nothing more than a war of secession. The Constitution of Seventeen Eighty-Seven was the real revolution. The Bill of Rights? It isn't worth the paper it was printed on. Making a document trying to say what the government cannot do, they have always found ways around it. If you are going to have a government, what you really *need* is a schedule of government powers. Then you make sure that document clearly states, 'Anything not specified in this document, the government cannot do.' Lincoln killed what validity the republic might have had by using force to return the Southern states to the Union. This country is an oligarchy. Yes, all empires fall. Those who think this country cannot collapse should look to the example of the Soviet Union. Where is it now? The day of the superpower is ending."

Bob Moore folds his hands on the desk. "Well said, Victor. Those are powerful words that even I ought to reflect on. Correct though you might well be, right now, it is people like myself and the people who support people like myself who are still in charge. Like the old Soviet commissars and the KGB, we might well lose that grip. When or if that happens, it will likely come quickly, and most people will be caught off guard. Myself, I still hold out hope that the nation can be turned around, not that the results of the last election please me. Victor, I have been elected to ten terms now. Maybe this will be my last term. My seniority gives me a lot of flexibility. I want to shake my colleagues up. I want you to be on my staff."

"Doing what exactly, Congressman? As entertaining as it might be, for a brief while, I am not interested in a job where all I would be doing is arguing with people who not only disagree with me but won't present logical counterarguments to my position. I enjoy debate, not futile shouting matches."

"I have read a detailed summary of your master's thesis. Some people whom I respect have read your paper in its entirety. The scholarship is sound, beautifully researched, sources cited appropriately. However, there is one real flaw to it, one missing piece. Do you wish to venture a guess as to what that is?"

Victor leans forward, a deep scowl crossing his face. "I'm all ears, Congressman. Tell me what you view as being the one real flaw in my thesis."

"Beyond voting, you have no direct experience in the political system. You have never gotten your hands dirty, never looked the beast directly in the eye. True, you did some direct research on the local and state level, but that is not where the game is really played. You want to see that? Then you need to come to Washington. You need to wallow in it. You need to see where the deals are cut. Go see the empire in all its decadence, in all its putrid glory. By being on my staff, you will see direct proof of what you wrote about. Then, you will really *know*. You will be able to speak with authority, with experience, hands on. No, Victor, I don't expect to change your mind. I don't expect you to suddenly love people like me. You will understand us better though. You will see how it really is. Perhaps this will allow you to take a leading role in building a better society once this all does collapse, stop history from repeating itself."

"You do have a valid point, Congressman. Having direct experience would take my thesis up a step from academia. Working for you would certainly be an opportunity to learn and probably would harden my resolve, though it would humanize my views. So, just what is this position?"

"It is a staff liaison position. You would be able to observe the lobbyists in action, spend some time in the house gallery as an observer, go to functions at embassies and special interest group parties as my representative, go to New York on occasion to observe some United Nations meetings that I have an interest in, do research in the Library of Congress. You would also have plenty of free time.

I suspect you would enjoy touring the Smithsonian. As part of my staff, you would have access to areas that the public does not get to see. You could even meet the new president, if such suited you."

"I don't know. This just seems like making a deal with the devil. I mean, truthfully, I have more respect for organized crime than I have for the state. I believe this offer is on the level, but is it really in my rational self-interests? Would I be able to look at myself in the mirror and not feel like a hypocrite?"

"Those questions you will have to answer yourself. Besides decent pay, the job also includes a furnished studio apartment in Georgetown. Also, if you do come to work for me, after six months of employment, a third of your student loans will be forgiven. After a year, another third goes away. If you stay with me for the full two years, the entirety of your loans will be written off. That is what I offer you."

Victor's jaw drops. "You can really do that, get the millstone of those student loans off my back?"

"Yes, Victor. I have that kind of pull. You work for me for two years, and they are completely gone. Even if you get sick of me after six months, a third of them will be gone, and I know even that will make a big difference. What do you say? The position is yours to take. I am not considering any other candidates because you are the best fit for this."

Victor ponders this for a few moments. "This is a very generous offer. Can I have a couple days to mull it over, talk to some trusted friends? I promise you a firm answer by Friday morning."

Bob Moore stands up and extends his hand. "That will be just fine, Victor. Call me directly by Friday morning and let me know what you decide."

Victor stands up and shakes hands with him.

Aurea is reading an alternate history novel when her cell phone chimes. Seeing that it is Cliff Nash, she pushes the send key. "Yes, Cliff? What news do you have for me?"

"Bob Moore just called me. Said he made the offer to Trent. Predictably, Trent asked for some time to think it over. However, Moore is confident that Trent will take the job. So, Aurea, you were right; he didn't turn the Congressman down flat."

"I was quite certain that he would not. Well done, sir. Your payment will arrive this evening. You earned it, and I thank you for your efforts."

"Are you sure this is all you need me to do for you? Rather a steep price to have paid if he does decline."

"As I said before, that is not your concern. If it appears that he will decline the offer, I have another friend in the OC whom I believe could be of assistance in convincing him. I am quite confident that he will take the job though. Take care, my friend."

"A good day to you as well, Aurea. May your venture prove stunningly successful."

The evening shadows deepen as Jean-Jacques Mondair pulls into the driveway of Phillipe La Mer's house. He has worked for La Mer for ten years now, and he plans to become a vampire in another year or so. Something just feels off to Mondair as he gets out of his car. It is too quiet, there is a whiff of a smell of burnt flesh, and the house just feels empty. Cautiously, he unlocks the door and enters. His eyes are immediately drawn to the large writing desk as he notices items that are not normally there.

He reaches the desk and sees the note addressed to him. His eyes widen, and his mouth drops open in horror as he reads it. Composing himself, he picks up the phone and makes the call that Phillipe had requested he make.

"Hello. This is Jean-Jacques Mondair. I am, or rather was, employed by Phillipe La Mer. May I speak to Francois Petard? I have news of import for the Vitzameri, Kristano Pa Anovas."

"This is Petard. What would that news be?"

"La Mer destroyed himself this morning. He left several letters, a will, and a DVD that his letter to me states contains his detailed confession regarding his role in the assassination of one Vetrina Pa Anovasa on October 16, 1753. I gather this individual was the Vitzameri's sister."

"Indeed, she was, Monsieur Mondair. Can you hold for a moment?"

Mondair answers in the affirmative. A couple minutes later, Petard comes back on the phone.

"If you have no objections, sir, I will come over and examine this material. If this checks out, then I am directed to have you come with me and speak to the Vitzameri in person. You do realize how grave a matter this is?"

"All I really know right now is that my friend and employer has confessed to an act he committed over two hundred and fifty years ago, and he was convinced that suicide was the only honorable course of action open to him. I have no objections to you coming over here. It will give me time to compose myself so I won't look like an idiot when I have to meet the Vitzameri."

"Very well. I will be there in about a half hour."

After his interview with Representative Moore, Victor drives down to Trestles Beach down near San Onofre. There are very few people there. It is cold. A brisk breeze is coming off the steel-gray Pacific. A fog bank hovers just off the coast. He is seeking solitude, a quiet place to think things over and come to a decision. He looks up at the railroad trestles that give the beach its name and scowls, perplexed. He starts muttering to himself.

"On the one hand, taking this job would be directly working for the enemy. There is no arguing that point. On the other hand, there is the fact that it would get me away from my parents, and I would get out from under the blasted student loans I had to take out. So, I can choose to sell out and become financially solvent or turn them down and hope something opens up that pays decently so that I don't have to stay with my parents another five years. That is my dilemma."

He sits on a rock and watches the waves crashing on the beach. No one disturbs him in his intense reverie. He decides to call his sister, Zoe. He also knows that she is in class, so he leaves her a voice mail. Sighing, he decides to call his uncle, Reggie.

"Victor, my man! How are you doing?"

"I have a dilemma, Reggie. I'm hoping that you can help me figure out what I need to do. For me, this is one of those watershed events that will have a major impact on the rest of my life."

"Wow. You really do sound perplexed. Tell me what's on your mind."

Victor tells his uncle all about the interview with Representative Moore and the job offer. He speaks of the moral qualms he is having as a result.

"Reggie, I feel like if I take the job, I will be selling out on my principles. If that is really true, I would not be able to look at myself in the mirror. On the other hand, it is an opportunity to get out from under my parents' thumb, get the millstone of my student loans off my back, and actually see the imperium's political process in action. Is getting direct knowledge that valuable? Do I hold my nose and take the job or stand on the moral high ground and turn him down?"

"You sure don't end up with simple problems, do you, Victor? Curse of the intelligentsia, that is what it is. I won't tell you what to do; that decision is yours. As to what I think, well, if this was coming from someone besides you, I would have thought this was some kind of weird joke just as you admit that you thought it was at first. It's kind of funny thinking about you hanging up on that politician's administrative assistant like that. As to what I think, no, I don't think that if you take the job that you will be selling out on your principles. Frankly, there are very few jobs anymore that pay decently that don't involve some level of government intrusion. Such is, sadly, the nature of the Keynesian mixed economy, the mercantilism that most people accuse of being capitalism. True, this position would be in the belly of the beast, and you would likely observe events nearly every day that you will regard as immoral and unethical. Being there would certainly have its impact. No doubt about it. Think of the political papers you could write afterward. You are a great observer. It is like you can make yourself invisible to the people around you when you want to. That is a fine ability in that situation."

"Those are certainly good points, Reggie. Sounds like you think I should go ahead and take the job."

"I think you should take whatever course of action supports your long-term rational self-interests, Victor. It would get you away from your father's constant harping on how you earned an allegedly useless degree. I know that must be getting really old. Arnold wouldn't be able to keep bumming rides off you when his car breaks down. You wouldn't have to worry about keeping the peace, trying to figure out what to do for the good of the order. What you *would* have to be concerned about is making sure that you did not get tempted to sell out. Knowing you, though, I don't think you have much to worry about there. You really believe; you live by your principles. You take a stand knowing what it means and what the ramifications of doing so are."

"Thanks for listening, Reggie. Thanks also for the food for thought. I will definitely weigh your words carefully."

"I hope it helps, Victor. No matter what you decide to do, I will be here for you. Take care."

Victor ends the call and goes back to watching the waves. After a while, he stands up and wipes the sand off his pants and heads back to his car to make the trip back to Orange.

Near midnight in Avignon, a car silently pulls up in front of a gated townhouse. Francois Petard exits first, going back to the trunk to take a large valise out. An obviously frightened Jean-Jacques

Mondair exits from the passenger side. As the two men approach the house, the door opens and Pa Anovas's porfo majere, Claude Duviere, comes out and motions for Petard to step aside.

"This is the smoking gun, isn't it? This is going to turn the Vitzameri's world upside down. You know that."

Petard nods. "I know that. I am convinced that La Mer was telling the truth in his statement. Bodellini was innocent all along, as just about everyone except the Vitzameri understood. No, he won't be happy, but the truth will prevail, and that is what is important here."

Duviere looks over at Mondair, who is visibly shaking with fear. "I see Monsieur Mondair is frightened. In his position, I would be too. We know he has nothing to fear from the Vitzameri, but he doesn't, and he would not believe us if we told him that." He sighs and leads both men into the foyer and closes the door. "I will let the Vitzameri know you have arrived. Wait here." Duviere then goes through another door.

Petard looks over at Mondair. "Calm down, man! I assure you, you are completely safe. Nothing La Mer said implicates you in any way. The Vitzameri is a fair man; he doesn't believe in guilt by association."

"You don't understand. On top of losing my friend and employer, I am now about to have an audience with the eldest vampire on the planet. We will be telling him things that we both know he is not going to want to hear. I mean, how old is he? La Mer mentioned fifty thousand years or something. I saw what La Mer could do. I bet the Vitzameri could end my existence with a mere thought, a wave of his hand."

Petard lets out a long sigh. "The Vitzameri is fifty thousand and forty years old. He is not going to vaporize you or harm you in any way. I give you my solemn vow, my word bond, that you are perfectly safe here."

Mondair is about to reply, but he falls silent when Duviere opens the inner door and ushers them into an ornate sitting room. Paintings adorn the walls, as do several shelves of books. A large chandelier hangs from the ceiling. Seated in a comfortable red chair is the Vitzameri, Kristano Pa Anovas. With brown hair, brown eyes, lean frame, the eldest vampire looked to be in his midforties. He is wearing black pants, a black shirt, and black shoes. He has a noncommittal expression on his face, but one could clearly see the concern in his eyes. Those were eyes that had seen so much, happiness and pain alike.

Duviere clears his throat. "My Lord Pa Anovas, your barrister Francois Petard and the porfo of the late Phillipe La Mer, Jean-Jacques Mondair, are here to speak to you about a very grave matter of utmost importance."

Pa Anovas nods. "Thank you, Claude." As Duviere leaves the room, Pa Anovas looks over at the other two men. "Gentlemen, please take a seat. Monsieur Mondair, I welcome you to my home. I am sorry it was not under better circumstances. Now, gentlemen, besides the suicide of La Mer, what is the issue that clearly has you all so troubled and confounded? Please speak freely, friends."

Petard looks over at Mondair and then back at Pa Anovas. "By your lordship's leave, then. As we all now know, Phillipe La Mer ended his existence this morning. Apparently, he believed this was the only honorable course of action left to him after he decided to confess to his transgressions."

Voice choking with fear and remorse, Mondair chimes in, "My lord, it seems that this, his suicide, was the only honorable act during his entire existence. What a monster! I can't believe it!"

Pa Anovas looks over at Mondair and scowls. "Since you only worked for La Mer for ten years, Monsieur, you are in no position to judge how honorably he conducted his entire existence. I, on the other hand, did know him for his entire five hundred-plus years in Order Ruby. So, Petard, what have you found out that La Mer did that would elicit such a reaction from his loyal porfo?"

Petard takes out the DVD La Mer left behind and puts it in his laptop. He turns the screen toward Pa Anovas. "Well, my lord, let's let Phillipe speak for himself, shall we?"

Phillipe La Mer's face appeared in the screen. He looked haunted, fearful, and apprehensive. "Vitzameri Kristano Pa Anovas, Plaz Seschni. My lord, I have decided to put an end to my existence on this plane this morning. I wanted to simply go out with the first rays of the dawn sun, but I have been around long enough for that to be a long and painful demise, and I am too much a coward now to do that. I have some gasoline to help me along. Given my moodiness and reclusiveness these past few years, I doubt my suicide comes as any surprise. However, the reason why will.

"Remember the night of October 16, 1753, the night of your true sister's demise? No doubt it is forever etched on your memory. The reason I am ending my existence is because I can no longer handle the dreams, no longer stand the guilt. My lord, your sister, Vetrina Pa Anovasa, was assassinated. We all know that. The assassins were I, Jacques Vachon, and an Order Sapphire psychopath named Albert Thorne. As you really should have known from the Plinthi, with yourself and that tribunal, Aurea Octavia Bodellini was utterly innocent of any wrongdoing. Why you believed Vachon and myself over the essentially foolproof sharing in Plinthi, hell, over the mere word of Aurea, was and is beyond me. She was Vetrina's best friend and blood sister to you both. I mean, your first clue should have been that Vachon and I refused to submit to Plinthi, but you kept on believing us. Thorne said the grief would render you irrational, and, brother, he was so right.

"So, why did we assassinate your sister and frame Aurea? We wanted both of these influential women out of the picture. We hoped your grief would render you malleable enough to start a movement to restore vampire slavery, create a vampire government and create a more favorable settlement for Order Sapphire. We merely wanted you to banish Aurea. That is why I told you to put her on trial. I could not let you destroy her as you had threatened to do. Anyway, we never got the changes we sought, so that part of the plan was a dismal failure.

"You need not seek out Vachon and Thorne. They were destroyed by mortals in Paris in 1857. In a way, I felt relieved when I heard about this. I had no qualms about doing this until a few years ago, when the dreams started. Your sister started haunting me in my mind. Then the guilt set in. The gravity of what I had been a willing party to started to weigh on my soul.

"So now it comes to this. I go now, into the void, until the karmic wheel spins again to take another shot at life. I am certainly not expecting, nor do I ask for, your forgiveness. I trust you will exonerate Aurea, as I said she was completely innocent. My estate is yours, as per the will. I recommend you liquidate it and use the proceeds to compensate Aurea. As for Mondair, he is a fine and honorable man, and I hope you will offer him some suitable employment.

"Farewell, my lord. My suicide is my apology, my escape from these dreams. It was the only honorable course of action left to me." With that, Phillipe La Mer bowed, and the computer screen went blank.

The room is silent for several minutes. Pa Anovas glares at the blank computer screen. Petard arranges the papers from La Mer. Mondair sits silently in fear, wondering what is to become of him. Finally, Pa Anovas looks over at Petard.

"La Mer was telling the truth, wasn't he? He seemed so haunted, so frightened. He dreamed about my sister?" He looks over at Mondair. "Monsieur, did he ever mention these dreams to you, anything at all?"

"He spoke of disturbed rest, my lord, but no, he never said just what it was. I admit to being very concerned about Phillipe these past few months. However, he never told me any of this. I will submit to Plinthi if you wish."

Pa Anovas shakes his head. "That will not be necessary. I know you are speaking the truth. I know La Mer is also speaking the truth. What a fool I have been. This is monstrous. This is inexcusable." He looks over at Petard. "Please start going over the lists of properties seized by me from Aurea Bodellini in seventeen fifty-three and fifty-four. Claude can show you where those records are kept. I want a complete reckoning." He then looks over at Mondair. "If you are still interested in working for us, in becoming one of us, I will find you a suitable position. I insist, however, that you take a month off once we have La Mer's affairs settled."

As Petard nods and leaves the room, Mondair stands up. "I would be honored to work for you, my lord. Yes, I am still interested in becoming a vampire, in joining Order Ruby. I might put it off for a year or so."

Pa Anovas stands up and shakes Mondair's hand. "You are an honorable man. I am sorry to see that you were very probably right about La Mer's character. Now I have to make amends for a grievous error made two hundred and fifty-five years ago, probably the biggest error I have made over the millennia."

Victor arrives home and has dinner with his parents. The meal is passing more peacefully than usual. Then Robert Trent looks over at his son.

"So, how was the interview? Had they made a mistake and called you instead of the right person?"

Victor smiles at his father. "Actually, the interview went very well. Congressman Moore told me I was the only candidate being considered for the job. Pay would be good. It includes a furnished studio apartment in Georgetown. And if I stayed with them for his full two-year term, all my student loans would be forgiven."

Robert looks at his son in astonishment. "You, the one who wrote a master's thesis trashing politicians? Moore wants you in Washington? Guy must be nuts. Wow, though. What an opportunity. You would have connections, be able to send some business my way. In this economy, that would be a godsend."

Susan Trent frets. "So what did you tell the Congressman, Victor? Are you going to take the job?"

"Of course he will take the job, Susie! Not even Victor would be silly enough to turn down an opportunity like this!"

Victor looks at both of his parents and sighs. "I told Representative Moore that I wanted a couple of days to think it over. I do have some moral and ethical issues to consider, though the offer does certainly have its merits. I told him I would make my decision by Friday morning. Frankly, I would feel better taking a job in organized crime because they are more honorable than the politicians, more ethical than the government. Still, the Congressman gave me a lot to think about."

Victor's cell phone rings, and he sees it is Zoe's number. He gets up from the table.

"If you two will excuse me now." He walks into his room and takes the call. "Thanks for calling me back, Zoe."

"Of course, Victor. You sounded so forlorn, so perplexed. What's this all about?"

Victor then tells Zoe about his interview with Representative Moore and the conversation he had had with Uncle Reggie about it.

"I went in there believing it had to be some set up for a reality show. Then it turned out to be legitimate. In some ways, I feel like I would be selling out to take the job, but Reggie said it wouldn't be, and I see his point on that. Moore is right as well; it would give me the opportunity to see politics in action on the federal level. Getting out from those student loans would be such a relief. What do you think I should do, Zoe? I want to do the right thing."

Zoe's reply came swiftly, without even a note of hesitation. "Victor, take the job. It is your ticket away from Mom and Dad, and I know they are dragging you down, especially Dad and all his allegedly cute, snide comments. They don't appreciate you. This will give you the opportunity to look those creepy politicians in the eyes and expose them for what they really are. I know that you feel like you will be moving directly into the lions' den. That is true. The perks, though: direct access to the Smithsonian Institution and the Library of Congress. The United Nations stuff doesn't sound very exciting, but you could take in a Broadway show. The embassy parties, well, go learn to dance. It won't hurt you. Heck, sometime in the summer, I could come up and attend such a party with you. I'd like that. Really though, Victor, if you don't take the job, you will be kicking yourself for years to come. Dad will never let you hear the end of it. I agree with Reggie that this would not be compromising your principles at all."

"This would be working directly for the enemy, taking the king's schilling. Still, Reggie was saying that government intrusion into the economy is so prevalent that it is next to impossible to escape it on some level."

"Reggie knows what he is talking about, Victor. Think about it. You had to go to a public university, a government school. We have to use government roads, and we are forced to pay our debts with their fiat money, which only has value because they back it up with the full force of arms of the state. Given these federal bailouts lately, one can only wonder how much longer Federal Reserve notes will be accepted as payment for anything. Taking that job will give you inside information that we can use when the time comes. Come it shall. You know it will."

"That I know only too well. It's funny, but Dad is having visions of government contracts if I take the job. He is forgetting that Moore is not a member of the incoming majority party. He is so shortsighted for an intelligent man. This is just so hard, Zoe. I feel like I am making a deal with the powers of Hades itself."

"Nah. You will just be getting a front row seat to witness the collapse of the imperial bureaucracy. You will get to see people fight over what portion of a store room belongs to their department. You will see people justify their jobs by creating useless forms. You will see how horrible it all really is. This edifice is tottering, Victor. In view of your long-term rational self-interests, you owe it to yourself to get out from under those blasted loans. Take the job, Victor. Take it with a clear conscience."

"Thanks, Zoe. I knew you could help me sort this all out. I will sleep on it and make my final decision in the morning. I won't wait until Friday to make up my mind."

"You are the best, big brother. You deserve this opportunity. Get out from behind the Orange Curtain. See another unreal part of the country, the fabled land within the Beltway. No matter what you decide, you know I will always be here for you. I love you."

"Thanks, Zoe. I love you too. Good night." Victor ends the call and then sits at his desk and becomes deep in thought.

He has made his decision.

In the house on Staten Island, Carol Ann and Aurea are having a rather animated conversation. "What is your plan if Victor does not make his decision on Thursday? I can't imagine you not trying to influence him in some way if he does not decide tomorrow. I know he told Moore he would decide by Friday, but still, really, you know?"

Aurea laughs as her friend paces. "The way you are acting, you would think this is *your* project instead of mine. I do have a plan, certainly. I have already arranged to have Brenda go and sit outside his bedroom window and influence his dreams Thursday night if he has not already committed. Somehow, I think that he will commit on Thursday. Not with intense enthusiasm, but that is not relevant. All that matters is getting him to take the job, get him into Washington. *Then* we will see what he is really made of. Is what Brenda and Silk saw him do just an unusual fluke, or is he really something special?"

"You are too clever for your own good, my friend. No wonder so many fear you. You play games within games. You stay several steps ahead of everyone. That must be part of the secret to your longevity."

"I have many secrets, Carol Ann. I have learned the hard way that one needs to keep their friends close and their enemies closer. Well, except maybe for our very own 'High Lord of the Seas' the Vitzameri. I would rather stay very far away from him. Try not to worry about Victor Trent. I'm not, so why should you be?"

"I just know how important this is to you, Aurea. I just hope all this expense and effort is worth it."

Dawn comes to Avignon on Thursday the fourth, finding Pa Anovas brooding in his study. He has not rested since the meeting with Mondair and Petard. He looks at the painting of his sister on the wall. A tear runs down his cheek.

"I should have known better, Vetrina. Aurea never would have harmed you. She would have died in your place if she could have. I know that now. How do I make this right?"

Claude Duviere enters the room. "My lord, Monsieur Petard has gone home to rest. He will be back this afternoon to continue his work on the accounting for the Bodellini seizures. Can I get you anything?"

Pa Anovas smiles wanly. "No, Claude. That will be all. You should get some rest too. It was a long night and a very trying one. When will Lady Maurana be back in town?"

"I believe she plans to return on the solstice, my lord. Do you want me to contact her and see if she would come back sooner? Under the circumstances, I am sure that she would."

"No. She is entitled to this time on her own. By then, we should have a full reckoning, and then I can have an intelligent conversation with her regarding Aurea. Rest well, my friend." Claude bows and leaves the room.

Kristano proceeds to pace and mutter under his breath. "Yes, Maurana will know what to do. This will have to be handled very carefully. I can't just call Aurea." He laughs to himself. "Yeah, that would go over *so* well. I doubt she would even take my call! That much time, two hundred and fifty-five years. Yes, to really screw something up, you need a high elder."

Victor wakes up to the sound of his alarm clock at 7:00 a.m. He does not need to be at the store until 10:00 a.m. today, but he likes having this time to himself. His parents had both left earlier that morning, so he has the house to himself. He gets ready and has breakfast. He is still having qualms about the job offer, but he has made his decision, and he is going to call Representative Moore at 8:00 a.m. and let him know.

"This is the right thing to do. It is what is best for me over the short and long term."

Presently, it is 8:00 a.m. He takes out the card that Moore had given him and calls his direct line.

"Bob Moore speaking."

The time is now. Victor takes a deep breath. "Representative Moore, this is Victor Trent. I have made my decision regarding the job offer."

"A day earlier than promised. I appreciate that. What have you decided?"

The words catch in his throat. There is so much turmoil in his mind. "Representative Moore, I am accepting your job offer. I will work for your Washington, DC office."

"You made the right decision, Victor. Can you come by the office today and finish the paperwork? We will need to make arrangements to ship your car to DC and whatever personal effects you care to bring."

"Sure. I can do that. I will just call my boss and let him know I will be late. Then I will give them my two weeks' notice. That is only fair."

"Of course it is. You don't need to be in DC until the twenty-ninth. So you will be able to spend the holidays with your family. See you in a little while, Victor."

After Victor hangs up the phone, he runs to the bathroom and vomits.

Shortly thereafter, Aurea receives a phone call from Cliff.

"So, Cliff, I gather you have heard something from Representative Moore regarding Victor Trent?"

"I am astonished to relay the message that Victor Trent has accepted the position. I really didn't think that he would. I guess the lure of getting out from under those loans was sufficient."

"Oh, I'm sure it was more than that. Victor is a very complex fellow. I guess that means I need to call Brenda and let her know that I don't need her assistance after all."

CHAPTER 3

Tuesday, December 23, 2008, a blustery winter night in Orange. At ten o'clock, Victor Trent and the rest of the staff at Dasher's are shutting the store down for the night. A couple of employees walk by and say farewell, shaking Victor's hand as they go. Victor is pensive and melancholy. The day of the move to Washington is swiftly approaching. First, however, he has to survive the great Christmas family reunion that his mother has arranged, sparing no effort and expense. Harold, the manager at Dasher's, is handing Victor his last paycheck.

"I'm gonna miss you, Victor. You were a really great employee. Thanks again for giving two weeks' notice and helping train Anneliese to take your place. I doubt she will be as good as you, but she should do all right."

At that point, Anneliese Bryce comes out of the employee break room. She has a brown trench coat on for the blustery weather outside. Petite, well-endowed, small waist, brown hair, and piercing green eyes, Anneliese is indeed attractive, but not proper material for consideration to become a vampire in the eyes of the elders. She is a young soul with much to learn. That is why several other vampires snicker when Cliff refers to her as porfa. On this night, though, she is walking toward Harold and Victor, smiling, getting an ego boost from their appreciative glances.

"She'll do all right, Harold. Just have to make sure she stays focused. Sometimes she flirts outrageously with the customers. Sure, sometimes that will make a sale, but still…"

Harold nods as Anneliese walks up to them. "Night, Harold. See you at eight tomorrow. Should be a hoot dealing with the last-minute shoppers on Christmas Eve." She then favors Victor with a smile. "This is your last night of freedom, Victor? Buy you a drink? There's this little place called Marcus's. It's just over in the Town and Country center across from Main Place. Good food, nice crowd. I think you'd like it."

Victor thinks it over briefly. Actually, Marcus's on Main was the sort of place he normally avoided, but he figures, *What the heck, it is either this or go home and start dealing with arriving relatives.* "Sure, Anneliese. I'll follow you over."

"See you there in a few then." She walks out the door, putting an enticing sway into her hips. Harold and Victor watch her as she leaves. Victor can see that Harold is actually jealous of him.

"Dude, you are *so* lucky. She is hot, and she wants you. Play your cards right and you will score tonight for sure."

Victor just shrugs and heads toward the door. "She is easy on the eyes, Harold, and possibly in other ways as well. She really isn't my type though. I find intellect attractive. I could be mistaken, but Anneliese strikes me as being more the cheerleader type." Harold just shakes his head as Victor leaves the store and walks out to his car.

Victor heads south on Tustin to Chapman. He turns right on Chapman, heading west. While driving through the famous circle of the Orange Plaza, he notes with sadness the large number of empty storefronts. *It's so sad. Every one of those vacant stores is like the end of someone's dream.* Shortly, the edifice of the Main Place Mall appears on his right. To his left is the more subdued Town and Country Plaza. He turns left and parks in front of Marcus's. Anneliese had arrived a few minutes before and has a table near the bar. She waves to him as he enters. Victor does a double-take. She has taken off the trench coat, revealing a very short red dress with a low-cut blouse that leaves very little to the imagination. Victor nods approvingly. *She looks hot.*. He waves back at her and then comes over and sits down.

As he sits down, Victor notices the envious looks he is getting from many of the other men in the restaurant. He laughs in his mind at that thought. Anneliese smiles and leans forward on the table, making sure he had a good view down her blouse while trying to make the move appear accidental.

"I'm buying tonight, Victor. Thanks for being such a sweetie over at Dasher's. You're really smart, you know? I like smart guys. You know how to treat a girl right. So, name your poison."

She motions, and an overly perky cocktail waitress comes over. Victor orders a Cuba libre while Anneliese orders a mojito.

When the drinks come, Victor looks at Anneliese's right hand and notices the ruby ring she wears. "That's a beautiful ring, Anneliese. It looks very old, heirloom quality. That's definitely a natural ruby."

Anneliese holds her hand out so Victor can get a closer look at the ring. "My, um…friend Cliff gave it to me a few months back. He said it was about five hundred years old, you know? He might be right, but it really is pretty, isn't it?"

Victor gives her a rather quizzical look. "Cliff must be some really great friend to give you a ring like that. I am sure it is very valuable. Is he your boyfriend?"

Anneliese puts her hand down and laughs that little teehee-style laugh that many men find endearing but grates on Victor's nerves.

"No, Cliff isn't my boyfriend. Not even a lover, not really anyway. I see him a couple times a week, but he's really busy, you know? He deals with all these boring politicians and their cronies. He seems to like it, though I don't know why. I've met some of his friends. They don't seem to like me at all. Bunch of stuffed-shirt meanies."

Victor shakes his head. "So what made you choose to work at Dasher's anyway?"

"It's something to do. I like working with the public. Besides, it's close to where I will be going to school next year, you know? I'll be attending class at Chapman University. My parents will be paying my way. Still, I need money to have fun and buy some supplies."

"Chapman is a really good school."

Victor takes a sip of his drink and then looks over at the dance floor. A few couples are out there, dancing to some tunes from the 1980s. Anneliese looks out toward the dance floor and smiles.

"Come dance with me, Victor."

They both get up and head to the dance floor. So long as it wasn't techno or country western, Victor truly enjoyed dancing. Guys on the dance floor look at Victor with envy, some of the women glare over at Anneliese. They dance to at least a dozen songs. Victor enjoys watching Anneliese dance, and she smiles and moves seductively. After about a half hour, they take a break and return to their table.

"You're fun to dance with, Victor. So many guys just won't get out there and dance. You do. That's special."

Victor just smiles. "Years ago, I used to be really self-conscious about dancing. I had to get really drunk before I would hit the dance floor. Then, one night, I went to a nightclub and just watched people dance for a while. I found out that about ninety percent of them didn't dance any better than I did. So, ever since then, when I get the opportunity to dance with someone, I do it."

They spend the next half hour talking about family, the holidays, life in general. Victor basically finds Anneliese to be endearing, though the constant "you knows" and the teehee laugh do grate on his nerves. Victor checks his cell phone and sees that it is nearly midnight.

"Sadly, I think I should be heading home soon. I have a lot of relatives coming into town. My mother decided she wanted to get the whole family together for Christmas. They wanted to give me a sendoff before I go to DC on Saturday."

Anneliese looks crestfallen. "Do you have to go, Victor? It's been so nice to spend an evening with a guy who actually listened to what I said, a guy who wasn't trying to grope me every chance he had. You really are one of the nice ones. That you have in common with Cliff, you know?"

Victor takes out one of his new business cards and writes down his e-mail address and his new mailing address in Georgetown and hands it to her. "I hope you will keep in touch. If you ever find yourself in DC in the next couple of years, let me know."

Anneliese opens her purse and takes out a card. "Here's my e-mail address and my cell phone number. Next time you are in OC, please let me know. We can get together, maybe go to the beach. I know you'd like seeing me in a bikini. Please? Promise?"

Victor nods and puts the card in his pocket. Anneliese beams. They get up, and Victor helps her with her coat. He then walks her out to her car. He extends his right hand.

"Thank you for the drink, the dancing, and the conversation, Anneliese. I hope you do well at Chapman."

Instead of taking his hand for a handshake, Anneliese gives Victor a hug and then a big sloppy kiss on the lips. She enjoys the surprised look on his face. "I can shake hands with anyone, Victor. You are my friend. I hope I will see you again soon." With that, she gets into her car and drives off.

Victor watches Anneliese drive off before he gets into his car. *Harold was probably right. She would have let me take her to one of those dive motels on Main and have my way with her. Just didn't feel right. I want the first time to be really special. I will know when the time is right.*

At about three in the morning on Christmas Eve in Avignon, a taxi pulls up to Pa Anovas's house. From it exits Maurana. As she is paying the driver, Claude Duviere comes out of the house. He reaches her as the taxi pulls off, and he waves the cab through the gates. Maurana is all smiles until she sees the look on Claude's face. She could read his surface thoughts easily enough; he was not trying to conceal them.

"Why are you so distressed, Claude? What has happened here in my absence?"

Claude grabs a couple of Maurana's suitcases. "It's best that we go inside to talk, my lady. Monsieur Petard is also in. I know he has been eagerly awaiting your arrival. As to the Vitzameri, you'll soon see."

Clearly distressed, Maurana follows Claude into the front salon. Petard is seated at a desk, running a calculator. He has a large pile of files next to him. He stands up and bows in acknowledgment of Maurana's presence. "You have returned, my lady. We were hoping to see you by the Solstice. I trust you had a pleasant holiday? Your grandson Dennis is doing well?"

Maurana is perturbed about the small talk. "I was delayed, sadly. Dennis is fine. However, we clearly have more important matters at hand. What has been going on? Why is Kristano distressed? What are all these files about? I want answers, gentlemen, in fairly short order."

Claude and Petard then proceed to tell Maurana all about La Mer's suicide and confession regarding the death of Kristano's sister back in 1753.

Once explained, Petard gestures toward the files. "The Vitzameri has had me comb the archives for all material related to the Bodellini seizures. Apparently, she owned quite a bit of property in France, Italy, and Switzerland. I believe I have a final figure to provide the Vitzameri with as regards proper compensation." He hands the summary to Maurana for review.

Maurana looks over the summary and hands it back to Petard. "Your fiscal review is sound, Monsieur. Sadly, though, this matter is far more about honor than about money. Aurea was wronged two hundred and fifty-five years ago, and now Kristano has to make this right. Where is he, Claude?"

"He's been in his private study upstairs for the past week, madam. I am sure he knows you have returned, so unless I miss my guess, he should be arriving here momentarily."

Claude's statement is confirmed by the sounds of footfalls on the stairs.

As the inner door opens, Maurana rises in respect, along with Claude and Petard. Maurana has been Pa Anovas's confidant for about a century. She is 16,532 years old, looks about forty. She was the youngest princess of the Vas Zolan dynasty, the rulers of a small late Atlantean kingdom. She is of average height and has light brown hair, piercing green eyes, and narrow hips, a classic beauty by the standards of that time. Pa Anovas values her for her keen mind and sound intellect. Pa Anovas enters the salon, looking worn and haggard.

"Sit down, my friends. Welcome back, Maurana. I presume you have been informed regarding the disaster I have on my hands?"

Maurana nods with a look of concern crossing her face. "With all due respect, Kristano, I never believed that Aurea Bodellini was responsible for Vetrina's death. The whole case never made sense to me. La Mer, the few times I saw him, he struck me as being a real scumbag. Now I see that I was right."

Pa Anovas sits down and turns to Petard. "So, my friend, do you have a final figure for me to work with regarding the Bodellini seizures?"

"Yes, my lord. The current value of the properties, if they were all intact, would be thirty-six million Euros. Figuring in lost rents, value of furnishings and such, we are looking at financial compensation of ninety-seven million Euros. Should you care to try and figure in punitive damages, defamation of character, wrongful accusation, and pain and suffering, well, a modern court would likely award her in excess of two hundred million Euros."

Maurana stands up and paces the room. "This is all well and good. However, the primary issue here has very little to do with financial compensation. This is a matter of honor, Kristano. A serious blood debt is owed here. You wronged Aurea Bodellini by accusing her of killing Vetrina in spite of hard evidence to the contrary. She underwent Plinthi several times. She was your sister's most loyal friend, and how was she rewarded? By loss of standing, loss of property, and exile. No amount of money can make up for that."

Pa Anovas nods morosely. "Thank you, gentlemen. If you wouldn't mind, Maurana and I need to discuss this matter in private."

Claude and Petard bow and leave the room.

With pleading eyes, Pa Anovas looks over at Maurana. "What in the world am I to do? How can I possibly make things right with Aurea?"

"You want to make things right, Kristano? I would say you are about two hundred and fifty-five years too late to do that. Best you can hope for now is to save face and make her whole. Aurea holds the blood debt, so it will be her decision to make, not mine. I doubt she will make you pay the ultimate price, but it is certainly within her rights to do so."

"I know that, Maurana. I have been asking myself how I could have been so blind, so foolish. I have stared at that painting of Vetrina in my study for hours, hoping it would speak and tell me what to do. I know I can't call her, nor do I think it would be prudent for me to just show up on her doorstep. This transgression cannot be allowed to fester any longer. I am in the wrong, and honor must be served."

Maurana sits down and thinks for a few minutes. "Well, I think I know where to start. I will contact Carol Ann Vincent. She is Aurea's best friend, and they are sharing a house in New York City. In the meantime, have Petard's agents purchase the eight properties that are still intact if the present owners will sell. Given the state of the economy right now, I would guess at least half would be receptive. Liquidate La Mer's assets, and hold those funds in trust for Aurea. I don't know how this will play out, Kristano. To say this is bad would be a vast understatement. As you say, though, honor must be served. That it shall be."

Early in the afternoon on Christmas Eve, Victor takes a break from the family and heads over to have lunch with his friends Matthew and Oscar at his favorite restaurant, the Imperial Thai Chrysanthemum.

He gets a bit misty eyed when he walks in the door. *I am really gonna miss this place.* He perks up when he goes in and sees Matthew at a table waving him over. He crosses the room and sits down.

Matthew's cell phone beeps, and he reads the text message. "Oscar's caught in traffic. He'll be here in a few minutes." He regards Victor solemnly. "So, how are you, my man? I'm still having troubling believing that you are going to be working for a Congressman. I mean, wow, it just seems so not like you."

"I'm fine, Matt, really. I am a bit overwhelmed and still in shock about what awaits me. So much change in such a short time. No, I never even considered working for a politician and yes, I do have reservations about it. In the end, shall we say, Moore made me an offer I couldn't refuse. I spend two years on his staff and my student loans are paid in full. That and it is a way to get away from my parents, at least for awhile."

Oscar finally arrives, looking harried but still smiling. "Hi Victor. Hi Matt. Geez, the traffic on Tustin is brutal! You'd think it was Christmas Eve or something." He sits down, shaking his head. "Oh yea, that's right. It *is* Christmas Eve!"

Victor smiles contentedly. "Glad you could make it, Oscar. It's been a long time since the three of us have been able to get together."

Oscar pats Victor on the back. "Couldn't miss this, my man! The wife told me to get over here and toast your escape from the OC. So, here I am! Congrats on the job! I bet your old man is just blown away by this, isn't he? I know how he kept browbeating you for the major you chose."

"My father and I have been at odds for many years. My choice of majors was simply the most visible dispute. He is suddenly treating me much better, but I know it is all an act. He looks at disagreement as defiance. I just didn't want to pursue an MBA."

Matt nods. "I really get that, Victor. If you look up the term 'control freak' in the online dictionary, your dad's picture should be there.

Seriously, though, why did Moore hire you? If he read your master's thesis, he would know what you think."

Victor chuckles. "C'mon, Matt. You know that Members of Congress don't actually read anything. He did tell me he had read a summary of my thesis, and he has stated several times that he admires me for having principles and being willing to speak my mind. As to the real reason why he hired me, that still perplexes me. I mean, this can't be winning him any brownie points with his party caucus. I was told that Homeland Security actually tried to convince him not to hire me. He told them to 'pound sand.' So, maybe I'll figure it out, or maybe I won't. It's hard to say."

Oscar shivers a bit. "Oh yeah, man! About a week ago, a couple dudes from Homeland Security came and interviewed me at the house. Dark suits and sunglasses, really spooky! They asked me if you were loyal to the United States. I told them you are a man of your word and you were as loyal as anyone these days."

Matt sighs. "I feel left out. None of those guys came to see me."

"I don't know why they bother with that kind of background check. I passed their drug check and the polygraph. I suppose many there in DC will find me to be annoying, but a threat? They need to get real. I am a man of words. I want to convince people to think and encourage lasting, peaceful change. Those who choose violence are playing into their game. Frankly, I don't intend to play it."

Presently they order their meals.

Later that evening, Carol Ann Vincent is taking a stroll through Central Park. The crowds are sparse, but she has been able to feed without incident, taking a pint of blood from this forlorn-looking man sitting on a bench. Now she has to make a phone call that she finds perplexing. Earlier that afternoon, she had received a coded text message from Maurana requesting she call her when she could, away from the eyes and ears of Aurea. Aurea was preoccupied with the Trent project, so she left and went to Manhattan for the evening. She punches in Maurana's private number and waits for the answer on the other end.

After two rings, a familiar voice answers. "I thank you for calling me. I trust Aurea is not nearby?"

"She is nowhere near, Maurana. Why all the secrecy? Why did I have to make sure Aurea was nowhere around? Is there some other problem to vex my friend out of Avignon, some other accusation the Vitzameri wishes to lay at her feet? With all due respect to him, of course."

Maurana clears her throat. "I am calling regarding the Vitzameri, yes. However, he is not accusing Aurea of anything. No. He has been slapped in the face by the truth, if you will."

Carol Ann's normally excited voice falls to a whisper. "You mean that the Vitzameri has finally acknowledged the facts, that Aurea had nothing whatsoever to do with the death of Lady Vetrina?"

"Exactly so, Carol Ann, as Phillipe La Mer confessed to everything. He gave detailed information that only someone directly involved could have known, gave the names of his co-conspirators, gave motive, and described method used. Now the Vitzameri feels like a complete idiot, as he should in this case, and he knows the gravity of the blood debt that he owes to Aurea. Honor must be served."

"I must be missing something here then, Maurana. Why aren't you calling Aurea and telling her this? She has a right to know this now. You know how much she has suffered over these decades, how she still pines over the death of her best friend, and how she feels betrayed by the Vitzameri. You know, she actually considered changing her name until she was vindicated. I managed to talk her out of doing that."

Maurana sighs. "Carol Ann, do you really think that Aurea would talk to me about the Vitzameri right now? Would they have an intelligent, frank discussion about discharging the blood debt and serving honor? Can you really tell me that would happen?"

Carol Ann is silent for a moment. "I see your point. I can just see her saying, 'Well, if he wants to serve honor, tell him to walk into a furnace.' While the protocols would give her that right, it would be an emotional response to a hideous wrong. We would end up with two dead high elders instead of our present one. Very well, Maurana. What do you want me to do?"

"Since you asked, what I *want* you to do is somehow convince Aurea to reconcile with the Vitzameri and make it like none of this actually happened, like it was some kind of mass hallucination, some kind of nightmare we all finally woke up from. Before you say anything, I know you can't do that. Nobody could do that. Therefore, I am asking you to intercede on *my* behalf. Tell her what I have told you. Once she gets the 'tell the bastard to walk in a furnace' out of her system, have her contact *me* to discuss this. I don't think it would serve anyone's rational self-interests for her to converse with the Vitzameri until a face-to-face meeting can be arranged as this is just so delicate. Does this make sense to you?"

"I can see your line of reasoning, Maurana. I don't know if this is the best course of action, but I don't have an alternative to offer. I will intercede on your behalf. I will let her know what you have told me. I somehow doubt this will prove simple or pleasant for anyone involved. Can I tell her that La Mer finally met a suitably violent demise? Surely the Vitzameri tore him to shreds after all this."

"La Mer's end was doubtless painful, but alas it was by his own hand. He doused himself with gasoline and went out with the dawn. He left all the documents and his confession on a DVD for his porfo to find. Poor man is still badly shaken by these events. Who can blame him? Petard did yeoman work figuring out La Mer's legacy and then having to go through all the documents relating to the properties seized from Aurea. Petard is a good man. Too bad he does not care to become one of us in this lifetime. I have already sent you copies of the confession via the network, secure channel. You and she can watch it together. Once the blood debt is settled, the confession will be made available to all vampires."

"We should consider making it available to our porfi as well. Once it becomes open channel, it will get out to them anyway. In the end, the Vitzameri will need to make a public statement about what really happened and give Aurea a public apology. As to the rest, well, I will not second guess her. I know how much this has hurt her. She deserves this vindication."

"I concur, my friend. I'll not take up more of your time tonight. I consider this a very special favor. Call it in when you have need of it. Farewell."

The conversation closes, and Carol Ann puts her cell phone back in her purse and then hails a taxi to get back to Staten Island.

It is midafternoon Christmas Day at the Trent house. Victor looks at all the festive decorations and mutters, "Humbug," under his breath. Zoe hears him and smiles and then gives him a silent tsk tsk. His mother and Grandmother Azalea are busy in the kitchen. The food is plentiful and smells good. His Aunt Cyndi Lou and Uncle Glenn arrived an hour ago. Both of them are watching the football game on the big-screen TV in the living room with his dad, Uncle Clyde, and Grandfather Fred. Victor looks with disapproval, having long regarded football as not just boring but as the modern equivalent of the Roman bread and circuses. The doorbell chimes, he answers it, and there is Uncle Reggie, whom he greets with a warm hug. Right behind Reggie are Victor's maternal grandparents, Norman and Abigail Croft. He greets them warmly as well. Before he shuts the door, Victor looks down the street to see if Arnold and Kat have shown up yet. As there is no sign of them, he shuts the door and then joins his Uncle Reggie at the table.

"So, Reggie, how's the paranormal research project going? Did you get to investigate the house in Torrance you were telling me about a couple weeks ago?"

"In fact, yes, my team and I did get to investigate that house, Victor. It was quite intense. Found three spirits there. They were all using this old, silver-lined bedroom mirror as their portal. Turned the thing around and made it face the wall. They tried coming through. The mirror shattered. So that house is now quiet. It's always so much more interesting when there is actually something there. Most of the time, there isn't."

Victor nods in agreement. "I think I will do some research while I am in DC, maybe take a trip down to Fredericksburg and Richmond or up to Baltimore or Philadelphia. There's lots of history there. I've read about several haunted locales in metro DC. Have to get some worthwhile activity while I am there."

"You will do fine, Victor. You will learn a lot, possibly about things you had never really considered before. What you will learn about how the imperial political system works firsthand could turn out to be doctorate material, if you want to go for that degree. If not, it is certainly prime material for a book."

Victor rolls his eyes, and Reggie mutters as Cyndi Lou sits down at the table with them.

"Why aren't you guys watching the game instead of wasting time talking about ghosts? They are all really demons from hell sent to torment wicked humans anyway. The Bible says so!"

Reggie smirks at that. "Most ghosts, if you will, are just place memories, echoes from the past. When someone sees an apparition doing the same thing without fail, over and over, rarely is that a spirit. Strong emotions, violent acts, can create such hauntings easily. Most spirits are just people who, for whatever reason, refuse to cross over. Generally, that is due to fear. The case I recently dealt with was a trio of angry earthbound spirits who simply refused to accept that they were no longer corporeal and that the house was no longer theirs. Nothing demonic about them though. They were agitated and confused."

Cyndi Lou looks perturbed. "That was just Satan fooling you, Reginald. Those were demons. Rely on that. Unless you used holy water and a blessed Bible, they will be back at that house soon with reinforcements!"

Before Victor can interject, his mother comes over to the table. "Leave the boys alone, Cyndi Lou. I might not approve of their paranormal research, but I don't think it is satanic. This is supposed to be a nice family gathering, and I intend to keep it that way, no matter what it takes!"

Muttering, Cyndi Lou gets up from the table and goes back into the living room to watch the football game.

Zoe and Victor help set the table in the formal dining room. As Victor pours the wine for those who want some, Arnold and Kat finally arrive, late as usual.

"I swear, Zoe, if those two were ever on time for anything, I would likely faint dead away."

"They are what they are, Victor. Not everyone values time the way you and I do. Besides, I think Mom figured they would be late as always. That would explain why dinner is only now ready to eat."

Christmas dinner was a polite affair. The conversation stayed light, mostly about mundane matters. The occasional quick glances and other body language showed how tense the room truly was. It had been years since all these people had been in the same room together, and Victor strongly suspected that the only reason his mother had been able to pull this off was because of his impending departure to DC. Susan Trent managed to have her dream dinner after all.

Once everyone was sated and the table was cleared, everyone gathered in the family room for the gifts. Per the family tradition, Arnold passed out the presents. Victor was pleased to receive a couple books, a nice silver bullion coin from his Uncle Reggie, and other practical items. His grandparents gave him some cash, which was particularly welcome, given his pending move. Zoe gave him a computer RPG that he had been looking at for a while. Aunt Cyndi Lou gave everyone cologne or perfume, as always. Some people were just imminently predictable in their gift-giving.

People quickly drift away from the living room and the Christmas tree once the gifts are opened and the trash collected. Victor saunters into the kitchen where his mother and Grandmother Abigail are putting food away and cleaning off the dishes. "Can I lend the two of you a hand with that?"

Abigail smiles warmly and shakes her head. "No, dear. Your mother and I have this under control. You go and mingle."

Victor turns around and looks at the various groups. Reggie and Zoe are chatting quietly out on the patio. His father is engaged in yet another absurd political debate with Uncle Clyde. Aunt Cyndi Lou is over in another corner hectoring her husband, Glenn, while Grandfather Norman watches in amusement. Finally, he notices Grandfather Fred motioning him over to sit and talk. Grandmother Azalea smiles as well. Victor makes his way over to the couch to join them. *They have long been a safe haven.*

Fred clasps Victor's hand as he sits down. "How are you, old timer? Are you all set for the move to Washington?"

"I'm doing all right; honestly I am very anxious and nervous about the move." The din of the argument between Clyde and his father drifted over. "However, I am glad for the opportunity to be out on my own." He sighs. "Don't get me wrong, I love my parents, but it seems like we just can't communicate. Maybe the distance and the time apart will help. Yes, I am so ready to be on my own."

Azalea nods curtly. "I understand, Victor, I really do. I don't understand why my son treats you and Zoe with such disdain, heck, and open hostility while treating that shiftless skunk Arnold like he is the most special child on the planet. We didn't raise him to be like that; I don't know where it came from. He may be an astute businessman, but when it comes to being a good father, well, something's missing."

"I certainly don't blame you and Grandpa Fred for any of that." He smiles wistfully. "My childhood memories of the times I stayed at your home are ones that I cherish. I remember the soft coo of the mourning doves in the morning, all the lovely rose bushes you had in the back yard. Those classic toys, especially the old tin gas station. You were like sanctuary to me and I appreciate it."

Fred nods. "We love you, Victor. We believe in you." He collects his thoughts. "I know some of how you feel about the world of politics, but I hope this new job opens up other opportunities for you. I really hope you make some new friends and maybe find someone special. You deserve to be happy."

"That's easier said than done for me, Grandpa. It's not easy for me to reach out because I get disappointed easily. As for romance, well, you know how picky I am. I so want it to be right. If I get married, I only want to do it once."

Azalea gives Victor a serious look. "I know you are an introvert, and yes, in many ways you are better than most people. You are too intelligent for your own good sometimes. Take some advice from an old woman: when it comes to finding that special someone, trust your intuition, not your reason. Let yourself fall."

Victor nods, sensing the truth in her words.

At about the time the Trent family Christmas party is winding down, over on Staten Island, Carol Ann and Aurea are sitting in the office, discussing the conversation Carol Ann had had with Maurana the day before regarding La Mer's confession. Aurea is very attentive, appearing numb about the news that she was finally vindicated in the matter of Lady Vetrina's death. She simply nods when Carol Ann offers to play the confession on her computer. They watch this together in silence. When it is over, Carol Ann notices that her friend is weeping quietly. She hands her a handkerchief, which Aurea daubs her eyes with.

"Somehow, it is aggravating that La Mer chose to commit suicide rather than facing me. It proves that the man was every bit the coward I knew him to be. Poetic justice, after a fashion, that

Thorne and Vachon were killed in some altercation in Paris in 1857. Is that everyone, though? I wonder if other Sapphires had a hand in Vetrina's assassination. Sounds like something the Society of Redemption would have loved to pull off. I wonder what Vetrina ever did to those three. Me, I know why they would try to frame me. La Mer and Vachon and I faced off several times on order business. They looked at me as being an upstart female who did not know her place. All those years ago, Carol Ann. I will never, ever forget it."

"You might have a point there, Aurea. Perhaps there were others involved. La Mer might not have known what other agents were in the employ of his Sapphire confederate. I'll contact Maurana and see what she thinks and find out what, if anything, has been done to investigate this possibility."

Aurea shakes her head. "No, my friend. I will contact Maurana myself. It is time for me to break the silence in a civil manner." She notes the shocked look that crosses Carol Ann's face. "No worries. I will not talk to her about what I want the Vitzameri to do as regards discharging the blood debt and satisfying honor. I am too outraged to give that matter proper consideration. If he came to our door now, I would likely tell him to disintegrate, and he would comply. I do need time to compose myself and think that through."

Aurea then turns to her computer and connects with Maurana's office. A rather startled-looking mortal female appears on the screen.

"Madam Aurea, is that you? By the gods, it *is* you! Lady Maurana told me to expect a contact from Carol Ann Vincent. It is an honor to serve you. I shall put you through to her at once!"

The computer screen goes briefly to the coat of arms of Order Ruby. Then, a rather surprised-looking Maurana appears onscreen.

"So Beatrice was not mistaken. I am honored that you have contacted me directly. I hated to impose on Carol Ann, but I did not think it would be prudent for me to contact you first, not for something as delicate as this. It was wrong that you had to suffer for this for any time at all, much less two hundred and fifty-five years.

Outside of Plinthi, I can only guess at the emotional turmoil you are going through now. How may I be of assistance?"

"I have a few specific questions regarding La Mer's confession. First, has there been any investigation as to whether others were involved besides Thorne and Vachon? I doubt any other Ruby vampires were involved, but this sounds like something the Society of Redemption would have had a hand in."

"Monsieur Petard has contacted Order Sapphire headquarters. Dr. Sancia Olos Parana's representative will only acknowledge that Thorne did exist and was killed in Paris in 1857. They insist he was the only Sapphire involved. Suffice it to say that we doubt Sapphire is telling us all they know. We are having experts go over what remains of the Redemptionist archives to see if anything comes up. I will let you know either way. Since you helped smash the Redemptionists, you might well have already smote anyone else involved."

"My second question has to do with the dreams La Mer said he was having prior to his suicide. Was his porfo able to shed any light on them? If I know La Mer, he likely kept some sort of journal."

"Monsieur Mondair has been completely cooperative in the investigation and most helpful in the disposition of La Mer's estate. He said that La Mer only complained to him of disturbed rest, that he was never specific about its nature. However, you are right; La Mer did keep a journal, which was found at his residence a few days after his suicide. It was most revealing reading, especially the last month. He said Vetrina herself was haunting his dreams. A week before his suicide, he wrote that someone who looked very much like Vetrina accosted him in the Casino de Monte Carlo. It is certainly possible that she has cycled back through. In fact, that is likely. We are looking into this. We have some agents in Monaco."

"I very much want an unabridged copy of La Mer's journal, Maurana. Depending on what it contains, I might well make a trip to Monaco myself. I knew Vetrina very well. If she is back and shows up in Monte Carlo, there is a chance that she would know me. That would establish lineage per the protocols."

Maurana nods in consent. "I will have Petard send you a copy electronically before this day is over. On another matter, I am pleased to say that we have obtained title to your villa outside Naples. We have made offers on six others that belonged to you. Petard is having the title made out to you, and the Vitzameri is covering all taxes and fees personally. I know the financial part is probably not your highest concern, but he is attending to that."

Aurea smiles sadly. "It would be nice to go back to Napoli. So very near Pompeii, so near home. I wonder if I could stand to actually walk those streets again. There are so many ghosts." She pauses and composes herself. "I have one demand to make at this time, Maurana, as regards the blood debt."

"The Vitzameri is in no position to bargain as regards this matter. Voice your demand, and I will relay it to him immediately."

"I want La Mer's confession released to the general nets within the hour. I know very few of the Vamphyri ever believed that I actually had anything to do with Vetrina's death, but I want the words of the assassin made public, straight from his mouth. I want it to have no restrictions. The Vitzameri need not say anything at this time, but I am insisting the release of the confession not wait until our final settlement."

"I expected you to make this demand. He told me that if you made this demand to go ahead and put the confession into general release, even make it available to Sapphire net." Maurana presses some buttons on her keyboard. "You will see it on Ruby and Emerald networks in about ten minutes. Is there anything else I can do for you tonight?"

Aurea wipes a tear from her eye. "No, my friend. I will be in touch about discharging the blood debt once I am ready to talk about it rationally. There are so many emotions to deal with."

Maurana weeps as well. "I understand, Aurea. Do let me know if you decide to make a trip to Monte Carlo. I could meet you there."

Both women sign off.

About two minutes later, as Aurea and Carol Ann are watching the general information feed on the Ruby network, a special bulletin comes up regarding La Mer's confession. Aurea clicks on the video, and they sit and watch it again. It was, as promised, in general release, completely unedited. As Aurea expected, the telepathic chatter increased. She was vindicated but felt no joy in it.

Midmorning on Friday the twenty-sixth found Victor and Zoe Trent wandering through the little boutique shops and galleries that lined Pacific Coast Highway in Laguna Beach. Zoe drove because Victor's car was on its way to DC. Congressman Moore's staff had arranged for it to be picked up at Victor's house on the morning of the twenty-fourth. The weather was too rough this time of year for cross-country travel by car to be desirable. Victor and Zoe walked hand in hand. People observing them thought they were just another young couple in love, enjoying an unusually fair late December day. Victor always felt at peace with his sister. He knew that she really understood him and accepted him for what he was. For her part, Zoe always felt understood, respected, and valued for her mind with her brother. So many guys insisted on talking to her breasts. Victor always looked her in the eyes. As lunchtime approached, they decided to dine at a small café near Main Beach. Being a winter day, the beach was not crowded; just people strolling along.

After they placed their orders, Victor looked wistfully toward the beach, watching the waves hit the shore. Zoe smiled at him, noticing that faraway look in his eyes that meant he was deep in thought. She knew every line on that face. Yes, they were closer than most brothers and sisters, and she knew why. A competent psychic confirmed it, but it really came as no surprise to either of them. They were a step above soul mates. They were twin flames. They were destined to complete an important task in this lifetime, though as of yet they had no idea what that was. Being brother and sister, they knew that they would never consummate their relationship, tempting though the idea was to both of them. Well, their future life partners would simply have to understand the special nature of their relationship. So far, no one else had measured up in her eyes. She knew the same was true with Victor. In their most recent past life, they had been husband and wife and they had loved each other deeply.

Victor sighs and smiles at Zoe. "I will miss this place, Zoe. I have had a lot of fun down here, wandering through the Sawdust Festival, gawking at the Pageant of the Masters, wandering the boutiques and galleries. Laguna Beach, Dana Point, Trestles Beach, these are truly special places."

"I really appreciated it when you pointed out the paintings by Cherise Oly-Patlin, the mother of Uncle Reggie's late friend Clark Oly-Patlin. Such a unique concept! Look at one side, see one image, and look at the other, completely different image. It is truly a rare talent. Reggie said that Clark used to help his mother make those paintings. How sad that he is gone. I would have enjoyed meeting him."

"I met Clark in December of 2000, a few months before he died. He had a keen mind and sharp wit, was very intelligent and dedicated to his causes. He had a rather novel political concept of libertarian monarchism. He did a lot of work with the homeless. The man practiced what he preached. That's for sure. I didn't agree with his political aims, but I will say that his kingdom ideas would beat out our present corporatist police state hands down."

Their meals arrive. Zoe takes a sip of wine and watches a guy playing Frisbee on the beach with his dog. She points them out to Victor. He looks over and smiles.

"You know, Victor, it really is the simple things that matter, that make life worth living. Don't lose sight of that when you are living in the imperial city. There are plenty of parks there, and Northern Virginia has plenty of open space, not to mention all the history.

Don't let them drag you down. I know it will be a challenge, but you can do it."

"I won't let them drag me down, Zoe. I promise you that. I will make sure I get away from DC whenever feasible. When I can't, I will make sure I get away from the office for at least a little while. Georgetown is supposed to be nice. I guess I will know how true that is soon enough. I'm flying out of John Wayne late tomorrow afternoon. I'll get into Ronald Reagan National around ten. Someone from DC staff will pick me up and take me to my apartment. I will have Sunday to myself and then straight to work on Monday. It should be ever so memorable. Get a week's worth of orientation. So much fun, I'm sure."

"I'll be able to make a trip out in early April. You can take me to a party at one of the embassies, go and play tourist, not worry about weird comments from Mom and Dad. I want to see some of the Smithsonian museums, go and visit the Vietnam War Memorial. I hear that is very sobering."

"That will be great, Zoe. By then, I'm sure I will be desperate to see a familiar friendly face. I know it will take me a few weeks to settle in and orient myself. I will be a stranger in a hostile strange land. As much as I don't like the southland sometimes, it is still home. This is my comfort zone, bizarre as it often can be. I will have to set new routines, figure out what makes those people tick. I'm sure though that my ability to basically vanish in a crowd will serve me well."

They finish their meals and pay the bill. Hand in hand, they go out and stroll Main Beach. At least for today, Victor is happy. No matter what the future holds, he is happy now. Zoe feels the same.

Later that evening, in the house on Staten Island, Aurea and Carol Ann have concluded a discussion about the relevance of La Mer's journal and are once again discussing Victor Trent. Paulina Wong,

Carol Ann's porfa, is present as well. She has been sworn to secrecy and fully informed about the project. Now that the day is nearly here, Aurea is giddy with excitement. Carol Ann finds her friend's intense excitement to be most disconcerting. Paulina gives them her complete attention, convinced that she is now part of a grand adventure. Carol Ann is about to give voice to a concern when Zack's face comes up on Aurea's computer screen. Aurea looks over and smiles at the young man.

"I see you aren't alone, Madame Aurea. Is this a good time? I could get back to you later if need be."

Aurea smiles and shakes her head. "Not to worry, Zack. Unless this is some personal problem you want to speak of in private? Like perhaps you have decided you prefer Ruby over Emerald?"

Zack grabs an energy drink and chuckles. "Nah. Nothing like that. It would break Sydney's heart if I changed my mind about that. Pest though she can be, she's the best, so I will go Emerald when I am ready. No. This has to do with updated information regarding the man we never spoke of."

Aurea nods. "I see. Is it anything really game-changing?"

"No. It's just his flight schedule and his new address in Georgetown. His flight is scheduled to arrive at Reagan National at ten oh three p.m. Davis Grayson from Moore's office will be picking him up and taking him to his new apartment. Nice studio, good neighborhood, excellent access to the Washington metro. There was one somewhat amusing matter. It seems Homeland Security did not like the fact that Trent was such a staunch critic of the American political system. They tried to talk Moore out of hiring him. Moore told them that criticism isn't terrorism, that if they could not somehow prove that Trent represented a tangible threat to national security, they had to approve him. Of course, they had to cave."

"Excellent, Zack. Keep me posted if you find out anything noteworthy."

Zack's face leaves the screen.

Aurea then turns and looks at Carol Ann. "So, who do we have that lives in the greater Washington metro area? We need to have a firm notion on just who it is that Victor might be dealing with."

Carol Ann punches a few keys, and a list comes up on her computer screen. "Best numbers that we have right now for greater Washington for vampires in residence are seven Ruby, five Emerald, and two Sapphire. There are always a few others passing through. The imperial city really isn't that popular among our kind. Especially after nine eleven, that place is just paranoia central."

Aurea taps her fingers on the desk. "I'm not concerned so much with the Emeralds and Sapphires. Unless I miss my guess, they won't be factors to be reckoned with for this blind test. If one of the Emeralds does discover him, I will call Patsy and have her talk to them. If one of the Sapphires finds him, he will probably be dead, sadly, and then I will hunt down said Sapphire and destroy him or her, as the case might be. Who are the Ruby vampires there? What do we know about them?"

Carol Ann presses another key, and seven pictures appear on the screen. "Adler, Cassandra Mae. Age one hundred and sixty-seven. Plaz since 1867, she is somewhat reclusive in that she has never had a porfa or porfo. She is regarded as stable and polite by her peers. She frequents the balls and parties of the Washington political circles and is originally from the Charleston, South Carolina, area."

Paulina looks over at Aurea. "I've met Cassie Mae. She's very nice, a really good friend of Midnight Silk. Very intelligent, and she plays it close to the vest."

Carol Ann clicks on the next picture. "Brown, Kathleen. Age two hundred and sixty. Plaz since 1778. She has a porfo at this time. She is gregarious and frequents the clubs of metro DC. She is known as temperamental and often dismissive of mortals. She was originally from Boston, Massachusetts."

Aurea nodded. "She's intense, that one. I will not be surprised if Kathleen sticks around long enough to become a high elder. She can play the intrigue games with the best of them."

Clicking on the next picture, Carol Ann continues on. "Dustin, Lester Henry, age fifty. Plaz since 1988 and lives with his mortal son, Chester. Very cerebral. Tends to frequent museums and historical sites. He's not very sociable according to his peers. Born and raised and still residing in Alexandria, Virginia."

Aurea raises an eyebrow. "He could be a problem. Let's hope Victor does not run into him on some bad night. The consequences would likely be fatal."

Carol Ann goes to the fourth picture. "Martin, Oscar, age one hundred and twelve. Plaz since 1922. Wealthy. Owns a sizable estate outside of Bethesda, Maryland. Has a porfa. Frequents clubs and attends plays and concerts. He is considered stable and reliable by his peers with a calm disposition." Carol Ann turns and faces Aurea. "I have stayed at his house a few times over the years. He is a very gracious host."

Aurea waves her hand, so Carol Ann turns back around and clicks on the fifth picture.

"Penn, Rachel, age two hundred and seventy-five. Plaz since 1755. She is considered by most to be the friendliest, most outgoing of the DC Rubies. Frequents parties, goes to clubs, and attends social mixers, which, of course, we all already knew. Rachel does come to New York City rather frequently. She came from Philadelphia originally."

Paulina nods. "Rachel is nice, though I sometimes wonder about her sincerity. When I am around her, I perceive games within games. I say watch your back around that one."

Carol Ann clicks on the sixth picture. "Sidney, Albert, age ninety-eight. Plaz since 1935. Born and raised in the district proper, he now lives in Silver Springs, Maryland. He is rather formal, tends to hang out at upscale clubs. He does have a porfo."

Aurea shakes her head. "I never have met the man. He sounds completely nondescript."

Carol Ann clicks on the final picture. "Well, we all know her. Van Clerc, Johanna, age seven hundred and one. Plaz since 1331.

Came from what is now the Netherlands. Skilled accountant. Works for many Ruby and Emerald Vamphyri. She's very well-to-do but very private. No porfa or porfo for over a hundred years. Currently resides in Arlington. She's pleasant, kind, considerate, and very professional."

Aurea looks over the pictures again and nods. "These are the people who will decide if Victor is what I think he is. They're quite a group, appropriate for a blind test. Some will say this is not fair, but then, what is? I bet he does something by late spring that will make it necessary for him to be put to the final test."

Carol Ann looks over at Aurea. "I would hope it happens sooner than that. Victor will get used to DC and become comfortable there. If he does that, our window of opportunity will pass. As you said, Aurea, the test works best when the subject is uncomfortable. Then again, I'm not sure Victor will ever get wholly comfortable in DC. It really isn't his kind of place."

Aurea looks over at Paulina. "You look like you have something to add here. Please do."

"I think it would be prudent to consider contacting Patsy. The sheer number of Emeralds in metro DC makes it a high possibility that Victor could run across one of them instead of one of us. Under the present circumstances, you have a lot of political capital, if you will. Look at it as insurance. Also, there is the ever-present issue of his sister, Zoe. They are very tight. She will need to be evaluated if Victor does pass the tests and chooses to join us."

Aurea smiles. "Point taken. I will give the matter of contacting Patsy some more thought. You certainly could be right. As for Zoe, she is already under evaluation." She turns and looks over at Carol Ann. "Victor and Zoe could be twin flames, so, yes, if Victor does join us, she will have to be approached rather soon thereafter. She will not be shut out of Victor's life on any level for long."

Carol Ann stretches in a fluid, feline-style motion. "I guess we will know when Victor is in the air tomorrow and when he arrives in

Washington. Have the airline website saved in my favorites for now. I guess you are off to the gym now, Paulina?"

Paulina stands up. "Actually, I am off to the karate class. I've just about qualified for my black belt. So much fun taking some of those guys down who think they can wipe the floor with me because I am small. You should see the looks on their faces!"

Aurea leaned back in her chair. "The wait is nearly over. Tomorrow, the game really begins."

At 2:00 p.m. on Saturday the twenty-seventh, Susan Trent drops Victor off in front of the terminal at John Wayne Airport. He walks in and glares at the huge statue of John Wayne. As he had checked in online and only had a small carry-on bag, he is able to walk past the long lines of holiday travelers at the ticket counter. He gets into the security checkpoint line and takes off his shoes and waits. After fifteen minutes in line, he is up to the TSA officer. He keeps a dead-pan look as the TSA personnel check his bag. Another minute and he is through. He sits down and puts his shoes back on and walks over to the gate. His flight to Washington is listed as on time, but he has an hour to wait.

He sits and reads a novel by L. Neil Smith. Occasionally, he looks up and observes the people around him. Mostly, he just keeps to himself and watches the time, seeing if the flight status stays the same. To his amazement, it actually does. The gate opens twenty minutes before departure, and the boarding process begins. After a few minutes, his boarding group is called. He puts his book away and boards the aircraft.

Once on board, he finds his seat, a window seat in the emergency exit row. He puts his carry-on under the seat and takes his book out again. Fifteen minutes later, right on time, the plane pushes away from the terminal. He looks out the window at the buildings near the airport, thinking about what lies ahead for him. He fidgets in his seat, drumming his fingers on the armrest, which earns him a glare from a nearby passenger. Yes, he is nervous.

A few minutes later, the plane takes off in the strange fashion dictated by the Orange County authorities, up at a swift speed and steep angle, followed by a brief cutoff of the engines. Once that is over, Victor breathes a sigh of relief.

The guy sitting next to him mutters, "I hate the takeoffs from this airport."

At about this time, Carol Ann goes into Aurea's room. "Victor's flight is in the air."

Aurea nods in affirmation. "That is excellent news. Let me know when his flight arrives in metro DC."

CHAPTER 4

Saturday, 27 December 2008, just before 10:00 p.m. Victor's flight is now on final approach to Reagan National Airport. He is staring out the window at the lights of Northern Virginia, thinking, pondering, wondering about the future. Truly, how is he to thrive spending the next two years in the belly of the beast? He looks around the cabin as some other passengers put laptops and game consoles away.

The captain's voice booms over the intercom. "Nice night for December in the Washington area with clear skies and a balmy thirty-three degrees with light winds. We will be on the ground shortly and will arrive at the gate on schedule. Thank you for flying with us, and we hope to see you again soon."

Victor smirks at that and then goes back to looking outside. Soon enough, the airport buildings and the runway come into view. The landing is smooth, and the captain is right; the plane reaches the gate on schedule. Once he disembarks, he sends a text message to Zoe, letting her know he has arrived safely. Then he calls the number of the staffer who is to pick him up and take him to his new apartment.

"Davis Grayson here. From the phone number and the time it is, I presume you are Victor Trent."

"You are correct, sir. The plane has landed, and I am in the terminal. Where will I find you?"

"I'm just beyond the security checkpoint. You can't possibly miss me, Victor. I am the only seven-foot-tall white guy out here. OC staff sent me a picture of you, so I will know you when I see you."

"Sounds good, Davis. See you in a few minutes."

He puts his cell phone back into his pocket and walks toward the security checkpoint. Victor passes by some newspaper kiosks, glances at the headlines, and walks on. Just before going through the checkpoint, he notices a sign that he thinks is ridiculous. It reads, "Warning! Passing beyond this sign is leaving the security zone. Travelers are prohibited from turning back once they pass beyond this sign." Victor sees a bored-looking TSA officer sitting just beyond this sign. For a moment, he thinks about asking him if the sign would apply if he just put a toe beyond it or if he actually had to step beyond it. Figuring such sarcasm would only cause problems, he just keeps going and emerges into the main concourse. Davis sees him and walks over.

The two men shake hands. Victor is impressed by Davis's firm, friendly grasp. Definitely not the limp handshake he had come to expect from career bureaucrats.

"Welcome to the district, Victor. Well, not quite, not yet. We're still in Arlington. You have anything to pick up at baggage claim?"

Victor shakes his head. "Nope. I only brought this carry-on with me for the flight. Don't need to deal with those blasted carousels. Not this time anyway."

"Good going, my man. Let's blow this joint and get you to your new place. It's a nice studio apartment in Georgetown. I think you'll like it." Victor walks out to the parking lot with Davis. They get in Davis's black SUV, and Davis drives them into DC.

As they cross the bridge over the Potomac, a chill goes up Victor's spine. He's in the imperial city for the first time in his life.

"You know, Davis, if someone had told me on the first of this month that I would be ending the month living and working in DC, I would have told them they were completely insane. Well, here I am, working for a Congressman. This is just bizarre."

Davis chuckles. "I like your sense of life, Victor. We'll get along fine. You should do some of the tourist stuff tomorrow, get a feel for the city. We'll only be working three days next week. Bob gave the staff Friday the second off as well. The week after, when the new Congress is seated, that will be a real grind."

"I'm sure it will be, but I'll wager it will pale in comparison to inauguration week. With the change of administration and all, I'm sure that will be quite the challenge as well. Do we have to attend any of those events?"

"Well, back in oh five we certainly did. That was the second term, and our guy was in the Oval Office. Now, we are on the outside looking in. However, yes, we are expected to attend the inauguration itself and likely one of the minor balls. I doubt we will get any invites to the really good parties this time around."

Shortly thereafter, they arrive at the apartment building in Georgetown. It is very neat, very practical. Davis walks with him to the door.

"Well, Victor, this is the place. Here are your keys, and here is your metro pass. Your car should be here on Monday, but using the metro bus to get to the Rayburn Building is a lot more practical. Parking is at a premium there. See you Monday morning at the office." Davis shakes Victor's hand again and walks back to the car.

Victor opens the door and enters the apartment.

Carol Ann and her porfa, Paulina Wong, are walking in Times Square, taking in the sights and sounds and doing some window shopping. From appearances, one would likely think that Paulina is Carol Ann's bodyguard. She is the one with the hard stare, wearing a black pantsuit while Carol Ann wears a long, red dress, only the edge of which is visible under the trench coat she is wearing. They are just out for the evening, taking a break from all the intensity and intrigue surrounding Aurea. There are quite a few people out in spite of the late hour.

Paulina points out a man lurking in the shadows across the street. "That one is trying too hard to be cagey and inconspicuous. I think even most of the unaffiliated mortals hereabouts sense his presence on some level." Paulina locks eyes with the man.

He cringes and walks off.

Carol Ann beams with pride. "You did that very well. Better than some of the Vamphyri I know. You are already a force to be reckoned with. You will be very powerful indeed when you become one of us."

Paulina's expression softens. "I was good at that even before I met you folks. Your training has made it more effective, certainly. I think that guy was some newly minted Sapphire. He didn't register or act like a mortal usually would. What say you?"

"Yes, Paulina, he likely was a Sapphire with only a few weeks under his belt. Have you decided when you want to become one of us yet?"

Paulina was looking at some display mannequins in a dress shop, admiring the dresses. "I was thinking about February of 2013, shortly after I turn twenty-five. I think that would be the best time to do it. I'm trying to do like Aurea has recommended and have a child before I undergo the transformation, to help preserve the bloodline. I agree that my genes should not be lost to the human gene pool, and besides, it is something I want to do. Finding the right guy has proved rather troublesome."

Carol Ann laughs. "I think you tend to scare most of them off. That look you can give will turn people's blood to ice. You don't have to limit your choices to the affiliated, although that does lessen the complications. It would be so exciting to see you happy, be with child, and bring life into the world. Once you become one of us, that opportunity passes. We can take life, we can save it, but we cannot create it. Something to do with what the transformation does to the body. Rather a shame, I think."

At that point, Carol Ann's cell phone beeps, indicating that she has a text message. She reads it and shows the text to Paulina. It is from Aurea. It reads, "Victor is now in Georgetown. The blind test is under way."

"I don't understand all the reasons why this Trent fellow has to be tested like this. You folks didn't do anything like that to me." She pauses when she sees the look on Carol Ann's face. "At least, I don't remember it that way. Certainly not so elaborate, was it?"

Carol Ann puts her arm around Paulina's waist. "Honey, no one even gets invited into our circles without undergoing some kind of test. Yours had to do with strength of character and resolve. Granted, it was nowhere near as elaborate as what Victor is being put to, nor anywhere near as dangerous. The stakes are higher for him as well. If Aurea is right about him and he is discovered by the right vampire, he could have a fascinating future if he joins us. If he runs into a hostile vampire or ends up failing the final test, then that is the end for him. Granted, Aurea could be wrong, and Victor could just serve the two years on Moore's staff and go back to his life with his student loans paid off. Aurea being mistaken isn't very likely."

"She seems obsessed with him. I mean, the issue with the Vitzameri also has her attention, but Trent even trumps that. It can't just be that she thinks he is likely a returned vampire. From what you have told me, this has happened many times before. She has always struck me as being passionate, but now, its just overwhelming and a real epic phenomenon wow sort of situation."

Carol Ann whispers in Paulina's ear. "She thinks Trent might be a returning ancient Atlantean vampire, one that would be highly prized by Avignon. If he passes the tests, Maurana will have to be consulted. The reward would be quite sizable, as would the prestige Aurea would gain. You might think that Rachel plays the intrigue games well, but she does not hold a candle to our Aurea. Watch her well."

Victor does not spend his first Sunday in the District doing "tourist stuff." He chooses instead to attend to more mundane concerns. He gets his computer set up and goes online. He chats awhile with Zoe and Arnold. He sends an e-mail to Anneliese. Then, he calls home and talks to his mom, letting her know he is alright.

After lunch, he decides to take a walk around the neighborhood to get the lay of the land. He is pleased to see that the bus stop is right in front of his complex. Soon, he is satisfied that he has a decent grasp of the overall situation. He takes a bus down to the Washington Harbour and walks along the banks of the Potomac. He notices how bare the trees are. He marvels when he spies a few hardy souls out sailing on the river. He looks over at the other bank into Virginia. *It's soothing to go for a walk and think.*

He ponders this deeply. *I really am alone here. I have no support system. Everything that I know, my friends and family, are clear across the continent. I need to get a grip and figure this out. Surely there are some free-thinking individuals around here.* He continues to walk, then steps into a small café for dinner. Then, he heads back to his apartment and stays online until late in the evening.

Just after midnight on the twenty-ninth in Avignon, Maurana and Francois Petard are meeting with Oliver Scott, a Ruby Order vampire who knew La Mer, Thorne, and Vachon. He is there to provide background information and insight, as Plinthi had shown that he had no direct involvement in the assassination of Lady Vetrina. Mr. Scott appears very composed, though he carefully maintains a respectful demeanor. Maurana is making no effort to conceal her surface thoughts, and he feels her contempt. Petard is ever the professional, the shrewd lawyer he has been for several years now.

Maurana glares across the table. "So, Mr. Scott, were you in Avignon on October sixteenth, seventeen fifty three?"

Oliver looks Maurana in the eyes. "My lady, I had already left France by then. I was in Genoa the entire month of October that year. I left Avignon in July of seventeen fifty-three and did not come back through here until the summer of seventeen fifty-nine. France was not my favorite spot in Europe to spend time in then or now."

Petard looks up from his laptop. "You seem rather well traveled for that era, sir. Was it through business dealings that you met the three assassins?"

Oliver arches an eyebrow, somewhat miffed at Petard's choice of words. "Yes, I met La Mer and Vachon through various business dealings. Since I know you'll ask, during that time, I was involved in the Roman antiquities trade, legal and black market. I met that Thorne character because he was often with Vachon. I never saw him alone, nor did I transact any business with him."

Maurana nods slightly. "Did any of them ever talk to you about the assassination, speak of Lady Vetrina or Aurea, gloating, remorse, anything?"

"Well, sometime in 1843, springtime, I would think, when I was passing through the Lyon area, I spent a couple days in the company of Thorne and Vachon. Thorne spent much of the time ranting and raving about how they should travel to the States and knock off Aurea because the demise of Lady Vetrina had not accomplished their ends. I asked Thorne if he really meant that. He went on to say that Order Sapphire was always getting a raw deal. I laughed out loud at that statement, and he just glared at me. Then he sneered and said that Lady Vetrina's death had unhinged the Vitzameri's mind, just like he said it would. I asked him if he cared to elaborate, and at that point, Vachon came into the room and Thorne just clammed up. Later, I asked Vachon about what Thorne had said. He just looked at me and said I should pay no heed to Thorne's babblings, that they were the onset of some weird Sapphire psychosis. That was the last time I ever saw those two. Thorne definitely was a psychopath. Vachon was simply an opportunist."

Oliver looks at Petard and then at Maurana before continuing. "As for the last time I was in contact with La Mer, oddly enough, it was on October sixteenth of this year. I was in Geneva at the time, and sometimes he would come up and meet me there to trade in some precious metals. At any rate, he did not show for our appointment, so out of concern, I called him. He was very apologetic. He said he would not be able to make it to Geneva to transact business. Since I was heading down to Monaco anyway, I offered to stop by his place, but he declined. He sounded awful, frightened, so I asked him what was wrong. All he would tell me was that he was having horrible dreams when he attempted to rest, but he did not tell me what they were about. He thanked me for my concern, but he said he didn't think there was anything anyone else could do."

Petard keyed some more notes into his laptop. "So you thought Albert Thorne was a psychopath and Jacques Vachon was an opportunist. In your dealings with him, what did you think of Phillipe La Mer?"

Oliver just shrugs. "He seemed like a decent enough fellow. He always traded fairly. He was ambitious, but what is the harm in that? I was not the least bit surprised to find out that Thorne and Vachon had a hand in the demise of Lady Vetrina, but finding out La Mer was involved surprised me. I did not know the man well, but this really seemed out of character. Had I known, back in 1753, that he was contemplating anything like this, I would have notified Aurea. She would have heard me out and checked into it and likely would have been able to prevent it. I certainly never believed she had any hand in it."

Maurana's look went from hostile to neutral. "The vast majority of the three Plaz never believed that Aurea was the assassin of Lady Vetrina. I don't know who really did, besides the Vitzameri. Mr. Scott, I thank you for coming and talking to us. You have been most helpful."

Oliver stands up and bows to Maurana. Petard stands up and shakes hands with him. He then takes his leave and shows himself the door.

Maurana looks over at Petard. "I think we can close the book on anyone else being directly involved in the assassination. Would have been helpful to have found an eyewitness, but anyone in that tavern would have been blasted into a cinder. If a high elder like Vetrina was taken out, the device must have been quite spectacular for that era."

Petard ponders this. "My lady, I respectfully disagree. Given the era, that device was just too powerful and too specific. It really just took the tavern out. No other buildings suffered anything but minor damage, and no one came out of there alive. I might never be able to prove this, but I think someone gave La Mer a functional Atlantean device that was then used to kill Lady Vetrina. I'm not sure she was the original target. Perhaps Thorne and Vachon talked him into employing the device that way. With your permission, I intend to keep looking into this possibility."

Maurana nods. "Far be it from me to talk you out of it, especially since you could be right. Just don't get in over your head. If you find solid evidence that someone with access to such devices was involved, come to me. If another high elder was actually involved, this could get very ugly."

Victor arrives at the Rayburn Building on Monday the twenty-ninth about a half hour before he is scheduled to start work. He prides himself on being on time, and he is not about to change his habits now. The numbers of workers appear to be rather skeletal, but he figures that was because it is a holiday week. The line to get through the building's security checkpoint moves swiftly. Victor shows the guard his aide ID, and they wave him through. He then joins a few other folks in the elevator and heads up to the floor where Moore's office is. The building is rather quiet. He knows that that will not be the case next week when the hundred and eleventh Congress convenes. Then, he is sure this building will be a madhouse.

He reaches the office door, opens it, and goes inside. The receptionist's desk is empty. He sees only two people in the office: Davis

Grayson and a woman whom he had not yet met. Davis sees him and walks over.

"Great seeing you again, Victor! Settling into the new place all right? See you figured out the transit schedule. Moore expects punctuality. Not that it would have mattered much today, but, well, you will see come next week."

"Great to see you again too, Davis. Yes, the new apartment has been easy enough to settle into. The boss doesn't need to worry about my punctuality. It is an old habit that I am not in any hurry to break."

The woman walks over. She is tall, rail thin, wearing heavy makeup, and looks to be in her early forties. She shakes Victor's hand. "A pleasure to meet you, Victor. I'm Daphne Surratt, manager of Bob's office here in DC. I have been informed of your background and of the position that you will have here. You might think that going to embassy functions and up to the United Nations will be fun. Well, sometimes, possibly, but I think you will find most of those people dreadfully dull. You will have to get used to pretending to like them."

Victor nods. "It's a pleasure to meet you as well, Daphne. I think I'm prepared for the reality of that part of my job function. I guess I should treat it like a role playing game." He looks around the office. "So, which desk is mine? I should put my stuff in order and start training on what I need to know. Business as usual resumes a week from tomorrow, and I don't want to be blindsided. This wasn't the type of employment I ever expected to have, but if I am going to do this, I intend to do it well."

Daphne looks a bit startled. She points at a desk near the window. "That desk is yours, Victor. Your computer is up and running. You have been approved up for full clearance. A word of warning though: don't send any e-mail out that you don't want anyone besides your recipient to read. Everything in this place gets looked at, and you don't want to talk to the DHS folks any more than you have to. I guess the best course of action for you today is to run the tutorials about the basics, get a feel for what being part of a Congressman's staff is really all about."

"Thank you, Daphne." Victor sits down and logs in. He spends the morning going through various online tutorials, taking all the quizzes that come after each installment. Daphne is startled by the fact that Victor keeps acing the quizzes, but he expects it. After all, much of this regards political theory and function, and that he knows well.

Lunchtime comes, and Davis invites Victor to join him. He accepts, giving a nod of farewell to Daphne, who is sitting at her desk, eating a sandwich and reading a mystery novel. Davis and Victor just go to the building's cafeteria, where only a few people are sitting and eating. They get their lunches and sit at a table that has a view of Independence Avenue.

"Well, Victor, you really have impressed Daphne. She didn't expect you to ace the tutorial quizzes. Nobody ever has before. Guess she forgot what you wrote your master's thesis about."

Victor smiles. "It's really pretty basic stuff. Nothing in there was all that challenging or revealing. Anyone who passed Political Science 101 in college should do well on those quizzes. So, I'm hoping that impressing Daphne is a good thing?"

Davis chuckles. "Yes, you want Daphne to think well of you. Makes things in the office go more smoothly. She is still mystified that Bob hired you to replace Terrance. Then again, everyone wonders why Terrance just up and quit after the election. I mean, no one has heard from the guy. I guess he went back home to Baltimore, but no one knows for sure. It's really quite odd."

"Daphne isn't the only one who is mystified about Moore hiring me. I still find it hard to believe I am actually here, working for a US Representative. Did the Orange County office tell you what happened when Mathilda first contacted me about the position?"

Davis stifles a laugh. "I do know because she called me and told me all about it. You hung up on her because you thought this was some kind of practical joke that your brother had put them up to. She told me that it took awhile after you did come for the interview before you were convinced it was real and not some bizarre reality show sham. Not that I blame you at all. Had I been in your shoes, I would have felt very much the same. Bob thought it was quite funny afterward. He's convinced you will make a solid addition to the staff. I think he made a sound choice."

Victor shrugs. "As they put it, I was the only person they were considering for the position. I still don't know why that was the case. Likely I never will know."

They finish their lunches and head back to the office.

Victor arrives back at his apartment at about five thirty. As promised, his car was delivered and safely parked. He goes to the manager's apartment and retrieves his car keys and obtains his parking sticker, which he promptly places on the back bumper of the car. He then goes inside, has some dinner, and then goes online and chats with his sister, Zoe, and his Uncle Reggie. He responds to an e-mail from his mother, letting her know that he is doing all right and adjusting to life in DC.

Later that night, Victor has the strange dream that he has had several times over the past few years. It was always very vivid, with the feeling of being very real. He sees a large, white room with many people busily running back and forth, grim determination on their faces and intent in their action. He sees himself with a small, handheld computer, punching in information as he directs these people in their task. Some he recognizes, others he does not. There is a woman standing at the far end of the room, whom he is sure was his sister, Zoe, even though she did not look like she does now. Everyone is speaking a language that is not English or any other tongue he was familiar with. In the dream though, he always understands it. Wherever this place is, they have technology far beyond what is presently available. He noticed an alarm wailing in the distance. A face shows up on his handheld's screen, a male face deeply troubled.

"Tectonic shift continues to destabilize this landmass, Commander. We might not be able to clear out the vaults in time. Fleet command says the ships will have to fly if the situation deteriorates any further."

"Understood. Tell them to give our people as much time as they can but if the landing zones are compromised to get out of here. I will get as many people out of here as I can." He looks over at the woman at the far end of the room. "Start the general evacuation, Lataritna. Get yourself and as many of the others onto the ships as quickly as possible. I will go down and shut the vaults."

She looks stricken. "That could be suicide, even for one such as we are. Isn't there someone else you can send to tend to the vaults?"

Victor shook his head. "You know better, my love. I am the only one here who knows the codes. Go do what you know needs to be done. I shall do likewise." He blows her a kiss and runs down the corridor. He feels the ground trembling and sees more cracks appear in the walls. It would not be long now. Everyone he passes, he tells them to get moving, to get to the spaceport and get out of there. Most salute and run off. A few try to argue, but he will not stay and listen. He has to seal the vaults if he can.

By the time he reaches the bank of vaults, the area is empty. The temperature is rising swiftly. If he were an ordinary mortal, he could not have handled the heat. He gets into the main console and starts punching in codes. The vault doors start closing. Just as the final door shuts, there is a huge tremor and the ceiling collapses, trapping Victor. He sees his handheld computer flicker with the woman's face contorted in terror.

At least she is safe.

As he contemplates how to escape, magma fills the space, incinerating him.

As always, Victor wakes up at this point in a sweat, his heart pounding. He looks around and sees that he is safe in his apartment. He gets up and goes to the bathroom. As he drifts back to sleep, he wonders if that was really simply a dream or something far more.

Early morning December 30 finds Kristano and Maurana engaged in a rather terse discussion regarding Petard's theory on the cause of the demise of Lady Vetrina. Maurana has just finished laying out Petard's case. Kristano looks at her gravely and then nods slightly.

"Francois could have a point here, but not in the way he is thinking to be the case. He probably thinks it was some artifact from old Atlantis. Any explosive device that old would not function properly, if at all. What he does not know is that we still have some off-planet manufacturing going on. At that point, we still had operating facilities on Luna. What we need to determine is whether or not any such devices were shipped to Earth during the mid-eighteenth century."

Maurana walks over to a bookshelf and takes down a slender volume. She scans the pages quickly. Eventually, her finger stops on a line item. She stares at Kristano, looking bewildered. "According to this, on September 15, 1753, three such devices were delivered directly to La Mer. How can this be? Those devices would have cost more than what La Mer had. Further, I thought that back then, the off-planet trade was an even more closely guarded secret than it is now. Who gave him access? Where did he get the money? Did any of the other high elders have any reason to want Vetrina dead?"

Kristano ponders that for a moment. "Back then, La Mer was pretty tight with Cartosimo and Aureoso. Now, Cartosimo chose to cease to exist back in July of nineteen thirteen. No way to talk to him. Aureoso is still around. The only question is: Where is he now? I was never close to either of them. I don't think my sister was close to them either. Aureoso does not strike me as being the type to breach that sort of protocol, but it would be prudent to check this out. I will see if Cartosimo left any papers of note behind. For a high elder, he was rather dull."

Maurana went online. "I found Aureoso. He is residing in Berlin, Germany. Let's see if he will accept an online call."

A few moments later, the screen fills with the face of a male who appears to be about forty-five but who is really 41,761 years old.

"Ah, Maurana and Kristano! It has been such a very long time. I am sure this isn't a social call. How can I be of assistance?"

Kristano held the ledger. "My brother, we have an issue. It seems that the late Phillipe La Mer was able to order three explosive devices from the off-planet trade. The record shows he took delivery of the devices in September of seventeen fifty-three, about a month prior to the assassination of my sister. Since you were a friend of Phillipe's back then, I was wondering if you knew anything about this."

A look of concern crosses Aureoso's face. "My brother, I wish I could help you. If you go through the records, you will see that I have not ordered anything from the off-planet trade. I daresay, though, that you will find that our late friend Cartosimo did so with some frequency. Now, why he would order something like that for La Mer that mystifies me. I never once recall him saying anything negative about Vetrina. My guess is that La Mer obtained the goods through underhanded means. Perhaps he told Cartosimo that he needed the devices to do some mining. Perhaps he actually did use two of them for that stated purpose. One thing I do know is that Cartosimo would not have participated in an assassination attempt. Just was not his style."

Maurana nods. "What you say rings true, good sir. My apologies for having troubled you about this matter."

Aureoso smiles warmly. "No trouble at all. Justice needs to be served. If I recall anything at all that might be helpful, I will be in touch." With that, he broke the connection and the screen went blank.

"Kristano, I am going to direct Petard to have La Mer's house and property searched again. He might have kept the other two devices. I ran across nothing that showed that La Mer was involved in any mining ventures at that time or any other for that matter."

Kristano simply nods in consent.

Late afternoon on the thirtieth at Representative Moore's office, Daphne, Davis, and Victor are discussing plans for New Year's Eve.

Davis smiles wistfully. "I'll just be watching the show and waiting for the ball to drop at Times Square. Don't feel like doing much else this year. It's been rather a down year for me."

Victor just looks a bit perplexed. "I must admit I didn't give it much thought. Being in a new city and all, I figured I would just go to one of the clubs close to my complex and toast in the New Year that way. Last year, I went to Disneyland for New Year's. Quite the crowd, but the fireworks were awesome."

Daphne sighs. "I have tickets for the National Symphony Orchestra show at the Kennedy Center on New Year's Eve. It's always a killer show. Stuart bailed on me again, the jerk." She looks over at Victor. "You seem to be free. You want to go? I can pick you up at your place. That is, unless you don't like classical music."

Victor thinks about it for a moment. "I love classical music, Daphne. It sounds better than what I was expecting to do. That's for sure. Yes, I'd like to go. Can I pay you for the ticket?"

Daphne smiles and waves her hand. "No need. Stuart did pay for the ticket in advance. He's claiming he's out of town on business, monkey business more likely. I am so over him. You can pay for dinner beforehand. You'll need to wear a suit and tie. We can attend the grand foyer party after the show. There's dancing, balloons, alcohol until one in the morning. You'll get to meet some of the people you are going to have to pretend to like for the next two years. This is the city of smoke and mirrors. It's time you learned what playing the game of the art of the possible is really all about."

Victor nods. "I can handle that." He pauses and a confused look crosses his face. "Wow, Daphne. Are these people really so bad that you are even more jaded and cynical than I am?" Davis chuckles, and Daphne grins.

"Jaded and cynical? I suppose I am. As for the people here, they aren't all bad, per se. Watch your back, Victor. Look out for the knives. Everyone in this town is working an angle, trying to get something out of you. People climb up the ranks here on the backs of other people. Here, who you are and who you know matter far more than what you know. You know a lot, Victor. I'll grant you that. These next two years though, you will learn a lot more, probably more than you ever really wanted to know about power and politics. I've read your thesis. Bob thought that I should. It held up a mirror that I really was not prepared to face. I wish I could disagree with your assessments. You will find out just how right you were without any practical experience."

Davis looks at the clock. "We might just as well call it a day, folks. We're only working until noon tomorrow, right, Daphne? I can certainly work the day if you like, but I don't think there will be much call for our presence."

Daphne nods. "Yes, that's the plan. No one's coming in on Thursday, and Bob said to keep the office closed on Friday the second too. He does expect everyone to be here on time and ready to roll on Monday. New Congress will be seated on Tuesday, all the swearing in and such. What a pain."

Davis just smiles. "Well, let's enjoy the quiet while we can. Let's make tracks and get out of here."

Early in the evening in Alexandria, Virginia, three sharply dressed individuals are walking east on Prince Street, heading toward Becker's nightclub on the corner with Henry Street. They are going to see Midnight Silk and the Scott brothers perform tonight. They are also coming to feed. Cassie Mae Adler and Rachel Penn are wearing slinky black dresses under their long coats. Along with her ruby ring, Cassie Mae is wearing a necklace with a cross that has a large ruby in the center. Rachel is also wearing some large ruby earrings. With them is a male from the Emerald Order, their friend Tom Rice. Tall and lanky, he looks thirty-five, but he is now 219 years old. He dressed in a sweater and jeans and is wearing his emerald ring. It is not unusual for Cassie and Rachel to go out on the town together. Tom is Rachel's friend and joined them because he had not heard Midnight Silk perform live.

Becker's is an intimate nightclub popular with blues bands. Rachel is pointing out the crowd, definitely pleased to see that it would be a full house, good for the band, and easier to mingle and feed when the time came. When they reached the entrance, the bouncer nodded and waved them in. They found a table close to the stage, where they could see and be seen. As he is in the company of two beautiful women, Tom notes the envious looks he is getting from some men. He simply smiles about that.

In the back, Midnight Silk has just finished with her costume when she has the feeling that someone she knows very well is out there in the audience. Curious, she peeks out into the club. To her immense pleasure, she sees Cassie Mae out there with Rachel and Tom. She signals to Vernon and Walter, and then she saunters out to the table, smiling broadly. Cassie Mae gets up and hugs Midnight Silk tightly.

Cassie Mae is simply beaming, her dark green eyes sparkling. "It's so great to see you again, Sallie Jean. Oh, I know that you have met Rachel. However, I don't think you've met Tom before."

Tom rises and shakes Silk's hand. "A pleasure indeed, madam. I have long been a fan of your band. I am looking forward to the performance. How shall I address you? You and Cassie appear to be longtime friends, and I know I don't fit into that level of familiarity."

Silk is mildly amused by Tom's formal tone. "Just call me Silk, Tom. Cassie Mae is probably the only one around who calls me Sallie Jean. You could say we are longtime friends. It goes further than that for the two of us though. You see, Tom, I was born a slave on her father's plantation in South Carolina. Totally against the laws,

Cassie Mae taught me to read and write. A few months after South Carolina seceded, she helped me escape. I didn't see her again until the summer of eighteen seventy-seven, when I helped her avenge the murder of her family by her natro. We have stayed in contact ever since. Really, we're family."

Tom nods, clearly impressed. "That was a very sad time in the history of this nation. I lived in New England during most of the eighteen hundreds, but I did make a few trips South. Saw the peculiar institution in action. It never made sense to me. Who was your natro, Cassie Mae?"

Silk excuses herself and goes up to the stage, where Vernon and Walter Scott are making sound checks and getting ready to start the set.

Cassie Mae sighs and looks at Tom. "Rather delicate question, that. My natro was Major Clifford H. Cole, CSA. He was part of General Stonewall Jackson's staff, and he was mortally wounded days before the Battle of Chancellorsville in eighteen sixty-three. He had been left for dead, but he was turned by an unknown rogue ruby. I met him in March of eighteen sixty-seven. My family had managed to keep the Union troops from torching our plantation when they made their run up to Charleston early in eighteen sixty-five, but my father was barely hanging on. Still, we had the occasional dinner party, and he showed up at one. I found him intriguing. He gained my trust over the next few weeks, and he invited me to come to his place in April of eighteen sixty-seven. He resided in a bungalow in Charleston proper. Well, to cut to the chase, I became his foara on May 3, eighteen sixty-seven. We were together for nearly ten years, though it was a very stormy relationship. I left him in January of eighteen seventy-seven. He became enraged, tried to make me come back. He ended up killing my family in a fit of rage that June. I met up with Sallie Jean a couple weeks later, and we avenged my family."

Tom looks stricken. "I am so sorry, Cassie Mae. I had no right to inquire and inflict such pain."

Cassie Mae sees that the band was nearly ready to start the first set. "That's all right, Tom. It was a very long time ago. I was never really close to my family, but Clifford had no right to just slaughter them to get back at me. We tore him to shreds and burned his body. I haven't been back to see my old family home since that night. Don't know that I ever will." She smiled wistfully. "Here and now, let's enjoy the music."

The first set is marvelous. Midnight Silk and the Scott brothers are in rare form. They are performing for friends, which is always more gratifying. The audience is enraptured. The band never uses mind tricks when they are performing. They are top flight blues musicians. When the set ends, Midnight Silk goes back over and sits down next to Cassie Mae. Tom excuses himself, saying he has found a likely mark and he is going to feed. Rachel simply nods to him.

Rachel is bubbling with enthusiasm. "You guys are so great tonight, Silk. You always are, but tonight, everything really seems to be in sync."

Silk smiles. "I am pleased you are enjoying yourself. Do tell, Rachel, where did you find Tom? Seems like a nice enough sort but rather naïve. Or is that the right word? He never should have asked Cassie Mae about her natro in a public place. Yankees just don't seem to have manners. Know what I mean?"

Rachel looks across the club, where Tom is taking a woman aside for his pint this evening. "Tom's a nice enough fellow, Silk. He asked out of curiosity. There's not an ounce of malice in him. That is one of the reasons I like him. I find his enthusiasm refreshing. Yes, he can go too far. Cassie could have refused to answer if she wished."

Cassie Mae sighs. "It still hurts to think about it, Sallie Jean. I think it always will. I could tell he asked because he was genuinely interested. He looked so stricken after I did tell him. No harm done. No offense meant or taken." She opens her purse and takes out a couple pieces of paper and hands them to Silk. "Here is the song I was telling you about. I just finished it a couple of days ago. What do you think?"

Silk read it over quickly. “It’s nicely scored, Cassie. It has lots of feeling, remorse, regret, such intense sadness. This feels like something you lived through. I would guess this is about Cody, isn’t it?”

A small tear runs down Cassie’s cheek. “Yes, it is about Cody. Do you think I will ever stop missing him, Sallie Jean? He’s been gone since eighteen sixty-four. I haven’t really taken a shine to any man since then.”

Silk nods. “You know what the elders say; everyone comes back. If it was meant to be, you will cross paths again. Cody was a decent fellow. I know he loved you. Anyway, let me show this to Vernon and Walter, see what they think of it. I’ll be back in a couple minutes.”

Rachel and Cassie Mae watch Silk walk over and then start talking animatedly with Vernon and Walter. Vernon looks over at Cassie with an expression of astonishment. Rachel looks over at Cassie. “Girlfriend, they are definitely up to something. Silk has an ulterior motive. Mark my words.”

Tom comes back from feeding as Silk came back to the table. She is beaming. “Well, Cassie Mae, Vernon and Walter agree with me. This song is beautiful and heartfelt. It expresses your pain and your loss. We want you to sing it first here tonight, during the middle of the next set. What do you say?”

Rachel and Tom look at Cassie in shock.

Cassie is amazed. “You really think so, Sallie Jean? Can I do the song justice in front of this crowd?”

Silk clasps Cassie’s hand. “No one could sing this song better than you. We will be honored to perform it on the road. Here and now though, this is your moment. You will touch everyone here with the magic of your emotion. That’s what real blues is about, says I. Reckon you’ll do this then?”

Cassie Mae nods. Silk goes back up to the stage with Vernon and Walter, and the band starts the second set. Cassie waits on pins and needles as the middle of the set approaches. Tom looks at her in awe.

Rachel is impressed. Then, the moment arrives. Silk looks out at the audience, all smiles.

"We have a special treat for y'all this evening. My dear friend, Cassie Mae, has written a song. Vernon and Walter and I found it so moving that we wanted to have her be the first to sing it. Cassie, come up here and sing your heart out."

The audience applauds politely as Cassie walks up to the stage. Silk stands aside as Cassie takes the mike. She nods, and Vernon and Walter start playing. Cassie's voice fills the club. Silk was right; all felt her passion, her sorrow, her loss. When the song ends, Cassie is sobbing. As Silk returns to comfort her, the audience gives Cassie a standing ovation. There isn't a dry eye in that house.

Victor is waiting in his apartment for Daphne to arrive so they can get to the Kennedy Center for the evening's festivities. He has just spoken to his sister, Zoe, who somehow finds it hilarious that he will be spending New Year's Eve with a bunch of politicians and their lackeys. Victor remarked that the New Year's he had rung in a few years back with the family cat was probably much better company than he would have tonight. Zoe readily agreed and then said that she hoped he didn't get too nauseated by this.

Daphne is right on time. Victor walks out to her car and gets in. Daphne nods in approval regarding his suit. He admits that she looks elegant and stylish in her long dress. She pulls out and heads toward the Kennedy Center. Victor watches the scenery as Daphne gives him a thumbnail sketch of what to expect for the evening. Victor sees the Kennedy Center looming up ahead. He has a feeling of dread. Still, he has to admit, if these were the people he would be dealing with for the next two years, he best get used to it. Daphne pulls into a special parking area for VIPs, explaining that free parking was one of the perks of the job. She takes Victor's arm, and they walk into the restaurant.

Once inside the restaurant, Victor notes the rather ostentatious décor. Somehow, he does not find it surprising. The maitre d' had them seated quickly. Ever the gentleman, Victor holds Daphne's chair out for her. She beams with approval. They have their meal, engaging in polite small talk. Once done, they head over to the main auditorium. Victor has seen the place on television, but it is even more impressive in person. When he finds out they have seats in the orchestra section, fifteen rows away from the stage dead center, he is truly impressed and tells Daphne so. He settles down and truly enjoys the show.

It is at the Grand Foyer party that Victor expects to be most challenged. As such, he is on guard when he and Daphne enter. She keeps her hand on his arm and takes him to a table and sits down. Daphne looks at him rather intensely.

"Tonight has been a breeze until now, Victor. Look around and tell me who you recognize. Do so nonchalantly though. Don't attract undue attention to yourself."

Victor nods and looks around. He points out about ten representatives, five senators, and a few people from the outgoing administration. Daphne nods in approval.

"There's a few people from the incoming administration here tonight, a smattering of foreign dignitaries and a whole slew of lobbyists. I will take you around and make the introductions. You are far safer with me tonight than you would be alone with this crowd. I am a known quantity. I know how to play this game. You don't, not yet anyway. I think you will learn quickly. If you want to survive here, you best be a fast learner."

Victor nods. They get up and start walking around the room. Daphne could smile on cue, shake hands, and properly introduce Victor to these people. Once out of earshot, she would often mutter some dark oath or snide remark under her breath. Victor finds that amusing, but he keeps that to himself. Anyone looking at him would see his stern poker face, exactly as Daphne had suggested. After a couple dozen introductions, Daphne points at a woman across the room. The woman has blond hair and is wearing a ridiculously short black miniskirt. "Know that face well, Victor. Her name is Gretchen Denter. She's probably one of the most successful lobbyists on the Hill. She's poison. Stay away from her if you know what is prudent."

Victor notes the scowl on Daphne's face and the rather venomous way she passes judgment on this woman. Noting the men flocking around her, Victor shrugs.

"If you say so, I am inclined to take your word for it. What has this Gretchen done to you or to Bob?"

Daphne shakes her head. "Bob is definitely a sucker for a pretty face, big boobs, and great legs. Gretchen is shrewd. She does have one weakness though. She tries to bed all the new guys who come onto the Congressional staff. She does one-nighters, nothing more, never goes out with the same guy twice. Rumor has it that she has bedded some of the women too, though I have no direct experience in that regard. She did get to Davis a few years back. He found it all rather humiliating in the end. Do yourself a favor and steer clear of her."

Victor nods. "Very well, Daphne. Easy for me to do since she's not my type, and I have no interest in one-night stands anyway. I will do my utmost to not have anything to do with her. If I do have to speak to her, I will keep it on an entirely professional level."

Daphne takes his arm as the band starts playing and the dancing begins. "Do you dance, Victor?"

He simply smiles and takes her out on the dance floor. After a half hour of dancing, they return to their table and order drinks.

"You don't have the best sense of rhythm, Victor, but you are fun to dance with. Stuart never wanted to dance. I had to drag him out on the dance floor."

"Well, Daphne, I like to dance. Guys who don't just don't know what they are missing."

As midnight approaches, the countdown begins. All are standing. Most have various party favors and wear hats. Victor feels very alone in this crowd. All kinds of strange thoughts go through his head. At the stroke of midnight, with the announcement that 2009 has arrived, Daphne gives him a hug and a polite peck on the cheek.

"Happy New Year, Victor. I know you will find it to be most fascinating."

Meanwhile, across the room, Oscar Martin has used the New Year's kiss as an opportunity to feed from an all-too-willing female. He is sated. She feels a little weak and woozy and sits down. He looks over and notices Daphne, whom he has met on a few occasions. He sees Victor and notes that he is a bright and that he definitely feels out of place here. Oscar shakes his head.

"Heck, any ethical person will have issues with this city. I sense that man has a strong sense of fair play. DC will eat him alive, wherever it is that he came from." Oscar bade his female companion a fair evening and left.

Victor looks across the room and sees Oscar leave the building. He does not think anything of it. Daphne gets his attention by pointing out a few more lobbyists. This goes on until one o'clock, when they finally leave. Upon his arrival at the apartment complex, Victor thanks Daphne for a fascinating evening. As she drives off, he shudders on the inside.

"City of smoke and mirrors does not even begin to describe what this place is really about."

On New Year's Day in Avignon, Petard has completed his intense search of La Mer's home and property. He is now giving his report to Maurana and the Vitzameri.

"Well, as Maurana advised me to expect, we did find two more of the Atlantean devices. They were in a room that had been concealed by a large bookcase. We even found a very fragile receipt for three of these devices. They were purchased for La Mer by the late high elder Cartosimo. Now I do regard the case as being closed. I don't think anyone else among the living had any direct involvement in the assassination of Lady Vetrina."

Kristano leans back in his chair. "Thank you, Francois, for all the hard work. Now all the pieces fit. We still need to make things as right as possible with Aurea, but now we need not concern ourselves with chasing after other Plaz to see that justice can now be done. Honor can and will be restored."

Petard stands up and bows to both of them. "By your leave then, my lord and lady. Given that a high elder was involved, I'm sure there are matters you will need to discuss privately. Is there is anything else that you require from me today?"

Maurana waves her hand. "No, Francois. You have done more than enough. Go ahead and take a few days off. You have certainly earned it."

Petard left the room. Kristano turns to Maurana. "You know, I find it most interesting that Petard did not comment on the durability of the devices or even ask how Cartosimo came into possession of them. I am sure he is most curious about it. Why does he refrain from even inquiring?"

"Petard is a very good man, a shrewd man. He knows his place. That is to say, he knows when to ask and when to just let it go. Too bad he definitely won't cross over and join us in this lifetime. His services will be most valuable in the years to come."

Kristano looks thoughtful. "That does make sense. I have tried to get him to change his mind about becoming a vampire a few times. No such luck, I fear. I guess we must put that aside for now. Has anything new come out about Aurea? Is there any inkling at all as to how best to go about putting this grave injustice to rest?"

"I heard from Carol Ann a few days ago. She said that right now, Aurea is really throwing herself into an intense project that she is not at liberty to discuss, though she might be able to soon. She says Aurea has talked about you a few times. Carol Ann senses that Aurea is not yet ready to face you."

Kristano sighs. "I am not surprised to hear that. I hope she won't choose to draw this out. I hope she turns out to be more reasonable and practical about this than I was."

Maurana arches an eyebrow. "Well, I'm sure that she will be. You need to be patient. This is her issue to call, not yours. There are lots of feelings to sort out—a couple centuries worth, to be precise about it."

Victor spends the rest of New Year's Day at his apartment. He spends some time chatting online with Anneliese. He sends e-mails to his parents and to his brother, Arnold. He calls Zoe and Uncle Reggie and talks to them at some length. They are both very encouraging, both promising to come out and visit in the spring. Victor then spends a few hours familiarizing himself with the names and faces of the incoming Congress. In all, he has a productive day. He is going into the lion's den now, so he wants to be fully prepared.

How prepared can anyone truly be for the brutal art of the possible in the imperial city?

CHAPTER 5

Monday, 19 January 2009. Washington DC is all abuzz as the city gets ready for the inauguration. Decorations going up; security is tightened. All must be in readiness for the change of power in the imperium. Victor has been working hard and keeping to himself as much as possible. A few people on the staff of other representatives had tried to goad him into useless arguments, but he never took the bait. What Victor had the biggest issue with was the cold, with recent temperatures right around freezing.

That morning, Representative Moore calls a meeting of his entire staff. He is sitting behind his desk, looking smug. Victor is pensive, BlackBerry at the ready. Davis Grayson looks amused. Daphne is all serious as usual. Jennifer the receptionist is snapping her gum. George the analyst looks like he would rather be anywhere else but here. Andy, the representative's page, is awed. Moore leans back in his chair.

"Well, as our candidate always said, 'my friends,' good to see all of you this morning. Some of you might have been wondering whether or not we need to attend the inauguration tomorrow. After all, it's going to be really cold, and it isn't our guy who is getting sworn in. Well, as our vice presidential candidate was fond of saying, 'you betcha!' That is to say, yes, I expect all of you to attend the inauguration. I also expect everyone here, save young Andy, to attend one of the inaugural balls."

George moans loudly. "C'mon! I understand all of us going to the inauguration, but why do we all have to attend an inaugural ball? I can't stand dancing, and I hate crowded rooms!"

Daphne just smirks. "Nobody said you have to dance, George. Just go mingle, eat some food, and talk to your fellow analysts. Who knows? You might even make some connections with the new administration."

George shakes his head and mutters dark oaths under his breath. Davis has to suppress a laugh.

Representative Moore opens his desk drawer and takes out some tickets. "I have enough tickets here for each of you and a guest to attend either the Neighborhood Inaugural Ball or Western Inaugural Ball. My wife and I will be attending the Commander-in-Chief's Ball. Are there any other questions or concerns?"

Victor looks up from his BlackBerry. "I don't have a guest to bring. I don't suppose they will care if I were to come alone, would they?"

Moore shakes his head. "Not that they would care, Victor, but it just won't do for you to attend one of the balls on your own. It makes you too much of a target for some of the more unsavory types that go to the big political events. I don't think you want to get mired in pointless political arguments or come-ons from one of the folks on some lobbyist's staff. They will be there. You can be sure of it." He looks over at Daphne. "Are any of your friends available tomorrow evening?"

"I think Phyllis is. Let me call and find out." She punches the numbers on her cell phone and leaves the room.

"I trust that the rest of you have someone to attend the ball with tomorrow evening?" Moore scans the office as everyone else nods. "Very well then. All of you, save Victor, are dismissed."

As the others leave the office, Daphne comes back in. "Phyllis is free tomorrow evening, and she would be more than happy to go to the ball with Victor. Nathan and I could pick her up and then pick up Victor to go to the Western Inaugural Ball. That way, he doesn't have to drive in this cold weather."

Victor smiles. "I appreciate that, Daphne. I must admit that I haven't tried driving much since I got here. Just to places close to the apartment. I know it gets hot and sticky here during the summer, but right now, wow. It's never been this cold in Southern California. I don't think people there would know how to handle it."

Bob Moore leans back in his chair. "Then all is settled as well as it can be. Victor, I am sure you will find tomorrow's events to be most interesting, all the pomp and pageantry. So many people will be transfixed by them. I know you won't be. I will be most interested in hearing your perspectives about the inauguration and the ball. You will get to see the new president and first lady. Not very close, certainly, but close enough. You are the ultimate outsider here. You won't be kissing up to anyone. I know you will play nice, but after it is all over, I really do want to know what you thought of it."

"As you wish, of course, it should be a fascinating experience on so many levels. I've never even watched the inauguration on TV, at least not since I was a little kid. I seem to recall my parents making me watch the 1989 inauguration. We're sure to hear a bunch of chanting of hope and change too."

Daphne scowls. "That's all the better reason to bring earplugs. Yes, I know this supposed to be all so historic and all that, but really, when I think about it, our guy didn't stand a chance once the financial sector collapsed. Nothing could save the campaign after that."

Moore smiles wanly. "That's all in the past, Daphne. We must play the cards we have been dealt, not the ones we wish we had. At any rate, I'm sure you and Victor still have work to do. I know I do. So let's be at it."

Daphne and Victor leave the office.

That evening, Aurea and Carol Ann are sitting in their office, windows open, looking at the lights of the quiet Staten Island neighborhood. Both are peaceful, though Aurea's mind is churning, pondering, and anticipating when Victor will be discovered. That and the blood debt owed by the Vitzameri.

"I take it there still hasn't been anything exciting out of Washington yet. I know you would tell me if there had been. You don't seem to be very worried about it, not that you should be. Victor hasn't even been there a month yet. I doubt that he has been doing much socializing. He is so out of his element there."

Aurea stands up and looks out the window. "Would have been way too soon and very probably not a desirable outcome. Best window really is from February first to April thirtieth. Tomorrow is the inauguration. I will not be surprised if Victor ends up having to attend one of the inaugural balls. That would be just like Representative Moore. He is very big on protocol and making an impression on those who hold the power. If he can get an edge with the new administration, he will."

Carol Ann shakes her head. "It's likely to be a waste of time on his part. Still, few have played the game better than Moore, which makes me wonder why it was so easy for Cliff Nash to get him to hire Victor in the first place. I'm glad it worked, but it really seems like it ought not to have been that easy."

"Cliff is really good, granted. However, the more amusing fact is that a big-time player seems to not know when they are being played. Moore probably would have seen it had Cliff been a mortal. Moore does have a decent level of psychic abilities, even though he either doesn't know it or fails to recognize it. Anyone short of a bright has a very difficult time resisting an auto-suggestion from a competent vampire."

Carol Ann contemplates this. "I see your point, Aurea. That politician never really had a chance. That makes sense. Now for the flip side of the coin: his sister, Zoe. Are we keeping a sufficient watch over her? You know how close she and Victor are."

Aurea sits down in front of her computer. "She is being watched. There are a couple of students attending the university who are porfi and reporting back as warranted. So far, she has done nothing spectacular, nothing that leads me to believe we need to make a move on her right away. If Victor gets through the blind test and passes the test of crisis, well, then that will change things. This I do know."

"All this hurry up and wait must take its toll on you though, especially with all the drama surrounding the Vitzameri going on. That must be very aggravating."

Aurea sighs softly. "The blood debt certainly must be settled. I am coming to grips with it. I feel like making Kristano wait two hundred and fifty-five years for resolution, but I will not do that. It would not prove a thing, except that I could be every bit as stubborn and petty as he was. That would not honor the memory of my friend, Vetrina. Nor would there be any healing, which I sorely need. I'm sure he does as well. Once Victor's status is taken care of, I will move to make my demands to settle the blood debt. As for the hurry up and wait part of Victor's blind test, that was to be expected. One facet of existence that I have become very good at is patience. I knew this would take time."

Aurea's computer beeps, indicating an incoming contact. Aurea presses a button, and Zack's face comes on the screen. He is drinking yet another energy drink.

"Good evening, Madame Aurea, Carol Ann. I have some information about Victor Trent's activities tomorrow night."

Carol Ann nods. "Very good, Zack. What is poor Victor going to have to endure tomorrow night in the imperial city?"

A look of confusion crosses Zack's features. "Imperial city? I've heard DC called many things, some that I would not repeat in polite company, but that is a new one. I kind of like it. It fits. Anyway, he will be attending the Western Inaugural Ball. Seems his boss found him a date for the evening too, so he will be spending the evening with folks from the West Coast. Probably, he will get bored to tears or really irritated. Beyond that, there is not much to say. I will keep you posted when I hear anything else."

Aurea nods. "I do have a question, Zack. Who is giving you this information? It has all panned out. Your source is very reliable. When this is all over, I think they ought to be rewarded."

Zack frowns. "This source, if she knew she was a source, would likely not be very pleased to hear of it. I am getting this information via Anneliese Bryce's e-mails to Victor. Cliff Nash found out about it, and he was not pleased. He thought I should know for security reasons, to make sure she did not somehow compromise the blind test. I have a filter, and I am only reading the ones between her and Victor. Not the most honorable thing to do. I will put a stop to it if that is what you wish, madam."

Aurea thinks for a moment. "Keep no permanent records of these e-mails. Once the blind test is over, I don't want there to be any record of this. Until then, go ahead and keep doing it. The information is too valuable to simply pass on. Also, Zack, I only want to know about talk of Victor's schedule, his views on life in DC. If they are having any sort of romantic discussions…"

Carol Ann's jaw drops. "Are they having mushy correspondence, Zack? Is Victor showing any sort of romantic interest in Anneliese?"

Zack shakes his head. "She adores him, but the feeling is not reciprocated. He likes her, but I would definitely say there is little hope for a love connection there. She's not in his league, and I think that she realizes that. She confides in him. It seems like she feels slighted by Cliff. She says his friends belittle her."

Aurea nods. "Very well. Once this is all over, I will have a chat about Anneliese with Cliff. Perhaps she can be useful to us after all. If Victor gets through the test of crisis, and I truly think that he will, and then he will certainly want a mortal friend. Perhaps she can fit that role. Thank you, Zack. That will be all for tonight." Zack nods and signs off.

Carol Ann looks aghast. "Anneliese could be useful? You must be joking! She's so vapid, so superficial! She probably drives Victor nuts! How can she be useful if Victor joins us?"

Aurea laughs. "My dear, you are forgetting one very important point. Anneliese might be all the things you mentioned and have legions of other faults besides. However, she has one advantage over us. She is a mortal. Believe me. Victor is going to need to have someone that he can talk to openly about Plaz Seschni, someone he has some level of trust with. Oh yes, she will fit that bill nicely."

"I hadn't considered that angle. You could very well be right. I will have to think about that."

Inauguration Day dawns crisp and brutally cold. Davis Grayson picks Victor up at his apartment and drives him to the area where other members of various Congresspersons' staffs were gathering. They are then taken to their area along the parade route. Their position is fairly near the Capitol. They are not just to view the parade but to watch the swearing-in ceremony. Victor nods when Daphne and Jennifer show up. He notices George off to the side having an animated conversation on his cell phone. Davis is watching the crowd, occasionally chuckling to himself.

"Well, Victor, you are about to see that this city does know how to throw a big party. Pomp and circumstance. Every four years, they make a really big deal out of it, spend lots of money. Impressed so far?"

Victor shivers. "I'm impressed by some of the audacity, perhaps. Look at that motto: 'A New Birth of Freedom.' Who are they fooling? Celebrating Lincoln? He was one of the biggest tyrants in the history of the country. States have the right to secede. The Civil War didn't change that fact."

Davis nods. "This city does not lack for audacity, which is for sure. Have a care how loudly you speak against Lincoln. I actually agree with you, but the vast majority of people around here consider the man to be some kind of saint. The truth? Most of them would not recognize it if it came and bit them on the behind. The masses couldn't care less about the truth. They don't want to have to think about it."

Daphne walks over and shows Davis and Victor the CNN feed on her laptop. "Look at the crowds lining the Mall. I don't think this city has seen an event like this. All these people! Where are they all staying? Talk about a logistics nightmare. What must the Bureau and the Secret Service be doing to keep order and guarantee security? I sure am glad that is not our job."

Victor just stares in amazement. "The Founders were looking to create an idealized version of the old Roman Republic. Instead, the country has turned into an insane version of Imperial Rome. All we need now is to have a herald walking behind the new president saying, 'Remember thou art mortal.'"

Victor gives grudging admiration to many of the bands as the parade goes by. They do know how to perform. This is the new administration's time to shine, and Victor knows they will stop at nothing to make that happen. He hears the crowd roar as the new first family came walking down Pennsylvania Avenue, waving to the throngs.

Victor looks over at Davis. "Isn't this just the new president? From the way this crowd is acting, you would think he was some great hero! Don't they realize this guy is nothing more than yet another in a series of lying politicians?"

Davis rolls his eyes. "You are forgetting the words of Dr. Goebbels, my friend. The bigger the lie, the easier it is to get people to believe it."

A stricken look crosses Victor's face. *I remember the words of Dr. Goebbels only too well. Not that anyone here would believe the reason why.*

Victor watches the swearing-in ceremony in silence. Power has been transferred to the new administration. The crowd listens attentively to the new president's speech. Victor keeps a sarcastic counter-dialogue running through his head.

When the ceremony is over and the crowd starts to disperse, a young woman, obviously a true believer of the new administration, comes up to Victor. She is all bubbly and excited.

"Wasn't that just the most amazing speech you ever heard? I think he will take the country in the right direction, heal the wounds inflicted by the previous administration. People around the world will respect us again! They will like us instead of hate us! It's a new beginning! Aren't you just glad to be here today? It's history in the making!"

Victor glares at the woman, and her enthusiasm just drains out of her. With ice in his voice, he replies, "I fear you have been sold a bill of goods, madam. Will things change under his rule? Some will, certainly. Will it be any better? I very seriously doubt it. Enjoy your day in the sun, but don't expect me to share in your joyous expectations. The empire is dying, and there is nothing he can do to stop that."

She scowls at Victor. "You voted for the other guy! You're just angry because he lost! Get over it!"

Victor laughs at that. "No, I did not vote for 'the other guy,' as you put it. I voted for a Renaissance fair puppet. I rather like most of his platform. I have the t-shirt for his campaign. Would have worn it today, but I was told that that simply would not do." With that, Victor turns and joins his fellow staff members, leaving the young lady simply staring in bewilderment.

Maurana and Kristano are discussing recent events in his study. Maurana looks up at the portrait of Vetrina. "The artist did well. He captured the true beauty of your sister. The one of you looks rather stern, haunted, not like you normally are. When did you sit for that portrait?"

Kristano looks at the portrait of his sister and shakes his head. "We sat for those portraits in 1532 and 1533 for a young, talented artist named Spuccini. He was on the staff for a couple of decades.

I offered to make him into a vampire, but he turned me down. I have not run across him since. As for how I looked, well, those were troubling times. Not as troubling as now, but troubling nonetheless. You discern no happiness in my portrait? I often wonder if Spuccini painted the subject as they really were on the inside."

"That's an interesting thought, Kristano. I've had many portraits done over the millennia. I still have one that I sat for in 1816, shortly after the Bourbon Restoration. I don't think it is all that flattering. Then again, given the styles we had to deal with then, it was probably the best the artist could do. The clothes were uncomfortable. I was uncomfortable. The portrait captures that. Now, I can go about wearing Atlantean style robes, and no one thinks anything of it. Perhaps not much is better now, but that suits me."

"Well, time to change the subject and deal with the current crisis. Petard has informed me that Cartosimo left nothing of any value behind—no notes, no clues, no nothing. So, since he was in fact the one who purchased the explosive devices for La Mer, he must have thought they would be put to proper use. I only met the man a few times over the millennia, but I find it difficult to believe he would have wanted my sister to be harmed in any way. So, somehow, La Mer did convince him of honorable intentions."

Maurana sighs. "Further investigation would likely be a waste of time. Somewhat sad, actually, that there is no one that can be held accountable for this heinous act. The only one who paid a price for this is someone who never should have been suspected of any of it. What really happened that night, Kristano? Why did you believe La Mer and Vachon over Aurea? The whole mess just doesn't add up for me."

"If you are looking for a logical explanation, a rational excuse, you will not find one, Maurana. I did everything wrong and then compounded it by letting the issue sit and fester until the day that La Mer committed suicide and forced me to confront it. In the weeks prior to Vetrina's demise, Aurea and I had had words. She was pushing for ending the practice of using mortals as mindless thralls for servitude. The practice was on the decline among the Ruby and Emerald Order vampires, but she wanted me to take a stand. Aurea thought my influence would help bring the debate to a close. I wanted to let the practice simply die out. Vetrina agreed with Aurea, but she was not pushing me to take a stand, at least not publicly. Everyone knew though, and the quarrels were often quite heated."

Maurana nods. "I remember the debates. In many ways, they were more heated than the ones that preceded the Order Amethyst extermination or the ending of the practice of creating slave vampires. As I recall, La Mer and Vachon were on the side of using mortals as thralls. In fact, they wanted to expand on the practice. La Mer mentioned finding vast amusement in it. I'm sure Thorne felt the same way."

Kristano shudders. "Amethyst. There's a horror I have not thought about in ages. Aurea earned her nickname 'The Enforcer' from that campaign. She rooted out hundreds of the poor wretches. You are correct about La Mer and Vachon's views. In fact, they wanted me to make a public statement in support of making mortals into thralls. I refused to do that. I did not see the two of them for a few weeks prior to Vetrina's assassination. In fact, I did not see those two again until that fateful night."

"I have certainly heard much of the events of that night, Kristano, but I think you understand why I am saying I need to hear it in your words. Your perspective is the one I am missing. I know you are pained by this exercise; however, I am trying to get a feel for your state of mind at that point."

Kristano bows his head. "In that case, Maurana, I think it is time that I did what La Mer and Vachon refused to do that night. I want you to understand the whole thing in graphic detail. I don't want you to miss anything or make a factual error. I request Plinthi."

Maurana looks startled. "Very well, Kristano. Let's get right to it."

Victor is dressed for the ball when Nathan's car pulls up at his apartment complex. Daphne is up front with Nathan, so Victor gets into the backseat with Phyllis. Nathan simply nods to Victor and pulls back out into traffic as soon as he is buckled in.

Daphne turns around and looks at him. "Victor, this is my friend Phyllis. Phyllis, this is my colleague Victor. Please make sure he stays out of trouble at the ball. We don't need another incident like we had this afternoon. Not that I blame you, Victor. That woman was asking for it. You don't want to make enemies tonight. People attending the ball will remember."

"Well, Daphne, all I have to say about that incident is that she asked. I didn't go up to her and get into her face about what a ridiculous farce I regarded the inauguration parade to be and what a buffoon I think the new president is. Not that anyone here should infer that I held the outgoing president in high regard."

Nathan laughs. Daphne just rolls her eyes and turns back around. Victor looks over at Phyllis. She has flaming red hair and dancing green eyes and is wearing a tasteful green taffeta gown. She looks to be in her midthirties. He smiles at her.

"Don't worry, Phyllis. I will stay out of trouble at the ball. I plan to mind my own business, not talk to anyone besides present company, and get in some dancing. I will respectfully applaud when the president and the first lady come in for their dance. There's nothing to worry about."

Phyllis beams. "No, Victor. We will mingle. This will be a tougher crowd than most of the other ones you will deal with, granted. I am a veteran of such affairs. You will see and be seen and make a lasting impression. Just stick with me, and I will keep you away from those who would do ill to you."

Victor simply shrugs. "Very well, Phyllis. I am in your hands this evening."

Shortly thereafter, they arrive at the inaugural ball. Overall, the mood is festive. There is electricity to the crowd, as if this event is something truly special. Once they enter the hall, Nathan and Daphne go over one way toward some people they know. Phyllis takes Victor's arm and leads him into a group of dignitaries and legislators from California. Victor recognizes several of them, a few of whose activities had made mention in his master's thesis. This group is talking rather animatedly about an incident at the inaugural luncheon.

"I hear that the senior senator from Massachusetts is still in the hospital. They suspect the poor fellow had a seizure during the luncheon."

"His health is just so fragile. I know he worked hard during the campaign, but he really needs to take better care of himself. The president is counting on him to get health care reform passed this year."

This is when Phyllis chimes in. "The man has terminal brain cancer. Hard to know if he will be able to live out the year, much less work. As for health care reform, it will surely be quite the challenge to pass it this year, especially with the economy on the skids."

There are polite nods all around, save for this one rather stern-looking fellow. "Madam, we will have a de facto supermajority in the Senate this year, once that mess in Minnesota gets sorted out. The president will have no problem getting his agenda passed. We will transform America and clean up the mess left by the previous administration. He already made good on his promise to close Gitmo!"

Victor chuckles, and all eyes turn on him. "Well, frankly, it is one thing for a president to issue an executive order. It's quite another thing at times to have it implemented. He might even be totally sincere in his desire to close the prison camp. Does he have the clout to actually make it happen? I guess we will have to wait and see. Equally true about the other items on his agenda. Everyone in the House and Senate has an agenda of their own. Will they all follow the president? Not likely."

While the group digests this, Phyllis leads Victor away and heads toward a refreshment station. "I see you haven't developed the knack to speak without really saying anything. I gather you don't aspire to making a career in electoral politics?"

Victor gets them both some punch and hands a glass to Phyllis. "No, I have no intention of trying to make a career out of politics. As to being able to just engage in small talk, I can do that, but those people needed to be politely taught a lesson in reality, which is what I did."

The band starts playing, and Victor takes Phyllis out on the dance floor. Unbeknownst to him, they walk right past Ruby Order vampire Albert Sidney. Albert notices Victor in passing and then gives Phyllis an approving once-over, earning him a cold glare from his partner. He shrugs, smiles, and works his charm on his companion, who is soon all smiles again.

By the time the president and the first lady show up, Victor and Phyllis are resting, indulging in idle conversation with some other congressional staffers. All rise to applaud the first couple. Victor does as well, albeit with very little enthusiasm. Phyllis notices, but she only smiles. As they dance, Victor studies the president and the first lady, watching their expressions and their body language. Once they make their exit, Victor looks over at Phyllis.

"You know, he really believes in his own rhetoric. He thinks he truly is an agent of destiny. The first lady, now she is scary. She is driven and has few scruples. They are both dangerous people. They will change things, and not for the better. Rely on it."

The rest of the evening passes quietly. Phyllis finds that she admires Victor, even though he is so clearly out of place in this city.

Around the time Victor is leaving the inaugural ball, Carol Ann and Paulina Wong are walking through Central Park. Every so often, they have been accosted on these late-night walks, which generally mean one less mugger or thug for New York to deal with. Tonight's walk is very uneventful, which pleases Carol Ann but leaves Paulina feeling vaguely disappointed.

"I was hoping to put some of my martial arts training to practical use. I need the practice, and there is more than enough human scum in this city. They must all be hiding tonight."

Carol Ann looks over at Paulina. "Looking at you, if I was someone who made their living by harming others, I would definitely go off in search of easier prey. Someone would have to be insane or suicidal to not see that you could destroy them. Me, on the other hand, I look all sweet and innocent and defenseless."

Paulina laughs. "That would be a most fatal assumption on their part. I guess I will have to try dressing more provocatively, show some more skin, try to act more demure, appear to be a victim instead of being the consummate predator." She attempts to bat her eyes and pout. "Do you think I could pull that off?"

Carol Ann giggles. "You pull off looking and acting like a victim? That I would pay to see because it would be the show of the century. You would have to learn to really bat your eyes and giggle at bad jokes guys tell."

Paulina snorts and is about to speak when Carol Ann's cell phone rings. She stares at the number and takes the call. "Yes, Lady Maurana?"

"Are you alone right now, Carol Ann, or at least out of earshot of Aurea? This can wait if she is close by."

"Yes. I've been walking Central Park with my porfa. Aurea is back at the house. Paulina is with me. I can send her away if you wish it."

There is an audible sigh at the other end. "No need to send Paulina away. I wanted to fill you in on what has been developing here in Avignon. Kristano had me do a Plinthi session with him regarding the night that Vetrina was assassinated. It was very odd, very strange. I went away from it even more shocked, if such is possible. Not the result that I would have anticipated. No, not at all."

Carol Ann looks puzzled. "How do you mean? Was the Vitzameri actually able to defeat Plinthi?"

"No. That part was valid, as has always been the case. I was just amazed at the pettiness, at the abject stupidity that was revealed to me about that night. I mean, he nearly destroyed Aurea for a crime she did not commit. He had no reason to believe La Mer and Vachon, absolutely none at all, yet he still did it. They showed up at his estate first and convinced him that Aurea did it. Aurea underwent Plinthi three times that night. La Mer and Vachon refused. This is common knowledge. What people did not know is that Vetrina's death left Kristano mentally unhinged and unstable for years. Fortunately, his porfo majere at the time was able to keep him from doing much harm."

"Mental instability is rare among our order. Do you think the Vitzameri is unstable now? Or has he recovered? Can he be trusted? Are you going to call a conclave of high elders?"

"I think he is safe enough, Carol Ann. It seems that seeing La Mer's confession brought him back to his senses regarding the issue. I am just amazed though. He had been angry with Aurea's meddling, as he put it, at that time. Vetrina's death pushed him over the edge. La Mer and Vachon did not get what they wanted though. He never came out and endorsed having mortal thralls. Now he is obsessed with meeting with Aurea and discharging the blood debt. After that, it's hard to say. I think he has had enough and is ready emotionally to let go and take another turn at the wheel. Kristano is really a young soul, and he has a lot to learn. So, tell me, how is Aurea doing?"

"She's doing quite well. She is keeping busy with her projects. I think she will travel to Naples in the spring and visit Pompeii. She is concerned about doing that, as she says she hasn't walked those streets since about a year prior to the eruption. I think she will be ready to face the Vitzameri well before the year is over. She has told me as much anyway."

Maurana sighs. "Better than I expected to hear. You and Paulina get back to whatever you were doing. A fair day to you both." Carol Ann presses the end button.

Paulina looks at her expectantly. "Want to talk about that? How often does Lady Maurana call you?"

"She calls a couple times a week. She has been for the last few weeks. It has to do with the Vitzameri having been a complete putz back in 1753 and blaming Aurea for the death of his sister in this big explosion at a tavern outside of Avignon. I think he was the only sentient being who believed that at all. It was a tragedy all around. I remember it all only too well."

As they resume walking, a look of puzzlement crosses Paulina's face. "Not to sound stupid, but exactly what does Vitzameri mean? I know that is not the name of the eldest."

Carol Ann hails a cab for the trip back to Staten Island. As the cab pulls over to the side to pick them up, she looks over at Paulina. "Apparently, it is a title he was given back in old Atlantis. It translates to 'High Lord of the Seas.' Apparently, he likes it, so that is what most of the Order calls him. Ruby never developed a title for the eldest. There never really seemed to be a need for one."

They get in the taxi and head home.

Early in the morning on Wednesday the twenty-first, Zoe is taking her morning run along the beach in Santa Barbara. It is a very cool morning, with light fog creeping in from the ocean. The sea is placid, waves very small and unremarkable. Zoe enjoys those days when the waves are crashing along the shore from some storm way off the coast. She had heard from Victor awhile ago, pleasant conversation about how much he had not enjoyed yesterday's events. Still, he seemed to be coping well with it all. She can feel Victor's presence even when he is not there. He said he felt her presence often during the day, and it helped him get through it all. Zoe starts running faster, shaking her head while doing so.

"Of all the fickle tricks the Weave shall weave. My twin flame is my brother in the lifetime. Really tends to complicate matters."

Not far away on the beach sits one Cassidy Yale, porfo to Nina Parks. He is one of two who are charged with keeping an eye on Zoe to see if she does anything that will warrant further study by the Plaz Seschni. They are also there to protect her if need be. Cassidy is a student at the same university and is in a couple of Zoe's classes. Cassidy knows how to be very invisible, which makes him valuable on an assignment such as this. If Zoe ferrets him out, he will lose face, and that he does not intend to do. Nina said this was important, and he intends to please her. He wants to prove his worth to her.

Zoe often feels the eyes of others when she is out among people. Sometimes she will catch snatches of thoughts. There are no threats today, which is certainly of some comfort. She heads back up the beach and walks toward her parked car. She feels invigorated from the run, loves the endorphin rush from it. As she approaches her car, she looks over and sees a solitary figure sitting on a bench not too far away. She recognizes him as a student in her European history class. She acknowledges him with a nod and a wave. She then gets into her car and drives off.

Cassidy watches Zoe drive away. He sits there for a few minutes longer. He has no need or call to actually follow her that closely, no need at all. He knows she will be in class in about an hour. He likes living in Santa Barbara; it's so much nicer than Encino and the San Fernando Valley. He knows he will have to go back there in due course. He just hopes it won't be anytime soon.

She is beautiful; that's for sure. She's very intelligent too. No wonder they are so interested in her.

He sends Nina a text message about his observations this morning. He receives an acknowledgement a couple minutes later. Satisfied, he heads back to the university.

Victor is sitting alone, eating lunch in the cafeteria in the Rayburn Building. The place is definitely abuzz now, filled with Congressional staffers and a few representatives. He is reading a copy of the local paper, scowling now and again at the drivel the mainstream media claims is news.

Daphne comes over with a tray of food. "Mind if I join you, Victor?"

Victor puts down the paper and looks up. "Not at all, Daphne. I just finished my own lunch and read the paper. Delightfully old-fashioned, I am told. Newspapers are definitely on the decline."

Daphne sits down. "Why do you eat lunch alone so often? Just makes you look so alone. You should try to mix just a little more. It makes things more interesting. At least, that's what I would think."

Victor just smiles. "I have very little in common with most of the people here. I like people who can carry on in-depth conversations, who have something meaningful to say. There are a few such folks here, such as yourself and Davis, who can do that. Vapid, meaningless conversations just hurt my brain. I might be alone, but I am never lonely. I am definitely good enough company for myself."

Daphne lets that sink in for a moment. "Hmm. You know, you do have a point there, Victor. There are lots of shallow and vapid people here. You always have to watch for the knife in the hand people keep behind their backs. Hard to trust anyone here, and it is healthier not to." She takes a piece of paper out of her pocket. "Anyway, I have some rather interesting news for you. Phyllis and I talked after the ball. She really likes you, so much so that she asked me to give you her phone number. I was surprised. I mean, you are about ten years younger than she is and all. She told me to get with it. Older women with younger guys is becoming more the rule than the exception. I called her a cougar, and she just agreed. So, what do you say? Interested at all in seeing her again?"

Victor takes the slip of paper and puts it in his pocket. "Phyllis was pleasant company. She helped keep me out of harm's way a couple of times last night. I could certainly use another friend in this town. So, what about you and Nathan? You see any future with him? He seemed rather stiff and formal, if you don't mind me saying so."

Daphne shakes her head. "I don't see any future with Nathan. He's just a friend of a friend, and I needed an escort for the ball. He was not stimulating company. He actually tried to get me to invite him into my place after we had dropped you and Phyllis off. He's a real cad with no couth. I know I won't be going out with him again. No way."

Victor looks perturbed. "I am sorry that happened to you, Daphne. You deserve better. Frankly, I think you deserve better than anything this city has to offer you. There are so few honorable people here."

Daphne pats his hand. "I appreciate that, Victor. Sadly, I am a creature of the federal district. This is the life I chose many years ago. If you turn out to be right and this whole mess unravels, I will have to reinvent myself. *Honor*, well, there's a word you don't hear very often in the halls of Congress. Oh yes, they all call themselves the 'Honorable' this or that, but most of them would not know honor if it came and hit them in the face." She checks the time on her cell phone. "We'd best be getting back to the office."

When she arrives home from Dasher's that evening, Anneliese turns on her computer to see if there will be an e-mail from Victor. Sure enough, there is one. She opens it up and hangs on every word of his narrative about having attended the inauguration and going to one of the inaugural balls. She is saddened that he did not have a good time, but then she has come to understand more about him over the past few weeks, so this came as no surprise. Victor is intelligent and sensitive, apparently nothing like those people in Washington.

Anneliese didn't really understand the way government actually works, and what little she did grasp did not make her happy. That it seems to make Victor miserable she definitely objects to. She would like nothing better than to have Victor all to herself, to have his children. Sadly, she also knows that would never happen. She just isn't in his league. In her heart, she knows that.

She sits down and composes an e-mail in reply.

> Hi, Victor! You know I am always glad to hear from you. Sorry DC is such a pain for you, but I know you are learning lots. All the gang at Dasher's does really miss you. Cliff has been sweet lately, but his friends are still stuck up. One of them told me I should just stay in the bedroom and be his plaything! They don't get that Cliff and I haven't done it, not really. Sometimes I feel like just up and walking out of Cliff's life, but I won't let his friends scare me away. Arnold came by the store the other night with his fiancée. What was her name? Oh yeah. Katrina. He spent most of his time ogling me instead of paying attention to her. What a jerk. Then you told me that he was. He is attractive physically, but I don't like his spirit, his sense of life. I send you a kiss from behind the Orange Curtain. Hope that I can come and see you in April. Much love, Anneliese.

Anneliese gets a bit teary eyed after sending the e-mail. She always does. She truly likes Victor. She freshens up and checks her appearance in the mirror. Feeling good, she leaves and goes over to Cliff's house for the evening.

Aurea is sitting in her room, contemplating how events are unfolding. She feels like a spider in a giant web. Once the web is struck, she will be able to act swiftly. Until then, she has to remain patient, which is something she is rather good at. She looks at some photos of the ruins of Pompeii on her computer. Some of the buildings are intact enough that she remembers them well. She didn't recognize any of the people that they had made casts of out of the volcanic ash, at least not yet. She did not have many friends in Pompeii when Vesuvius erupted. Still, it hurts her heart. She has to go and walk those streets again. Now that her villa outside of Naples is back in her hands, she has a place to stay. Getting there would take a bit of doing. Certainly not impossible. Nowhere near as hazardous as the crossing she made back in 1753. That took weeks. Fortunately, she had mortal friends who were up to the task.

She walks over to the window and looks outside. The neighborhood is peaceful at night. She prefers this to the frenetic pace of Manhattan. She can easily afford to live there. There are just too many people there for her liking. Crowds make for easy hunting, but that really isn't a problem for her. She only feeds twice a week, and she never has an issue finding a willing mark. She is thirsty tonight, so she will be going out soon, probably hit on some local guy at a bar nearby. Staten Island does not lack that form of night life.

She puts on a slinky black dress that accentuates her curves. Her skirt ends just above the knee. She puts on a pair of pumps comfortable enough for the short walk to the bar she has in mind. She slips on her favorite long, black coat and then looks at herself in the mirror. She preens and is satisfied with how she looks. In fact, she feels like she is dressed to kill, though that is not her intention. A pint will be enough to slack her thirst. No one need die for that. She leaves the house and heads to the bar, Chez Marc's.

Chez Marc's has a pretentious name, but it is really quite the dive. There are only a few people there this night. A couple of worn-out hookers sit at a table in the back. Some guys are playing darts and drinking beer, typical male bonding behavior. Aurea scans the bar and sees some likely prospects. She walks over to a table and makes a production out of shedding her coat. Most of the men in the place, and a couple of the women, take note, which is exactly what Aurea wants. Most of the time, she finds that she does not have to use psychic suggestion to get people to notice her; it is all in the presentation.

A rather harried-looking cocktail waitress comes over, chomping on some gum. "What'll ya have?"

"Bring me an Irish coffee, dear. I need something to warm the insides on this cold night."

Aurea feels one set of eyes looking at her intensely. She glances over and sees a rather timid-looking, balding, paunchy fellow with sad eyes. He looks away quickly when he sees her looking at him. Aurea feels warm inside. She nods when the cocktail waitress brings her the drink. Once she turns away, she feels the man's eyes mentally undressing her. She catches some of his thoughts of what he would like to do to her. She laughs at that on the inside. She can tell the man would never act on those desires even if a woman was willing to indulge him. Sexually, he is definitely not her type, not even for a tryst. For a quick infusion of blood, he will do nicely. She looks at him again and smiles coquettishly, giving him a come-hither look that even he cannot misinterpret. Still, he looks shocked. A few seconds later, he walks over to her table.

"May I join you, young lady, buy you a drink?"

It generally strikes her as amusing when men call her young lady. She often feels like telling them she used to watch the lighthouse keepers stoke the fires and clean the mirrors at Pharos, the famous lighthouse of Alexandria, and that she also used to spend time at the library there, not that any of them would believe her. She coyly looks up at the man.

"Yes, kind sir. Please join me. I don't need a drink though, as I already have one. Some company would be welcome."

As he sits down, she purposely lets her skirt run up a bit, exposing more of her thigh. He notices, as she knew that he would. This guy will be easy to get her pint of blood from. Still, she decides to play with him for a little while.

"So, tell me, what's a nice guy like you doing in a dive like this?"

The man laughs. "I'm a regular here. Name's Steve. Yeah, it's a dive, but it's comfortable. Good prices and they don't water down the booze. Not like some of those snooty places in the city. That's no place for a working stiff like me. Give me Staten Island any day."

Aurea leans over slightly, making sure he gets a good view down her blouse. "Lived here all your life, Steve? Got any family?"

Steve sighs and takes a swig from his mug of beer. "Nah. I wasn't born here. I was born in Jersey. Newark actually. Lived there until I turned twenty, and then I moved here. I met my Mattie a few months later. I got two kids, both in their teens. I had to work late tonight, so I came here for a couple drinks. Then I saw you, and it started to get interesting. You are beautiful. You remind me of a gal I used to know from Italy."

Aurea preens and looks at him. She can tell the booze is starting to hit him. It's just about time to make her move. Still, she can play a little longer, and that appeals to her. She is hungry but far from starving.

"My family was from Italy, near Naples, actually. Tell me, Steve, since you are married, why are you hitting on me?"

"My Mattie, she's great and all, but she just doesn't understand me." He looks over at two hookers and grimaces. "I don't like dealing with the working girls. Never know what you might catch from them. You, you're different. I know you aren't from here. I think you understand me."

Oh yes, Aurea understands him very well. His surface thoughts are giving her lots of images of what he'd like to do with her. She isn't interested in that kind of play, not with the likes of him. It's time to make her move, feed, and get on her way. She looks him in the eyes and uses a very simple psychic trick. Now he looks rather glassy eyed.

"Steve, why don't we just go over to that corner in the hall? I'll give you what you need there."

Steve nods and stands up when Aurea stands. As they walk to the hall, Aurea gives an, *Ignore us*, suggestion to the rest of the people there. As there are no brights that evening, the suggestion takes hold and, and they do what she wants. She guides Steve up against the wall and stares into his eyes.

"Relax, darling. You will really enjoy this."

Steve nods and closes his eyes, fully relaxed and under her control. She looks hungrily at his neck. She watches his carotid artery pulsing strongly. Smiling, she lets her fangs extend fully. She embraces him and slowly sinks her fangs into the artery. As Steve is fully relaxed, he simply sighs as she does this.

Aurea sucks slowly, savoring the taste, the texture of the warm, hot arterial blood. She swallows and enjoys the warmth as it oozes down to her stomach. The alcohol is just hitting his blood, so it is not diluting the rich flavor.

There is something positively euphoric about feeding, Aurea muses.

She feels the pull of Steve's heart, the hum of his blissful thoughts. Feeding is, indeed, a very intimate act.

After a couple of minutes, she is sated. She withdraws her fangs, deliberately piercing her right index finger as she does so. She puts a drop of her blood on both of the wounds on Steve's neck, and they close rapidly, leaving no marks. Her fangs retract, no longer visible. She looks at Steve. His eyes are barely open.

"You will stand here for a couple of minutes and then go to the bathroom, freshen up, and go home. You will remember only that we had a pleasant conversation. Good evening to you, my friend. Thank you for the meal." Aurea walks away and leaves the bar.

When she is about a block away from the bar, this punk kid jumps out from an alley with a knife in his hand.

"Hand over your purse, or I'll cut you bad!"

Aurea just scowls, looks in his eyes, and says, "Die."

The punk's eyes bug out, and he clutches his chest and falls down dead. Shaking her head, Aurea continues her walk home without further incident.

Thursday morning at about ten o'clock finds Victor having a meeting with Bob Moore in his office. The representative is sitting behind his desk, looking very relaxed, almost amused. "So, Victor, what do you think of our new president?"

"I don't like the man, and not just because he is the president. He believes his own lies. He is very arrogant. Some would likely say he is gullible, but I think he knows that he was set up to take the fall."

"That's an interesting angle, Victor. Why do you think he was set up to take a fall? It doesn't seem that you buy into the 'making history' aspect of this at all."

"It seems pretty clear to me, actually, sir. The establishment knows the days of this oligarchic republic are numbered. They set him up because it was expedient. When it all collapses, they will make sure that he takes the blame for it, even though his role in it will be relatively minor. The problem is, I think he knows that is what these people think, but he is so arrogant he thinks he can stop it from happening. He might be able to slow down the process, but he is in no position to stop it."

Moore thinks about that for a moment. "You could well be right, Victor. If you are, my colleagues in the other party are more devious and callous than I would have thought. So, any impressions you care to share with me about our new first lady?"

"Watch out for her. She is so much stronger than he is—it isn't even funny. No, I don't mean physically, though she certainly could be that as well. She is driven and determined to push her agenda of social justice. She is a true believer in the righteousness of her cause. I strongly recommend keeping a wary eye on her."

Moore smiles. "I knew I hired you for the right reasons. You aren't afraid to speak your mind. I appreciate that. Next week, I will have you spend a couple of days in the House galleries. You can watch some of the ongoing debates. There is going to be a session at the United Nations in February that I will have you attend. It has to do with health and human welfare, old-fashioned touchy-feely issues. For now, I thank you."

Victor stands up, nods to Moore, and returns to the office to continue his workday.

CHAPTER 6

Sunday, 22 February 2009. There is a relatively small crowd this evening at Becker's in Alexandria. Smilin' Joe Fritz, a local blues artist, is performing, setting the proper tone. Sitting at a table toward the back is Kathleen Brown, very into the music and enjoying herself. Also with her is Lester Dustin, looking dour and totally out of place, as usual. They are waiting for Johanna Van Clerc to arrive so they can dispense with having their taxes done for the year. Kathleen is smiling and moving to the music. Lester is glaring and unnerving some of the other patrons. Kathleen notices and taps on Lester's hand.

"You need to chill, Lester. You are making some of the mortals nervous. Loosen up and have some fun."

Lester snorts. "Let them be a little nervous. I'll not harm them. I promise. I will hunt after Madame Van Clerc arrives, and we can finish this dreadful business. Keep having to pay taxes. Geez. I was hoping I could get out of doing that once I became a vampire. No such luck."

Kathleen nods. "You could if you want to go entirely off the grid, go live in the woods or something. If you want to stay in civilization though, it is prudent to tithe the temporal powers some small amount. Johanna is quite good at this. Then again, I guess if you stay in the same trade for centuries, you are bound to get exceptionally competent at it."

At that point, Johanna arrives. She gives Kathleen a peck on the cheek and shakes hands with Lester. She definitely looks like an accountant, wearing a business casual outfit and carrying her laptop. She places the computer on the table and starts punching in numbers and bringing up electronic forms. She turns the screen toward Lester.

"You did pretty well last year. Sadly, most of your income generated quite the paper trail. Try investing in more precious metals and get more of your cash flow off the books. Did what I could to minimize the hit, but you are taking one with the Feds. For Virginia, you came close to breaking even." She prints a couple forms. "Sign these, and we will set the electronic transfers to trigger on April fourteenth. No sense in paying them sooner, unless you actually want to."

Lester shakes his head as he signs the forms. "No. That will be fine. No need to hand the money over to the thieves until I absolutely have to." He stands up. "Ladies, if you will excuse me, I must be about my business for the evening. Much to do can't waste more time on this sort of frivolity."

Johanna and Kathleen watch as Lester leaves the club. The mood of the place became much cheerier once he left the premises.

Johanna looks dumbfounded. "Some people accuse me of being a stick in the mud. Compared to him, I'm the life of any party. Is he always such marvelous company?"

Kathleen laughs heartily. "For him, this was a positively cordial evening. I don't associate with Lester often; he's generally very rude and obnoxious. Makes me wonder how he actually survived his first twenty years as a vampire. He's just a few months past that allegedly magic number. Johanna, nobody would ever accuse you of having bad manners. You are shy and reserved, yes, but you are never rude."

Johanna grimaces. "I'm not shy; I just don't like most people. I know I don't like Lester. I don't even think Lester likes Lester. Have you ever been intimate with him?"

A look of puzzlement crosses Kathleen's face. "Intimate? With him, it was purely a physical release, and not all that pleasing of one at that. There was certainly no spiritual connection in any sense. He's not even fun to play with."

Johanna turns her attention back to her laptop. "Okay. I have your federal and district returns ready, all under the proper alias. You'll get a small amount back from the federal and just owe a negligible sum to the district. Just sign these forms, and you are finished with this silly chore for the year."

Kathleen signs, as directed by Johanna. Then she takes a gold maple leaf coin out of her pocket and hands it to Johanna. "I know it's worth more than you usually charge, but it is so appropriate. You are the best. What do you have planned for the rest of the evening?"

Johanna quickly pockets the coin and looks around the club. "I'm free the rest of the night, actually. No other appointments until tomorrow. Should be a busy week, but that's how it goes for accountants during the tax season. It's so nuts now, all the different tax authorities. They keep changing the rules. I don't know how mortals keep up with it all. It makes my head spin, and I have over seven hundred years of experience in bookkeeping." She takes Kathleen's hand. "What did you have in mind?"

Kathleen is moving to the beat of the music in her seat. "I love this club. The bands are always good." She looks over at Johanna. "I propose we get out there on the dance floor. We'll get some guys whom we can get our pint from. Then we can go back to my place. I have this lovely bottle of Drambuie we can share. Then, well, we can do whatever strikes our fancy. What do you say?"

Johanna turns off her laptop, grinning mischievously. "Sounds like a very nice idea." She makes a fake pout. "Are you trying to get me drunk and take advantage of me?"

Kathleen laughs and takes Johanna's hand. "Shall we dance? Lots of folks we can feed from tonight."

They stand up and head out to the dance floor.

ꕥ

At about that time, Victor is at his Georgetown apartment, chatting with his sister on his cell phone. Zoe is filling Victor in about recent events at the university.

"There have been these two students, one guy and one girl, who have been watching me the past few weeks. I think they think I don't know that they are, but I have been aware of them for quite some time. I don't think they intend me any harm. They've never even tried to talk to me. I'm sure it has something to do with where you are and what you're doing."

Victor scratches his head absently and sighs. "You could be right, Zoe. Have you thought about approaching either one of them? Do you think they know each other?"

"I've nodded and waved to the guy a few times. His name is Cassidy, and he is in a couple of my classes. You know how huge some of the classes are. The woman's name is Dianne Spence, and I usually see her at the library and the student union. They are both legitimately registered university students with declared majors. I don't think they know each other. I only saw them in the same area once, at the student union, and there was literally no interaction between them. If they do know each other, then they are very good at handling their body language. I really get the impression they are there to observe and protect."

"Well, I trust your judgment, Zoe. Still, at some point, you might just want to approach one of them and see if you can figure out what they are really up to, who they are working for. Even if they are feds, it would be very difficult for me to figure out which agency sent them. I've ruffled some feathers here, but nothing major. Just trying to do what Moore hired me to do."

Zoe laughs at that. "So how are things with you, Victor? Gone out with Phyllis recently?"

Victor moans at the mention of Phyllis. "We went out again on Friday night. We went to a nice little café here in Georgetown. Pleasant enough evening, talked for a few hours. Then she suggested we go back to her place for a nightcap. I declined politely, citing a project that I was doing on Saturday for the representative. She looked very disappointed by that. We kissed when I took her home. It was nice, but not in a way that made sparks fly. Frankly, I was more moved when Anneliese kissed me. I like Phyllis, but I know I don't want to lose my virginity to her. I want that to be special, with someone I really care about."

Zoe sighs. "Yes, that would be ideal. I'm sure there is something truly magical about being able to be truly intimate with someone. Sex alone is fun, but you want the whistles and bells too. I get that. The right person is out there for you. Whether or not you will meet that special someone there in the imperial city, well, you can never tell, can you?"

"That's true, Zoe. I still feel out of my element here though. I'm definitely still out of my comfort zone. I am learning how to put up with and deal with the denizens of this city. Find love here? I suppose it is no less likely than it was behind the Orange Curtain. People, by and large, are such phonies here. They make the silly plastic people of the OC look genuine and sincere by comparison."

"So tell me, how was New York City? Did you go and see anything besides the United Nations and the hotel you stayed at?"

"New York City was very strange, Zoe. I did make a brief stop at the area near Ground Zero, but I couldn't make myself stay long. It was like hearing thousands of people scream. There are definite earthbound spirits there, people who refuse to cross over, refuse to believe it is time to move on. I still don't think the government had anything to do with those attacks, but I do believe that they knew the attacks were coming and they could have stopped them if they had wanted to. Since it helped them expand the power of the police state, they let it happen. I didn't do much else in the city. I spent all day at the UN listening to this conference about sanitary conditions in Africa. Took the train back to DC that night and made my report to Moore the next day. I hope sometime to be able to stay long enough to at least catch a Broadway show."

"That would be fun, Victor. Maybe I can come over there during the summer and we could do that together, see some sights, dine at some snobby restaurant in Manhattan."

"I'd like that, Zoe. Just have to figure out when you can travel and when I can schedule a few days off."

At about one in the morning on Monday the twenty-third, Aurea is talking animatedly with Maurana over the computer link.

"I am planning a trip to Napoli as soon as I have everything tied up neatly over here. I have so much going on. It really has been most interesting. It's something that just hasn't been so for quite a while."

Maurana looks thoughtful. "It is certainly marvelous to see you in high spirits. You definitely have been preoccupied by issues that appear to have no bearing on the blood debt. Not that I'm faulting you at all. Certainly not, given how long it took the Vitzameri to realize the error of his ways. Justice needs to be done, and he needs to pay the price, and the sooner this happens, the better it will be for all of us. I wonder if you have given much thought to exactly what you want from him. The restitution you would receive anyway, you are certainly entitled to full compensation for the material losses. Do you intend to make him wait much longer before you make your settlement demand?"

A smirk crosses Aurea's face. "How much longer he waits depends upon a great many things. I must see my present project through to its conclusion. I must go back to Italy and wander the streets of Pompeii and face the ghosts of my past. Once that is done, I intend to demand that the Vitzameri make a public apology and fully admit his errors in regards to how he treated me after Vetrina's death. Therein lies the rub though, as I want this to be an event attended by several hundred of the Plaz. I want this to happen in North America. Yes, I am going to insist he come to me. I will not just show up in Avignon for this. Once this event has happened, I will consider the blood debt discharged, as I owe it to Vetrina to let this end."

Maurana nods. "That is very generous of you, far better than he actually deserves. A few weeks back, he submitted to Plinthi. Looking back at the events of Vetrina's demise and the turmoil afterward, as he perceived them, really seemed like watching some horrible soap opera. I still don't understand how he let his grief override his judgment like that. I understand passion, but he should have known better. On some level, he must have because once La Mer confessed to everything, the Vitzameri's world simply collapsed. Some days, he doesn't even come out of his study. He will look at Vetrina's portrait and weep." A wry grin flashes across Maurana's face. "You might take some pleasure in this. He has re-hung your portrait in his study, apparently where it was prior to all the madness. It's really quite good. You could demand that he give that portrait to you as part of the settlement."

Aurea chuckles and shakes her head. "That I will not do. It is a striking portrait, granted, but it was Vetrina's favorite. It should be hung there. If Vetrina comes back and is found and rejoins us and she decides she wants me to have it, then I will accept it. I have been considering sitting for a portrait to be done by Robert D'Anse once the blood debt has been settled. The man does excellent work."

"I thought sculpture was more his style, Aurea. I have seen his rather twisted vampire animal series. The vampire rhino was really quite spectacular. I hear he is planning on making a limited edition of bronze castings for that one. That should make the man even richer."

"I will definitely be putting an order in for one of those. I enjoy his sense of whimsy. With his sculpture, he sets his inner child free.

With his portrait work though, he captures the essence of his subject. His studio is in Philadelphia. Next time you are over here, I'd be happy to take you there."

Maurana nods. "That sounds like a most intriguing idea, my friend. I hope I can make it soon."

Victor is sitting in Representative Moore's office at ten o'clock Monday morning. As usual, Moore is quite upbeat while Victor looks nondescript. People often find Victor to be an enigma. It confuses and bewilders them that they can but rarely read his emotions. Moore hands Victor an envelope.

"I know this is very short notice, but tomorrow evening, they are having a reception at the Spanish embassy. I was planning to attend in person, but we are having caucus meetings, and the whip says attendance is pretty much mandatory, so I need you to go there in my place. Generally, they have good food, and the embassy staff are good folks. You don't need to stay long; just a couple of hours will be fine. Just make sure you speak to the ambassador and convey my regrets."

Victor nods and puts the envelope into his pocket. "Not a problem at all, sir. Will there be anyone else there that I should speak to or someone that I should avoid?"

"There's no one that I can think of, Victor, since you already know most of the players by sight now. Just use your best judgment and trust your intuition. Looking ahead to next week, I will be sending you to New York again to attend a three-day conference at the UN. You will be able to just sit and observe in the visitor's gallery. It's an environmental conference, talking about global warming and such. The current administration is making a big deal about this. I expect them to try to get through cap and trade as well as strengthen the regulatory reach of the EPA. This conference could give us some idea what to expect."

Victor nods and enters notes into his BlackBerry. "That is fine with me. It will give me some time to see more of New York. The conference does sound interesting, at least in the fashion of knowing what your adversary is up to. I'm sure the scientists assembled will be the types who are claiming that this climate change is being driven almost entirely by human action. The facts don't really bear that claim out, but then, when did that ever matter to the political class? No offense intended, sir."

Moore smiles. "No offense taken, Victor. I know your opinions, and while I don't agree with many of them, I do respect them. What I will say as far as the climate change issue goes is that I tend to agree with your side. I will vote against cap and trade and against strengthening the EPA. However, right now, it seems the president has the votes to bulldoze his agenda through the House and Senate. Perhaps someone with your perspectives will see or hear something at that conference that I can use to change a few minds."

Victor looks at Moore. "Even if you do manage to change a few minds, even if the House and Senate actually vote the current climate change and cap and trade legislation down, it won't be enough to save the country from ruin. I will be attentive and take notes. On that you may rely. I will bring back information. What you do with it is entirely up to you. One thing I have noticed is that the United Nations is even stranger than the federal government. These people who want a new world order have really chosen the wrong vehicle to implement their desires. Basically, it is an impotent body that has delusions of grandeur well beyond its actual utility. It is fascinating to watch, kind of like observing a train wreck."

Moore leans back in his chair and laughs. "Well, I'm sure you have other work to attend to, so have at it and enjoy the rest of your day."

Victor stands up and walks out of Moore's office, entering notes into his BlackBerry as he goes.

Shortly after sunset, Aurea is sitting in her office, reading a vampire novel, shaking her head as she goes along.

"This one's even weirder than the other one I read," she mutters under her breath. "They sparkle in daylight? What nonsense is that?"

At that point, her computer beeps, signaling an incoming transmission. Seeing that it is from Zack, she accepts it and his face soon appears on her screen.

"Good evening, Madam Aurea. I have some more news of Victor Trent via Anneliese Bryce. It's simply news of his upcoming travel schedule and various gripes about the imperial city, but still useful."

Aurea nods, putting her book aside. "What is his schedule, Zack? Where is he traveling to and why? Must have to do with congressional staff business. It's far too soon for him to have any time off."

"He's going to be attending that United Nations conference on climate change as an observer. That is being held on March third through the fifth. He will come up via the train late on the second and return to DC on the evening train on the fifth. I did read over the rest of the e-mail, but it held little of value. He still thinks politicians are a bunch of crooks and that they do not have the best interests of the populace in mind." He snickers. "Guess that is part of why I have just steered clear of politics. I just don't see what there is to gain by participating in a system that is very clearly rigged."

"Your observations are on target, Zack. Just remember that there have been few formal governments that actually did any good for the general populace. The desire for power is very great. Be sure that you understand that of the Plaz too. Emerald and Ruby don't have formal lines of control, but the cliques do exist, and there are certainly those who wish to rule. Usually, those folks get careless and thus are neutralized. Mind your place and mind your step, Zack. Always keep your wits about you."

Zack is taken aback. "I hear you, Madam Aurea. Sydney has told me something of the Order Sapphire and their rigid caste system. She was talking to me the other night though about the great lady of the Emerald Order, Madam Sybille, the one they call First Speaker because she is the only one that the eldest will converse with. Isn't his name Satchna? It's truly fascinating."

Aurea smiles. "I have spoken with Lady Sybille on several occasions. She is indeed very gracious and very intelligent. She's been around for twenty-four thousand five hundred and twenty-seven years, so I've been told, and I have no reason to doubt that. I trust that Syd told you not to address her as First Speaker, should you ever meet her. She really hates that. Satchna is a recluse, has been one for about a millennium now. He is over thirty-eight thousand years old. I have seen him but have yet to speak to him. As to why he became a recluse, no one seems to know."

Zack clears his throat. "By your leave then, Madam Aurea, I have quite a full plate this evening. I will keep you informed when I learn more, as agreed."

Aurea nods and Zack signs off.

Victor is having lunch Tuesday afternoon at the office cafeteria, sitting with Daphne and Davis. "Phyllis has taken ill, so I guess that means I will be going to the Spanish embassy party alone this evening. She sounds like she has the flu. It's really a shame, as she seems to actually like attending these parties. She has kept me from putting my foot in my mouth a couple of times. I really do appreciate that."

Daphne pouts. "Sorry to hear she is ill, Victor. I'll have to call her later and see how she is doing. Still, I think you will be okay on your own at the Spanish embassy. We are on good terms with the ambassador, there has never been an unpleasant incident there. There are generally lots of women there who won't mind dancing with you if you are so inclined. Just remember that the reception is semi-formal, which means a jacket and tie. Thank the fates it isn't a formal affair. Then you'd have to rent a tuxedo."

Davis laughs. "Ever worn a tux, Victor? It isn't much fun. Be ready though. I'm sure Bob will send you to some formal reception well before the end of summer. That can be really brutal, having to wear a tux here in the summer. It gets really hot and steamy here then."

"I haven't had to wear a tuxedo yet; however, I am fully prepared to do so when the need arises. In fact, I am thinking about actually going ahead and buying one. It seems like it could be a worthwhile investment. I think that I will check out some of the stores near Manassas that I heard about. I wouldn't want to buy in Georgetown. There really aren't any bargains there."

Davis looks thoughtful. "I don't think you even need to go that far from the district for a good deal on a tuxedo. Some shops down in Fairfax could do it for you. If you are actually going to buy a tux, Victor, then you want it tailored especially for you."

"For once, Victor, I agree with Davis. I'm sure he can get you a couple of referrals with some good tailors down in Fairfax. I don't blame you for not wanting to shop in the Georgetown boutiques. You are just paying for the privilege of buying in a snooty location. It still amazes me how some people vie to buy stuff just because it has a high price. I mean, if you really want a Coach purse, you can find it at the thrift store for a mere tiny fraction of the cost new."

Victor smiles. "I will keep that in mind if I am ever in the market for a Coach purse, Daphne. Davis, let me have a couple of tailors' names down in Fairfax, and I will check them out in the next couple of weeks. No sense in drawing this out. The sooner I own a tux, the better." Victor picks up his meal tray. "Got to finish up in the office and get ready for tonight."

The cab drops Victor off at the embassy gate at about six o'clock. He promptly walks over to the gate guard, who checks the invitation and Victor's ID and waves him through. He looks sharp in his brown jacket and white shirt. He chafes at wearing a tie, but he is getting used to it. People are gathering inside, and the mood appears festive. He shrugs inwardly and makes ready to spend a few hours socializing.

At least I will get a meal and maybe a few dances, he thinks. *I just hope someone asks. I really hate making the first move. Socially awkward, that's me.*

Another in a series of cabs arrives at the embassy gates at about six fifteen. The passenger door opens, and out comes a very stylishly dressed Cassie Mae Adler. She looks calm and assured, wearing a stylishly cut black dress with low-heeled pumps. Her ruby ring is prominent on her right ring finger. She is also wearing small ruby earrings and a necklace with a small silver cross. While she does have an invitation, the gate guard simply smiles at her and waves her through, the advantage, she thinks, to being known, to being on friendly terms with the ambassador's son. She strides purposefully toward the embassy building and the reception that is already well underway.

Victor is standing in the foyer, nursing a drink and watching the people. They are simply mingling, engaging in small talk and greeting friends and acquaintances. He does note the presence of the notorious lobbyist Gretchen Denter chatting up some of the embassy staff. He can see right through her, but he knows she talks a good game. She is quite attractive and knows how to use her looks to her advantage. He turns his attention toward the front entrance and watches the arriving guests. It is then that he notices Cassie Mae reach the front door. He sees her exchange pleasantries with the doorman, who smiles as she walks in. Victor smiles and nods to her as she walks toward him. She smiles, not breaking her stride.

Cassie Mae does note Victor's presence as she enters the embassy, so bright, in their parlance, that he would have been impossible to not notice. She favors him with a smile as she continues walking toward the reception hall.

Decent-looking fellow, she thought. *Disaffected intellectual. He feels so out of place here. He's definitely not part of the political class. Alas, he's not the type of mark that I had in mind for tonight.*

At this point, her preternatural senses go off. Out of the corner of her eye, she sees Victor flinch, staring at her with a look like a deer in headlights.

Victor's mind is racing. *Did I actually hear what that woman was thinking?*

Cassie Mae stops and slowly turns toward Victor. Her mind is racing too, trying to assess the threat level that he represents. *I think he heard my thoughts! I wasn't directing that internal dialogue toward anyone! Who is this mortal?* She walks toward Victor, looking him in the eyes. She notices that he is starting to sweat nervously. He is clearly rattled. As a test, Cassie Mae thinks, *Sir, if you can hear this, please say, 'Yes,' out loud. Just say, 'Yes,' nothing more.*

Victor gazes into Cassie Mae's eyes, feeling the fear rising in him. He had heard her. He utters one word, a trembling, "Yes."

She studies him a little more and then extends her right hand. "Well, that is quite unusual. Do you hear people's thoughts often, sir? I'm called Cassie Mae."

Victor shakes Cassie's hand, calming down slightly. "I definitely don't hear people's thoughts often. I get impressions from time to time, a word here or there. There was this one time at this blasted nightclub back in Orange County, but that seemed more like a psychic assault." Victor regains some composure. "Where are my manners? My name is Victor Trent."

Cassie Mae smiles and offers Victor her arm, which he gently takes, and they walk together into the reception hall. They are both calming down. She is becoming certain that he has no idea what she is and thus does not represent an active threat. However, she has to make sure, as this is something that she has never experienced before. "So, Victor, where are you from? I can tell you aren't from around here."

"I'm from California, a far cry from this place." He looks at her a moment. "I would guess, from your accent, that you are from South Carolina." Cassie Mae nods. "That's true, Victor. I was born outside of Charleston. I grew up there. I've lived near the district for quite some time now. So what brings you here this evening?"

"Oh, I'm here because my boss, Representative Moore, could not attend the party. He wanted me to come and be sure to convey his regrets to the ambassador."

"I'm somewhat surprised that you work for a Congressman. I hope you don't take offense, but you just don't strike me as being the type who finds power politics honorable or stimulating in any way. You just look so out of place here."

"You are right; I am no fan of partisan politics, and yes, I feel like a fish out of water here. I took the job because it was a ticket out of Orange County, a way to get away from my parents and get on with my life. I have a master's degree, and the only work I was able to get out there in this economy was as a sales clerk at this little second-hand store called Dasher's. Sometimes this place is a nightmare, but I am learning a lot."

Cassie Mae sees the ambassador and waves. He nods and walks over to them. He bows and kisses her hand and then gives Victor a hearty handshake.

"It's so nice to see you again, Senorita Cassandra! Who is this fine gentleman you are in the company of?"

"Ambassador, I'm Victor Trent. I'm part of Representative Robert Moore's staff. He asked me to attend the reception tonight in his place and give you his regrets. House business requires him to be on the Hill this evening. He hopes you and your family are doing well, and he is looking forward to seeing you soon."

The ambassador nods. "You are certainly welcome here, Senor Trent. Tell Robert that I understand completely and look forward to meeting with him again as well. Please, enjoy our hospitality. Eat, drink, and dance." He turns to Cassie Mae. "My son, Eduardo, will be here in about an hour. He is looking forward to seeing you again. It's always a pleasure having you here. So, if you two will excuse me, I must greet and speak with the others here. *Adios*!" The ambassador bows and takes his leave.

Victor looks at Cassie Mae and studies her. She seems just a little pale, but her eyes are amazing to him. They have such a piercing quality. He feels like he could drown in those eyes. He feels like they could see through to his very soul. The way she moves and comports herself reminds him of mannerisms more common in a more genteel society than that of Washington DC. He is still rather shaken by the clear telepathy, still trying to wrap his mind around how that could happen.

For her part, Cassie Mae is studying Victor as well. She is still wary after the overheard internal dialogue, but she is comfortable enough in the belief that he is no threat to her and her kind. She can feel the turmoil in his mind, but he is closely guarding his thoughts, so she is only catching glimpses from him. She can tell he is a very ancient soul. She will definitely contact Johanna about this.

"So, you're a friend of the ambassador's son? I guess that means you come here rather frequently."

Cassie Mae shrugs. "I regard Eduardo as being more like a friendly acquaintance. Ambassadors come and go. I think it is best not to try for deep relationships with such a transient population. I suspect you are much the same way. You likely have many acquaintances but only a few true friends."

Victor holds up his right hand, showing four fingers. "There are four people that I call friend: my sister Zoe, my Uncle Reggie, Matthew, and Oscar. The last two I met back in high school. I did not make any lasting friendships at the university. I think most people really overuse the word *friend*. To me, a friend is someone who is a true confidant, someone you can rely on, and they can rely on you. That represents a considerable investment in time and emotion."

"Your sentiments echo mine, good sir." She notes a man from the embassy staff looking their way, and she waves him over. As the man approaches, she turns to Victor. "Do you mind if I have Juan take a picture of us with my cell phone? I'll be happy to e-mail it to you as a memento."

Victor nods as Juan reaches them. Cassie Mae hands Juan her cell phone and then stands next to Victor. Juan takes their picture and hands the cell phone back to her.

"Now, I just need your e-mail address to send you the picture. It's quite nice actually."

She shows him the photo, and he nods. Victor reaches into his wallet and pulls out a business card and then writes his home e-mail on the back and hands the card to her. She smiles and puts the card in her purse. The music starts, and people start heading to the dance floor.

"Do you care to dance, Victor?"

Victor relaxes a little. "You sure Eduardo won't mind? I don't want to insult our hosts."

Cassie Mae smiles and takes his hand. "Eduardo won't care at all. I always dance with several of the men here. It's a party. I know the evening started strangely, but why let that continue?"

They head out to the dance floor and dance for a while. Victor enjoys watching her move. For Cassie Mae, she notices the kindness in his eyes. Yes, she can clearly see that Victor is someone special, a matter that she definitely intends to discuss with Johanna. She no longer has any doubts about that. No, she would not kill him; there is no need for such drastic action. Nor will she feed on him. Eduardo would do for that. He has donated a pint to the cause more than once.

As they walk off the dance floor, Victor checks the time on his cell phone. "I guess I'd better head for home. It will be a busy day at the office tomorrow." He holds out his hand. "Well, it certainly has been a most extraordinary evening, Cassie Mae. I hope the rest of the evening goes as you expected it to and nobody else overhears what you are thinking about."

Cassie Mae grins and shakes Victor's hand. "Don't dwell on it. In the end, no harm was done. I'll get that picture e-mailed to you soon. Perhaps we can get together sometime and meet for drinks? I'm sure there's a nice little bistro you like going to. I would really enjoy that."

"Maybe we could in a couple weeks. I have to make a business trip to New York to observe a UN conference on climate change. I'm sure that will be a most mind-deadening experience. After that, I will want some intelligent company." With that, Victor turns and makes his way out of the embassy.

Cassie Mae quickly goes to a quiet alcove, sending an, *Ignore me,* suggestion to the crowd. She pulls out her cell phone and calls Johanna. She then proceeds to tell her everything that happened at the embassy with Victor. Johanna has her upload the photo and then says she will call back. About a minute later, her cell phone rings, and it is a number she does not recognize, but she had the impression that it was very important that she take the call.

"This is Cassie Mae."

"Good evening, Cassandra Mae. I do believe we have met before. This is Aurea Bodellini. Johanna told me that you have had an incident with one Victor Trent, who is indeed a mortal of interest. Specifically, an incident involving him overhearing your thoughts that were not directed toward him and that you confirmed it by doing it again and having him respond verbally. You then determined that he was not a high risk to the Plaz Seschni, had no idea what you were, and thus, you let him leave. Does that cover it?"

A look of concern goes across Cassie Mae's face. "Yes, Madam Aurea. Did I act improperly? Is he actually a threat to us? I know where he lives. He seems like a decent fellow, very pleasant."

"No, Cassandra. You did the right thing. Your evaluation was sound. You see, I had Victor sent to DC for a blind test. I will explain myself tomorrow. Carol Ann and I will be taking the train down to DC tonight. She's called Oscar Martin. We will be staying at his house. I'm going to be calling the other metro DC Rubies on the way to get together at Oscar's place tomorrow night about seven thirty to discuss this incident and Victor Trent. You will be there, won't you? It's rather vital."

"Of course, Madam Aurea. It wouldn't make sense to have a meeting about an incident I experienced without me being there."

"Very good, my dear. I will see you tomorrow night."

At the house on Staten Island, Carol Ann and Aurea are rushing to pack some bags and have Paulina take them to the train station. Oscar Martin will be picking them up when the train arrives in the district. They rush down the stairs and into the car, and Paulina heads out. Aurea is talking animatedly on her cell phone. Carol Ann watches the range of emotions going across Aurea's face. Some of the calls are cordial. A couple are rather terse. By the time they reach Grand Central Terminal, Aurea has finished with the calls.

"Well, they will all be there. Lester and Kathleen were a bit difficult, but in the end, I convinced them that it will be worth their while to attend. Lester was particularly difficult. At least I was able to pique Kathleen's curiosity in the end."

As Aurea and Carol Ann exit the car and grab their luggage, Paulina looks over at them.

"I have one suggestion, Aurea. Since, as they like to say in the military, the balloon has gone up, perhaps it would now be prudent for you to contact the Emerald Order? Now that Mr. Trent has been noticed, we might want to have their support and possible protection. It's your call, of course."

Aurea looks thoughtful. "I think you are right, my dear. I will call Patsy once we are on the train. We will only be gone for a couple days. I don't intend to impose on Oscar's hospitality, and, frankly, I do so detest the imperial city."

Paulina nods and drives off.

About a half hour later, the train pulls out of Grand Central Terminal. Carol Ann is looking intently out the window. Normally lively, she is now very quiet and pensive. Her mind is racing. So much is happening at once. At least the waiting for the shoe to drop is over. Now, though, the stakes are higher.

Aurea sits back and takes out her cell phone and calls her Emerald counterpart, Patsy Plontz. While she lives just outside of New York City, Patsy is the Emerald elder who kept watch over matters concerning DC as well. Patsy picks up on the third ring.

"Aurea, my dear! Such a rare pleasure to hear from you! How are you?"

"I'm doing well, Patsy. Thank you. How have things been for you and yours recently?

Patsy sighs audibly. "Everything has been rather quiet here on the Eastern seaboard since New Year's. I know you heard about that blasted hunter Van Arpel destroying Louise in Philadelphia on New Year's Eve. It was a tragic loss. Louise was such a treasure. For some reason, we just can't flush this creep out. He's destroyed two of ours and three of yours in the past year."

"Yes, Patsy. That mortal is a menace. It's like he doesn't actually exist. No one seems to be able to pick up on his mental signature. Not even his sister Abigail has been able to help, and she is just devastated. At any rate, I am calling to discuss a matter of rather high importance that requires the utmost of discretion."

"Certainly, Aurea. How can I be of assistance to you?"

Aurea then explains to Patsy all that has been going on over the past few months regarding Victor Trent and how he has now done something rather extraordinary for a mortal and how she is holding a meeting tomorrow night with the Ruby vampires in DC to discuss the blind test and the final trial for him. Patsy listens very intently without interrupting.

"So, Patsy, the great favor that I need from you is, will you talk to your people in the DC metro area and have them be aware of him and see that he is not harmed accidentally? I would hate to have gone to all this time and effort and expense to see it end in tragedy."

"Certainly, Aurea. I will advise my people of the situation. Right of self-defense acknowledged, but I am sure that I can have my people be on the lookout for Mr. Trent. You may rely on their discretion, certainly. I wonder though, with something this important, why you didn't tell me about it sooner. You know that you can trust me to keep a confidence."

Aurea pouts. "It's kind of ironic, Patsy. Paulina Wong, the porfa of my associate Carol Ann, recommended that I contact you as soon as we knew that Victor was going to take the position and move to DC. I just wanted to be sure, absolutely sure, that Victor was what I thought he might be before I started taking actions that I regard as being asking for favors. I owe you one, Patsy. Next time you need assistance on a major project, I will be there for you."

"Of course, Aurea. I will contact my people while you have your meeting tomorrow night. I wouldn't want any of them accidentally discussing this with your folks prior to them being informed. It will be quite the marvel if you are right, Aurea, and Victor turns out to have been an ancient Atlantean vampire of some standing. Then Avignon will need to get involved. I suppose that would mean Maurana. I don't think Pa Anovas is really up to the task, even if you and he settle the blood debt soon."

"On that we are agreed, Patsy. Thank you for your help. I will devote some more effort to flushing out that complete jerk Van Arpel and avenge the blood of our brothers and sisters."

Oscar Martin is standing in the waiting area of Union Station in DC when the train from New York City arrives shortly after one in the morning. He looks at his fob pocket watch, noting that the train is a mere fifteen minutes late.

"Not bad for Amtrak," he mutters.

He stares across the room at the young woman whom he had fed from about a half hour ago, noting that she still looks dazed. The place is rather empty and quiet at this hour of the day, which suits him fine. The mortals that frequent the train station are not his usual crowd. He watches the people file off the train. Aurea and Carol Ann are in the middle of that group. With some disappointment, he notes that Paulina Wong is not with them.

She will be a fine vampire, that one. She really has what it takes. Once Aurea and Carol Ann enter the waiting area, he approaches them with a smile. "Ladies, welcome once again to the capital of the American imperium."

Aurea smiles thinly and gives Oscar a hug. "Under the circumstances, I am pleased to be here. I appreciate your hospitality and your understanding with this being such short notice. It just couldn't be avoided, and the issue needs to be dealt with. I'm sure you've had to field some rather odd phone calls."

Oscar helps them with their bags, and they start walking out to the parking lot.

"I've heard from all of them tonight, if that's what you're asking. Most of them, with the exception of Cassie Mae, tried to pump me for more information. Of course, I had none to give them. Kathleen was rather clipped and terse, but that just seems to be normal for her. Rachel and Albert needed directions because they had never come out to my place before. The only one who was really rude was Lester. That guy needs to learn some tact. He kept complaining about you pulling rank and that it clearly wasn't any of his concern. To be blunt, he's an idiot. I don't know how he survived his first twenty years as one of us."

They get into the car, and Oscar drives off. Aurea turns back toward Carol Ann. "You are still being incredibly quiet, and it certainly isn't because you are meditating. You might have your mental defenses up, but I can tell your mind is churning. You are dwelling on the possible negative endgames. That just doesn't become you. Cheer up. I think everything is going to turn out very well."

Carol Ann sighs. "I hope you are right, Aurea. I want to meet him and see what really makes him tick. I believe you when you say he is an ancient soul. I'm more concerned about the meeting tomorrow night. That could so easily turn into a circus. Just be prepared."

Victor wakes up a few minutes before his alarm goes off. He had slept fitfully that night. The telepathy incident with Cassie Mae at the Spanish embassy has him perplexed and anxious. Talking with Zoe last night afterward has helped somewhat. As he shaves in the process of getting ready for work, he starts thinking out loud.

"If something like that happened between Zoe and me, I wouldn't be the slightest bit surprised. Heck, we tend to know what the other is thinking anyhow. With a total stranger! That is just so bizarre on so many levels that I don't know where to begin."

After he cleans up and gets dressed, Victor signs on and checks his e-mail. Sure enough, there was one from Cassie Mae with the picture from last night attached. It wasn't a bad picture at all, seeing as how it was taken with a cell phone. The note was brief but cordial. It read, "Victor, thanks for a very unusual and eventful evening. Hope to see you again soon. Fondly, Cassie Mae."

Victor thinks about that for a moment.

I must admit that I find her to be fascinating, but I need to come to grips with that incident. Will it happen again? Do I want it to happen again?

He decides not to reply immediately. He signs off and heads for the bus stop to go to work.

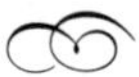

Zoe is having lunch in the student union when she feels someone staring at her rather intently. She slowly turns and sees that it is

Dianne Spence. Dianne twitches and then goes back to pretending to read a book. Zoe knows it is an act. After the incident Victor told her of last night, she is more concerned about these two people whom she knows have been watching her. Zoe decides it is time to blow their cover, consequences be damned. If her brother is threatened, she will put a stop to it. She gets up and walks over to the table where Dianne is sitting. She pulls out a chair and sits down. Dianne puts down her book, a look of surprise and concern crossing her face. Zoe glares at her.

"Something I can do for you, Ms. Spence? Was there something on the back of my head that was ever so fascinating?"

A look of despair crosses Dianne's face. "I'm sure I don't know what you are talking about, Ms. Trent, is it? I was just scanning the room, looking for my friends. If I somehow bothered you, I am truly sorry."

Zoe breathes, calming down just a bit. "Look. Let's cut the crap, shall we? You and this guy have been watching me ever since the semester began. Don't try to deny it. I had you both made almost as soon as you started. A normal person might well have never figured you out, but for me, it was easy. You both have a rather clear pattern. I don't think you two know each other, so here's the guy's name so you can check it out with your employer: Cassidy Yale."

Dianne breaks into a nervous sweat and laughs without sincerity. "Do you know how paranoid this sounds? Why would people be hired to watch you? What makes you think you are so special?"

Zoe simply glares at Dianne, unblinking. Dianne starts to sweat profusely and shakes a bit. She can't maintain eye contact with Zoe.

"Want to try that again? I can tell you don't work for the government, but this does have something to do with my brother, Victor. I love my brother, and I want to know what this is about, what the heck has been going on. I want answers, and I want them now."

Dianne looks up, tears in her eyes. "Please respect and understand that my employer means you and your brother no harm, Zoe.

Please don't make me tell you his name. I really am a student here, and I was hired to simply watch you and to protect you if someone did try to harm you. Your brother is special, as are you. I should have guessed that you had me figured out. I don't know who this Cassidy is, nor do I want to. My employer will not be pleased by this failure. I am sorry. We meant no disrespect and no harm."

Zoe weighs Dianne's words and sees the truth in them. "I apologize for being harsh, Dianne. When it comes to my brother, I will do anything to protect and assist him, even if it were to cost me everything. I know he would do the same for me. If you understand the concept of twin flame, then you will know where I am coming from."

Zoe smiles, and Dianne calms down.

"Tell your employer that I said I will be willing to meet with him and discuss whatever needs to be taken care of. I must admit to being very curious about all of this cloak and dagger stuff. I will take you at your word that my brother is not in danger from your employer." Zoe stands up. "Enjoy the rest of your day, Dianne." Zoe walks away.

Once she regains her composure and is sure Zoe is gone, Dianne whips out her cell phone and sends an urgent text message to her employer, Dave West. It reads: "Sir, the whole Zoe operation has failed. She had me pegged from the beginning, and some guy named Cassidy Yale as well. I did not tell her your name, but I must request to be relieved from this assignment. I am clearly not as good at this as I thought."

She hits the send key and waits for a response.

It comes about a minute later. Dianne reads it with some trepidation. "Zoe was craftier than we had anticipated. I will let Nina know that the cover for her porfo was blown as well. Will have to consider what the next move ought to be. We'll discuss it more tonight. Try not to be too upset. This would have happened sooner or later. A bright sensitive like Zoe…well, what were we thinking? You are relieved, Dianne."

She puts her cell phone away and walks out of the student union.

It is about five o'clock, and Aurea is working on getting everything ready for the meeting tonight when her cell phone goes off. She recognizes the phone number of Nina Parks and takes the call.

"Yes, Nina? What do you have for me?"

"Regrettably, Madam Aurea, I must report that the covers of both porfi assigned to watch Zoe Trent have been blown. It turns out, at least according to Zoe, that she knew she was being watched from the very start. She basically crushed Dianne Spence. I called Cassidy off once Dave West told me what had happened. Dianne did say that Zoe offered to meet with us and discuss issues."

Aurea grimaces. "She's a clever woman indeed. It seems that I underestimated her. She is likely every bit as clever and probably as old a soul as Victor. Many forces are in motion now as regards Victor Trent. In a week, I will be able to tell you more, especially if the outcome is favorable. For now, I believe it is prudent to trust that Zoe Trent knows full well how to fend for herself. After I sort out issues here, I might well have you meet her and evaluate her for me. Thank you for your assistance. Tell Dave he has my thanks as well."

"Very well, Madam Aurea. I will await your further instructions."

The call ended, and Aurea put the cell phone back into her pocket.

Shortly after seven thirty, all the Ruby vampires in metro DC have assembled in the formal dining room of Oscar Martin's estate. The walls of the room are covered in cedar paneling. Several oil portraits also decorate the room. Aurea is seated at the head of the table. To her right sits a clearly nervous Cassie Mae. To her left sits Oscar Martin. Rachel Penn is seated next to Cassie Mae, picking at her nails. Albert Sidney sits next to Oscar, looking placid, very unconcerned. Seated next to Rachel is Lester Dustin, who is scowling and muttering dark oaths under his breath. Next to Albert sits Johanna

Van Clerc, working away on her laptop, looking up every so often to see what is going on. Kathleen Brown is seated next to Lester, frowning at him as he continues his mumbling diatribe. Standing behind Aurea, setting up a large-screen monitor is Carol Ann, who is in a much more positive frame of mind than was the case the night before. She signals Aurea that all is in readiness.

Aurea rises from her chair, making eye contact with all assembled. Everyone looks back at her, even Lester. "Thank you for coming. I know at least one of you thinks I am pulling rank and wasting your time by calling this meeting. I believe otherwise, and once this evening has come to its conclusion, I'm certain that all of you will agree."

Lester lets out with a loud snort. Everyone turns and glares at him. Kathleen sends a quiet hiss his way. He sinks back into his chair. Attention then returns to Aurea.

"In November of last year, a mortal by the name of Victor Trent was brought to my attention." She presses a button, and his picture comes up on the large screen behind her. Gestures of recognition were made by most of those assembled. "I see Cassie Mae is not the only one of you who crossed paths with him. I guess he didn't do anything particularly memorable when you did. I'm not surprised. At any rate, the first one to contact me about Mr. Trent was my foara, Brenda Rennert. She ran across him at some nightclub in Buena Park, California. She said he noticed him right away. He's very much a bright. She wasn't going to bother him, but he was thinking disparaging thoughts about the crowd, so she got irritated and hit him with a rather harsh psychic blast. She said he closed up his mind in defense so fast it was astonishing."

Rachel winces. "Were Brenda's observations enough to make you take action? I mean, that is clearly most interesting and highly unusual, but psychically aware individuals know how to defend themselves against a psychic attack. It sounds like she caught him by surprise."

Aurea shakes her head. "I was fascinated by what Brenda told me, still more fascinated by the video she shot with her cell phone. I could tell by his mannerisms and the intense look in his eyes that he was clearly an ancient soul. No, I wanted more before taking any decisive action, before interfering in his life. After all, not all ancient souls have karmic ties that have anything whatsoever to do with the Plaz."

Johanna nods. "So what happened that made you decide to act, Aurea? What was the second piece of the puzzle? I know that Cassie Mae's experience is the third link in the chain."

"It was the very next night, actually." Aurea presses the button, and a picture of Victor, Zoe, and Reggie sitting and talking with Midnight Silk shows on the screen. "This photo was taken by Vernon Scott. As most of you know, besides being an incredible musician, Silk is a very talented empath. She can gauge quite accurately how old a soul she is dealing with. She told me that all three of the Trents pictured are brights. She said that Victor is an ancient soul, with Zoe only being slightly younger. Reggie Trent is very old as well. Of keen interest though is that Silk watched Victor psychically browbeat one of the bouncers. Victor saw this bouncer was being disrespectful of the female patrons, and he was not about to let his sister be treated in such a fashion. Silk said the man mumbled and was extremely polite the rest of the night."

Albert nods. "It seems to me that Victor and Zoe are very close. The karmic ties are fairly clear from the body language that I see in that picture. I can see why you took interest in Victor after hearing from Silk. Zoe though, she is definitely also an individual of interest. Do you not agree?"

"Yes, Zoe is definitely of keen interest. Victor was the higher priority because of what he was seen doing. Zoe is very clever, and the time will come when we will very definitely put her to the test. One item of keen note that Silk told me is that she sensed the strong likelihood that Victor and Zoe had been Plaz Seschni in at least one of their previous incarnations. All of this put together decided my course of action. I had one of our California people convince Representative Robert Moore to offer Victor a position on his DC staff. Even though Victor can't stand politicians, the offer was too good for him to pass up."

Oscar looks rather intense. "I have read some of Mr. Trent's work. He basically tore the political establishment apart. What did you have this self-described representative offer that actually made him take this position?"

Aurea pushes the button, and a picture of Victor standing in front of Dasher's in Orange appears. "He was working in a dead-end job with few prospects. He was living with his parents, and they did not respect him, especially his father. That guy is a piece of work. None of those reasons would have likely been enough on their own to get him to actually work on a Congressional staff. No. He owes many thousands of dollars in student loans. If he works for Moore for the entire two-year term, all the loans are forgiven."

Johanna nods as she punches some numbers into her computer. "Given the degree he has and the present job market in Southern California, I can see why he accepted the offer. I bet he resents it every day."

Cassie Mae chimes in. "That was the impression I had from speaking to him last night. He definitely has no love for the oligarchy and their political charade."

Aurea clears her throat. "To conduct an ultimately successful blind test, it was necessary to get Victor out of his comfort zone. No matter how much he chafed in Orange County, that was a known quantity. I needed to have him someplace where he would not be comfortable. For a man with his attitudes, this city was the most logical choice. Would you not all agree?"

Everyone in the room laughs and nods. Aurea smiles and presses the button again. Up comes the picture of Victor with Cassie Mae at the Spanish embassy from the prior evening.

"As I suspected would be the case, he did tip his hand. Now he has done three things in the presence of our brethren that require him to be put to the final test, as I am certain all here will agree once Cassie Mae tells her story."

Aurea nods to Cassie Mae, who then stands up, looking at everyone with rather frightened eyes, wringing her hands to gain some composure.

"Last night, I attended a reception at the Spanish embassy. They know me there. I've been several times. It's an easy place to get a pint from a willing donor. Well, shortly after I walked in, I noticed Victor glancing my way. I favored him with a smile, and then I was going to continue into the main hall. I thought that he was a nice-looking sort for a disaffected intellectual but that he wasn't the type of mark I had in mind for the evening. The trouble is I saw him flinch after I thought that. My senses told me that he had heard my internal dialogue."

Silence hangs in the room for a brief moment. Then it explodes in uproar.

Lester literally snarls. "He overheard a thought in passing, not directed toward him? Why does he still have a pulse? If that doesn't represent a threat, I don't know what does!"

Rachel scowls at Lester. "Don't be such a boor, Lester. I'm sure Cassie Mae satisfied herself that Victor was not a threat. She knows how to handle herself."

Albert looks thoughtful. "This is *most* unusual. It definitely raises the bar for the possibility of Victor having been one of us before. How intriguing an event this is."

Kathleen winces. "I agree that Lester is certainly overreacting; however, in the spur of the moment, if it had been me this happened to, I probably would have killed him just to make sure he wasn't a threat."

Johanna sends a harsh look Kathleen's way. "Then I am very glad that Victor was fortunate enough to not run into you and instead had the good fortune to meet up with Cassie Mae."

Oscar sighs. "Enough with the outbursts, people. Let's show Cassie Mae some courtesy and let her continue with the presentation. I, for one, want to see how this all played out."

The room quiets, and Cassie Mae resumes speaking. "I tested him just to make absolutely certain I was not mistaken. I thought to him that, if he heard me, to simply say, 'Yes.' He said it. I then spent the next couple of hours with him, evaluating him, getting to know what made him tick. I determined he was not a threat, at least not an immediate one. He had no idea that I was a vampire, and no, I certainly didn't tell him. I must admit that I found him to be personable, if very cerebral. I called Johanna after he left, and then she had Aurea contact me, and, well, here we are tonight."

She sat down, and then all eyes were on Aurea.

"The blind test established that there is a high likelihood that Victor was once a vampire. How long ago is very hard to say. I suspect he is an ancient soul with a history of coming back frequently. Now we have to find out if we can trust him." Aurea turns toward Cassie Mae. "Since you are the one who found him, so to speak, it is necessary that you take the lead role in this final test. Do you understand why?"

Cassie Mae nods. "I think so, Madam Aurea. I will do it. However, if he fails the final test, I do not wish to be the one who has to take him out. It would be most troubling and, in my mind, just so unfair."

"We are what we are, Cassie Mae. However, I don't think Victor will fail, but if he does, I will do the deed. That is fair, as he is my project."

Oscar frowns. "What will his final test be? What is suited for an individual of his likely power?"

For the first time that evening, Carol Ann speaks up. "He will face the test of honorable behavior. Cassie Mae will be dressed very sexy, and she will drop less than subtle hints of interest in a sexual encounter. That evening, over drinks, she will proposition Victor, using enhanced charm glamour. If he declines, he passes and he finds out about us and we offer to make him a porfo. If he accepts, he dies. It's harsh but effective. Why is that? Because if he is a truly ancient soul, then he is not so impulsive and chooses to take the time to get to really know his partners."

Albert looks shocked. "I don't know if I could pass such a test even now! My god. I feel for the man."

"Well, we have an opportunity to do this next week. Victor will be in New York City attending the UN conference on climate change. He will be dreadfully bored and will likely welcome the break. I have procured a couple of tickets for an off-Broadway show the evening of Thursday March fifth. Afterward, Cassie and Victor can go to Clyde's, a pleasant little bistro around the corner from the theatre.

"This is intimate theatre, which should be more to Victor's liking. This leaves only one action more that needs to be taken this evening." Aurea pauses and looks at Cassie Mae with expectation in her eyes. "Make the call now, Cassie Mae. We need to have this all neatly tied up so we can move forward and see what the universe has in store."

Cassie Mae takes a deep breath, nods, and stands up. She wipes a tear from her eye and then glares at Aurea. "I just hope you know what you are doing, elder. There is kindness in his eyes and passion in his soul. The world will lose a lot if we end up having to extinguish it."

She then turns and walks over to a quiet alcove, feeling the eyes of those assembled staring at her as she leaves the room. She sits down and takes her cell phone out of her purse. She finds herself trembling, so she does some deep breathing to calm down. That done, she dials Victor's number and waits, almost hoping he will not answer.

On the third ring, Victor answers. "Victor Trent speaking."

Cassie Mae swallows hard and then puts a smile into her voice. "Hi, Victor! It's Cassie Mae. How are you doing this evening? Trust that it has been less stressful and calmer than last night was."

Victor chuckles nervously. "That it has been. Just been doing some online chat and responding to e-mails. Thanks for sending the picture, by the way."

"Glad you liked it. Say, a friend of mine gave me tickets to see a play next Thursday night at a little off-Broadway theatre in New York City. Care to join me? It should be a nice change of pace after the second day of observing that climate change conference at the United Nations."

There is a brief pause before Victor responds. "After that mind-numbing conference, I think that would be most pleasant. Yes, I'd be honored to join you."

A tear runs down Cassie Mae's cheek. "Great! Afterward, we can go to Clyde's for drinks and conversation. I'll e-mail you all the particulars. Enjoy the rest of your evening."

"Thank you, Cassie Mae. See you then."

After Victor hangs up, Cassie Mae stands and puts her cell phone back in her purse. She then returns to the room where all are looking at her expectantly, except for Aurea. With the smile on her face, Cassie Mae knows for sure that she already knows what has happened.

Johanna speaks up as Cassie Mae sits down. "So, what did Victor say? Will he go to the play with you?"

Cassie Mae scans the room. "He accepted the invitation. I guess that means that I better get ready for a trip to the Big Apple. Will I be staying with you, Madam Aurea?"

Aurea nods and then makes eye contact with all assembled. "Very well then. It would be prudent for all of you to not seek out Mr. Trent, not until the final test has been completed at any rate. Possibility of accidental contact is acknowledged. However, should this happen, minimize it." She pauses and glares at Lester. "He is not to be harmed in any way, unless he somehow comes to attack you, and, believe me, you had better be willing to submit to Plinthi if you wish to make such a claim. Do we understand each other?"

All assembled nod in assent, and Aurea is satisfied. Carol Ann turns off the computer, and the picture of Victor and Cassie Mae goes away.

"Very well then. Our business is complete."

CHAPTER 7

Wednesday, 4 March 2009. Early that evening at the house on Staten Island, Carol Ann and Paulina are helping Cassie Mae with wardrobe choices for her date with Victor Trent tomorrow. The atmosphere is rather tense and electric, although with Aurea out hunting, it is quieter than it had been. Cassie Mae is standing in front of a wall mirror, wearing a slinky black dress while Carol Ann fusses over various pieces of jewelry.

"You do look marvelous in that dress, dear. I wonder if it meets the criteria of being daring and sexy enough. This has to be done just so, just right."

Paulina snorts. "A normal heterosexual mortal male would fall for the ugliest vampire using charm glamour. You could wear a burlap sack for all such a one would care. I know Victor is special, but still…"

Carol Ann looks in the mirror and nods in approval. "Yes, I think that this one will do. A micro-mini just isn't your style, and I think such would freak Victor out. This one shows just enough thigh to be enticing." She eyes the front and then looks over at Paulina. "What do you think, PW? Shows enough cleavage? Could find a push-up bra, I'm sure."

Cassie Mae pouts. "Oh, for crying out loud! I know my breasts aren't huge, but they show well enough. I'm supposed to look like a woman on the prowl, not some kind of cheap, sleazy hooker!"

Paulina laughs. "I agree with you, Cassie Mae. You look marvelous. The dress is certainly revealing enough, Carol Ann. We don't want her looking like she's about to fall out of it."

Carol Ann scans the jewelry on the table. She holds up a delicate necklace with a cross containing a ruby. She shows it to Cassie Mae. "I think this necklace would look great on you. Old silver cross with a ruby. It's just so chic."

Cassie Mae takes it and puts it on. "Not bad at all, unlike these blasted pumps I have to wear. I really prefer a lower heel or even flats. I don't mind not being tall."

"I can't stand high heels myself, Cassie Mae. Until I do become a vampire, I don't intend to wear them. They play havoc with the hamstrings and the lower back." Paulina reaches behind herself and rubs a sore back muscle. "Think I overdid it at the gym tonight. Oh well."

The office door opens, and Aurea steps in. She has a satisfied look on her face.

"The night's hunt was most successful. No fools tried to mug me on the way back from the bar either."

She walks over to Cassie Mae and walks around her, appraising the outfit. Cassie Mae stands motionless, as does Carol Ann.

"Cassie Mae, you look beautiful. This will be fine for tomorrow night."

Cassie Mae steps away from the mirrors. "Well, I'm rather thirsty now, so I will change into something a little more understated and head out. Are you heading into Manhattan tonight, Carol Ann?"

"Well, we certainly can do that, get a cab and head up to Times Square. Are you doing anything special tonight, PW? Want to go scare folks off?"

Paulina shrugs. "I'm game. Whenever you two are ready, just say the word."

Aurea holds up her hand. "I'd like a word alone with Cassie Mae, if you two wouldn't mind."

Paulina and Carol Ann leave the room. Cassie Mae looks over at Aurea with worry clear on her face.

"So, my dear, are you prepared for tomorrow night? So much of this hinges on how well you perform. I expect Victor to pass, and I very much want him to pass, but this test is important. I expect you to use all your natural wiles as well as charm glamour to the fullest. I really think I am right about him having been an ancient vampire, but if I'm wrong, I need to know that. This test is the best way to make sure. I know this is harsh, and I apologize for how it has affected you. I know you did not ask to be the one to find Victor."

Cassie Mae shakes her head. "It is what it is, Madam Aurea. There is such depth to Victor. I've read a lot of his works over the past few days. His vision is simply phenomenal. I'm not sure I follow all of it, but he argues eloquently and backs up what he says with hard facts. Your contact in California must have some wicked skills to get this Moore character to hire someone like him. I agree that this test is necessary. If he is what you think he is, then honor is important to him. If he is a cad who has fooled you and my dearest friend, Silk, well, then he is a threat that must be dealt with. I will put on the necessary performance. I promise."

Aurea smiles wanly. "Of course you will. Remember, Paulina will be in the theatre audience to watch out for possible threats. I don't expect Sapphire to make a move. I don't think they know anything, but it doesn't pay to not cover all bases. I am told there will also be an Emerald operative, but don't expect this person to tip their hand unless a situation arises. After the show, Clyde's is just around the block from the theatre. I will be there with my associate, Scott. Paulina will come to Clyde's after the show as well. Presuming Victor does pass, it will be you and I and Scott who will be talking to him. I don't want him to feel overwhelmed, though that might be unavoidable. Anyway, you'd best get changed and go catch up to Carol Ann and Paulina. May your hunt be successful and uneventful."

Cassie Mae starts to head for the door but then turns toward Aurea. "You know, I wonder if you have considered the fact that if you do end up having to eliminate Victor, you will have to deal with Zoe in a similar fashion. She is his twin flame; they are joined at the hip. She would hunt us down with all the fury she could muster if anything happened to Victor." She then turns and leaves the room.

Aurea sits down and stares at her computer. "Yes, I have considered that fact. I already have Nina prepared to shadow Zoe tomorrow night. If he has to die, they die together."

Victor is in his hotel room, entering notes of his observations from the first day of the climate change conference into his laptop. As he had expected, it had been quite challenging to stay awake through much of it. Other times, he had been so exasperated that he wanted to throw things at the speakers.

"What a load of rubbish," he mutters under his breath. "Climate change runs in cycles. Yes, humans affected it, but really, if they want to know the real driver of this, they should be paying attention to the sun."

His cell phone rings, and caller ID shows that it is Zoe.

"Hi, Sis. How are things with you?"

"Doing all right, bro. I watched some of that conference you have to observe. My god! What a bunch of pompous idiots! Is there an honest individual among the delegates at all?"

Victor closes his laptop. "I really doubt it. Trouble is, there are some sincere folks attending. The lies and half-truths have been told so many times that they actually believe they are telling the truth. It can be sad, really, except I tend to find it all rather exasperating at best and infuriating at worst."

"Well, things have been really quiet here since I confronted the woman who had been observing me. I haven't seen her or the guy since. It's almost strange being all by myself again. I still haven't heard from the people who employed them. I wonder if I ever will."

"I guess it ultimately depends upon whether or not they see any need to, Zoe. I sense you really embarrassed them by letting them know that you had them figured out from the beginning. I would think they will be craftier next time, now that they have some idea what you are capable of."

"I'm sure you are right, Victor. So, tomorrow night, you are going to see that play with the woman you met at the Spanish embassy? That should be most interesting. That still seems eerie to me, to actually hear in your mind what someone else was thinking. I mean, you and I, we often know what the other is thinking in general, even when we are apart. To literally hear it, I mean, wow, that is still incredible to me."

"I have given that incident a great deal of thought, Zoe. I wonder if it had something to do with my being alone that evening, something to do with the atmosphere, the fact that I had never been there before. I was very sensitive that evening, very keen on observing my surroundings. It was important for me to make a good impression on the ambassador. According to Moore, I did very well in that regard. I am somewhat surprised that she wanted to see me again. I mean, you know she called me the very next night. I will certainly be wary and on my guard. Still, I hope I have a good time. She certainly seems like good company, and the play sounds intellectually stimulating. We will certainly have a lot to talk about afterward."

"So Cassie Mae is from Charleston? I've heard that that is a beautiful city. If you two actually hit it off, you should go down there and see it. Haven't you had some dreams about the place that you think are really past life memories?"

"I've had some, Zoe. Most seem to involve standing in front of some warehouses near the wharves, looking out at Fort Sumter and seeing the federal blockade fleet keeping the port shut down. I am sure if I did go there, I would probably end up going someplace that sparks a memory, if that is what they are, and I have no reason to believe otherwise."

"Well, I better get back to studying. I'm working on a research paper. It needs to be done next week, and I have only finished reading the books for the background material. At least my professor approved my topic. I'm doing it on nineteenth century American alternative communities. There were so many different ones. It was quite a time in the history of North America."

"That it was, Zoe. I hope you will let me read it once you have it completed. That shows how warped I am. I actually enjoy reading research papers. Well, depending on the topic, that is."

Zoe laughs a laugh that seems like music to Victor's ears. "I love you, Victor. Let me know all about tomorrow night. This Cassie Mae had better treat you right, or she and I will have some words and a score to settle. You are the best. Don't let anyone tell you differently."

"I love you too, Zoe. Good night."

Around 11:30 p.m. in Times Square, Paulina, Carol Ann, and Cassie Mae are walking along and watching the people, making fun of some, remarking about the beauty of some others. Paulina keeps hoping to find someone who would try to harm them, but few seem to care to approach. Carol Ann and Cassie Mae have fed, so they are just passing some time. None of them will rest well, not with the events of tomorrow night being on their minds. Carol Ann's cell phone chimes. She sees that it is Maurana calling. "You two go up ahead a bit. I need to take this call." She then pushes the receive button. "Yes, Maurana?"

"Ah, Carol Ann! I figured I should call and see if perhaps you could help clarify some matters, answer a few questions, and put my troubled mind at ease. You see, I have been hearing strange things out of North America for the past week, and I can't seem to shake the notion that Aurea is largely responsible."

Carol Ann bites her lip. "What sort of strange things have you been hearing? Aurea's project is coming to its conclusion, but I would say that she has been much too busy to stir up trouble."

"What have I been hearing? DC metro and Greater New York are buzzing, Baltimore and Richmond are uneasy, and Greater Los Angeles is rumbling. There's so much psychic energy. No one has spoken to me directly, but this must have to do with her project, unless I am way off the mark. Unlike poor Kristano, I do not simply jump to conclusions. I need to know if this is something that is going to destabilize our communities and make it necessary for me to intervene. Should I be flying out?"

"No, Maurana, the culmination of the project will not destabilize our community. Change the paradigm, quite possibly. After tomorrow night, I will be free to discuss everything with you per the word-bond agreement that I made with Aurea. It would be a disaster to put the brakes on it now. Please trust me on this. I really think this is vital to the future well being of Order Ruby."

Maurana sighs. "You have proven yourself to be trustworthy many times over, Carol Ann. I will stay over here for now. Try to make sure this does not escalate out of hand. I know Aurea is an incredibly intelligent and passionate woman. I will expect to hear from you, if not from her, once this is all sorted out. In fact, I would rather hear it from her. Do give Paulina my regards. Good night, my friend."

Carol Ann presses the end button and catches up with Paulina and Cassie Mae. "I'm so glad this is coming to a close. I don't think I care to handle many more calls like that one."

Paulina raises an eyebrow. "So Avignon is getting suspicious? No wonder, actually. There must have been an explosion in psychic activity over the past week."

Carol Ann nods. "She mentioned DC and New York really buzzing, with lesser disturbances in Baltimore, Richmond, and Los Angeles. I told her that all would be culminated tomorrow night, and she did calm down. She was thinking about flying over. Can you believe that?"

Cassie Mae sighs. "It will all be over by this time tomorrow. I just hope it is the ending that Aurea is looking for. We will either radically change a man's life tomorrow or end it."

Early Thursday afternoon, Victor is sitting in one of the cafeterias in the United Nations complex, eating a rather tasteless lunch. His ears are still ringing over the morning's presentations and arguments. He looks around and sees no familiar faces, which suits him fine. He wants to be alone with his thoughts. He is feeling some anxiety about his date tonight with Cassie Mae. He is fascinated with her and perplexed and frightened by her at the same time, which clearly leaves him uneasy. He stares out a window, looking at New York, so deep in thought that he jumps when his cell phone beeps for an incoming text message. He takes the phone from his pocket and reads the message. It is from Cassie Mae.

> I'm looking forward to seeing you tonight, Victor. I'll meet you in front of the theatre. See you soon.

Victor smiles slightly and sends a text back.

> It will be nice to have some intelligent company after all this, Cassie Mae. See you tonight.

Then he puts the cell phone back into his pocket and resumes eating. He looks at the people in the cafeteria. A few do catch his eye momentarily, but none are worthy of much scrutiny. He overhears arguments in many languages, most of which he does not understand at all. He opens up his laptop and checks his e-mail. There is a message with a couple of document files attached from his Uncle Reggie. It reads:

> Hey, Victor! Hope you are doing all right. Really miss having you nearby. The attached files contain documentation on some hauntings that I researched in LA a few months ago. I have some pictures you might find intriguing. Read these over and let me know what you think. Take care, my friend.

There were a few other e-mails, all ads for various products. He closes his laptop and finishes his lunch. He looks at the clock and sighs. "It's time to head back to the observers' gallery."

By four o'clock, the loft of Scott MacAllister is literally abuzz with activity. The solar proof shades are in place, so none worried about exposure. This loft is a mere three blocks from the theatre where Cassie Mae will be meeting Victor. Aurea's mind is racing on several tracks, and she is on pins and needles.

"This is it, Scott. In just a few hours, we will know whether or not Mr. Trent was worth all this effort."

Scott has a serene and content look on his face. "I suspect this will prove to be a most interesting evening, very interesting. I think we will all learn a lot. Being a gambling man though, I am willing to wager a considerable sum that you are correct about Mr. Trent and he will pass the test. Having to fight full press charm glamour will be most challenging, but I think he is up to the task."

Aurea looks over at Cassie Mae, who is getting ready with assistance from Carol Ann. "I wonder if she will be too easy on him and not hit him with a full effort. A lot of this really depends on Cassie Mae. I just hope her heart is in this. She has never had to test a mortal before. Most never have to subject anyone to this kind of test. This is only the third time I have been involved in this level of testing."

Scott looks intrigued. "How did the other two tests pan out? I am most curious."

“The first test was a dud. She fell for the charm nearly instantly and thus was unceremoniously shuffled off this plain of existence for another turn at the wheel. The second test, about five hundred years ago, was an unqualified success. Alphonse has gone on and fully embraced his legacy. I hope to see him when I visit Italy in a few weeks. That test was very trying on all concerned. I doubt this one will be much different.”

Scott nods. “Cassie Mae will give you the full effort, Aurea. She is very proud, and she only wants Mr. Trent to end up in the Order if he is, in fact, honorable and thus worthy of our trust. I think she will let go of the bitterness once the test is over. For now though, we should make sure we are very prepared to play our roles in this event.”

At that moment, Paulina enters the room. She is wearing a short skirt and high leather boots, an unusual choice of attire for her. Carol Ann notices and smiles. A look of surprise crosses Aurea’s face. As for Scott, he nods in approval. Cassie Mae simply shrugs, not knowing this is anything unusual.

Paulina strikes a pose. “So, Carol Ann, what do you think? Is this a good look for going to see a play?”

Carol Ann starts giggling. “I have never seen you look so feminine, PW. You definitely look fine. You won’t stand out dressed like that. Very chic. Very cool indeed.”

Aurea looks at her cell phone as a text message comes through. “I have been informed that there will be two Emerald operatives joining us, one at the theatre and one at Clyde’s. They will make themselves known to us via the general protocols. Victor won’t know those, so that should be acceptable.”

Cassie Mae smoothes out her dress and checks everything in the mirror. She puts a bracelet on her right arm and puts on some lip gloss. “I’m as ready for tonight as I am ever going to be.”

Aurea looks over in approval. “You look great, Cassie Mae. Sunset will be in a few minutes. Paulina, you go ahead and get to the theatre. I sense that Victor arrived a few minutes ago. I’d know that thought matrix anywhere by now. I sense a level of impatience and expectation. That is good."

Paulina waves and leaves the loft. Carol Ann looks over at Aurea. "Are you sure you don't need me at Clyde's tonight? I'd like to see how this all turns out. I mean, really, I've been part of this since nearly the beginning, and now I am feeling shut out of the climax. How fair is that?"

Aurea thinks it over. "I don't want Victor feeling overwhelmed by the presence of several vampires in the event that he passes our test. By the same token, I don't want anyone to go into hysterics in the event that he fails and I have to take him out. That said, perhaps your presence would be a plus, help lighten his mood when, as I suspect, we have a positive outcome." She looks over at Cassie Mae. "You have any objection to Carol Ann being at Clyde's? I think you should have the final say on this."

Cassie Mae smiles at Carol Ann. "I don't have a problem with it. Since you want to be there, be there."

As always, the vampires feel it when the sun sets below the horizon.

Aurea looks at all of them with expectation. "Time we were about our business."

Victor has arrived at the theatre and is waiting out front for Cassie Mae. After all, she has the tickets. He has changed into something more casual in the hotel room. As this isn't a fancy Broadway show, he figures business casual will be fine. He has finished checking in with the office and is now scanning the people walking by. He's read about this play, and it sounds quite good. The sun sets, and twilight starts to set in. It is a cool evening but not cold, which truly pleases Victor.

Cassie Mae has left the loft and is walking toward the theatre. She can feel Victor's thoughts probing the crowd, his eyes scanning and taking everything in. She is carefully shielding her thoughts in the hopes of managing to surprise him. She wants to give him something to ponder. She smiles as the crowd is just thick enough that she will be able to approach him from behind. She simply uses her preternatural stealth.

Arriving behind Victor, she thinks, *Hello, Victor.*

Victor hears Cassie Mae's thought and turns around. "Good evening, Cassie Mae. Why am I not surprised that you did that? Still, I'd rather actually talk, if it's all the same with you."

Cassie Mae smiles and takes his arm. "That's fine, Victor. I just couldn't help myself. Had to see if it would still happen or if what happened at the embassy was somehow a fluke." She looks over and sees a tall man in the lobby who gives the signal she expects. She now knows who the Emerald operative is. "So, how was your day at the UN? Everything you were expecting and then some, I'll bet."

Victor scowls as they walk in the door, and Cassie Mae hands their tickets to the usher.

"My day there was as irritating as I expected it would be. Thank God I just have one more day of that conference. I swear the people there are convinced that human activity is the main driver of climate change. No one has even tried to present evidence to the contrary. I think that if someone did try, they would be shouted down at best and flogged at worst." He smiles. "At least thinking about tonight gave me something to look forward to. I really appreciate it."

They make their way to their seats. Cassie Mae notes that Paulina is seated five rows behind them.

Cassie Mae snuggles into Victor. He looks mildly surprised, but he does not object. His body stiffens and then relaxes. She smiles and sighs contentedly. Victor looks at her with a slightly bewildered look. He then watches the other people filing in and sitting down.

"Your friend had some nice seats, Cassie Mae. Thanks for asking me to join you. Wow. Entertainment and intelligent company. I haven't had that in a while."

"You have no one special in your life, Victor, not back in California or in DC? I find that hard to fathom."

Victor shrugs. "I suppose you mean by 'someone special' you are asking if I have a girlfriend. I do not have one, not in the imperial city and definitely not back behind the Orange Curtain. There are a couple of women I know whom I suspect would like to have that title. One is Phyllis, a friend of my office manager. The other is back in OC. Her name is Anneliese. I like both of them as people, but there is no romantic potential there."

"I'm genuinely curious to know why, Victor. What do they lack that you are looking for in a serious relationship?"

"Phyllis is intelligent and really knows her way around the Washington social circles. This makes her very valuable as an escort, not as a girlfriend. We went on a couple of dates. We have very little in common. She doesn't understand my concerns or viewpoints. As to Anneliese, she's a very sweet girl, a tragic figure. She means well."

Cassie Mae looks at Victor and nods. Her voice is sultry and silky. "Guess that means I have a chance with you then. This pleases me."

Victor raises an eyebrow in surprise. "This is our first date, right? We have a lot to learn about each other before even considering going down the road less traveled. For now, let's enjoy the play."

Aurea and Scott are sitting at a table in Clyde's. Carol Ann is sitting at the bar, speaking to the bartender, reveling in idle banter. At about nine forty-five, Aurea's cell phone rings.

"Yes, Paulina?"

"Play is over. Cassie Mae and Victor are en route to Clyde's. ETA about five minutes. I will be about two minutes behind them. Victor has not made any of us. Cassie Mae has done well in keeping his attention focused on her."

"Thank you, Paulina. We will be ready here." She puts the cell phone back in her purse. She sends a thought Carol Ann's way. *Stop flirting with the bartender and find a seat. The show you wanted to see unfold will be starting in a few minutes.*

Carol Ann nods and takes a seat.

Scott looks over at Aurea. "Is your California contact ready?"

"Yes. Nina is shadowing Zoe Trent. She is ready to act in the event that the fates prove unkind and I am made to look foolish." She looks out the window and sees Cassie Mae and Victor approaching the door. "Well, here we go. In about fifteen minutes, we will either be sitting and talking with him or he will be having a quick trip to the other side. May the fortunes smile on us."

Victor holds the door open for Cassie Mae, who smiles and enters. They walk toward a booth in the back of the restaurant. She keeps her eyes down, not making eye contact with the other vampires present. She is mustering her psychic energy to perform the task that has to be done, one she takes no joy in. They reach the booth and sit down.

The waitress brings them their drinks. Victor has his usual Cuba libre. Cassie Mae simply orders a soda that she has no intention of drinking. Cassie Mae breathes in and centers herself, stilling her genuine emotions and making ready to hit Victor with full power charm glamour. She looks deep into Victor's eyes and smiles, licking her lips suggestively.

"Tell me, Victor. Do you find me attractive?"

Victor gives Cassie Mae a rather dumbfounded look. "Yes, you are very attractive. More important for my standards, you are intelligent and fascinating company."

Cassie Mae keeps direct eye contact and starts the charm glamour. The air seems to electrify in the restaurant. Aurea sits at her table with Scott, waiting expectantly. Carol Ann sits at another table, biting her lip and trembling slightly. Cassie Mae looks like the paragon of composure.

"Do you want me Victor? I'm free the rest of the night. You can take me to your hotel room, and I can deflower you. I can show you pleasures you have only dreamed of."

With that, Cassie Mae hits Victor with the full psychic power of her charm glamour. Aurea has her cell phone at the ready to contact Nina either way regarding Zoe's fate.

Victor is rendered speechless. He can't keep from looking into her eyes. He feels compelled to accept. On the animal level, he truly does want the carnal pleasures she is promising. He is tired of being a virgin. However, he feels himself falling into his core, the strength of his being. Time seems to stand still. He feels a presence that calms him, seemingly like Zoe.

Decline, Victor. She might turn out to be the one, but this is not the time. You will know when it is right. Trust in your intuition.

He slowly comes back into full consciousness. To Cassie Mae's surprise and relief, he breaks eye contact and shakes his head.

"I really like you, Cassie Mae. You are great company, a breath of fresh air. I see a lot of potential here. Maybe we will take the road less traveled. However, I am not going to take you back to my hotel room and have my way with you, though the offer is attractive. I need to get to know you a lot better. I need to know that I can trust in you and confide in you. When it does happen, I want more than the physical act. I want all the deep emotions, all the whistles and bells. I'm sorry, Cassie Mae, but no, I don't want you tonight, not that way. I hope you understand and will honor my wishes and drop the subject for now."

The atmosphere in the restaurant clears. The tension is dissipated as Cassie Mae terminates the charm glamour. Aurea texts Nina, calling her off of shadowing Zoe, as there was now no need. Victor has passed the test most convincingly. Aurea and Scott and Carol Ann stand up and start walking toward the booth where Cassie Mae and Victor are seated.

Cassie Mae is beaming. "I do respect and honor your wishes, Victor. It is very rare to meet someone who actually lives by their principles and has any idea what honor entails. My congratulations to you. You have passed the test of crisis. You get to live, and you get to hear a most amazing story."

At that moment, Aurea and Carol Ann and Scott arrive. Victor and Cassie Mae scoot over, and they all sit down.

Victor looks at them all quizzically. "I get to live? I passed a test of crisis? I get to hear a most amazing story? What's this all about? For that matter, who are these people?"

Aurea looks at Victor and mutters, "Fade."

Victor notices the restaurant start to shimmer briefly, and then it comes back into sharp focus.

Aurea arches an eyebrow. "Impressive. That glamour did not work on him either." She turns to Scott. "Did it take with the other patrons?"

Scott nods. "It worked fine, except, of course, for Paulina and the Emerald operative. As far as the others are concerned, this booth never existed and we are not here."

Aurea gives all present a satisfied glance and puts her laptop on the table. She then looks at Victor, studying him. "You are in full defensive mode, Victor. You don't need to be, though I understand why you are. Introductions and a full explanation are clearly in order. I am Aurea Bodellini. You will hear the others address me as Madam Aurea. I do not expect you to do that." She motions to Cassie Mae. "You already have made the acquaintance of Cassie Mae. Next to her is my housemate, Carol Ann Vincent."

Carol Ann reaches across the table and shakes Victor's hand.

"Next to me is Scott MacAllister."

Scott reaches over and shakes Victor's hand as well.

Aurea stills herself and collects her thoughts. "Victor, it is an honor for me to finally meet you. I hope that once we are done here tonight, you will understand and appreciate why I am saying this. Right now, you probably feel like you have been ambushed. Am I right?"

Victor looks at Aurea. "Actually, I feel very confused, almost like I want to feel hostile, but my intuition is telling me to welcome this encounter. I have learned the hard way what happens when I don't abide by my intuition. I can also sense you are not trying to flatter me. Please continue."

Carol Ann claps with glee. "It seems you were right all along, Aurea! What a find you are, Victor. The fates were kind to us when Brenda found you in that silly nightclub."

Aurea shoots Carol Ann a withering glance and then turns on her laptop. She turns the screen toward Victor, and he watches intently. It was the video that Brenda Rennert had shot that evening at the Orange Curtain.

"I'm sure you haven't forgotten that night, have you?"

"Er…no. How could I? That was the night I was hit broadside by a very harsh thought pattern. I had made a judgment call on the quality of the clientele when I was hit by a thought that soundly chastised me. I spent several minutes trying to identify the source but could not. So you are telling me this video was shot by your associate Brenda? Was she the one who blasted me?"

Aurea presses another button, and a picture of Brenda appears on the screen. "Yes, Victor. This is she, my foara." She pauses. "Forgive me. You don't know our internal language yet. That loosely translates to "child." She sent me this video. I studied it rather closely and decided to learn more about you and your family. You see, this showed that you are what we term a "bright." It means you are very psychically aware and powerful, and you know it. You have worked on your skills instead of trying to bury them as most people are inclined to do. Yes, Brenda did bring you to my attention. However, it took the observation of yet another before I decided to take action and actually interfere in your life."

Aurea presses another button, and the picture of Victor seated at a table with Midnight Silk; his sister, Zoe; and his Uncle Reggie comes up.

"I'm sure you remember this night very well. Midnight Silk is a very good friend of mine. She is also a blood sister to Cassie Mae. Silk called me, and she was very impressed with your entire family, especially you and Zoe. She said the two of you were definitely ancient souls with incredible karmic ties. Your uncle is just a bit younger. I know you accept the validity of karma and past lives and soul progression."

Victor nods. "That I do. Zoe and I know we are twin flames, which means we messed up badly in a very recent past life since we are brother and sister this time around. I notice that Silk is wearing a ring very similar to the ones all of you are wearing. Clearly, that is a symbol of profound significance."

Cassie Mae interjects. "It is indeed, Victor. And yes, Silk is the best friend that I have. She was eager to tell me about you, but Madam Aurea swore her to secrecy until just last week."

Aurea closes the lid on the laptop. "Before I can go on with my explanation, it is time for us to show you what we are. Otherwise, it simply won't make sense, and I don't care to have to dodge the topic any longer. Tell me, Victor, what do you know of what is commonly called the paranormal?"

"Well, my Uncle Reggie and Zoe and I have studied such phenomenon extensively for years. Even my brother Arnold does some ghost hunting on the side. I don't believe in ghosts. I know there are ghosts. I gather you are speaking of other denizens? The fae? I suspect that they do exist, though I have no direct experience of them. Lycanthropes? Sketchy historical evidence, so it's hard to say. Undead? No, that doesn't make sense to me. I mean, they proved that zombies were really created by drugging people. Angels and demons? I am certain they are out there. Then there are the entities that are presently the rock stars of popular fiction, if you will: vampires. I'm sure that they do exist. Too much circumstantial evidence for me to easily dismiss."

The others around the table start looking at each other.

Aurea decides the time is right to reveal their true nature. She looks over at Victor. "You are correct, Victor. Vampires do exist. However, just about everything that you ever read about us in popular fiction, and likely most of the research papers you have read, simply aren't true." She then casually bares her fangs. Once she is sure Victor has had an eyeful, she retracts them back into her mouth. "We are vampires, Victor. I strongly believe that you were once one as well for a very long time."

Victor actually does look shocked. He looks over at Cassie Mae. She nods and bares her fangs.

"It's a stupid question, but, may I touch them?"

Cassie Mae nods, and Victor touches them rather tentatively and carefully.

"They are so smooth, so sharp."

Cassie Mae blushes and retracts her fangs.

"This is just astonishing. I never thought I would actually knowingly meet a single vampire, let alone four of you." He turns and looks at Aurea. "You think I actually was a vampire elder? I presume that is the correct term."

"I think it is highly likely, but that will be a long while proving or disproving. I'm sure you understand that past life regression gets more complicated and more dangerous the further back you go. Yes, I am an elder. I am two thousand one hundred and twenty years old. I was born in Pompeii. I was turned at age thirty-two. My friend Carol Ann comes in at five hundred and thirty years old. Scott, he's three hundred and thirty-one years old. Cassie Mae is the youngest one of us present."

Cassie Mae smiles and looks at Victor. "Like the others though, I am well preserved for my age. Don't you think? I'm a hundred and sixty-seven years old. I'll be turning a hundred and sixty-eight on April twenty-ninth. I was turned in eighteen sixty-seven. My natro, 'father in darkness,' I guess is the best loose translation, has been off this plain of existence for some time. Until the last few years, I really did my best to stay on the periphery of the Order and stay out of the politics." She looks over at Aurea. "Now, here I am, involved in what is likely the biggest event in North America in quite some time. To think, all I was looking to do that evening at the embassy was dance and dine."

Aurea puts her purse on the table and opens it. "Well, just to satisfy curiosity and all for you, Victor, here goes." She pulls out a small cosmetic mirror and opens it. "Well, gee, I *do* have a reflection! Imagine that!"

Victor laughs. "That one never made sense to me. If a being actually had no reflection, you would never see it. Everything we see with our eyes is due to reflected visible light." He thinks a moment. "Do you folks see beyond this, perhaps into infrared and ultraviolet?"

Carol Ann nods. "We do have a great deal of low light vision, which I guess would be infrared. Emerald vampires do have true darkvision though. That is their sole advantage over us Rubies."

Aurea smiles. She takes a solid silver cross out of her purse. "Nice cross. Don't you all agree? Nope, silver and religious emblems don't bother us either." She looks over at Cassie Mae. "You likely had that one figured out too. Cassie Mae is wearing one on her necklace."

Victor just shakes his head. "I never believed that one either. I asked this one fundamentalist Christian why an atheist vampire would be afraid of a cross, asked a Catholic why they would care about being doused with holy water, except maybe one would not care to get wet."

Aurea takes out a garlic clove. "Anyone here care about this?" She throws it over to Carol Ann. "Nope. That doesn't work either. Running water doesn't stop us. We don't have to ask to be invited into someone's home or wherever to ply our craft." She frowns. "And no, we don't sparkle in the daylight, we don't turn pasty white, we don't sweat blood. Yes, we do breathe. No, we aren't undead. Have I covered the essentials?"

Cassie Mae laughs. "You forgot about the things we wish we could do! We can't shapeshift ourselves into bats or become mists and go through keyholes. We can create convincing illusions, certainly. We can't turn into dogs either. I've never tried commanding swarms of rats telepathically. Possibly could do that under the right circumstances. Don't know why I'd want to though."

Victor scowls. "So, tell me this. Are you folks actually immortal? Are you affected by sunlight?"

Scott coughs. "I'll answer this one. Everything eventually dies one way or another. The soul is immortal; the body is not. However, for a vampire, there is no such thing as dying of natural causes. We are not affected by disease. It seems the transformation confers this on us. So, we always end up coming to some sort of violent end, whether by forces of nature, at the hands of another vampire, or by a mortal. As for the affects of sunlight, well, that part is somewhat true. Solar exposure, direct sunlight exposure, can be disastrous for younger vampires. As one grows older, one develops a resistance to sunlight. At my age, I'd be okay for roughly half an hour. Aurea could stand about four hours of direct sunlight with no ill effects. There is an ointment that we have that will provide protection from direct sunlight in the event that we have to go out in it." Scott took a pair of heavily mirrored sunglasses out of his shirt pocket. "I would definitely have to wear these too. It's important to protect the eyes."

Aurea opens up her laptop again. "I believe it is now appropriate for me to continue with my explanations as to why we sought you out and interfered with your life. After what Silk told me, I knew we had to take action, find out if you were what I thought you might be. To do it though, it was necessary to remove you from the familiar, take you out of your comfort zone."

A recent family picture shows on the screen.

"As much as you detested your father and found your mother irritating and your youngest brother needy, they were known quantities, as was Southern California. I decided to get you to move to the city that you never would have chosen to live in, the center of what you regard as the great malignancy."

Victor's jaw drops. "You did well. I am still very uncomfortable in DC. You know I never would have accepted the position with Moore if I had had any real job prospects. The forgiveness of the student loans was simply too good to pass up. Felt like my psychic powers grew there because they had to. How did you convince Moore to offer me a position, given my political views?"

"It wasn't all that difficult. An associate of mine, a Ruby by the name of Cliff Nash, had a conversation with Representative Moore. He persuaded Moore to offer you that position, to you and only to you. Likely that made the whole interview rather surreal to you. As for the loan forgiveness, Cliff made special arrangements at my direction. The funds are held in trust. When Moore advises Nash that you have reached the specified time thresholds, money is sent to the Department of Education on your behalf. Of course, a contribution is also made to Moore's campaign fund. According to Cliff, Moore was very easy to deal with. In psychic parlance, he is very dim. Far from stupid, Moore is shrewd, a survivor, a brilliant politician. We probably could have made him hire you as chief of staff, but that wasn't where we wanted you to be."

Carol Ann looks over at Victor. "Yes, we had to have you in a position that required you to mingle, attend embassy parties, get sent here to New York City every so often. I suppose we could not have planned the timing of this final test any better than if we had actually set your schedule. Everything happens for a reason, and I guess it was time for this to take place."

Victor sorts all this out in his mind. "So if I am hearing all of you correctly, you believed that if you got me to move to a place where I would be out of my comfort zone and I became more psychically sensitive, I would be more likely to do something that would require this kind of test." He looks over at Cassie Mae. "So what brought tonight about was that I heard your internal dialogue there in the foyer of the Spanish embassy. That was so shocking, caught me completely off guard. I sensed it did the same to you."

Cassie Mae nods. "It did more than that, Victor. You see, an unaffiliated mortal who thinks on our wavelength, who can hear a thought that was not directed toward them, well, that's a threat. To be blunt, I had to do an on-the-spot assessment. I quickly determined that you had no idea what I was and had no intention of causing me harm. So, after we parted, I contacted Johanna and let her know what had happened. She called Aurea, and, well, here we are."

Aurea opens her purse and takes out a small box. She then looks very intensely at Victor. "Yes, you passed the test. You even did better than Alphonse, the last person I had subjected to this. Cassie Mae hit you with full power charm glamour, and you took less than a minute to recover and fight it off. You are definitely a force to be reckoned with." She opens the box, which contains a rather sedate ring set off by a natural ruby of roughly a half carat. "I think I can speak for all assembled here this evening when I say that it would be an honor to have you become a porfo in Order Ruby. I know you would find it fascinating. It will open many doors to you. You will be among people who will really understand you. Even as a mortal, you can learn to use your psychic powers so much more efficiently. Are you ready to take this step? Will you accept our invitation?"

Victor looks longingly at the ring. He studies the faces of all assembled. He feels very comfortable with them. Still, he does have a couple of questions.

"What will become of me if I were to decline?"

Aurea frowns. "We here would not raise a hand against you. On that you can rely. However, word will get around the Plaz community. There are those who will regard you as a threat. Without being a porfo, you will not have any protection from them, and we will not be able to raise a hand against them. You've been outed, Victor. Many eyes would be looking your way, and a lot of them would not be friendly."

"That is about what I expected you would say." He sighs. "What about Zoe? Will you be extending this invitation to her as well?"

"Zoe will continue to be evaluated. She shows a lot of promise. I am most impressed by how she knew from the beginning that she was being watched by two of our most promising porfi. Zoe crushed Dianne. She is completely shattered and will likely never be the same again. Cassidy was disappointed by the failure, but he has taken it in stride. When the time is right, Zoe will face a test. That time has not yet arrived. I suspect it will rather soon, but until it does, we will need to rely on your honor. You can tell her just about everything, but you must not tell her you know that vampires exist until she has been properly tested."

Victor nods. "I can see the reasonableness of what you are saying. I will honor your request."

He looks longingly at the ring. The others look at him expectantly. He goes deep into thought. *Well, this is certainly a huge decision. What they have said rings true. It sure makes a lot more sense to me now how I ended up in DC. This really feels right to me.* He looks back at all of them, studying their faces. *This really means a lot to them, especially the elder, Aurea. I can feel that to the depths of my soul.* He takes in a deep breath. *Is this what is best for me? My gut instinct is telling me it is. I've paid a very steep price every time I've gone against it.* His eyes brighten.

"I presume I will have to start addressing you as Madam Aurea, elder. I accept your invitation."

Aurea beams. "I give you leave to address me as Aurea except in formal gatherings, where it simply would not do." She looks at Victor's glass. "I think you could use another drink." She mutters, "Restore," and the waitress immediately takes note of them and rushes over.

"I'm so sorry! I completely forgot about you folks! Anyone want another drink or something to eat?"

"My friend would like another Cuba libre. The rest of us are all right for now."

The waitress nods and goes to the bar and swiftly returns with another drink for Victor.

Aurea hands him the ring. "Let's see how well it fits. I was told the previous bearer had hands very similar to yours, with long, slender fingers."

Victor puts on the ring. "It fits quite well. It looks good too, very old, heirloom quality, much like the ring that I saw Anneliese Bryce wearing." Victor looks perplexed. "You know, she said Cliff Nash was her special friend or something. So, actually, she is his porfa, correct? So, that raises the question of whose porfo I will be."

Aurea nods. "Johanna, the elder of metro DC, said that she would be willing to have you as her porfo."

Cassie Mae interrupts. "No, Madam Aurea. He can be my porfo. I'll do it. Seems like a far better idea. I mean, Johanna doesn't like mixing in public very often, and I don't mind doing that. I know Johanna has done this before and I haven't, but I think Victor will learn more and be more comfortable around me."

Aurea arches an eyebrow. "I must admit that I am a bit surprised, Cassie Mae. I thought you would want to be done with all of this after tonight. However, if Victor has no objections, I will honor your request and let Johanna know." She looks over at Victor. "Is this acceptable to you?"

"This is fine, but I do have one small request. I don't want to face the charm glamour ever again."

Everyone around the table laughs.

Aurea looks over at Cassie Mae. "See that this simple request is granted, Cassie Mae. From now on, whatever might happen, just be you around Victor."

Cassie Mae grins. "So it shall be, elder. I will not employ glamour of any sort against Victor ever again. I give my word-bond for this."

Scott stands up. "Well, I think I will take my leave of you folks. It has certainly been a fascinating and educational evening." He turns to Victor and shakes his hand. "Victor, I think you have an incredible future ahead of you. With us, you will learn and explore and truly broaden your horizons. Take your time though. I'm certain you will be a fast study, but experience is really the best teacher." Scott makes his farewells and leaves the restaurant.

Aurea starts typing on the keyboard of the laptop. "This is probably every bit as important as giving you the ring, getting you set up on Ruby Net."

Zack's face appears on the screen.

"Good evening, Zack. I trust all is well?"

Zack chugs an energy drink and nods. "Yes, Madam Aurea. All is well but definitely very busy. Some folks have contacted me asking questions about you and your project. Naturally, I told them I did not know anything that I could speak of. I see Victor Trent is seated next to you. I presume the evening was a resounding success and he is now a porfo?"

"Yes, that he is. I need you to activate an account for him in Ruby Net with standard porfi access. He will most likely be granted broader access in a matter of weeks, but this should be sufficient for now."

Zack furiously presses buttons and make entries on his end. "Okay. He's all set up. You are giving him this laptop, correct, Madam Aurea? He wouldn't want to try to connect with our network through his desktop at his apartment. There are too many federal spy programs and cookies in that box."

Victor looks indignant. "I thought that my spy sweeper and antivirus programs would take care of those. You have a program that could neutralize those things?"

Zack chuckles. "I could and I do, Victor. However, it would be more dangerous to you if those programs did get shut down. They would be even more suspicious of your actions, and believe me, they really have no love for you. Better that you just accept the gift of a laptop from Madam Aurea. It has an ultra-secure wireless network card. Our protection programs are second to none."

Aurea nods. "Thank you, Zack. I will let you know if we need anything else."

Zack waves and signs off.

Aurea then hands the laptop to Victor. "This is now yours. It will not work for anyone besides you or me. In twenty-four hours, it will only work for you, and only one of our network gods like Zack would be able to override the protocols." Aurea looks at Victor intently. "Are there any other questions you have that simply cannot wait, or are you ready to call it a night?"

Victor weighs his thoughts. "I just have two that curiosity insists that I ask. What are you vulnerable to? I would presume fire since solar exposure does have an impact. Also, what is the truth about the strength and speed that I have read so much about? I presume there is some truth to that since it is a universal element."

Carol Ann sighs. "Fire is definitely detrimental, as are caustic acids. Just about any other injury will heal rather quickly, but those can take a very long time and will generally leave scars. I mean, I could cut off my hand and it would be back within twenty-four hours. If it were to get burned off, well, unless I happened to be around a high elder, it would take months to regenerate. Decapitation, with a few noted exceptions, also is as fatal for us as it would be for you. Getting blown up, having your chest totally destroyed…stuff like that is certainly not desirable."

Cassie Mae looks grim. "As for the stake-through-the-heart thing, well, that doesn't have to be wood. Any object that stops the heart by puncturing it through is incapacitating to a vampire, it renders one totally helpless, which usually ends in one's demise because then one's foe will usually destroy your body. A few have survived being staked. I understand it is an experience even more terrifying than being turned."

Aurea smiles. "As for the strength and speed issue, after a few months, we end up having the strength of roughly ten strong men and are capable of speeds in excess of that of a cheetah in short bursts. Would you like a little demonstration of strength perhaps? Victor, go ahead and try to lift up this table."

Victor does as he is bidden. He does try to lift the table, but it will not budge. "This thing must weigh about four hundred pounds or thereabouts."

Aurea looks it over. "It is pretty solid." She shrugs and then effortlessly lifts the table up a couple of feet with one hand and then carefully puts it down.

Victor is clearly impressed.

"I could have lifted it higher and tossed it out the front window without breaking a sweat, but that would have made a scene and would have been terribly rude to our most gracious hosts. Don't you think?"

"That would be an understatement." Victor picks up the laptop. "Well, this has been a most eventful evening. I have learned a lot. I trust the next time I see you all, it will be under more cordial circumstances? That is to say, not matters of another life-or-death test?"

They all stand up. Carol Ann gives Victor a hug. Aurea politely shakes his hand, still taking his measure, with a satisfied smile on her face.

Cassie Mae gives Victor a hug and a peck on the cheek. "See you again in a few days. This will be a new experience for me as well, so we can learn together."

As they leave the restaurant, they let Victor take the first cab. After he is off, Paulina Wong joins the others.

"Our Emerald associate left shortly after Scott did. So, he passed the test rather convincingly I see. I figured he would. I took an instant liking to him. Not my type, but he does possess great strength of character. I am glad that Brenda and Silk found him, and I am most pleased that he was discovered by one of the sanest of our DC brethren." Paulina makes a slight bow of respect to Cassie Mae.

Another cab pulls up and takes them all back to the house on Staten Island.

CHAPTER 8

Sunday, 8 March 2009. Cliff Nash is enjoying a quiet evening at home when his doorbell rings. He looks out the door peephole and is startled to see that it is Aurea. He opens the door and puts a smile on his face. "Madam Aurea! What a pleasant surprise! Do come in! What brings you to Southern California?"

Aurea walks in silently as Cliff holds the door open. "We have some unfinished business, Cliff—important enough that I chose to come in person, unannounced."

She sits down on the sofa while Cliff sits in the chair next to it.

"What sort of unfinished business? I was told your project concerning Victor Trent has been quite successful. Do you require something else of me now?"

Aurea looks over at Cliff, studying him. "The project is going well. Victor passed the test, and he is now a porfo, which brings me to why I am here. You had Anneliese's e-mail account put under surveillance so that all of her communication with Victor was monitored. While this did provide us with useful information, it was a violation of protocol. Since I let it go on after being made aware of it, this makes me partially responsible and guilty of wronging Anneliese as well."

Cliff is taken aback. "I thought it was necessary! I was afraid she would say or do something that would jeopardize your project! She was so taken with Victor. I certainly was not trying to do her harm."

"I know you meant no harm, at least not consciously. I wonder if some jealousy was involved. From having read the e-mails, I noticed that she complained rather frequently about how she was being treated by your friends and how distant you seemed to her. Why did you take her as porfa? She so clearly is not suited to even consider becoming a vampire."

Cliff shakes his head. "I thought I could make her life better. She was just being passed around like some toy, a pretty bauble. I wanted to protect her. She reminds me of someone I loved dearly in a past incarnation. Perhaps she is that person. I just don't know. I was appalled by how my associates would treat her and especially by how they spoke of her behind her back." He chuckled nervously. "After she met Victor, she actually stood up to a couple of them, showed some backbone. As to unconscious jealousy on my part, that, Madam Aurea, I shall have to reflect on."

"At any rate, I don't intend to say anything about this to Anneliese. I had Zack stop the monitoring as soon as Victor passed the test. Still, things need to be made right." She looks at Cliff intensely. "I am requesting that you relinquish her as porfa and allow Johanna Van Clerc, the elder of metro DC, to take her in that capacity. Victor is going to need other porfi to talk to now, and he knows her well. I think this would be good for both of them. It will also take the pressure off of you. In time, we can have her investigate her past lives and see what the karmic connection is between the two of you."

Cliff sighs. "If that is what Anneliese wants, I won't fight about it. She should be here in a few minutes."

About ten minutes later, Anneliese walks in the door. She is wearing a tight red blouse and a red miniskirt and high heels, smacking on some gum.

"Hi, Cliff! How goes it?" She stops and stares when she sees Aurea. "My god! Like, you are that elder I have heard about! Madam Aurea Bodellini, right?"

Aurea nods. "That would be me, Anneliese. Please sit down. We have important matters to discuss."

Anneliese sits down and looks at Cliff, wincing at his pained expression. She then looks over at Aurea. "It must be really important if you are here. I mean, nobody told me you were coming! I would have worn something less informal for sure."

Aurea smiles. "It is not important, dear. You look marvelous. Tell me, how well do you know Victor Trent?"

Anneliese's face brightens. Her eyes sparkle. "Victor is a good friend. I really like him, you know? He treats me like I matter. He actually listens to what I say. We only went out once, just before he took that job in DC. We talk on the cell every so often, and we e-mail regularly. Why? Has something happened to him? Is the Order checking him out or something?"

"Ruby has done much more than simply checked Victor out. He is now a porfo. This means you can speak to him openly now. If you like, I can arrange it so you can see him again regularly."

Anneliese stares at Aurea. "He's a porfo now? Wow. That is wicked cool. You know, the night we went out, he asked about my ring. I had to make a lame excuse about it being from my friend Cliff." She looks over at Cliff. "He was astonished at your generosity." She looks back at Aurea. "What did you have in mind? I'd really like to see Victor again."

Now Cliff sighs audibly. "She wants you to move to DC and become porfa to Johanna Van Clerc, the elder there. She's an accountant, and you would work in her office. You would be treated better than you have been here in Southern California. I think this would be a good move for you. However, the decision is yours to make. If you want to stay here, Madam Aurea will respect your decision."

Anneliese looks stunned. "Madam Aurea, why would you do this for me? What's the catch? What would you expect me to do for you in return? I might not be the brightest person, but I do know that nothing is free."

"This is more for Victor than it is for you, Anneliese. He needs other porfi to interact with. Yes, there are several in metro DC, and he will be getting acquainted with them in short order. He knows you from the time before he knew for certain that vampires existed. He trusts you, at least on some level. You would be doing him and the Order and me a huge favor. This is your chance to shine and show people you really are somebody, really are a force to be reckoned with. What do you say?"

Anneliese tears up and walks over to Cliff and hugs him hard. "I hate to leave you, you know? You have done so much for me. If you think that this is really for the best though."

Cliff kisses her cheek. "I do, sweetheart. Best for all of us that you make this move."

Anneliese composes herself and looks at Aurea. "Tell Madam Johanna that I will be proud to be her porfa. When do I move?"

Aurea smiles. "I will have the particulars taken care of. Quit your job tomorrow. We will have you in DC by Friday. Let Victor know."

Anneliese grins. "You know, if it's all the same with you, Madam Aurea, I'll let Victor know once I get there. Then he will be surprised!"

Aurea shrugs. "Whatever suits you, my dear."

At about that time in a bistro in Georgetown, Victor and Phyllis are sitting down for a couple of drinks. She is doing her best to be seductive, shamelessly flirting with her eyes. Victor is perplexed, wondering just what he should do about this. He had no romantic interest in her before his latest trip to New York. Now he is certain that he will never have it. He isn't sure if he has a future with Cassie Mae, but he knows he has no love interest for Phyllis. He sighs and shakes his head.

Phyllis takes a sip from her drink and peers over. "Something wrong, Victor? You seem tense tonight, tenser than usual anyway. Did something weird happen over at the United Nations?"

Victor swirls the thin straw in his drink. "No. The United Nations conference was as irritating as I expected it would be, all these people acting like they knew what they were talking about when it was clear to me that they were totally inept. What the people there actually knew about global climate change was how to say the words. It was all politics, very thin on facts and evidence. They sincerely believe that anyone who disagrees with them is beyond the pale of human reason." He takes a sip of his drink. "Phyllis, I like you, and I appreciate all that you have done for me. You want more out of this relationship than I can give you. I hate to hurt your feelings, but there will never be an us."

Phyllis swallows hard. "Is it the age difference, something I said, something I did or didn't do?"

Victor shakes his head. "No, it has nothing to do with that at all, Phyllis. Women talk about the chemistry issue so often. The times that we have kissed, there has been no fire for me. It just isn't there, and there is no way to make it be there. I refuse to pretend, and you would know only too well if I did."

Phyllis sighs. "I wasn't necessarily looking for anything long term, Victor. I am not opposed to friends-with-benefits arrangements. I can see that such would not work for you at all. You are so different than most people, Victor, let alone most men. This city just doesn't abide by honor, but you do."

"You're right; friends with benefits would not work for me. Philosophically, I have no issue with it, but emotionally, I do. I have to be true to myself, and doing that, for me, would not be."

Phyllis wipes a tear from her eye. "I hope we can still be friends. If you need someone to go with you to one of those balls or receptions, let me know. You are getting better at dealing with them, but you are still socially awkward. Don't let this city eat you alive."

"We can certainly stay friends, Phyllis. I hope you meet someone soon who appreciates you and makes you happy, someone who cares about you. You deserve better than just another fling."

Phyllis laughs. "I'll take what I can get, Victor. At my age, I don't worry about being wined and dined. Romance is fun, but I'll take the physical release. You have a lot of depth. Most people don't."

They finish their drinks and leave the bistro, going their separate ways. Victor does not expect to be seeing Phyllis again socially. He looks at the ruby ring on his right ring finger.

This is the world I need to get to know better, and very quickly.

Early on Monday morning, Maurana walks into Kristano's study. She finds him just staring out the window, brilliant sunlight filling the room. She sighs and shakes her head. Sunlight held no peril for those as old as they were, and she rather enjoyed its warmth. Kristano turns to her and nods.

"It looks peaceful out there, kind of reminds me of better days in the past. Sometimes this city reminds me of an old provincial town in Atlantis. It makes me homesick sometimes." He looks back out the window. "Is there anything new and interesting to discuss?"

Maurana joins him at the window and takes his hand. "Actually, there is. I have news from Aurea and her associate, Carol Ann Vincent. No, not regarding discharging the blood debt, but I believe you will find this most interesting and worthy of giving notice. I think it might, over the next few months, provide a path to putting things back in order and letting you move forward, but only if you act with utmost care."

Kristano looks at Maurana. "Pray, continue. For you to speak in such a fashion is intriguing enough. You have my full attention, and I am very inclined to act in accordance with your judgment, especially in any matter that concerns Aurea."

They sit down on the divan, and Maurana collects her thoughts. "It appears that Aurea might, and I emphasize might, have found a returned Atlantean elder. His name is Victor Trent, and he passed one of the harshest tests we ever subject anyone to. He is now a porfo, and she hopes to start having him explore and authenticate some of his more recent past lives in a few months. There is, of course, the trust issue that they need to overcome with him. That in itself will take time."

Kristano looks thoughtful. "Hmm…a returned elder. Rare indeed that we manage to find such a one again, though it has happened. What was the test that she had this man subjected to?"

"Full force charm glamour. She said that he managed to break eye contact and shrug it off in well under a minute. She sent me the details about that and what had brought him to her attention. He is a most interesting individual, and I think she is probably on the mark about what he is."

Kristano considers this carefully. "What kind of man is Victor? What is his personality type? If history has any precedent here, I am willing to wager that he is an introvert, most likely a disaffected intellectual, a man who does not make friends easily and makes people earn his trust and respect."

Maurana arches an eyebrow. "One would think you have already read Victor's files, but I know that you have not. You appear to be correct on all counts. Aurea pulled strings to have Victor move to Washington, DC because she knew he would be uncomfortable there and thus likely enhance his psychic abilities by putting him outside of his comfort zone. It worked because he actually heard a vampire's thoughts when they were not directed toward him in any way. That vampire was one of ours, Cassandra Mae Adler, and Victor is now her porfo."

"That would be where the trust issue comes into play. However, I think it was wise to place Victor with Cassandra Mae because they already know each other." Kristano stands up and starts pacing. "Obviously, Aurea hopes to gain by having done this. If she has found an old Atlantean, gain she shall. Even if she has simply found an exceptional intellect to have join the Order, gain she shall." He looks over at Maurana. "Are you going to be seeing Aurea anytime soon? I'm talking about an in-person meeting, not over the network.

It's time to take an assessment of where her head is at. I'd do it, but she isn't talking to me."

"As it happens, I should be seeing her on Thursday. She is flying into Rome on Wednesday. She will be staying at her villa outside of Naples and visiting Pompeii on Thursday evening, the first time she has been there since the city was destroyed by Vesuvius. I will be meeting her there. It will certainly be a very emotional experience for her." Maurana looks sternly at Kristano. "It is also her first visit to Europe since her exile. I think though that you are grasping why I believe that an opportunity for reconciliation between you and Aurea might well lie through Victor Trent. I am confident that he will be curious enough to seek us out directly once he has established himself within the Order. I don't think that will happen overnight, but sometime this summer, I am sure that it will."

Kristano nods. "I do understand completely. I will have to let him make the first move, tempting though it would be for me to initiate first contact. Who knows? Perhaps he will prove to be a long lost comrade. Yes, this could open the door for reconciliation." He sighs heavily. "Then, perhaps, I will wrap up this incarnation and take another turn at the wheel, see where the Weave puts me. After this, I think I will need some fresh perspectives, and those are only going to come from a new life."

"If that is what you choose once the blood debt is discharged, so be it. That would be your right."

After a very busy Monday morning in the office, Victor is sitting down to lunch with Davis and Daphne. Davis is his usual gregarious self, Daphne somewhat reserved and distracted. Victor is frazzled and conflicted but glad to be back in his normal work routine.

Daphne looks over at Victor. "Bob was pleased with your report about the conference. I hope that the event was at least of some interest, though, considering where you were, it probably wasn't."

Davis chortles. "Bah! The United Nations? What a crock that all is. One of the planks of the Bircher platform that I do agree with is that the United States should leave that outfit. It's a big waste of time. I don't know why Bob insists of having someone from our staff attend some of those conferences. Very few other House members even bother with it."

Daphne shrugs. "Bob is a very shrewd politician. You know that, Davis. He is always looking for an edge, a way to advance his career. As for the UN, I used to believe it was a force for good. Now, well, I doubt that it is. I think the new administration is really buying into the concept of a new world order. I hope that I'm wrong." She pauses and looks at Victor's ring. "That's quite a handsome ring, Victor. Where did you get it? That's a natural ruby, isn't it?"

Victor nods. "Yes, it is a natural ruby. I met with a very old friend in New York, and she gave me the ring as a keepsake. She said it suited me well." He smiles. "I think I agree. I've never been into rings or any sort of personal ornamentation for myself, but I like this one."

Davis smiles. "You know, I agree with you, Victor. It is elegant and masculine at the same time. It's probably quite valuable too. Definitely looks very old, and it has probably changed hands several times. Is this friend really old, or is she someone you have known for a very long time?"

Victor amuses himself with the thought of answering Davis truthfully, knowing he would not believe it. "She's very old, and I have learned quite a bit from her. Because of her, at least my evenings in New York were not aggravating and mind numbing. That conference, my god, it was horrible, all the posturing and pseudoscience. There certainly wasn't anything productive that came out of it."

Davis laughs heartily. "Of course something productive came out of that conference! It kept a bunch of scientists and diplomats occupied arguing about a topic that really has no political solution. Sadly, most people actually believe that the governments of the world simply must do something. They will, and it will be something incredibly stupid. Probably end up calling this the war on climate change."

Victor chokes on a sip of water. "Point taken, Davis. The trouble here and now is that the administration will use this material to justify trying to push through cap and trade legislation on carbon emissions. They will probably also use it as an excuse to throttle the coal industry and forbidding building new coal-fired power plants. Pollution is really a technological problem. It certainly can and should be addressed. In the meantime, the economy is still shot and unemployment is still rising, so, yes, the populace does expect a grand gesture out of the federal government, and soon."

Daphne stands up. "We need to be getting back to work, gentlemen. See you back in the office."

Davis and Victor get up and clean off the table and head back toward the office.

Shortly after sunset, as Victor is getting ready to have dinner, there is a knock on his door. Perplexed, he gets up and looks out the peephole. To his surprise, he sees Cassie Mae standing there with another woman. He opens the door and smiles.

"Good evening, Cassie Mae. Please come in."

Cassie Mae shakes her head. "No, Victor. You grab a coat and come with us. My friend Rachel and I are taking you down to our favorite blues club, Becker's, down in Alexandria. I know you like blues music, and I'm sure you need to unwind after your day at the office."

"I won't argue about that. Some blues would be marvelous."

Victor grabs his coat, and they head out to Becker's. The traffic was not bad, and they arrived well before the band was scheduled to perform. Victor takes in the atmosphere of the club and finds it to his liking. They take a table close to the stage.

Rachel stretches. "So, Victor, what do you think of us so far? Were you shocked to find out we really do exist? You seem to be adjusting to being among us rather well. You aren't frightened. I can tell."

Victor shrugs. "Should I be frightened of you? I know you intend me no harm. I would certainly be wary of any vampire I had not been introduced to until I got to know them, same as I would anybody else. What do I think of vampires so far? I am very curious. I am enjoying learning and am eager to learn more. Was I shocked to find out you folks do exist? No, definitely not shocked by that. Figured there had to be some truth in the old legends. I was surprised to find out that I had been observed and sought out." He frowns just a bit and looks over at Cassie Mae. "The test was brutal. Necessary, I concur, but brutal nonetheless."

Cassie Mae sighs. "It was brutal for me as well, Victor. I did not want to have to put you to the test even though I also saw it was necessary. I had to throw everything I had at you psychically while, at the core of my being, I was hoping you would prevail. To my surprise, you did. Yes, I was surprised because I have never seen anyone shrug off full charm glamour before." She smiles. "I like to think I am pretty good at that. Wouldn't you agree, Rachel?"

"Of course you are, Cassie Mae, darling! I heard that Aurea had full faith in your abilities even though she knew you did not want to put Victor through the test. He passed, and now he is of the Order. I was a bit surprised that you decided to take Victor on as porfo. I figured you would want out of the matter once the test had been concluded."

Cassie Mae smiles brightly. "I am not ashamed to say that I find Victor to be a very fascinating individual. It has been awhile since I could say that about any mortal I have met. Heck, many vampires are vapid and shallow and just driven to enhance personal power and control when you come right down to it. It's refreshing to meet someone with depth. Yes, having a porfo is quite a responsibility. However, I think I am up to the task. It should prove to be most interesting."

Victor looks around the club. "It's a decent crowd for a weeknight. Who's playing?" He stops speaking and he grins when he sees Midnight Silk and the Scott brothers come out.

Cassie Mae waves, and Silk comes over to their table and gives each of them a hug.

Silk lingers with Victor, he eyes sparkling with tears. "You poor dear, what you and Cassie Mae ended up getting put through because of me!"

"I'm fine now, Silk. Yes, it certainly was quite the event and, no, I would not care to go through with anything similar ever again if it is all the same with you."

"I wasn't expecting Aurea to put you through anything like that. I've been involved in some tests before, but what they put you through, well calling it brutal would be quite the understatement."

Victor nods. "Yes, it was a vexing experience. However, because of it a whole new world has opened up to me. There's so much I will be learning. I will get to confirm past lives and discuss history with people who were actually there. I really appreciate what has come after. I feel like I belong."

Silk flicks a tear from her eye. "I just hope you don't hold any of this against me."

Victor hugs Silk again. "I don't hold it against you. I'm getting comfortable with you folks, and besides, I got this wicked cool ring in the bargain!"

Cassie Mae and Silk embrace again. "I can only imagine how hard it was for you to not tell me about Victor, Sallie Jean. I mean, we are sisters in the blood, and you are the very best friend I have in the world! No doubt Aurea made you swear to keep your mouth shut."

Silk nods. "Oh yes. She made it very clear that I was not to discuss this with anyone else until after the blind test was completed. Somehow, I am amazed that Aurea was able to keep this under wraps so well. Secrets are very difficult to keep among us. We are no better than the mortals we sprang from in this regard. Sometimes, I think we tend to be worse. So, the end result was quite good; however, I do not agree with the scholar Machiavelli, though perhaps Aurea does."

Victor frowns. "Ah yes, the old saw of the politicians and the bureaucrats: the ends justify the means. No, I don't agree with that either. I don't know Aurea well enough to judge her on that. I will say that she seems very driven, very determined. She also has a wicked sense of humor."

Silk takes her leave of them and joins the Scott brothers on the stage, getting ready for the first set.

Victor looks over at Cassie Mae. "So Silk is your best friend? Looks like an incredibly strong bond between the two of you. Couldn't help but notice that you called her Sallie Jean. I would gather that is her birth name? How did you two meet, if I may inquire?"

Rachel excuses herself as Cassie Mae sighs. "When I was growing up, my family owned a large rice and indigo plantation in South Carolina. My father owned over three hundred slaves. Among those slaves was Sallie Jean, whom everyone now knows as Midnight Silk. Her mother was my wet nurse. They were house slaves. As we grew up, she and I were nearly inseparable. I never felt like she was my property, although, legally, she was. She became, clearly, a strikingly beautiful woman. She became the hostess of the manor house. I taught her to read and write, which was highly illegal then, but my father approved, said it made her even more useful to him." She smiles thinly. "Bit more of an answer than you were expecting, I take it? Want to know what I thought about slavery? I will admit that when I was very young, I did not think anything much of it. It just was. As I matured, I started to question the institution. My father tried to explain why it was just and proper for us to own people, but the arguments rang hollow. By the time South Carolina seceded, I was determined to work for a peaceful end to the peculiar institution because I was convinced that it was morally wrong to own people."

Victor takes it all in thoughtfully. "I do understand, Cassie Mae. It takes awhile to even think to question mores and social systems that one grew up in."

Rachel returned to the table, which Victor acknowledged with a nod.

Victor goes on. "I was a Boy Scout, made Eagle. I really believed in the American way. When I participated in flag retirement ceremonies, I would weep. Now, I know that most of what this country allegedly stands for is nothing but lies, smoke and mirrors Yes, I keep hearing it is worse in other countries. But even if that is true, what of it? This is where I live, so this is what is most relevant to me. One of my fervent beliefs is in the right of secession. No, I certainly would not endorse chattel slavery. However, the Southern states had every right to secede. I firmly believe that the day is swiftly coming when states will secede from the union again. I just hope that this time it will be peaceful."

"Have you told Victor about how you helped Silk escape from the plantation? I think he will appreciate that part of the tale," Rachel said.

"It was late March of 1861. Even before South Carolina seceded, Sallie Jean and I had been scheming to find a way that she could escape and gain her freedom. She would be able to use her looks and charm—even as a mortal she had that in abundance—and she had the further advantage of being able to pass for white. As a manor house hostess, she spoke as the planter class did, not with the patois of the field slaves. We had our opportunity on a stormy night. There had just been a shipment, and the wagonmaster insisted on getting his load out of there and on the road. We spirited Sallie Jean onto that wagon, and she was on her way. My father was shocked that she left. He thought she was happy. At any rate, I did not see her again until late July of 1877. Since then, we have stayed close. For me, she is family."

At that point, the band starts playing. All in the house pay attention to Midnight Silk and the Scott Brothers. The music is rapture to Victor. Rachel is enjoying it too. Cassie Mae always enjoys Silk's music; and while tonight is no exception, she catches herself looking over at Victor, watching his reactions. She still isn't completely sure what to make of him. She has a feeling that she has known him in some previous existence, but when? Perhaps someday she will know, but tonight will not hold that answer. Victor looks over at her with a smile and then returns his attention to the band. Cassie Mae relaxes a bit, and then she does the same.

Zoe is walking along the beach in Santa Barbara. It is a typically cool evening with some light fog. She hears the waves lapping quietly along the coast. There is no wind, so the sea is very smooth. She has passed a few other people during her walk, nothing unusual. She is deep in thought about her brother, Victor. He is holding something back from her, and she has no idea why. Normally, nothing he does is surprising to her, but this omission is. She decides that he has good reason and, since he is not being deceptive, she will respect his privacy and wait for him to tell her.

While she is in this reverie, a tall, slender woman walks up to her. She is smiling, no menace in her stance or in her eyes. Zoe studies her a bit, noticing the depth in her brown eyes and the fact that her skin seems just a shade paler than she would normally expect. She definitely finds this woman to be fascinating.

"Hello. Very peaceful evening, is it not?"

"Yes, it is very peaceful tonight." Zoe looks at her more intently. "Have we met?"

"Not before now. I'm Nina Parks. You are Zoe Trent, correct?"

"Yes, I am. And you know this because?"

Nina smiles. "You remember having flushed out Dianne Spence a few weeks back at the Student Union, correct? Well, I am one of the people you requested to meet."

Zoe feels no fear, but Nina now has her full attention. "Of course I remember Dianne. So, are you saying that you are one of the people who were having me watched, or are you saying that you represent them?"

"I am one of the people who were having you watched." She sighs. "We seriously underestimated your abilities. You really had her figured out right away?"

"That I did. Cassidy, he wasn't so bad, but Dianne had this way of just staring. I finally got fed up with being followed and confronted her. How is she anyway?"

"The poor dear was crushed. She hasn't been the same since."

Zoe shrugs. "I'm sorry that she is faring poorly. I didn't have to be so brutal, but she was a very poor liar. She couldn't even hide her deep thoughts from me."

Nina nods. "No worries, Zoe. It isn't your fault. She has chosen to react this way. Cassidy, the young man who was also tracking you, was simply disappointed by the outcome. He is doing fine, and he asked me to wish you well. Yes, I am one of those who were involved in having you watched. So, shall we walk? No sense in just standing here on the beach. Private enough for what we have to discuss. No prying eyes or ears."

"True enough," Zoe says as they resume walking along the beach. "Part of why I enjoy my evening walks along this beach this time of year is the solitude. Just try finding that here during the summer!"

They walk in silence for a while, Zoe deep in thought about what she wants to say.

"Yes, solitude is difficult to find here during the summer. It seems like everyone wants to be at the beach then. I think, to experience the true majesty of nature, one needs to be free of the crowds, not necessarily alone. In fact, I have found that most experiences are enhanced when you can share them with a friend or a loved one. Unless I miss my guess, Zoe, some of your favorite, most cherished memories are of things you experienced with your brother, Victor."

A fleeting smile crosses Zoe's face. "I won't deny that, Nina. However, that is not what we are here to talk about. You were going to explain why I was being watched and how it involved my brother. Yes, Victor and I are very close. I would do anything to protect and assist him, even if it cost me everything I had. I know he feels the same way about me. I believe I said as much to Dianne that day. No one should have any doubt how far I will go. Is he all right? He has not been as forthcoming recently."

Nina studies Zoe, noting her body language, which still shows tension. "Victor is doing very well. Sadly, there is much that he is learning of that he cannot discuss with you, or frankly the vast majority of people, at this time. Don't be alarmed. It has nothing to do with the government. He will benefit greatly from this. I am certain that in a few months, you will also be brought into this. For now, I am hoping we can rely on your discretion and have you give me your word that you will not push Victor into divulging more information than he volunteers to you about his new associates."

Zoe looks over at Nina. "I will do anything for Victor. You know that. I see that you also know that we are twin flame, which means you should know how hard this is. I can feel his emotional turmoil. Often, I get glimpses of what he is thinking. I feel his presence even though he is clear across the continent. Tell me why I should trust you, Nina. You haven't even told me who you represent and why it is I was being watched and protected because of Victor. You are going to have to give me some reasons, something that I can hold onto, a reason to respect you enough to cooperate with you."

They approach a bench, and Nina motions for Zoe to sit down, which they both do.

"I'm going to stick my neck out and tell you some things that I could get into very serious trouble for revealing. I am certain it is the right thing to do, as I can tell, just by having spent time with you, that you are also a very ancient soul and likely to be every bit of interest to us that your brother is. Aurea casts her nets too narrow at times."

Zoe stares at Nina. "Aurea is one of the names Victor did mention to me. He said that she was very old and venerable, also very driven and precise. He found her to be fascinating and disconcerting at the same time. He has taken a liking to a Cassandra Mae. Do you know of her too?"

Nina nods. "I am familiar with the name because of Aurea's work with your brother. Yes, Aurea is very old and very powerful among us. She is an elder of high standing. Her enemies often refer to her as The Enforcer. She is not one to be taken lightly. You should tell your brother to watch his back around her and to do his utmost not to cross her." She notes the look of concern on Zoe's face. "I can assure you that he is fine and likely to stay that way. He just needs to be prudent. Cassandra Mae, who goes by Cassie Mae, I am told is a pleasant woman who originally came from South Carolina. She is the best friend of one Midnight Silk, whom I know you have at least a passing acquaintance with."

"You are referring to the blues artist?"

"Yes, that would be her."

"I met Silk once at a little club in Burbank. I saw her show with Victor and my Uncle Reggie." Zoe smiles. "This is starting to sound really good for my brother, all these interesting and intelligent, talented people he gets to be with. Getting back to Aurea, what do you mean by she 'casts her nets too narrow'?"

Nina frowns. "I am only agreeing with what some in Aurea's circle have already said. I was told that Silk tried to convince Aurea to bring you and Victor in together. The karmic ties between the two of you are so intricate, so deep, that in the end, you will rise and fall together. You two will not allow yourselves to be emotionally and physically separated for any great length of time. Such is the nature of twin flame." She holds up her right hand, her ruby ring prominent. "Have you seen rings like this before?"

Zoe studies the ring intently. "Silk wore a ring very similar to this one. I recall that the Scott brothers were also wearing ruby rings. Dianne also had a ruby ring, though the stone was not as large as yours." She studies the designs on the ring. "The craftsmanship is simply phenomenal. May I touch it?"

Nina nods, and Zoe runs her fingers along the sides of the ring and then settles on the ruby.

"This ring has presence; it has its own energy field. I would surmise that these rings have a great deal of meaning beyond being beautiful. You are all part of some group, right, a special organization that now includes my brother?"

"Correct, Zoe. The rings do mean that we are part of a special organization, one in which confidentiality and trust is essential. My intuition tells me that I can trust you. I almost feel like I have to, regardless of the consequences. You should be among us, just as your brother is." She takes a deep breath and ponders. She takes off her ring and hands it to Zoe. "Put on the ring. Tell me if it makes you see or feel anything. Consider this to be a test."

Zoe stares at the ring with a look of disbelief. She puts the ring on slowly, marveling that it fits well and looks good on her hand. More than that, it looks like it belongs there, had, in fact, once been there. She closes her eyes.

"I feel like I'm someplace else, like in this dream that I have had, it is just so vivid. I see what must be me, even though it isn't me now. I'm talking to a man that must be my brother, but not as he is now. It's some kind of major disaster. He's telling me to get out. I don't want to, but I know I have to." She looks over at Nina, tears in her eyes. "I know this is a vision of a past life. It always ends the same way. I and many other people escape and leave the planet. He manages to secure some vaults, and then he gets killed by magma. I see it happen on a video feed. Victor has had the same vision." She looks at the ring, startled. "We were wearing rings similar to this in that past life!"

Nina looks deep into Zoe's eyes. "I am now certain that you were. This seems to be a vision from a very long time ago. Probably several millennia have passed since that event. I know people who can help you explore that."

She stops and looks at the ring on Zoe's finger. Zoe looks down as well. It was glowing rather intensely. With preternatural swiftness, Nina takes the ring off Zoe's finger and places it on her own.

"This is a distress call, as you probably remember from your vision. I fear I am too late to help." She kisses Zoe on the cheek. "I will see you tomorrow. Come back here about the same time if you can. I will have to trust in your discretion for now."

With that, Nina is gone so quickly that Zoe has trouble fathoming it.

Zoe is awestruck. *Wow. That was incredible. I will have to take my time and digest it.*

As she starts walking to her car, she vows to be back on the beach the same time tomorrow night. She is no longer afraid for her brother. If anything, she is intrigued.

Two vampires and two porfi arrive at the Encino home of Dave West fairly swiftly, but they are clearly too late. Cliff Nash is the first Ruby on the scene, followed quickly by Brenda Rennert. Their porfi remain in the cars. Cliff is waiting beyond the front door, clearly sickened by what he sees. Brenda enters and a look of horror crosses her face.

Brenda gags. "Who in the nine circles of Hades could have done this to Dave and Dianne in his own home? I've seen some ambushes, but, really, this is a piece of work." She looks into the living room of the well-appointed suburban home. What is left of Dave is smoldering in the middle of the room.

Cliff cautiously moves forward, his preternatural senses working overtime to make sure that they would not have the same fate befall them. "It looks to me that he was hit by a large amount of caustic acids without warning. It had to have been at very close range. How could he have not sensed the presence of an intruder in his own house? Are we dealing with someone who can actually totally mask their presence, not just their thoughts, from the likes of us?"

Cliff walks into the bedroom and carefully carries Dianne out. She is horribly burned, her right arm and left leg amputated. She is still breathing but unconscious.

"She won't survive this. Only a high elder could give her strong enough blood, and she would be disfigured by the burns." He looks at Brenda. "Do we try to bring her back to consciousness to tell us what happened, or do we let her pass?"

At that point, Nina arrives on the scene. She looks over at Cliff. "I see that she still lives. Put her on the couch. Cruel as this is, I need to try and rouse her. We need to know if she knows who did this."

As Cliff complies, Brenda comes over, carrying a note.

"Perhaps not, Nina. Take a look at this. I think it is from the maniac who did this. If so, this is his first hit here on the West Coast."

Nina takes the note and reads it out loud. "'I come from the shadows and smite another of you undead fiends and his mortal slave. They both died in the agony they deserved. I shall not rest until I have cleansed the face of the Earth of your foul presence. Yours most respectfully, Van Arpel.'"

Cliff shudders. "Van Arpel. I have heard of that guy. No one seems to be able to tell when he is around. It is like he doesn't exist, yet very clearly, he does. I wish we could flush him out." He scowls. "We need to contact the Ruby motherhouse in Richmond, Virginia. If this was really his work, then he has called his sister Abigail to gloat about it."

Brenda takes out her cell phone. "I'll call the motherhouse in Downey. They would know if anything has happened in Richmond." She walks over into a corner and speaks in a hushed tone once the phone is answered. A couple minutes later, she comes back, looking stricken. "It was definitely Van Arpel. He called Abigail from here, using Dave's phone. Cliff missed him by about five minutes."

Cliff pounds his fist on a table, shattering it and sending splinters all over. "How does this guy do this? Have we ever faced a mortal like this? Most of these so-called hunters are complete jokes. This guy, I mean, he has to be stopped."

Nina walks over to the couch and wipes the sweat from Dianne's forehead. Nina whispers to Dianne, and she stirs. Her right eye, the one not burned out by caustic acid, opens by a slit. "Can you speak, child?"

"I…think so, Nina. I hurt so much. There was…nothing I could do. This man, he was already here. I did not feel his presence until he grabbed me in the bathroom. He's so malevolent, so evil, so hateful. He accused me of being Dave's thrall and accused him of being an undead fiend." She coughs and looks at Nina. "There's no hope for me, is there? He did so much damage, cut off an arm and a leg and then seared the endings with fire. Then he threw acid in my face. He…killed Dave, didn't he?"

Nina wipes a tear from her eye. "Yes, he killed Dave. I'm so sorry about all this. I wish we could have stopped this fiend. Are you ready for another turn at the wheel? This body will not survive much longer."

Dianne shivers and then nods. "I so wanted to be one of you. I wanted you all to be proud of me. So much that I wanted to see and do." Her breath catches and then finally ceases. Nina weeps openly, as does Brenda. Cliff stands there in numb silence. As Cliff is about to speak, two men wearing black suits arrive on the scene.

Brenda sniffs. "Ah, I see that Order Security has arrived. Good evening, gentlemen. Not much for you to do here but clean up this mess and decide if you want to alert the temporal authorities, the denizens of the police state. Given this situation, I would recommend against it, as there were no witnesses."

The taller of the two agents looks nonplussed. "We shall be the judges of that, madam. We would appreciate it if you folks vacate the premises so we can do our work."

Cliff glares at the agent. "Show some respect. These people are our friends. You have no right to be rude. I will be reporting this to the motherhouse accordingly." He looks at the others. "Let's get out of here before one of us does something we regret." As they slowly file out, the tall agent stares at Cliff.

Zoe is walking along the beach on Tuesday evening. She is very expectant this night, absolutely certain that Nina will show up. No doubt she will have a tale of great loss to impart. Zoe, however, is confident that she now knows the whole story. As twin flames can, she melded with Victor's mind last night while he slept, a bit more complicated since they were clear across the continent from each other, but still very doable. It was amazing, and she is certain that after tonight, she will be able to speak openly with Victor all about it. She is willing to keep the secret from everyone else, which is not an issue. She jumps just a little when Nina appears next to her. She smiles tentatively.

"A fair evening to you, Zoe. Sorry that last night's conversation had to come to such an abrupt end."

They start walking.

"There's nothing to apologize for. I am deeply saddened by your loss." Zoe notes the look of shock on the other woman's face. "Your body language and vocal tones gave you away if you thought to try and conceal this from me. It is one of my gifts, as some would say."

"You are a very intriguing individual, Zoe. Yes, last night ended very badly. I lost two good friends. Dianne was murdered, as was her employer, in a very cold-blooded fashion. It was ghastly."

Zoe nods. "That was a tragedy. I had no quarrel with Dianne. I really didn't. However, she was no more an employee of Dave West than Cassidy Yale is your employee. I believe the collective term you folks use is *porfi*. The rings represent the Order, of which there are three: Emerald, Ruby, and Sapphire. There was a phrase I have heard in several dreams that I am certain are actually past life memories: 'Plaz Seschni.' I believe that means 'Order Ruby' in a very ancient tongue." She sees the look of amazement on Nina's face. "I see that I must be correct because you have heard the term. Shall I tell you what you are, or do you want the opportunity to tell me?"

Nina is stunned. "How could you know these things? I didn't even tell you Dave's name! You know our terms! Did Victor tell you these things?" She studies Zoe's face. "No, he didn't. What are you? By the gods, Aurea was so wrong to not take you in when she took Victor. You are every bit as powerful as he is. Silk essentially said as much." She smiles. "Fine. I will tell you what I am, what Aurea is, what Silk is, and what you were and likely will be again. I'm a vampire."

"Well, that is the honest answer. I have long surmised that vampires must exist, though certainly not as most fiction writers have depicted them. I mean, you aren't undead, I know you have a reflection, and I seriously doubt you can turn into mist or into a bat." Zoe grins. "Although there would be certain benefits to having those abilities, wouldn't there? Let me see your fangs please."

Nina lets her fangs come out. Zoe touches them tentatively. She retracts them, and they resume walking.

"Now I either have to ask you to join Order Ruby as a porfa or I have to kill you." She smirks at that. "I know killing you would not be prudent. It would derange Victor and deprive the Order of a returned elder. The day will come when I will have to address you as Lady Zoe. She pulls a ring out of her pocket. "What do you think, Zoe? Do you want to join Order Ruby as a porfa? Be honored to have you as mine. Cassidy has mentioned wanting to be reassigned to Portland, so that won't be an issue."

Zoe puts the ring on and smiles. "Yes, Nina. This feels so right. Victor will be pleased that he can speak openly to me again without fear of reprisal. You know, you folks really need to study up on the twin flame. He could not have kept this from me much longer. I was able to meld with him and become one with his mind while he slept last night. He can do the same with me. There really can't be any secrets between twin flames. I think that you, at least, understand that now."

Nina chuckles. "I know what I have experienced these last couple of nights." She pulls out her cell phone. "I think we need to call

Aurea. In fact, I know we do. I sense she is thinking of me." She dials the number.

"Good evening to you, Nina. I am saddened beyond words by the loss of Dave West and his porfa. That it was at the hands of that devil Van Arpel just makes it crueler still. I sense, however, you have something very important to tell me, something that has nothing to do with that tragedy."

"Indeed I do, Madam Aurea. Order Ruby has a new porfa as of a few minutes ago, one that I know will make a huge impact, just as Victor is certain to do."

There is a brief pause on the other end. "Someone that significant is very rare indeed. Who is she?"

A sly grin crosses Nina's face. "Tell you what. She's right here. I think she speaks very well for herself, and I think you will agree with me that bringing her in was a wise choice." She hands the phone to Zoe.

"Good evening, Madam Aurea. This is Zoe Trent, Victor's sister. I trust you are well."

Zoe hears some hushed whispers on the other end of the connection.

"Welcome to the Order, Zoe. I trust you know how important discretion is among our ranks. Yes, you certainly can talk to Victor all you like. While I am surprised, I am sure this is a very sound move. Could you put Nina back on?"

Zoe hands the phone back to Nina.

"Yes, Madam Aurea?"

"I have been pondering this for a while, especially since Carol Ann started looking into the matter of twin flame and sharing the research with me. Also, I have been having some visions concerning Victor and Zoe. Silk was right; I should have had the foresight to bring them both in at once. Is she going to be your porfa?"

"Yes, she will be. Frankly, I suspect that I will be learning a lot more from her than she will be learning from me. I will contact the network administrator in Los Angeles and get her set up. She can have Dianne's old laptop. It is still in good shape. Arpel must not have realized that there was anything special about it."

Aurea sighs. "I already decided to postpone my trip back to Italy for a couple of weeks after what happened last night. I might make a trip to DC in a few days. Perhaps we should have Zoe come out and see Victor. Yes, I think that can be arranged. They are going to want some actual face time after all of this. I know she is excited. Just try to keep her from becoming overwhelmed."

Nina looks over at Zoe, who is already talking to Victor on her phone.

"She's already talking to Victor about it. I'll do my best, Madam Aurea. On that you may rely."

Anneliese arrives at Johanna's home early Thursday evening. She rings the bell, and Johanna opens the door and bids her to enter. She picks up her suitcase and comes inside. She marvels at the preternatural grace that accentuates Johanna's movements.

"I am, like, so honored to be your porfa, Madam Johanna. Such a thrill to be here! Wow! Victor will be so surprised when he sees me!"

Johanna sits down. "Take a seat, Anneliese. There are matters that we need to discuss, such as my expectations of you and your expectations of life here."

Anneliese sits down. "Madam Aurea and Cliff told me that I would be working for you as, like, your secretary. I do know Word and Excel pretty decent, but I still just don't get Access. I am so willing to learn though, you know?"

Johanna sighs. "Yes, you will learn to be my office assistant. I know you can learn the job duties. You will also be living here with me. Your room is over there. You will find the kitchen fully stocked. You will also find a new wardrobe in the closet. I'm not saying you can't dress like that when you go out to clubs and such, but on the job, you will dress professionally. I have also scheduled a voice coach to come over and work with you. We will train you to stop saying *like* and *you know* constantly. You are worthy of respect, Anneliese. We just need to make other people look at you that way as well."

Anneliese nods. "I'd like that, Madam Johanna. Victor is one of the few people I know who respects me, and I know the way that I talk sometimes irritates him, you know? Geez, I said it again. I really don't have many expectations of you except shelter and work. I do want to learn." She looks at Johanna plaintively. "I don't suppose you can teach me enough to make me into the kind of woman that Victor would really want to be with, you know, for sex and companionship?"

Johanna smiles. "Victor is a very special person, very complex in all regards. No, I can't make Victor want you. However, perhaps you can. I am sure you will become the kind of person he will be proud to call friend, which certainly is no mean feat. When it comes to romance, I think that he will be a tough nut to crack for any woman. Besides, you are asking the accountant. When you really want to explore that side of the equation, you should talk to Kathleen or Rachel."

Anneliese sighs. "Oh well. For sure I can dream, right? Lofty goals are good to have. I will make you proud. I promise."

Johanna nods. "I'm certain that you will, my dear. Now, let's get you settled in your new quarters."

CHAPTER 9

Wednesday, 18 March 2009. Paulina Wong brings Aurea's private jet in for a smooth landing at a small airport outside of Naples, Italy. In the passenger cabin, Aurea is looking wistfully out of a window. Carol Ann is rousing herself from her slumber. Scott MacAllister is working away on his laptop, stealing a glance out the window as the plane taxis into a hanger. The plane rolls to a stop, and Carol Ann stands up and opens the hatch. The stairway slowly lowers itself to the ground. A security officer climbs up and boards the plane. He looks at them sternly and then chuckles as he raises his hand, showing an Emerald Order ring.

"Welcome to Napoli, Madam Aurea. I am Guido, porfo to Lord Marco. Alphonse let us know when you folks would be arriving, so they made sure I would be on duty tonight. I know you would have no problem with normal customs agents, but why not keep everything cordial?"

Scott stands up and shakes Guido's hand. "We appreciate Alphonse's and Marco's thoughtfulness. Is either one of them going to make an appearance tonight?"

"Sadly, Lord Marco has other pressing business this evening and sends his regrets. However, I am told that Alphonse will be meeting you folks at Aurea's villa."

Guido gestures for them to go ahead and disembark. Aurea goes out first and is nearly overwhelmed by the emotions she is feeling. Carol Ann rushes out to steady her, a little too quickly, as one of the ground crew does a double-take. Aurea waves her off, and she walks down the stairs and is standing on the hangar floor. She looks out the hangar door and sees the airport with the lights of Naples close by. A tear rolls down her cheek.

"I'm home. I'm really here again. I'm no longer an exile."

Carol Ann stands next to her. "This must be really overwhelming. I bet you wondered if this day would ever come. Well, it has, beloved friend. You are home, and this is right."

A large, sleek, black Mercedes limousine with tinted windows pulls up to the hangar door. A sharply dressed, tall chauffeur gets out and walks toward them.

"Madam Aurea and company, I presume? I'm Carlos. Signore D'Amato sent me to take you folks to your villa outside of town. Has your luggage cleared customs? I'll be happy to stow it all in the trunk if it has."

Guido guides a porter with a cart carrying about ten large suitcases. "Yes, Carlos, everything is in order. These folks are good to go." Guido turns toward Aurea. "Madam, I sincerely hope that you find everything in good order at the villa. Marco wants to be informed if anything at all is amiss. Anything needing repair, per Lady Maurana, is to be noted and charged to the Vitzameri's account."

Carlos opens the doors, and all but Guido enter. He waves farewell as they pull away.

Paulina looks out the window as they head onto the Autostrada. She smirks at the fire-breathing dog that adorns the sign on the fuel station they pass. "You know, this place reminds me of Southern California, except for the architecture. Guess it's because of the similar climate." She looks over at Aurea. "All the memories you have here. You grew up in this very area, didn't you? Late Roman Republic. Wow. That's kind of hard to wrap myself around. I believe it, but all that you have seen and experienced. Does it ever all blur together at all?"

Aurea sighs. "No, not really, Paulina. One of the benefits of the transformation is a clearer memory. I really do remember much of my childhood in Pompeii. That will be the most emotional part of my trip. Rome certainly was a fascinating place, but there are many fascinating places in the modern world too."

Carol Ann looks out the window at the changing scenery. Presently, the limo leaves the Autostrada and heads down a smaller side road that goes through wealthier neighborhoods. The houses get further apart as they go on. Carol Ann is pointing at some homes, and Paulina nods. Scott simply busies himself with his laptop, working on some report. Aurea is alone with her thoughts, looking absently out the window and noting the cloud patterns. The limo then makes a turn into a driveway with a rather high gate stretching across it. The driver punches in a code, and the gate slowly slides open. The driver turns back to his passengers.

"We have arrived, Madam Aurea."

As the limo drives toward the villa, Aurea is taking it all in. "My fountains have survived. The gardens look much the same, some different plant types but suitable." She looks toward the villa as the limo comes to a stop near the front steps. "I see the house itself was expanded. They still kept the lines though so that anyone who had not been here before would not know of the renovations. I should thank the previous owners. They treated the property well."

As they exit the limo, Carlos goes back and unloads the luggage from the trunk. The front door of the villa opens, and a tall, swarthy, well-dressed man steps out. Aurea's eyes sparkle, and a big grin crosses her face as she recognizes him.

"Alphonse! How marvelous it is to see you again!"

He smiles back and nods.

Scott reaches the top of the steps first as the limo pulls away. He shakes hands with Alphonse. Carol Ann comes up next and kisses him on both cheeks. Paulina gives him a hug and goes into the foyer. After the others are inside, Aurea races up the stairs and holds Alphonse in a warm embrace, tears staining her cheeks. Alphonse holds her, kissing away the tears. His eyes are wet as well. After a time, Aurea looks up into Alphonse's eyes and smiles.

"I'm finally home. My exile is over. My vindication is at hand. How are you, most beloved friend?"

Alphonse puts his arm around Aurea's waist and walks to the door. "I have been doing quite well. Thank you. I have kept busy with various projects, though the latest one has been most satisfying." He opens the door and waits until she has entered the foyer and then follows her. "Lady Maurana requested my assistance with finding and securing the available properties that you forfeited because of the Vitzameri's foolishness. As you will see, not only was I able to assist in getting this property back into your hands, but I also found much of the original furnishings. No small task, I assure you."

She and Alphonse wander the halls, looking into the various rooms. Aurea nods at the tapestries and marvels how many of the furnishings had survived the years.

"You did very well, my friend."

They approach what had been the master suite, which has its own private courtyard. She visibly trembles when she opens the door, and a look of awe crosses her face. She walks in and takes in the sight.

"My god, Alphonse! It is just like I remembered it!" She sits on the huge four-poster bed, running her fingers on the sheets. "I know these can't be my old sheets, but this is my old bed. I can sense it. There has always been something very intimate, very comforting about it."

Alphonse nods. "Actually, the bed never left the property. Everyone who owned this place liked it. The last owner actually wanted to take it with them. You might say I convinced them to leave it behind. This house just wouldn't be right without it."

Aurea licks her lips and stretches out on the bed. "Indeed, it would not be." She eyes Alphonse hungrily. "Join me, my love. It has been far too long, don't you think?"

Alphonse smiles and shuts the suite door.

Victor walks into a small café near work. Anneliese is already inside. She smiles at him and waves. He notices that she is dressed more conservatively than she has in the past. Her blue dress ends just above the knee, very tasteful and professional. He smiles and joins her at the table.

"So, how are you doing, Anneliese? I trust that Madam Johanna is treating you well. You look sharp."

Anneliese positively beams with pleasure. "Madam Johanna is the best boss I have ever had. You know, I get to live in her house. It is just so beautiful. She is also having a speech teacher work with me so I stop saying *like* and *you know* and such so much. She's going to make me into a proper polished lady, you know?" She grins sheepishly. "Well, I guess you do know. How's it going for you?"

"Not bad, all things considered. Frankly, now that I know how I got the position on Moore's staff, I don't look at him the same way. I almost want to feel sorry for him. Then I figure that Cliff just managed to play a player. When it comes to politics, be assured that Moore is a player. So I guess this is poetic justice."

Anneliese laughs, a sound that Victor does find pleasing. "Well, I hope you aren't concerned about the representative figuring out what happened. Cliff is the best with political types. I miss him."

The waitress comes and takes their order.

Victor taps absently on the table. "Cliff does strike me as being one shrewd operator. I will give you that. As for him being a decent sort, I will take your word for it. I don't know him at all. So how did you and Cliff meet, if you don't mind me asking?"

Anneliese takes a sip of her water. "Cliff used to hang out at this little club in Seal Beach. I used to dance there. Yes, I was an exotic dancer. Pretty successful at it too, you know? One night, he came up to me and said I could do better than this. I was like, huh? That was a pretty good gig. At least I thought so. He was so nice though, so after a couple of weeks, I took him up on his offer. I think I was with him for about a month when he revealed that he was a vampire." She takes another sip of water. "I gotta say that that was a real shock. I mean, gosh, real vampires? I didn't believe in them at all until I met Cliff. Once he showed me his fangs, I was totally convinced. Also frightened, you know? Geez. There I go again."

Victor chuckles. "Don't fret about it, Anneliese. That will come with time. You should check out some of the public speaking groups here. Good way to get training and make some friends. So you were an exotic dancer? That explains some of the way you moved on that dance floor, making all the guys stare and most of the women glare. It is interesting to hear that Cliff hung out at such a club. I would have figured him for one to go to the more upscale clubs and other places political types tend to congregate."

Anneliese smiles slyly. "You don't know much about the nocturnal wanderings of politicians, Victor. They will never publicly admit it, but they do go to dive strip clubs. A lot of them try to do it incognito, you know? Many deals have been cut in the kind of club I used to work at. I don't think that is where Cliff met with Moore, but it certainly could have been."

"Hmm…I heard such, but I did not give it much consideration. You know, I've never been to one of those clubs, not because I think they are degrading to women or horrible places or anything like that. I have my Uncle Reggie's attitude: why pay good money to get worked up when, in the end, you won't get to act on it? If anything, I think those places exploit foolish guys and part them from their money."

Anneliese finishes her sandwich. "I never felt like I was taken advantage of there, Victor. Some of the guys did try for more, but touching and fraternizing was strictly not allowed. We had some big bouncers there—strong, tough guys." She shudders. "Strange to think that Cliff and Johanna could easily toss them through the wall, you know? I always used to be in awe of the club bouncers."

"Yes, it does change one's perspective, doesn't it? I still find it very odd when I am out with Cassie Mae and a couple of the others walking through some rough neighborhoods and knowing I am completely safe. They all look very normal. Back to Cliff though. How did he take your moving out here?"

She looks at Victor and pouts. "He was very hurt by it, truly. He said that it would be for the best, and that is why I did it. Aurea promised Cliff that she would look into the possible karmic ties between him and me. You know, I don't know if I believe in any of that, but he sure does. He thinks that people here will treat me better than they did out there. I haven't been here long enough to make that judgment. Madam Johanna is very nice, as is Oscar Martin. Rachel is all right, but that Lester fellow, well, he's a real jerk, to put it mildly. Haven't met any of the others just yet, though I understand I will be seeing Kathleen this evening."

"I haven't heard anything good about Lester either, though I haven't met him yet. I like Rachel well enough, but Kathleen, well, judge her for yourself and see what you think." Victor looks at his cell phone and sighs. "Well, I best be heading back to the office. Thanks for joining me for lunch."

After they walk out the door of the diner, Anneliese gives Victor a hug, and he hugs her back. As they part company, Anneliese smiles happily.

I did just as Madam Johanna advised. Just gave him a friendly hug. When he actually wants a kiss, it will be quite clear.

Aurea and Paulina are watching the sunset in a field just outside the ruins of Pompeii late on Thursday afternoon. Carol Ann is staying in the car, insisting on waiting for sunset, which is just minutes away.

Paulina sighs and looks toward Vesuvius. "She knows that she could take this brief sunlight without any harm, yet she refuses to come out. Whatever shall we do with her?"

Aurea smiles wistfully at that, still swimming in her emotions. She looks up the slopes of the volcano and points. "That is where Herculaneum stood. I can see they are excavating there as well. I didn't visit there but a few times. Pompeii was a much more vital town." She shudders. "Just seeing it from here is more than a little unnerving. There are so many memories from my mortal days. I am glad I am not here alone."

"There is comfort in that, granted," Maurana says as she walks forward. She gives Aurea a hug. "It is so good to see you again." She shakes hands with Paulina. "It's a true pleasure to meet you as well. Carol Ann has spoken very highly of you. Speaking of which, isn't she here?"

Paulina gestures toward the car. "She refuses to come out until the sun sets. She still has trouble truly believing it would take more than an hour of solar exposure to harm her. I mean, we did bring the special sunscreen and all. Aurea and I have been out here nearly half an hour, and she hasn't burst into flames."

Maurana scowls and heads toward the car. "Get out of there, Carol Ann. The sun sets in three minutes, and I give you my word-bond that you will not singe or anything else untoward in the meantime."

As Maurana is about to grab the car door, Carol Ann timidly steps out, covering her eyes.

"I know I can do this, my lady, but on an emotional level, I find this to be very intimidating." She gives Maurana a hug. "I am pleased to see you again, and under less trying circumstances."

Maurana looks over at Aurea as she and Carol Ann walk toward her. "These are still trying circumstances, my friend. I can tell that Aurea is still an emotional wreck, even though she is putting on a brave face. By the gods of the ancients, what she has been through. Even when it is over between her and Kristano, it still won't be right. Nothing can fix that, even if Vetrina reborn is identified and chooses to rejoin Ruby. Believe it or not, that could actually complicate matters."

Once the group is all together, the sun slips below the horizon and Carol Ann relaxes visibly. A young man approaches from the direction of Pompeii, and Aurea's eyes widen.

"That can't possibly be who he looks like. Or could it be?" She switches over to late Republic Latin. "Cato Julian? Where have you been hiding out all these years?"

The man smiles and addresses her in the same tongue. "I have been keeping a very low profile until quite recently, Aurea Octavia. I will explain myself at another time." He looks toward the others. "Good evening. I am Cato. Like my friend, Aurea, I lived here in Pompeii as a mortal. I just barely missed the great eruption that destroyed this town. I will be your guide as we go through the ruins." He looks over at Aurea. "I can take you directly to the old neighborhood if you wish. It was excavated about ten years ago. I have found some items that I believe belonged to your family, which I will give you."

Aurea looks bewildered. "If they have uncovered our old neighborhood, then there is a lot of the town that they are keeping off limits to the tourists. Very well, Cato. Lead the way."

Soon, they are among the ruins. It is very still and quiet, as all the tourists have left. The security guards ignore them because they are making themselves psychically invisible. As there are no brights among the guards, this is a simple task. Cato is the perfect guide, pointing out sights of interest as they make their way toward Aurea's old neighborhood. Maurana is tense, watching the moods travel across Aurea's face. She is making no attempt to conceal the cascade of emotions. Carol Ann is noting them as well. Paulina is her normal stoic self, looking at the ruins and carrying herself with an air of authority.

They arrive at the entrance of the townhouse that Aurea had grown up in. She peers in the doorway cautiously. "I never expected to lay eyes on this place again. Last time I was even in Pompeii was about twenty years prior to the eruption. I came by here, and another family was living here. They kept the place about the same though, remarkably. I never thought my family had decorated the place that well."

Aurea leads the way inside. Paulina follows, marveling at the well-preserved frescoes. Maurana is scanning the room carefully, as if she fully expects something to jump out at them. Carol Ann steps in quietly, very concerned about Aurea's demeanor. Cato brings up the rear.

"This was a neighborhood of fairly well-to-do merchants and tradesmen. The ashfall from the eruption kept this area almost air tight and very well preserved until the excavations about a decade ago. This home is fairly typical of what you would see, although you will also note how quiet it is. No one died in here during the eruption."

They walk slowly through what had been the courtyard. A couple empty fountains and some statues sit in mute testimony to the pleasant garden that had once been here. They come to a small room at the far end of the courtyard.

Aurea turns around, looking rather mystified. "That was my room. I'd like to go in there alone for a few minutes and speak privately with Maurana."

The others nod assent and walk off, while Aurea and Maurana walk into the small, dark room.

For a few minutes, they both sit in the room silently. Aurea has her head bowed, tears silently running down her cheeks. Maurana sits calmly, waiting for Aurea to speak her peace. Aurea looks over at Maurana, eyes swollen with tears.

"This is a good cry actually, Maurana. Coming here has been cathartic, helping me come to grips with my past. A part of it, that is." She wipes her eyes. "Tell me of Kristano. Does he suffer much? Does he have any idea just how hideous, how monstrous an injustice he inflicted on me? Not just on me truly. He dishonored the memory of my blood sister and best friend. He should have known that I had nothing to do with Vetrina's demise. How could he have blamed me? Why?"

Maurana sighs heavily. "I will make no excuses for him, Aurea. There are none that make any sense at all. He does accept full responsibility, and yes, he is suffering. Though you will be made whole on a financial level, I know it does very little for you on an emotional level. He even consented to Plinthi with me, and, frankly, even that did not clear much of any of this up in my mind. It raised more questions than it answered. I realize that this is no real consolation, but no one I know of ever believed you were responsible for Vetrina's demise, not even Sapphires who detest you and fear your name. Everyone thought Kristano to be the ultimate fool, even the ones who were responsible."

Aurea stands up, having regained her composure. "I'm still not ready to see him and settle the blood debt. That is a confrontation I am not yet prepared for. I want to have a firm grasp of exactly what I want to say to him. I intend to look him in the eyes and tell him exactly what I think of his utter foolishness. Then, I intend to forgive him because I know that is what Vetrina would want me to do."

"That is far better than what he deserves, my friend, even though I am sure you are correct as far as what Vetrina would want you to do." Maurana chuckles. "I suspect though that she would want you to forgive him so she could soundly thrash him for having been so ridiculous. I don't know why he blamed you, Aurea. I suspect it had something to do with jealousy over how close you were to his sister. I suspect he was unnerved by the changes he saw coming among the Vamphyri. He is a young soul, after all, and I will say that he is really out of his element. Even he suspects the truth of that. He told me he thinks he is ready for another turn at the wheel, figuring a new life will help him get some new perspective. He might well do just that once this blood debt is settled satisfactorily."

They walk out of the room and rejoin the others in the courtyard.

Aurea looks over toward Cato. "I think we are ready to see the rest of the town. It was a beautiful place once, wasn't it, Cato?"

"That it truly was, my friend. At times, I still think about it with longing." He moves a stone over in the corner and takes out a small bag and then hands it to Aurea. "I believe these are personal effects from your family. I could be wrong, but they have the right feel to me. Tell me what you think."

Aurea opens the bag carefully and examines the contents. She takes out a small statuette of Minerva. "This was mine. I kept it in my room. Minerva was my favorite goddess." She goes over and gives Cato a hug. "Thank you, my friend. Until now, I have had nothing from my mortal days except the memories."

Van Arpel is staying at an old motel on the outskirts of Providence, Rhode Island. He has paid extra to not be disturbed by housekeeping and to get a late checkout. He looks at his watch and sees that it is two o'clock. He gets dressed and checks out. He is on the trail of his next target, a Sapphire vampire who calls himself Tomas Gilbert. This one appears to be rather wealthy, as he has a home in one of Providence's upscale neighborhoods. This makes his task more difficult, as it will be harder to just blend in. Arpel always plans his ambushes carefully, often preparing for weeks before making a move. Arpel reminisces about his last attack. It had only taken him a week to get into Dave West's place and off that undead scum and his mortal thrall. That one had been most entertaining.

"She was far too trusting. She was so shocked when I blasted her with the acid. The screams as I took her. Ah, that was sweet revenge."

He makes his way into downtown Providence. He walks down a side street that is lined with old storefronts, about a third of which are vacant. He walks with purpose and confidence, and people stay out of his way. He is headed for a small used bookstore on the corner. He arrives and enters slowly. It is a rather typical store for its type, shelves filled with books of different types. He notes that the largest section is of romance novels. He shakes his head in disgust. He walks down the rows, pretending now and then to be interested in a book. He is really keeping an eye on the cashier. A tall, thin brunette in her mid twenties, he figures. What interests him the most about her is the Sapphire ring she is wearing. He is certain that she is a mortal thrall who can lead him to his quarry.

Once the other customers have left, he walks over to the counter. The cashier glances over at Arpel warily, sizing him up to see if he is a threat. She decides that he is not, so she smiles at him.

"Can I help you find something, sir? Are you looking for a particular book or author?"

"I'm hoping to find a book by a man named Gilbert. First name was Tomas, I do believe. He is a very obscure author, and I don't know where I might find his work. I was hoping perhaps that your store might have something by him, but I did not see anything on the shelves."

The cashier looks momentarily flustered by the mention of that name, but she recovers quickly. She looks at Arpel's hands to see if he is wearing an Order ring, which he is not. She punches the name into the computer next to the cash register.

"I'm terribly sorry, sir, but I don't see any titles under that name in our stock at all."

Arpel nods politely as a couple of other customers enter the store. "How disappointing. I had been told that he was a local writer here in Rhode Island. I was hoping you folks might have something by him. Thanks, and a good day to you."

He then touches the side of the counter, placing a small bug on it. He walks out of the store, holding the door open for another customer and walks up. She favors him with a smile as he walks on down the block. Once he is out of sight of the store, he puts some headphones on and waits patiently.

After about an hour of hearing rather normal used bookstore conversations, Arpel's patience is rewarded. He hears the clerk suddenly calling on the store's landline, close to where his bug is planted.

"Master, I have had a rather strange visitor show up at the shop. This man claimed to be looking for a book allegedly written by you. He said you were an obscure writer from Rhode Island."

A throaty chuckle comes from the other end of the line. "Sounds like some lame attempt at a ruse to me. Did this fool look familiar at all, like anyone we are looking for?"

Arpel mutters under his breath about that remark. "That undead jerk is calling me a fool? Yeah right."

"No, Master, he did not. There was something different about him though. I can't really put my finger on it, except to say that he really did sound sincere about his desire to find a book by you."

"That is very odd, especially since I never have published anything. I wrote a few poems, but I never had them collected in chapbooks. Did you find him to be threatening on any level?"

"No, I did not, Master. Just found him to be odd. I could not really read him, but then that isn't my strong point yet. I still have much to learn for that skill."

"Well, should this avid fan of mine return to the shop, tell him that you know a collector who has a couple of my books, but he is not sure he wants to part with them, but he will be honored to show them to him. Then you will send him to my place, where he can be properly disposed of."

Arpel smiles at the audacity of the vampire's statement. "That undead fiend also is afflicted by the sin of pride. I shall take immense pleasure in doing the work of the righteous."

"Very well, Master. It shall be as you say. Your will is my directive. I live to serve Order Sapphire."

When the call ends, Arpel takes off the earphones and walks to a nearby diner for a meal. A smile crosses his face. "Before sundown tomorrow, that undead fiend and his mortal thrall will both cease to be."

Nina and Zoe drive up to an office complex in Downey.

"Welcome to the Ruby motherhouse of Greater Los Angeles."

They get out of the car and start walking toward the side entrance. Zoe looks quite perplexed. Nina laughs.

"Not exactly what you were expecting to see, is it?"

Zoe shakes her head. "No, it isn't. I really expected to see a very nice, large house. I know there are a few such homes in Downey. Maybe not a lot, but still."

She waits as Nina knocks on the door. A slat opens, and a pair of eyes stares out at them. A buzzer sounds, and the door opens.

Zoe nods at the guard as they enter the hall. Zoe looks around. "This place looks very utilitarian. I gather the windows have full blackout curtains for the occupants during daylight hours?"

Before Nina can answer, a tall, rather slim man with an air of authority approaches them. "Actually, we have the best in state-of-the-art technology for the windows. They polarize fully in daylight hours so no sunlight can get in. Not that it generally matters. Most of the sleeping chambers are in the basement, which is fully solar proof." He extends his hand to Zoe, who shakes it firmly. "I am Alexander Tewes, proctor of the Downey motherhouse. I am honored to meet you, Zoe. You have been spoken of very highly." He turns his attention to Nina. "I do apologize for the shoddy treatment you and your colleagues received from Order Security the night that Dave and Dianne were murdered. Those responsible have been properly disciplined. They should have realized you folks were likely friends of Dave, as he was well regarded."

Nina nods. "I suppose that is the best that I could hope for under those circumstances. I don't suppose that Arpel left behind any clue suggesting where he was heading off to next, did he?"

They walk down the hall to a rather plush office. Alexander takes his seat behind a large ornate oak desk. Nina and Zoe sit down in comfortable chairs on either side.

He wrings his hands. "Sadly, no, Nina, just like every other time. No fingerprints, a few skin samples, but nothing we didn't know before. We know what he looks like, but we can't track him because he always uses throwaway cell phones or the actual victim's phone, and he is psychically invisible to all of us."

Zoe shakes her head. "How can anyone actually be truly psychically invisible? I've been studying this guy, and he seems to be unique, which is bewildering since most people, heck, any being with some sentience, are throwing off random thought patterns constantly. Even if one shields one's thoughts, it does not render one wholly invisible on the psychic level. There should at least be a signature, a presence."

Alexander leans back in his chair. "I totally agree with you that there ought to be. However, he could not do what he has managed to do if he did. I mean, Dave should have known there was an intruder in his home. He must not have or he would not have just casually walked in to immediately get hosed with acid and then get decapitated. In his case, the weak spot was his porfa, who clearly was still distraught over her failure to successfully watch you." He notes the stricken look on Zoe's face and waves his hand. "Please, Zoe. You must not blame yourself. She made her choice as to how she reacted. Yours was certainly the superior skill set. We do, however, have a problem that we hope you can assist us with."

"Certainly, Sir Alexander. How may I be of assistance to the Order?"

Alexander chuckles. "Just call me Alexander for starters. No sense in me getting used to hearing honorifics from you Zoe. If even half what I have been told about you turns out to be true, you are a returned elder and I will be calling you Lady Zoe before too long. At any rate, it appears that Dianne's soul is refusing to move on to the next plane and is staying there in Dave's house. Some vampires and a couple of porfi have tried to talk to her, but they say all she does is weep and moan. Clearly, this is not good for anyone. I have been told your family has some fairly formidable spirit hunters in it. Also, we think that she would be willing to talk to you." He pauses and reflects. "Or, possibly, your presence would make her angry enough to lash out and we could have another sensitive call in a friend or loved one on the other side to convince her to make the transition. Are you willing to assist us?"

Zoe shivers. "This sounds like something that my Uncle Reggie or my brother Arnold would be very well suited to. I can certainly identify spirits. I have seen a few and know when they are around. Dianne must feel like she has unfinished business on this plane if she is refusing to move on."

Nina looks over at Zoe. "She does think that she has unfinished business. She feels like she failed the Order. She didn't, but that is not what she believes. Oddly enough, I do think she would talk to you, Zoe, and then she could be convinced to move on. We can't bring your brother Arnold or your Uncle Reggie into this." She smiles wistfully. "Although I have met Reggie a couple of times, he is a very intelligent man. He just isn't Plaz material. Arnold, from what I have been told, is simply annoying."

"Arnold being annoying is an understatement, Nina. However, for real surefire annoyance, you should go hang out with my parents." She looks over at Alexander. "I am willing to try to make contact with Dianne and see if I can get her to move on. When did you want to do this?"

Alexander smiles. "I believe I can get all the proper people in place by this time tomorrow."

That same evening, Victor and Cassie Mae are attending a formal reception at the Kennedy Center. Victor is walking rather stiffly in his suit. Cassie Mae looks resplendent in her simple gown. Just to spice things up, she is also using mild charm glamour. She enjoys playing with the mortals, especially the self-important ones who seem to abound at these Washington affairs. Victor waves as Davis Grayson approaches. As usual, Davis has a very jovial look on his face. Cassie Mae studies him intently.

Davis bows to Cassie Mae and kisses the air above her hand. "I'm pleased to meet you! You must be Cassie Mae, the one whom Victor has talked about. He's a really lucky guy to be with you."

Cassie Mae smiles demurely. "Why, thank you, good sir. It's so rare to meet anyone in this city with manners. Victor has spoken very highly of you as well. Is Representative Moore going to be making an appearance this evening?"

Davis scans the hall. "He said he was planning on stopping by." He waves when he sees Daphne. "There's Daphne and that Alfred fella."

Davis finds it difficult to take his eyes off Cassie Mae, a fact that she finds most amusing.

Daphne and Alfred make their way over.

Daphne shakes hands with Cassie Mae. "Great to see you. I'm the office manager for Representative Moore. I see you have met Davis. Are you enjoying the reception?" Daphne makes a face. "This one isn't really all that obnoxious. So many of them are."

Cassie Mae shrugs. "Its fine, Daphne. I have been to more of these affairs than I care to remember. So long as I have pleasant company, it is bearable. The ones where I have not, well, I am sure you know."

Daphne rolls her eyes. "Oh my, do I ever know what you mean, Cassie Mae. Well, must mingle. See you all later." She takes Alfred's hand and heads back into the crowd.

He keeps glancing back at Cassie Mae, a move Daphne finds to be most irritating. Davis goes off as well.

Victor looks over at Cassie Mae. "I know you are using charm glamour tonight. Not directed at me, so it doesn't breach the agreement made in New York. Still, I think it would be best if you stopped. You are stunning enough without resorting to the mind games."

Cassie Mae pouts. "Oh, very well. If you insist, you spoilsport." She puts a stop to the glamour. Her eyes scan the hall and fix on a woman wearing a very clingy and revealing gown. "Do you know that woman, Victor?"

He looks in her general direction. He nods. "I do know her. She is Gretchen Denter, one of the most successful lobbyists in this town, and that is saying something. What troubles you about her?"

She speaks in a very low tone. "Did you notice the ring that woman is wearing? She's a Sapphire porfa."

Victor's eyes went wide. "I must admit I never noticed that ring before."

At that moment, Gretchen looks over at them, puzzled, and then scowls and starts walking over.

"This could end up not being pretty. What are the rules of engagement in a public place?"

Cassie Mae stands her ground as Gretchen approaches. "Openly fighting in a public place is a serious breach of protocol. I think that I got her attention by pinging a hostile thought pattern at her. Just play nice, and don't fret about this. I know who her master is, and he would not be happy with her if she does make a scene. It would at least end her career. Likely, it would be the actual end of her as well."

When Gretchen arrives, she is wearing a very fake smile. "So, we meet again, Victor. I see that you have made a rather poor choice of companions. Ruby is decadent, permissive, and rotten to the core." She holds up her hand, sapphire ring prominent. "Sapphire teaches honor and discipline, something that I would think someone like you would find to be rather more appealing." She looks over at Cassie Mae. "Or does this strumpet from the Old South really do it for you?"

Victor keeps his composure. "Ruby is decadent and permissive? You know, regular people warned me about you as an individual long before I became involved with the Order and started wearing this ring, which I do with pride, by the way." Victor glares at Gretchen.

“I hear that you have bedded several of the staffers and many of the Congressmen here tonight to promote your clients’ lobbying efforts. Is this what you mean by honor and discipline? If so, you have very odd definitions of those terms. Sounds like something one of the more recent ex presidents of the imperium would have said. As for Cassie Mae, she is far from a strumpet. She is an honorable individual, and for that and other reasons, she has my respect.”

Cassie Mae stares coldly. “You are being rude, porfa. Perhaps I should speak with Seth, your master. I somehow don’t think he would approve of your behavior. The Orders are in détente right now, so it behooves you to keep the peace, don’t you think?” She smirks. “Go peddle yourself somewhere else, dear. The price for this man is far too high for the likes of you to meet.”

Gretchen bites her lip. “I will go, but you will get no apologies from me. I serve my Order well, and I serve my clients well.” She looks over at Victor. “It isn’t too late to change your mind. You do not fully belong to any Order until you are transformed. If you are wise enough to reconsider, you know where to find me.” She turns and walks back into the crowd.

Victor sighs. “Yes, Gretchen, I know where to find you. In the local sewer, partying with the other rats.”

Cassie Mae favors him with a smile.

During mid afternoon Friday, Maurana and Aurea are having a discussion at the villa.

Maurana is admiring the room they are in. “I am so pleased that we were able to find most of the furnishings that you had to leave behind. Those that we could not were replaced suitably, I trust.”

“That part is fine, my friend. It is nice to be back here again. I have been away for far too long.” Aurea sighs. “In a few more days, I will need to return to New York. For now, that is where I reside. It will never be home. This area, this place, is truly my home.”

Maurana looks wistfully toward the window with the drapes securely drawn. “My home is long gone. What remains of Atlantis is well beneath the waves. Some could be salvaged, but there is no way to make it habitable again. Once Kristano is gone, I think I will leave Avignon. Perhaps I will go off planet for a while. Costly, but I know it can still be arranged.”

“I never think much about leaving the Earth. Maybe once this is all over and the blood debt is discharged. Perhaps once I know for certain about Victor and his sister, Zoe, then I can consider such ventures. I have heard that Mars has a rather stark beauty all its own.” Aurea gazes at a tapestry. “I really think that Victor and Zoe are returned ancient elders and will prove to be powerful and valuable allies.”

“It is an intriguing possibility, Aurea. It would be most heartening to have such people back in the Order, if that is what they in fact are. Even if they are not returned elders, they certainly have the kind of aptitude and psychic skills that are desirable. My intuition tells me that you are correct, but we must move carefully. The further back one probes into past lives, the more complicated and risky it becomes. I trust they are both doing well with the brethren they are porfi with?”

Aurea’s eyes sparkles. “Oh yes. Nina Parks says that Zoe is simply amazing, a very fast learner and the very best porfa she has ever had. Cassie Mae and Victor are learning together. She has never had a porfo before. She finds Victor to be complex and most intriguing. I think she also has feelings for him that she is having difficulty coming to grips with. Midnight Silk, her best friend, thinks that Victor might have been someone Cassie Mae knew very well back in the Antebellum South, but she does not want to raise false hopes by saying anything. She is convinced that if Victor was that individual, it will come out soon enough.” She sighs. “The Weave is a very complicated mechanism, all those lives we live.”

“Truer words have never been spoken. So, do you have any message that you want me to deliver to Kristano? Any sort of timeline that you care to give me about discharging the blood debt? Please don't tell me you are going to make him sit there for a couple of centuries, brooding over it. He is really starting to get on people's nerves, especially mine. So don't do it as a favor to him; do it as a favor to me."

Aurea thinks for a moment. "Tell the Vitzameri that I know I am a better person than he is. I will forgive him his transgression. It will be in the fall of this year, and it will be in North America. I am certain there will be some kind of event that will draw many Ruby and Emerald together. I will want a public apology. Then I will expect him to conduct himself honorably until such time as he chooses to exit this plane and go through another life cycle. Given what you have said and what I have heard, he is very likely to wind up his affairs and shuffle off for a while. That will be suitable."

"I shall advise him of this when I see him tomorrow. What kind of event do you have in mind? Rarely does anything that we do draw that kind of crowd, mostly because, except under rare circumstances, it isn't a good idea. We are a fractious lot. For being so thin on the ground, we have so many cliques, and even with Emerald, there is a measure of inter-Order rivalry. Still, it is certainly your call to make. He won't object."

Aurea looks at her laptop. "Perhaps one of the gatherings of the Red and Green would be appropriate. I will talk to the commandant in New York. He might well have a suggestion." She pauses when she sees Carol Ann making her way down the hall. "We will be going into Rome tonight. Care to join us?"

Maurana smiles. "Yes, Aurea, I would be happy to join you and your companions for a night on the town."

A somber group lines up in front of Dave West's house shortly after sunset. Alexander is there, as is Brenda Rennert. When Nina and Zoe get out of the car, Brenda comes over to them.

"So you are Zoe Trent, the sensitive who will attempt to get Dianne to leave this house and this plane and move on? I'm Brenda Rennert. Nina and I were here the night of the murders. We probably missed Arpel by minutes, the wretch. Alexander has one of those Order Security folks setting up some equipment that I am sure you have some familiarity with." She sees Alexander going inside. "Well, no time like the present to get to the task."

As they walk toward the door, Zoe notices the hair on the back of her neck standing up. "She's definitely here, Nina. I don't think she is the only sentient spirit in there either. This should be an eventful evening."

Nina looks concerned. "There's more than one? I was told that Dave was off the plane before we even arrived on the scene. I wonder if it is a friend or relative of Dianne's who has come from the other side of the veil to try to convince her to cross over. Guess we will soon find out."

Zoe enters the living room and lets herself become accustomed to the surroundings. She closes her eyes briefly. She then points to the floor in front of her. "Dave died right at this spot. You are right. He isn't here." She looks over at a blank wall. "Dianne finally died over there, where I presume there was a couch until recently." She looks toward the bedroom. "However, she is in her bedroom. The other presence I felt is in the kitchen. It is a female, but I do not know who she is, nor is she offering to come forward." Zoe smiled. "It seems she isn't comfortable with vampires. Blames you folks for what happened to Dianne."

Nina ponders this. "It could be her grandmother. Dianne said that she would never have approved of her being with the likes of us. Would have called us undead fiends, monsters, demon spawn."

Brenda snorts. "Sounds like the same kind of ignorant tripe that most people who have some passing belief in us think. She probably believed blessed crosses and garlic and rosewood would kill us too."

Zoe feels a kind of psychic jolt. "Let's not antagonize the other spirit much more, shall we? I do believe you are right that this is

Dianne's grandmother Dorothy." She looks toward the bedroom door and sees an outline of a person. The others, save the porfo from Order Security, notice this as well.

A faint but audible voice comes from the bedroom. "I want to talk to the one who bested me, Zoe. Nina, Brenda, Alexander, please let her come in here alone. I will not bring harm to her." A faint chuckle fills the air. "How could I? I have no body to use anyway."

Alexander looks at Zoe. "You don't have to do this. No one here would fault you for just turning around and getting out of here. It is entirely up to you."

Zoe squares her shoulders. "I sense no threat. I will trust in my intuition and take Dianne at her word." She looks toward the room again. "All right, Dianne. I am coming in alone." She walks slowly into the bedroom and watches the door close behind her. She sits down on a chair in front of the desk and watches Dianne's spirit form into a nearly perfect apparition. "Very well, Dianne. I am here, and we are alone. You know that your body has died because of what that foul murderer Van Arpel did to you. It is time you accepted that and moved along. You know you will be coming back anyway. Why are you still here?"

Dianne is crying. "I didn't want it to end like this. It just isn't right. I had what it takes to be a vampire, and Arpel took that opportunity away from me. It isn't so much that I feel like I failed the Order. I know that I really failed myself. I should have been able to snap back from having been found out by you, but you know, I never was able to. I thought I should be invincible. Clearly, I was not."

Zoe looks at Dianne. "I didn't have to be so brutal that day back in the Student Union. I felt very bad about it afterward. It felt like my intelligence had been insulted. Since I have become a porfa, I understand more about what motivated them to send you and Cassidy out to observe me. Neither of you meant any harm. These are truly paranoid times, and I should have given both of you the benefit of the doubt. I am sorry, Dianne. I did not mean for you to be devastated."

A whiff of perfume from another era came into the room. Zoe looks over and sees another outline in the room.

Dianne looks over and smiles. "Yes, that's my grandma. She waited for me. She has been here nearly every day since I died, trying to convince me to join her, which I shall do shortly. Zoe, you don't need to be sorry. I apologize to you for not just admitting it when you confronted me. That was an insult to your intelligence. I see that now. You and your brother Victor are very special people. You will both be powers to be reckoned with once you do become vampires. You know that you will. Trust in that."

Insistent thought patterns came from the other spirit.

"I just have one favor to ask of you, Zoe, and then you can go out there and tell them that I have left this plane."

"If it is within my power to do so, Dianne, I will do it. What do you need to give you peace?"

Dianne starts to fade. "Promise me that you will seek me out in a new lifetime a couple centuries from now. Let me be your porfa. I won't let you down. I could learn so much from you."

Zoe nods. "You have a deal, Dianne. Now, go in peace and say hello to the guardians of the Weave for me. Pick out a new life in which you can live to a ripe old age and experience the fullness of being."

Zoe feels the planes shift as the two spirits leave. The house is now clear of spirits, with only place memories remaining. She composes herself and stands up and opens the door. She looks into their anxious faces.

"Dianne and her grandmother are gone. She will not be returning in spirit form."

Alexander breathes a sigh of relief. "I am very glad to hear that. Excellent work, Zoe. The motherhouse is in your debt. If you should ever be in need of some assistance, please contact me. If I can provide it, you will have it. Dave and Dianne were good friends, and I did not want her to suffer any longer."

As they walk out of the house, Nina notices that Zoe is deep in thought. "What happened in there? Is it anything that you can talk about? Is there anything at all that you care to share?"

Zoe sighs. "It's all so very hard to wrap my head around. She wanted to be perfect, demanded such from herself. She couldn't recover from her failure. I wish I could have talked to her weeks ago. Maybe then Arpel would not have found her to be such an easy target and she and Dave would still be here."

"An interesting thought, but we can't change the past. Have to learn from it and move forward. She will be back, and I have a feeling that you will be the one to find her. So you will be able to help her."

Arpel is walking back to the bookstore in the early afternoon. He is filled with his usual confidence. He is certain that he will be taking down yet another undead fiend and their mortal thrall today. After he is finished, he will call his sister with the news and then vanish to find another target somewhere else in the country. He smiles.

I could go up to Canada. That would throw them off a bit.

He enters the store and notes that there are several customers inside. Sally is talking to one of them while making a sale; however, she smiles slyly at Arpel when he comes in. He finds that most amusing.

Bet she thinks she is going to put one over on me. Won't she be surprised. Well, she will be meeting her maker soon enough, and I will triumph over her undead master.

Van is browsing the philosophy section, sighing sadly about the very sparse offerings. He notes with scorn that there are five bookcases literally filled with self-help books right next to the blasted romance section.

"This really says something about who bothers to read these days. What a crying shame."

A few minutes later, Sally is standing next to him. "Are you still interested in acquiring some of the published works of Tomas Gilbert, sir? I'm sorry. I don't believe I caught your name yesterday."

Arpel smiles. "Call me Frank. So, you managed to find some of Gilbert's work? Do you have the books here? However did you manage to find such rare works, Sally?"

Sally motions for him to follow her into the back. He notices that she has put up the closed sign and locked the front door. He finds that somewhat surprising. Still, he follows her into the back room and sits down when she offers him a seat. She sits across the table from him. "Well, Frank, I was contacted yesterday afternoon by a local collector. Said he had a couple of chapbooks of Gilbert's poetry. He wondered if I knew of anyone who would make him an offer." She smiles. "I immediately thought of you. I would have called you if you had left me your phone number. Well, this collector is elderly, so he would like you to drop by his home tonight around, say, eight? I am sure you will find it most interesting."

She pushes a slip of paper over to him with the address.

"Thank you so much. I will be happy to visit this fine gentleman and see what he has. Perhaps I can make him an offer he will be happy to accept."

When Sally gets up and approaches the door, Van stands up and takes a syringe out of his pocket. He quickly jabs it into her back and injects the contents. Sally gasps and then falls limp in his arms, unconscious. He puts her back in the chair and ties her up and then carefully removes the sapphire ring from her finger and gloats.

"Another one that I can add to my growing collection."

He then sits down and waits a few minutes while Sally comes to. He relishes in the look of horror on her face when she recognizes him.

"You are Van Arpel, the assassin! I should have known! When my master gets his hands on you, you will be finished. You hear me, Arpel? Finished!" She spits at him. "My ring will let him know I am in distress."

Van holds up the ring. "Not when you aren't wearing it, thrall. I learned very quickly how these things work. Cursed creations of demons, which is what they are." He leans in close. "You have a choice to make, Sally. You can die fast and relatively painlessly, or you can die slowly, in more pain than you can possibly imagine. I know this address tonight is for an ambush. I planted a bug here yesterday, so I know what you and he talked about. So here's the deal. Tell me where he is right now, and I will blow your brains out. Don't, and I will make sure that you suffer until you do tell me where the undead fiend is."

Sally's face turns into a snarl. "Do your worst, Arpel. I will gladly give my life to protect that of my master. Why you call him undead I cannot fathom. There really is no such thing as undead."

Arpel grins and slaps her across the face, hard. Then he tears off her blouse. "So be it, thrall." He takes out a small bottle of acid and dribbles it along her naked back.

Sally grimaces, but she does not give him the satisfaction of crying out.

"Impressive. No other thrall has endured that without screaming." He takes out a knife and cuts off one of her fingers. Still she does not cry out.

"I will give you no satisfaction, assassin. Ravage my body, violate me, flay me, kill me, do what you will. I will not tell you how to find my master." Sally stares at Arpel defiantly.

The possibility of this being his first failure is starting to eat away at him. He loses his composure. He takes out a knife and slashes her chest, her face, her arms, and her legs. Bleeding profusely, she still does not cry out. She manages to grin and chuckle.

"I will be remembered well, assassin. You are a fool."

In a fit of rage, Arpel cuts her throat deeply, ear to ear. Blood gushes from the slashed arteries for about thirty seconds, and then Sally is quite dead. Arpel tears the room apart. Disgusted by his failure to make her reveal Tomas Gilbert's location, he sets her body ablaze and then sets the bookstore on fire and swiftly walks away.

Safely away, he starts cursing himself. *I doubt they will think I did this. It doesn't follow my usual mode, and I am not going to call Abigail to brag about this. No sense in going to that house tonight. The undead fiend won't show since he did not hear back from Sally. I have to be more careful in the future, take my time. That hit in Los Angeles was just sheer luck."* He hears the wail of sirens approaching the bookstore. *Next time I will target someone really significant, one of the Emerald or Ruby elders. I think I will leave the Sapphires alone for now. Their thralls are truly made out of stronger stuff. Such loyalty!*

CHAPTER 10

Thursday, 9 April 2009. Lester and Kathleen are spending part of their evening at Becker's in Alexandria. Kathleen is all smiles, watching the crowd and enjoying the band. Lester, as usual, is scowling, making some people very nervous as they walk by the table he is sitting at. Kathleen looks over at Lester and sighs.

"Can't you ever just loosen up and enjoy yourself out in public? You scared that one poor kid so badly that he practically ran out the door. There's great music, we already fed, so why are you sulking?"

Lester glares. "I can't seem to stop thinking about that mortal upstart Victor Trent. He seems to be the man of the hour, the glory boy of our Order, all this rubbish about his great pedigree and interesting past lives. What a crock all of that is. You only live once, which is why I became a vampire. I want to get the most out of it. I still haven't met the man, and I can't stand him. Thinking about him is irritating enough."

"He's really not a bad guy, Lester. Tends to be rather quiet and reserved, but he certainly is very intelligent. Get him on the right topics, and he is downright passionate. I think Madam Aurea made the right decision regarding him. I surely did not at first; however, now I am quite certain."

Lester shakes his head. "I don't care. This Trent fellow will never win me over. Neither will the hocus pocus mysticism of the elders. What kind of crap are they trying to pull anyway? Giving people false hope like that. Karma indeed! Justice has nothing to do with life. It comes to those who can afford it."

Kathleen gives Lester a perplexed look and then quickly brightens as she sees Oscar Martin enter the club. She waves, and he comes over and joins them. Oscar smiles warmly. "It's great to see both of you this evening! This band is quite good. I really like their sound, the emotion, the tension. It sounds like they really feel it."

Kathleen is fascinated, while Lester keeps scowling.

"So what brings you out tonight, Lester? I must admit I am surprised to find you here at all."

Lester looks over at Kathleen. "She thought it would do me good to get out for a while. Since I needed to feed anyway, I figured, why not? I do come here every so often, Oscar. Granted, I do prefer my solitude, but there are times that it likely makes sense for me to mingle. Even though I just can't stand the hoi polloi, as I know you know only too well."

Kathleen preens. "I did promise him a most enjoyable evening afterward if he behaved himself. I guess he largely has, although he seems intent on picking on Victor Trent and mocking the elders. Lester does not believe in karma or past lives. His argument is you just get one trip around, so make the most of it."

Oscar raises an eyebrow. "Well, Lester, you are certainly entitled to your beliefs, opinions, biases, and the lot of it. Suffice it to say that you and I have gone over that ground many times, and I respectfully disagree with you. As for Victor Trent, I find him to be an admirable fellow. I believe he is an ancient soul, and I think it is highly likely that he is a returned elder. Who knows? I might have to call him Lord in a few years. If that should happen, I'm fine with it. You should be too, Lester. Your anger does you no merit whatsoever."

Lester snorts. "My anger is just. I think us vampires need to expand our numbers and be more aggressive. I'm not saying we should kill lots of mortals, but I do think we need to stop being so squeamish about it. As for Trent, I say the only thing that guy has going for him is his sister, Zoe. Now, she is something else again. She's beautiful and smart. Her I wouldn't mind spending some quality time with."

Kathleen giggles. "Zoe Trent would just give you a withering look, Lester. She would sense your hostility toward her brother and would likely only deal with you to the extent that she had to."

Oscar smiles benignly. "Well, as luck has it, Lester, you might get your opportunity to meet Zoe sooner than you thought. She will be flying in tomorrow morning. She is spending a few days with Victor, and she wants to meet all the metro DC Ruby vampires. I will be hosting a reception Sunday evening. I understand that she and Victor and some other folks will be here tomorrow night. It should be great, especially since Midnight Silk will be performing. I certainly don't intend to miss that. No sir."

Kathleen beams. "I'll certainly be at both. I wonder if Anneliese will be coming here tomorrow. She cracks me up. She is trying so hard to stop talking like a Southern California airhead. You know though? She is making some progress." She looks over at Lester. "How about you, sourpuss?"

Lester just groans. "It would be rude for me to not attend the reception at Oscar's. However, I intend to enjoy some solitude tomorrow. I find Silk to be far too intense for my liking."

Kristano is meandering through his garden in Avignon Friday morning, watching the sun rise. He finds such an environment quiet and contemplative. Kristano is thinking of several issues at the same time: Aurea, his sister, Order business, the blood debt, his incredibly long existence, what the future might hold. He is sitting on a bench, deep in thought, when suddenly, Maurana appears, sitting next to him.

"Lost in thought again, Vitzameri? That seems to be happening to you more frequently. It is an improvement over you sitting in your study and just brooding. That I will give you."

"I am trying not to brood anymore. I don't see the point of wallowing in sorrow. The blood debt will be discharged in a few months, and then I can decide what to do next. I really have pretty much decided what I intend to do once the blood debt is resolved. I think it is time to let go. I probably should have shortly after the demise of my sister. There is no excuse for how I acted. I do see that now."

Maurana nods. "Have you spoken of this with Aureoso at all? He is the oldest Ruby after you. Is he prepared to be our titular head? Has he even given it any consideration?"

"Aureoso and I have spoken of this before. I have not spoken to him of it recently. I don't think it would be prudent until the blood debt is settled and then I can formally seal my fate. I am sure he will be fine with it. I would not be surprised if he wanted to continue working with you. You have been my right hand for several decades, and I truly do appreciate it. Of course, you would not have to work with Aureoso if you do not care to. I don't think you have had many dealings with him."

"I have not had many dealings with Aureoso, true. As for working with him as I have worked with you, I would certainly consider it. I do intend to take a brief break after the blood debt is settled though, depending on developments regarding Victor and Zoe Trent that could change."

"How likely do you think it is that they are returning Atlantean elders? If they really are, they could have very useful information about some sites that might not have been totally destroyed in the upheavals that destroyed the landmass. Maybe one of them was involved in sealing the great vaults. If so, they can hopefully recall the codes. I know it is too soon to probe, but it is something to keep in mind."

"Far too soon for that, tempting though it sounds to jump the gun. Past life regression gets more difficult and more dangerous to the subject the further back you go. It takes finesse on the part of the one who is guiding the regression and deep trust on the part of the one who is undergoing it. I don't think that we have won

Victor's trust entirely. Zoe seems to very much trust Nina. I don't think Cassie Mae could really handle Victor in that regard. Silk or Johanna very likely could. I will have to approach the subject with Aurea in due course. Speaking of which, how do you feel about her idea of you making a public apology to her in front of a gathering of the Red and Greens?"

Kristano looks pained. "It really does not matter what I think of it. If that is what Aurea chooses to have me do and the society is willing to accommodate us, then that is what shall happen. Yes, I would prefer to have all of this done very privately. However, what I did to her was very public. So, I shall do precisely as she wishes. She was the one who was harmed. Rejecting Plinthi, actually holding a trial, by the ancient gods, I really want to know what I was thinking. Apparently, I was not."

"It was madness, pure and simple. That's very rare among us. However, you have been around longer than just two other vampires. The researchers kept insisting that we are not functionally immortal, but no one knows for sure how long we can endure." She takes his hand. "You are a very young soul, Kristano. You likely would have had several hundred more lives by now. You should have several before anyone seeks you out to become a vampire again. To the extent that I can arrange that, I shall. You should rest awhile on the other side before coming back. You must have had astonishing karma to end up on this side this long."

"What you say makes sense, Maurana. You have long been a great counselor and an outstanding friend. I shall certainly reflect on all of this." He stands up. "For now, there is much that I ought to attend to."

Early Friday evening at Becker's, Rachel and Cassie Mae are sitting and talking to Silk as the audience is trickling in. Cassie Mae is nervous, Rachel is intrigued, and Silk is talking animatedly. "I think that you two will really like Zoe. She is every bit as intelligent as Victor, and she is more outgoing than he is. She is very intuitive, and she can smell a lie a mile away. We are so fortunate to have found both of them when we did. I know they will be great friends to us and incredible assets to Order Ruby. I look forward to having them around the next several centuries."

Cassie Mae sighs. "I am still having issues with the whole concept of twin flame. I mean, I get it about serial lives and soul mates. What Victor and Zoe apparently are is just playing with my head. Knowing how close they are, I definitely want to make a good first impression. I mean, if Zoe doesn't like me, Victor is likely to ask for a transfer. You know, I find I am actually enjoying having him as my porfo."

Silk smiles. "Just be yourself, and I am sure Zoe will like you just fine. As for what they are to each other, twin flame is the ultimate soul mate. You have many soul mates. They are your cohorts, the people you spend a great deal of time with in your serial lives over the years. You only have one twin flame. There can be no secrets. It is an intimacy known only by a few. If you are with your twin flame, it means the two of you will be doing something vital during that lifetime. Victor and Zoe are vexed because they are brother and sister. The first time we laid eyes on them at that club in California, Vernon and Walter thought that that was a shame. The way they interact, they would make an incredibly solid couple."

Rachel looks perplexed. "Well, if that is what they want, then why don't they just do it? Many brothers and sisters are sexually intimate. Some even become vampires and carry on. What's the issue?"

Silk shakes her head. "Victor and Zoe are honorable individuals. Yes, you will see that the sexual tension is there. They don't try to hide it. However, since they are brother and sister, they would never act on it, not even as vampires I don't think. They both accept that their destiny this lifetime is to pair bond with a significant soul mate if, in fact, they do that at all."

She grins. "You will be in awe when you see them together. The energy is incredible. They will change the mood of this room. You can't help but notice them."

Cassie Mae just shakes her head. "I just wish I wasn't so nervous. It's all the anticipation." She stops for a moment. "They are here. I sense Victor's thought patterns. He is excited and nervous too."

They turn and face the door. Sure enough, there stand Victor and Zoe. Victor looks proud with his sister at his side. Zoe is looking around the club, taking it all in. The mood in the club, while pleasant already, lightens even further. Cassie Mae is indeed awestruck, finding the energy just incredible. Zoe breaks into a broad grin when she sees Silk. She takes Victor's arm, and they walked over to the table.

Victor smiles warmly. "Zoe, this is Cassie Mae Adler, my proctor. She is teaching me well."

Zoe smiles when Cassie Mae stands up. She gives her a hug, which catches Cassie Mae off guard a little. "I am so pleased to meet you! Victor has spoken so very highly of you! Thank you for taking good care of him."

Cassie Mae is stunned but quickly regained composure. "I am honored by your brother's kind words, Zoe. I think he has taught me more than I have taught him. He is a joy to work with—and a great friend as well. I am glad we crossed paths at that party at the Spanish embassy."

Rachel stands and shakes Zoe's hand. "I'm Rachel Penn, longtime friend of Cassie Mae and Silk. Welcome to Washington. Tonight will be great with Silk and the band. Tomorrow at Oscar's, well, that will be another issue entirely. Tell me, Zoe, were you surprised to find out that vampires are real?"

Everyone sits down after Zoe gives Silk a warm hug. "No. Discovering that vampires were real was not a surprise in any sense. My Uncle Reggie and my brothers often discussed the so-called paranormal. I thought that it was essentially inevitable that vampires existed. The surprise is the structure, how you folks came to be, the different orders, that sort of thing." Zoe laughs. "It was mildly disappointing to find out you couldn't turn into mist or shapeshift."

Everyone at the table laughs about that, brightening the mood still. Silk waves when she sees Oscar and Kathleen walk in. "Wow. It is looking like the big reception tomorrow night is getting upstaged by my band's show tonight. It's such a pity." Silk looks over at Zoe after Oscar and Kathleen introduce themselves to her and sit down. "I have been told that shapeshifting can be done, but I am also told it burns energy like mad and is so painful that it makes the transformation process seem pleasant. I don't know anyone who has tried it." She stands up. "I'd best be joining Vernon and Walter. Show will be starting soon."

Anneliese enters the club as Silk heads off to the back. She has come tonight in spite of Johanna's advice that she not attend. Her words still echo in her mind: "I certainly won't order you not to go to Becker's tonight, but you would do well to consider the dynamics of the situation you are likely to find. Zoe will be meeting Cassie Mae for the first time. Victor will be on pins and needles. All that will be over tomorrow when the reception at Oscar's home takes place. Much better environment, I would think, for your first meeting. Do what you think is best." Anneliese decides to go. She feels like she has to. Besides, this is a nightclub, right? This is her old environment. She takes a look around. At least she thought it would be. Clearly, blues clubs are not the same as dance clubs. She squares her shoulders and starts walking toward the table they are all sitting at. Kathleen notices her and motions for her to come over. Anneliese plants a smile on her face and sits next to Kathleen.

Cassie Mae looks over at Anneliese. "It's a pleasure to meet you. I understand that you knew Victor back in Southern California. How do you like working for Johanna?"

Anneliese perks up. "Madam Johanna is the best, Cassie Mae. I am learning a real trade from her. I'm also learning to speak properly so people stop thinking I'm some kind of ditz, you know?" She then looks over at Zoe, whom she can feel is assessing her. She extends her hand. "It is an honor to meet you, Zoe. Victor and Madam Johanna have spoken very highly of you. I heard you helped with the Dave West case."

Zoe shakes her hand firmly, her eyes seeming to look right into the depths of the other woman's soul and finding her to be quite wanting. "Yes, I was able to help Dianne see that she needed to leave this plane and take another turn at the wheel. You knew Dave, right? I understand you used to be Cliff Nash's porfa."

Anneliese nods. "I knew Dave fairly well, yes. I do miss Cliff, but he and Lady Aurea thought it would be for the best if I came out here. How are you getting along with Nina?"

Zoe remains cordial, but Anneliese can sense that she is purposely remaining distant. "Nina is intelligent and easy to get along with. She says she learns more from me than I am learning from her. Perhaps that is so."

The house lights dim, and the performance lights come on.

During the first set, Victor senses a level of tension between his sister and Anneliese. As far as Cassie Mae is concerned, he knows that Zoe accepts her. Cassie Mae is in awe of Zoe but looked upon Anneliese as being an outsider, an interloper, even a potential rival.

Victor catches Cassie Mae's eye and sends a thought her way. *So, what do you think of Zoe?*

Cassie Mae is startled but smiles and thinks back, *She is incredible, Victor. I can just feel how strong your ties with her are. I really am pleased that she likes me.*

After the first set, Victor excuses himself to go to the bathroom. Rachel goes off to talk to Vernon Scott. Oscar, Kathleen, and Cassie Mae get up to work the crowd and find themselves a quick meal. That leaves Anneliese alone with Zoe. Anneliese looks over at Zoe, who is again regarding her rather coolly.

"I really like your brother, you know? He is one of the few guys I have ever known who treated me nice, like I really matter. I really hope I can prove myself to you and that we can be friends. I'd like that."

Zoe regards her with a level of amusement. "You want to prove yourself to me and be my friend? You can start by not trying to play me. You do far more than like Victor; you are in love with him. You also know that while he likes you, he certainly doesn't feel the same. Victor will not give his heart easily. He might not marry the first woman he has sex with, but I can tell you that such a woman will be someone he deeply cares about. You think you can be that woman, Anneliese? Stranger things have happened. Learn to be honest around me because I will catch any falsehood, conscious or otherwise. I am sure you grasp that."

Anneliese looks at Zoe wide eyed. She is stunned. "Like, I did not know how transparent my feelings are, you know? I must be so easy for you to read it's just, like, pathetic." She catches herself and shakes her head. "You even got me so nervous that I slipped back into my previous mode of talking." She looks and sees that Victor is on his way back, as is Cassie Mae. "I will really think about what you said, Zoe."

After Victor and Cassie Mae sit down, she looks over at Anneliese and sees the emotional tumult going through her mind. She lightly probes her surface thoughts and finds them amusing. She smiles sweetly. "Are you enjoying the performance, Anneliese? I don't think this is really your preferred type of music, is it? I think you are more at home with the techno or dance clubs. Am I right?"

"You are right, Cassie Mae. I so rule on the dance floor. But the passion in Silk's music is incredible. They sing it like they really lived it." She frowns. "Duh. Of course they do. Because they did. I still have a problem grasping just how long vampires can live. I hear that Vitzameri dude is over fifty thousand years old. What he must have seen and experienced. That must be incredible. How long do most vampires live?"

Oscar laughs warmly as he sits down. "Well, Anneliese, we vampires have a saying, a rather callous one that tends to be true nevertheless. It goes thusly: if you can make it through the first twenty years, you will likely make it to about eight hundred years. Those first twenty years can be really rough." He looks over at Victor and Zoe. "For you two, I think it will be a cakewalk. You have both been down that road before, maybe even more than once. I know I will be expected to address you as Lord and Lady, and I shall defer."

Victor looks over at Oscar. "I will never expect you to address me as Lord, Oscar. It just doesn't seem to be proper. Even if all that Madam Aurea suspects to be true of Zoe and me is the case, it still doesn't ring right in my mind. Seems we could use a little more level playing field in the Order. Don't you think?"

Kathleen and Rachel return and sit down. Oscar looks at Victor thoughtfully. "I do know what you are trying to say, Victor. Perhaps all the sir, madam, lady, and lord does sound strange to you. They are titles of respect in the Order. There really is no such thing as a level playing field when it comes to vampires. As you know, with us, age is power. One becomes more powerful as one ages. Much fairer than what happens to the regular humans, I would say. An interesting phenomenon, and I have seen it myself, is that returned elders regain their powers shortly after transformation. It is really quite stunning. I envy you both in that regard." He sighs. "In other ways, I do not. Soon, you will be dealing with Avignon, most likely Lady Maurana. I am sure the Vitzameri will take a keen interest in you both for various reasons."

Zoe nods. "I look forward to meeting them both. To change the subject, I understand that the transformation process is very painful and changes one's appearance slightly. How bad is it?"

All four of the vampires at the table cringe at the memory of their transformation. Kathleen takes a small handheld computer out of her purse and punches in some data lightning fast and shows Victor and Zoe the result.

"The actual transformation is painful, but not terribly so. It is what happens a couple of hours afterward that is the stuff of nightmares. Your body undergoes a total purge. It takes about ten minutes, and it is horrible. As to the change in appearance, well, this is what you and Victor would look like if you transformed tonight. Your skin goes about a shade paler, and your eyes acquire what we call the vampire cast. On people with hazel eyes like you two, it is particularly marvelous." Victor nods, as does Zoe. The band starts its second set. Victor catches the tension between Anneliese and Cassie Mae even more. Zoe is essentially ignoring her this time around. He really feels caught in the middle. He shoots a thought over to Cassie Mae.

Do you think that Anneliese is really that pathetic?

Cassie Mae looks over at him and thinks back. *No, but she has a lot of growing up to do still. I think Johanna has done wonders with her. Just relax and enjoy the show.*

Victor nods and tries to do that.

Just before midnight, Van Arpel is wandering the streets of the south Bronx. He walks quietly, purposefully looking for some trouble. If he is really lucky, he reasons, he might even find a recently made undead fiend to destroy. He has seen a few people walking the streets, but no one seems to want to approach him. This is no surprise to him. The last guy who tried to mug him ended up very much dead and certainly not lamented. As he saw it, that was simply doing his civic duty.

He hears a commotion going on down a rather dark alley. With a shrug, he makes his way down to investigate. Luck is with him that night. He finds a very terrified thug who is about to be done in by a rather foolish young Sapphire vampire. Arpel knows the vampire was recently turned because those who had been at it for any length of time did not go for this sort of ambush hunting. He has terrified his victim, showing no finesse whatsoever. He agrees that this thug is scum and should die, but not like this. The vampire is not paying any attention to Arpel, who has removed a small, sharp, wooden stake from his jacket. Just as the vampire sinks his fangs into the neck of the screaming man, he quickly thrusts the stake into the vampire's back, piercing his heart. The vampire falls to the pavement in a heap.

The terrified thug looks at Van. "What in blazes is that thing, man? It had fangs! Did you kill it?" He looks on as Arpel takes a machete out of his coat, shaking his head as he bends down to the still form.

"Nah. The stake through the heart simply immobilizes them. If I took this out, this undead fiend would be in a lot of pain, but he would recover. Have to cut his head off. Then I will know I have sent this fiend's soul screaming to hell, where creatures of Satan such as he belong." He looks at the thug, who is still shaking. "What were you doing out in this alley this time of night? There are plenty of nasty folks out that make this guy seem almost tame by comparison, unless, of course, you would happen to be one of those folks?"

"Not me, man. I was just walking home from work, you know? Yeah, that's what I was doing. This alley was a shortcut!" He cringes as Arpel glares at him. Sweat pours off of him in spite of the cool evening, as he is frightened beyond belief.

"I should strike you down where you stand. You are a liar and a purveyor of products of death. However, I am feeling charitable tonight. Give me your stash and your cash and I will let you walk out of here. I don't care if you talk about vampires. They are real, and the more people understand that, the safer people will be. I would gather that no one would believe the likes of you. Do you want to live?"

The thug empties his pockets and hands Arpel a roll of hundred-dollar bills and several bags of cocaine. He pockets them and points toward the alley exit. The guy runs out of there quickly, never looking back. Arpel chuckles and then looks at the still form of the vampire. He has a very startled look on his face, eyes still wide open.

"I wonder if you can hear me, fiend. Your mere existence was a blasphemy in the eyes of the Lord. I am here as his instrument. In a few more minutes, your soul will be freed from this undead shell, and you will go to spend eternity in the eternal flames of hell." He bends down and removes the Sapphire ring from his hand. It is not glowing, so he knows no help will be coming for this fiend. He puts the ring into his pocket. "Guess I will add it to my collection." He stands up, raises his machete, and cuts the vampire's head off with one blow. Picking up the head, he tosses it into a nearby trash bin. He lights a match and ignites the contents. Once he is satisfied that the flames will consume the head, he walks out of the alley and back onto the street.

Van thinks deeply as he resumes his stroll. *I won't call my sister tonight. That youngster is not what I came to New York City to find.* He comes to an intersection where he can see some of the skyline of Manhattan. *I sense I will find the one that I seek here. I know there are important undead elders in this city. It's time I was about the Lord's work and thinned their ranks. Once I do that, then I will call my poor, benighted, undead sister.* He clenches his fists in rage. "I will not fail to destroy the undead fiend this time. This I swear!"

Shortly after midnight, Carol Ann and Paulina are making the rounds of Central Park. It has been an entertaining evening. Some kid who was high on angel dust had actually tried to jump Paulina, who had him literally dead to rights before Carol Ann was ready to feed. Paulina talked her out of it, saying that blood filled with dust chemicals just would not be enjoyable. They are approaching a rather dejected-looking elderly gentleman sitting on a bench. Carol Ann decides to approach while Paulina keeps a discreet distance.

Carol Ann sits down next to the man. She can smell that death is near for him, and from his surface thoughts, she can tell that he knows this.

He looks over at her briefly with sad eyes and then resumes starting at the ground. "Time was, young lady, that I would have much enjoyed your company. Sadly, now, well I could not function that way even if I wanted to. Nothing left for me anymore. No family, no friends."

Carol Ann puts on mild charm glamour, hoping to cheer the man up a bit. It does work somewhat, in that the man looks at her with some sparkle in his eyes. "It's hard for me to believe that an intelligent man like yourself does not have any friends. No family, well, that can happen. Want to talk about it?"

The man sighs. "What is there to say? My wife died a couple years ago. My children don't want anything to do with me because I have no money. The company I worked for went under five years ago, so I lost most of my pension. To top it off, about five months ago, I was diagnosed with an aggressive form of brain cancer. They said I had six months to live at most. So, I spend most of my evenings here in Central Park. Basically, people leave me alone. Even the punks can tell that I don't have anything worth taking."

Carol Ann shoots Paulina a pained look. Paulina just shrugs, gesturing that this is her call to make. Paulina knows what Carol Ann is going to do here. This person's life can be measured in days, and he has nothing to really live for in his mind.

"Too bad we don't have a fledgling with us. Someone who desires death makes a very convenient first kill. Not my time yet," she mutters under her breath.

Carol Ann looks deeply into the man's eyes, looking into the depths of his soul. "My name is Carol Ann. I can make this pain end for you tonight if you want it to. There is no need for you to suffer any longer."

The man looks at her with hope. "My name is John. You can end the pain? I have been ready for this moment for a long while. I miss my wife so. Maybe I will find her again on the other side. The only release from this pain would be my death. If it won't hurt very much and you can make it quick, then I will say bless you and please do it. The universe is kind after all."

Tears well in Carol Ann's eyes as she replies, "It won't hurt at all. I promise. Just go into the light once you see it. If you are meant to be with your wife again, then she will be waiting for you."

She bares her fangs and sinks them into his neck. His blood tastes of the cancer, but she forces herself to drink. She soon feels his heart slowing. After barely taking a pint, his heart stops. She feels his last breath and sees a smile on his face as his body goes limp. Paulina comes over as Carol Ann dissolves into tears, cradling the dead man in her arms. Shortly thereafter, a park ranger comes into view, and Paulina motions for him to come over.

The young man looks perplexed. "What has happened here, ladies? Is this man ill? Does he need help?"

Carol Ann lets the man go and stands up. "No. He is beyond anyone's help. He died in my arms as I was talking to him, the poor, dear, sweet man. He deserved a far better end to his life than this."

The park ranger takes out his radio. "I'll call for the coroner. I'll need statements from the two of you."

Carol Ann smiles at the ranger and looks into his eyes. "You don't need us to stay. You just found this poor man dead on the bench and discovered he was dead. You never saw us. We weren't here." He stands there mesmerized as she and Paulina walk out of sight.

"Well, that sure took most of the fun out of the evening. Are you going to tell Aurea that you just performed another mercy killing, or do I just chalk this up to yet another of your acts of kindness and just pretend like it never happened? You know that she would take a very dim view of this."

Carol Ann nods. "I will appreciate your silence on this matter. What Aurea does not know about, we don't have to hear about. She thinks I am too tenderhearted at times. Do you think so?"

Paulina sighs. "I think that you do what you believe to be best. You are true to yourself. You are not ruthless and ambitious like Aurea, although, I must say that I saw a different side of her there in

Italy. Going home has affected her in a positive way." She smiles. "I will keep silent about this, of course."

"Thank you, my friend. Let's get back home now and get some rest."

Early Saturday evening, Oscar is finishing preparations for the reception. He is a fastidious host, and he wants to make sure that all, mortal and vampire alike, will be comfortable. He enjoys having his home be the social center for Order Ruby in metro DC. Tastefully elegant, the estate reflects the man that he has become over the years. The rich draperies, the polished mahogany, the crystal chandeliers, the whole property speaks of the success that he has earned. He looks up the grand staircase to see Allison, his porfa, starting to walk gracefully down. She is wearing a full-length red ball gown with a bodice that leaves little to the imagination. She favors him with a smile, and he nods their usual form of greeting.

When she reaches the bottom of the stairs, he takes her hand and they walk into the ballroom. Plates of food line the tables, as do bottles of some of the very best wines of the world. Allison nods in approval.

"As usual, Oscar, you have outdone yourself. The porfi in attendance should be pleased with the selection. I gather our Vamphyri guests will have fed, or will feed, elsewhere?"

"That's very likely, my dear. Still, if one should be famished, I do have a few bags of blood in my private refrigerator." He scowls. "We will have to keep an eye on Lester. With all that anger in him, I wonder how he did manage to get through his first twenty years. I doubt anyone else will be a problem."

"I don't think that even Lester likes Lester. Best to keep him away from the wine, it would be wasted on him anyway, and he doesn't handle it well. Are any Emeralds coming tonight?"

"I have an acceptance from Tom Rice and Stephanie Moureau. They are very nice, cultured individuals, also very studious and scholarly. I think that Victor will find them to be most suitable company."

Allison smiles. "Victor is a very nice man. I have noticed that he tends to be quiet in groups, being very attentive to all that is going on around him. Some likely mistake him for being oblivious. Having been with him a couple of times, I know that is not true."

The doorbell rings, and Allison goes over and opens the door. Seeing Johanna and Anneliese, she curtsies and bids them enter. Johanna is surprised by the gesture, while Anneliese does not have the slightest notion what the other woman has done.

Johanna nods in approval. "Very well done, Allison. I have not seen anyone do a proper curtsy in many years." She walks over to Oscar and gives him a hug. "Great to see you again, Oscar. The house looks marvelous, as always." She looks over at Anneliese. "Go on into the ballroom, dear. I smell a feast in there that makes me long to be a mortal again. Well, almost."

"Thank you, Madam Johanna." Anneliese turns to Oscar. "Thank you so much for your hospitality, Oscar. Will Victor and Zoe be arriving soon?"

At that point, the doorbell rings again. Allison opens it. Victor and Zoe are standing there, arm in arm. Victor is wearing a dark suit and tie. Zoe is wearing a forest green gown that accents her eyes. Allison curtsies for them. Victor bows and takes Allison's hand and kisses the air above it. To the surprise of all but Victor, Zoe also curtsies properly.

"Please do come in. I am sure the others are right behind you. Madam Johanna and Anneliese are already here."

Victor enters and shakes hands with Oscar. Zoe gives Johanna a hug and shakes hands with Anneliese. True to Allison's observation, the others arrived in short order. First to arrive are Lester and Kathleen. Albert Sidney arrives next, closely followed by Rachel and Cassie Mae. A couple minutes later, Tom and Stephanie arrive.

Oscar and Allison direct all of them to the ballroom. Oscar is playing the ever-cordial host, and Allison is fulfilling the role of hostess perfectly. Both of them are clearly in their element.

Victor and Zoe are standing near the center of the room. Zoe is marveling at it, taking everything in. Victor has been here a few times prior. He notes Lester standing off to the side, staring at him. Zoe turns and looks at him as well. When she does, he looks away.

"That guy really doesn't like me. We've never even really talked. The others have told me to just pay him no mind. Hard to do when you are talking about a vampire, a being that could snap my neck like a twig. He really does worry me at times."

Johanna walks over, looks over at Lester, and smirks. She turns to Victor and Zoe and smiles. "Don't worry about Lester. He wouldn't dare harm a hair on your head, Victor. He wouldn't have to wait for Aurea to come down and destroy him. He knows what I would do to him, not to mention what Cassie Mae would do to him as well." She regards Zoe for a moment. "So, what do you think of the District?"

Zoe laughed. "I really see this city through a similar prism to Victor's. This is the modern-day equivalent of Imperial Rome. However, the architecture isn't anywhere near as good. As for the local Ruby community, you folks are not much different from the ones that I interact with on the west coast. Well, likely a bit more formal. I can't imagine a reception like this being put on by Nina or Cliff in Santa Barbara or LA." She looks over at Anneliese. "I understand that poor waif is now your porfa. How is she working out?"

"On the job, Anneliese is doing well. She is still learning the social graces, definitely. I know she went to Becker's last night even though I recommended she refrain from doing so. She acted rather embarrassed today. I hope that she did not make a complete nuisance of herself."

Victor tenses a bit, watching as Zoe nods.

"Let's just say that Anneliese and I had a very constructive conversation. I don't think she will be any problem. Victor knows I don't think she is his type." She notes Cassie Mae approaching. "Now her, on the other hand, she shows a great deal of promise."

Cassie Mae walks up and nods to Zoe and Victor. Johanna takes her leave, going off to talk to Oscar.

"You know, you two make a great couple. You really do. The energy, the synergy, it is all there. I am sure if you were not brother and sister, you would be a couple. What tricks the Weave plays on all of us."

Victor smiles. "Zoe and I have talked about all of this. Yes, we would be a couple if we weren't related. In this life, however, we were fated to be together, but not in that fashion. Has to do with karmic debt and what she and I need to learn in this incarnation. So, we accept our situation as best as we are able."

Cassie Mae lets that sink in for a moment. "What do you think happened that made it your karma to be together as twin flame and not be able to be a full couple in the classic sense of the term?"

Zoe sighs. "Victor and I were husband and wife in our last life. We lived in Germany during the reign of Hitler and the Nazis. We had a chance to make a positive difference there. We knew that what Hitler was doing was wrong. The promise of power was simply so tempting, especially after having hope crushed during the years of the great inflation in the Weimar Republic. As it happened, Victor and I ended up being high-ranking party members. We both worked in the propaganda ministry. We had authority, and we knew what was really happening. Sometimes our conscience bothered us, but not enough, sadly."

A look of disbelief went across Cassie Mae's face. "You sound so certain of this. Most people only remember bits and pieces of their past lives, even the most recent one. Do you remember your names? Did you have any children? Have you seen pictures of yourselves?" She blushes. "I'm sorry. You don't have to answer those questions. It's just, I have not met mortals before who were so matter of fact about this."

Victor nods somberly. "We have known since our middle teens. Uncle Reggie took us to a top-notch past life regression hypnotherapist in Los Angeles. Zoe and I suspected much, given the kind of dreams we had and the things that we just knew when we were young. Only took a couple of sessions for us to be sure. The therapist was quite profoundly shocked. Who were we? We were Helmut and Eva Strauss. Did we have children? Yes, two boys and one girl. Our daughter still lives, not that we would try to contact her. As for having seen pictures of ourselves, well, what do you make of this?" Victor takes a photo out of his wallet and hands it to Cassie Mae. She looks at it, looks at them, and hands it back.

"My God. It looks so similar to how you two look now, not exactly the same, but that is just incredible. I really only have solid recollections of my most recent past life, and that only came about several years after I became a vampire." She looks at them both with a sense of wonder.

Zoe smiles. "I don't know why more people don't choose to know themselves. A big part of that is learning the lessons of one's previous lives so that you can avoid making the same mistakes. That seems to be a tall order for most people. I don't relate well to the commons, granted." She notes Lester finally coming forward, being somewhat prodded by Kathleen. "Ah. This should be most interesting." She turns to Cassie Mae. "We will talk some more later. Have to deal with a snake now."

Cassie Mae steps away, stifling a chuckle as Lester and Kathleen approach.

Lester scowls as he extends his hand to Victor. Victor shakes it firmly. Kathleen nods to Victor and shakes hands with Zoe. The four of them look at each other intently, taking each other's measure.

Lester shrugs. "You are a formidable man, Mr. Trent." He looks over at Zoe. "You, madam, are both brilliant and beautiful. Seeing the two of you together proves some of the points my colleagues have made." He scowls as he looks back over at Victor. "You know that I was opposed to bringing you into Plaz Seschni. I thought that what happened that night at the Spanish embassy constituted a threat to all of us."

"I was told of your concerns, yes. You know, to an extent, I don't blame you for feeling that way. Still, I prefer very much still being alive, so I guess it was better that I did not run into you someplace and have that happen." Victor looks over at Cassie Mae across the room. "The fates were kind to me that night."

Lester did laugh at that, to the astonishment of most present. "Yes, it is preferable to be alive and well. I will go along with that. I might never buy into the official line that you and your sister are returned ancient elders, but I will say that you both have my respect. That is something I grant to very few. You need not worry about my intentions anymore, sir. If ever you require my assistance, I will be there for you."

Kathleen nods. "Same here to both of you. However, Victor already knew that from me. I had my reservations before we met, but once I did, I agreed that Madam Aurea chose the proper course of action. You know, I am somewhat surprised that she did not make an appearance tonight."

Lester and Kathleen take their leave as the two Emeralds, Tom and Stephanie, make their approach. They both greet Victor and Zoe warmly.

"Tom and I are thrilled to be able to meet the two of you. Believe it or not, you both have piqued the interest of many circles in our order. Why, I have been told that even the first speaker, Lady Sybille, has taken an interest in you." She shows off her Emerald ring. "You sure you two wouldn't rather be in our Order? We might not party as much as Ruby does, but you two strike me as being more studious types anyway." She smiles at Zoe. "The ring would look so good with your dress!"

Zoe laughs. "I see your point, Stephanie. You know though, I really do have an affinity for the Ruby ring. From the first time I wore one that night I met Nina Parks, it just really felt right. I have had a past life vision where I was wearing such a ring, as has my brother. So, I have to say we are sticking with Ruby."

Tom nods. "I didn't expect you to accept. Knowing what I do know about the two of you, though, I will not be surprised to see you doing joint project with members of our Order. As for Sapphire, well, that is a completely different matter. There are a few civil types over there, but on the whole, a rough crowd."

Presently, Allison is passing out drinks, as Oscar is about to propose a toast. All eyes in the room are focused on him.

He smiles warmly. "I propose a toast to Victor and Zoe Trent. May they have many fruitful decades among us."

All raise their glasses and joined in the toast.

Victor looks over at Cassie Mae and smiles, raising his glass to her in a salute. She grins and does likewise. She lets her gaze linger on Victor as he turns back around and starts talking to Tom again. She has an odd, warm, pleasant feeling as she thinks of him, and on some level, that scares her.

I really think I have known him before, she thinks to herself, carefully shielding. *Could he have been someone that I once truly loved?* That thought startles her. She will need to reflect on that for quite a while.

Aurea is visiting a friend in Manhattan that evening, specifically the local commander of the post of Red and Greens. Sitting in a drawing room in a penthouse apartment with sweeping views, Colonel Matthew Adams, CSA, is listening intently to Aurea's presentation. She is very animated, very intense.

"I think it would serve two purposes, making the Vitzameri discharge his blood debt to me at one of your functions. First, it would give me the satisfaction of having a public apology, and second, he would have to do it in front of a society that he has never been willing to fully embrace the legitimacy of, in spite of the fact that he meets all the qualifications for membership. I think the Vitzameri dismisses this group because it was not created while Atlantis still existed." She preens a bit. "The Red and Green came to be during the late Roman Republic, which I guess makes it too gauche, too nouveau for his tastes."

Matthew nods, his face still bearing an intense expression. "I can see your line of thinking here. We do have a couple of functions later in the year where there would be a good number of us all in one place. However, I wonder just how suitable this would be for one of our gatherings? How would it impact our younger members to see the Vitzameri humbled so? We could not restrict this to only the Ruby members. In this society, as in most other situations, Emeralds and Rubies have equal standing. If this is to be done at one of our gatherings, it will have to be an honorable affair. As a member, you know that. What the Vitzameri did to you was certainly not honorable." He looks directly into Aurea's eyes. "Believe me. I can see where making him do this would be tremendously emotionally satisfying. I find it to be viscerally enticing as well. So, tell me, what would you really be hoping to accomplish by doing this?"

Aurea pouts. "I want him to feel some pain, to show some remorse for what he did. I know you were not around when this happened, at least not as who you are now and certainly not as a vampire, in any event, but I know you are familiar with my case. Lady Vetrina was my best friend. I underwent Plinthi several times, even went through a staged trial. A trial among us! He nearly had the panel he convened destroyed for finding me blameless in her death. I only escaped physical destruction because La Mer, the real assassin, convinced him it would serve no useful purpose." Her eyes glisten with tears. "I guess I do want to see him be humbled in public. Does that fly in the face of honor?"

"Not necessarily, Madam Aurea. It would depend on a salient point that only you can really answer for yourself. It would be treading a fine line though. Do you want him humbled, or do you want him to be humiliated? You know, it is hard to know what he would feel. From what I have heard, he is already humiliated by this whole affair. I have heard other things as well. Some say he has been struck by a debilitating madness, which does happen to a few of our number. Very few have been around anywhere near as long as he has in a single incarnation. At least that is what I have been told."

Aurea thinks for a moment. "You show wisdom beyond your age, Post Commander. You are right; it was humiliation I sought, not simply humbling. That would not be honorable and thus not in keeping with the tenets of the society. I need to give this matter more thought. The blood debt needs to be closed satisfactorily, and, much as it would please me, humiliation and public ridicule is not the most honorable way to do this." She looks over at him. "Pray, if this was your blood debt, what would you do?"

A look of surprise crosses the colonel's face. "You don't ask simple questions, do you? I have never faced such a dilemma, and I hope that I never will. You suffered from the Vitzameri's callousness and, dare I say, stupidity for longer than I have been around thus far. I can tell you what I hope I would do. I suspect that I would approach the person who wronged me, once the blood debt had been acknowledged, and meet with them privately. I would proceed to tell them exactly how this had affected me, physically and emotionally. I would then tell them I expect them to act honorably in the future." He pauses briefly. "Then I would tell them that I forgive them but they had best never expect me to forget what had happened."

"That is a very admirable approach. I keep trying to figure out what Lady Vetrina would want me to do. She was so kind and gentle. If the Vitzameri was driven into madness, her assassination likely pushed him in that direction. It is hard to get over it since he took so long to come to his senses." She looks at the colonel. "I shall certainly consider what you have said. No need for you to talk to the council about this, as I am withdrawing my request. However I end up handling this, I must concur that it is not a proper matter for the society." She rises and shakes his hand.

"I hope that we will see you at the conclave in July outside of Richmond. We would be honored if you would give a presentation about the destruction of the Society of Redemption. That is still a very timely topic of great interest."

"I was certainly in the thick of that fiasco. Order Sapphire is still reeling over that. Serves the creeps right though. They had a few Order Amethyst folks in cold storage, hoping to use them as focal point assassins. They probably would have done it, had there not been a porfa who defected. I will be there, Post Commander. As for the talk, yes, I will give one. I think it is time for that sordid tale to be told."

Arpel wanders through the empty warehouse in Brooklyn. It had stood derelict for some years. Reasonably empty, no homeless people were taking shelter within its walls. As he examines the building, it seems that no one had walked around in there for quite some time. There are some skylight windows, all shattered long ago. There is a narrow corridor of rooms that he thinks will be perfect for setting up a trap in. He has some particular targets in mind. The other evening, he had found out, by speaking to a particularly drunk porfo at a bar in Queens, that Greater New York boasted two elder vampires, one from the Emerald Order and one from the Ruby Order. Perhaps God would favor him and he would rid the world of both of these undead fiends. He goes into what was once the foreman's office and sits down.

He has managed to obtain an adequate amount of very caustic acids. His machetes are razor sharp, and his .45 is in pristine operating order. Now, he just has to design a trap that will hold his prey. He knows about how strong these fiends are and how fast they can move. His advantage is that he is somehow psychically invisible to them. However, he knows that in all other ways, he is truly outmatched. He is doing God's work. He is certain of that. He bows his head and prays, hands folded in supplication on the battered desk. He looks around in the dim afternoon light. Yes, he is certain he can make the proper trap. He will take his time doing it to make sure that he does it right. He is likely to only get one chance at pulling this off. He also surmises that he is only likely to destroy one of the undead elder fiends. He is somewhat partial to taking out the Ruby elder. After all, they are the scum who have made his beloved sister Abigail into one of them.

He slips out the door quietly and heads down the alley. Yes, he has a lot to do. However, he has plenty of time and enough funds that he can stay at a decent hotel for a couple weeks if he wants to. He smiles about that. Rolling a few drug pushers and offing a couple of muggers has set him up fairly well. He reaches a major street and simply blends into the crowd. To the casual observer, he looks fairly nondescript.

"How little most of them know," he says under his breath. "Tell most of these fools that vampires are real and they would laugh hysterically. Not funny at all. No, sir."

Late on the afternoon of Easter Sunday, Victor is driving Zoe back to Dulles International for her return flight to Los Angeles. As they are nearing the terminal, Zoe is finishing her rundown of the various people Victor is dealing with here.

"I definitely do not trust Lester any farther than I can throw him. He will not move to harm you openly, but don't expect him to assist you if you are in trouble unless he sees a way that it would be of immense benefit to him. Actually, knowing Aurea, it probably would be."

Victor nods as he turns off the highway and gets into the airport exit. "Johanna told me that Aurea pulled him aside and warned him explicitly of a painful destruction if he harmed me. He is an angry one, but I do not regard him as being stupid. Still, I intend to give him a very wide berth."

"You can definitely rely on Johanna, Rachel, and Cassie Mae. Oscar and Albert too, for that matter. I just love Silk and the Scott brothers. I know they will be coming back to SoCal in a few weeks." She glances at her brother and smiles. "If all you wanted was to get laid, brother dear, Anneliese would do you in a heartbeat. I know that isn't what you want; you want all the whistles and bells. You will find that woman. I really doubt she will be the one though."

Victor pulls up to the curb and pops the trunk. He gets out of the car as Zoe exits. They embrace warmly and give each other a kiss. "I can handle Anneliese, Zoe. Don't lose a moment's rest wondering about that. She is very sweet, but no, she really isn't my type. Have a safe flight home." He returns to his car and drives off.

Zoe waves and blows him a kiss and then enters the terminal for the flight to Los Angeles.

CHAPTER 11

Monday, 20 April 2009. Victor is working out that evening at the gym a few blocks from his Georgetown apartment. He does this three nights a week. He finds his Monday workout to be a great stress release, as that is usually the most hectic day at the office. As he is working out on the leg press, he reflects that the day was not that bad. He is getting ready to make another trip to New York City on Thursday. On this trip, he was also invited to attend a gathering Aurea was putting on. He knows the invitation is a command performance, but he really doesn't mind. At least he will have intelligent company one evening.

As he is finishing up on that machine and having a drink of water, he notes a sudden change in the atmosphere. A couple other sensitives working out note the change as well. He looks toward the front door and is astonished to see Cassie Mae there, sweet-talking her way into the gym. She is wearing a blue scoop neck t-shirt and tight, black shorts that left little to the imagination. She bats her eyes at the clerk behind the desk.

"Surely y'all can make an exception for me? I simply forgot my card, and I so need a workout after the kind of day I had."

Well, it works; the clerk grins like an idiot and lets her through.

Victor nonchalantly walks over to the lateral pull while Cassie Mae makes her way over. Nearly all the males are looking her over, some getting evil looks from their wives and girlfriends who are also there. Some of the women regard her with approval as well. She appears at Victor's side and smiles.

"So, what brings you here this evening? I didn't think that you needed to do any of this. I was told that was one of the benefits of transformation, great strength without having to work out."

She makes a fake pout. "Don't tell me you aren't happy to see me? Actually, I do come here fairly regularly. It is an easy place to feed. Plus, I just have so much fun playing head games with some of the jocks who hang out here." She scans the gym. "Most of the folks here are pretty nice. You chose a good gym to join." She waits as Victor does his two sets on the machine, and then she sits down.

Victor grins. "What weight level do you want to set this at? I doubt the sixty pounds I had it set at would be any sort of challenge for you." He shrugs. "For that matter, I doubt the max would be either."

She looks over at a burly young jock and makes sure she has his attention. "Go ahead and set it at three thirty, Victor. I want to totally blow that guy's mind."

Victor puts the pin into the weight stack at the very bottom. Cassie Mae flexes and pulls down the bar effortlessly, lifting the weight stack with stunning ease. The young man blinks and walks over and watches for a bit. Cassie Mae isn't even breaking a sweat doing this.

When she is finished, the guy sits down. "No way is this machine set up right. Begging your pardon, miss, but there is no way that you can lift three hundred and thirty pounds and make it look that easy. I could barely budge that myself, and I use machines just like this every day." He grips the handle, expecting to have the same results. Sure enough, he can only budge the weight stack by a few inches. He breaks out in sweat, muscles shaking and face contorting. He lets the bar go and stares at Cassie Mae in disbelief. "How…I mean, really, that is just the wildest thing that I have ever seen." He walks away, muttering to himself and shaking his head.

Cassie Mae smiles. "Give me a few minutes. I think I can get my evening meal out of that guy. I'll promise to tell him my secret. See you by the elliptical trainers?"

Victor uses his towel to wipe the sweat from his brow. "That sounds like a very good plan."

Victor only has a few minutes left in his cardio on the elliptical when Cassie Mae comes back, looking quite sated. "So, you feel like joining me for a drink afterward at the bistro a few doors down? You should relax after the flood of endorphins you get from this."

After wiping the sweat off his face, Victor smiles. "Actually, I could use a drink. It has been a hectic day."

After they arrive, they sit at a table in the back. Victor orders a mojito while Cassie Mae just asks for a glass of water. She studies Victor's face, marveling at the worry lines on his forehead, an unusually high number for someone not even thirty years old.

"Is today a really strange day for you, Victor?"

Victor looks perplexed for a moment, and then a look of recognition crosses his face. "Ah. You mean because today is Hitler's birthday. Yes, it does lend a strange vibration to the day. It brings back odd, fractured memories from the last life. At times, I find it difficult to accept that I was part of his apparatus in my most recent previous life. I'm nothing like that this time around."

"I have been told by various teachers that one must not dwell on the errors of previous lives, as they cannot be undone anyway. True, everything that Helmut was is part of you, but you are more than that, so very much more. Of that you can be quite certain."

"I know that only too well, Cassie Mae. I do well to not dwell on it like I did when I was younger. I am sure that my previous life has much to do with why I am so passionate about my philosophical and political viewpoints now. Experience is a harsh teacher." He takes a sip of his drink and smiles. "Your birthday is on the twenty-ninth, right? Made any plans yet?"

Cassie Mae raises an eyebrow. "Nice change of topic there. No, I haven't made any firm plans for my birthday, though if I know Rachel, she will want to do something." She smiles sweetly. "You apparently have something in mind?"

"Actually, yes I do. There is a new art gallery opening up that evening down in Fairfax. An acquaintance of mine from California is having some of her work showcased there. I thought it would be nice to do something that had nothing to do with imperial politics or Order politics. It will just be the two of us."

"That sounds quite marvelous, Victor. It's a date."

Arpel is mingling with the crowds that evening in Times Square. He is lost in thought, reflecting on the chain of events he is starting here. He will strike one Order, and possibly two Orders, a truly stunning blow. He heads toward a small bar and slips on an Emerald ring that he has taken from one of his kills. *Just have to keep up this masquerade for a few more days. Then I shall have my victory.*

Arpel walks in, and his ears are assaulted by the loud punk rock music coming from the stage. He shrugs and walks toward a table in the back. As he expects, the boisterous young man he has been talking to the past several days is sitting there, drinking a beer. The man sees Arpel and waves. The young man's name is Alfred, and he is a Ruby porfo for some undead fiend named Clark. That one is not his target, as he is after elders. Once his deed is done, he will let Alfred live and face the consequences of being far too talkative, which Alfred tends to be, especially when he is drunk, like now.

Alfred smiles as Arpel takes the seat next to him. "How's it going, buddy? Want a beer? I'll buy!"

Arpel just nods, and Alfred motions the cocktail waitress over and orders a beer, which she brings over promptly. He looks over at Arpel.

"So, enjoying your visit to the big city?"

"Yes, it has been interesting. Quite different than the little towns in West Virginia, where I am usually living. There is certainly something to be said for the solitude one can find just outside of those towns. Here, it is all hustle and bustle. There are so many people here. Still, quite the learning experience for me." Arpel smiles. "So, you were telling me about your friend Zack last night. He runs the local network?"

Alfred laughs. "Yeah! He's the network engineer for the Emerald and Ruby nets. He handles the mid Atlantic and New England states. I think in West Virginia, you guys would be handled out of Charleston. He's one of the best, and he has pledged to Emerald, your Order." He grins. "Madam Aurea keeps trying to talk him into joining us instead. He won't though, because he's sweet on this Emerald fledgling named Sydney. She's cute, and I don't blame him for falling for her. How about you? You got a girl?"

Arpel shakes his head. "I stay out of relationships. I don't like to be tied down. So, is there any chance that I could meet Zack, go and see his network setup? Bet I could learn a lot from him."

"Visit him at the network office? Not a chance, my friend. That place is well guarded. No one that they don't know even gets near that place. Heck, I don't even know where it is. I suppose Syd would know, but I don't travel in her circles." His face brightens. "I remember him saying he was going to catch a show on Thursday night. That's right! He's going to be here. You could meet him then, man!"

Arpel smiles and nods. "That would be grand, Alfred." He ponders that and decides it will work out very well since he wants to spring his trap by Friday. "Yes, I will make sure I am here."

"Great, man! The band that night is the Czarista Cosmonuts! They are totally awesome!"

Aurea and Carol Ann are talking in the office at their home. Paulina is out for her martial arts class. Aurea finds that situation somewhat amusing.

"Why is she still taking instruction? She has proven her abilities time and again. She is planning on becoming one of us in a couple more months, right?"

Carol Ann shivers at the thought. "Yes, she will undergo the transformation in a couple months. Right on the summer solstice is what she asked for. She says it will be a good omen. I don't pretend to know why she decided to undergo it so much sooner than she had originally planned to. I hope she fully understands what she will go through. Just thinking about what I went through all those years ago still creeps me out."

"Paulina is twisted enough that she might actually enjoy it on some level. Frankly, the disciplines she has learned through all that martial arts training will help her get through that and the first several years as a vampire. I don't think she will have much anxiety about not going out in the daylight without the proper gear. As it is, she doesn't seem to go out much during the day anyhow. She's a perfect night creature, that one."

The incoming call light blinks on Aurea's computer. She presses a button, and Zack's face appears. As usual, he is downing yet another energy drink. He blinks when he sees Aurea and Carol Ann.

"Good evening, Madam Aurea and Carol Ann. Hate to bother you, but one Tomas Gilbert, a Sapphire from Providence, wishes to speak with you. He insisted on a secure connection, but that doesn't surprise me. He likely does not want Dr. Olos Parana's people to know he contacted you." He slaps his head. "Duh! You will want to know why he is calling! Seems his porfa died under mysterious circumstances a few weeks back, and he thinks that Van Arpel might have been responsible."

Aurea looks over at Carol Ann, who seems dumbfounded. Then she looks back over at the screen. "I will speak to him. Thank you, Zack. Patch him through."

Zack's face leaves the screen and is instantly replaced by that of Tomas Gilbert. He has a very pained expression and looks very worried.

"Hello, Tomas. I understand your porfa was killed recently. I extend my condolences to you."

Tomas scowls. "Spare me the sentimentalities, Madam Enforcer. Sally was an exceptionally good servant of the Order and would have made an exceptional vampire. She was prepared to undergo initiation in about six months. Yes, I was very fond of her. Some would say more than I ought to have been." He looks Aurea in the eyes. "However, that is not why I have sought you out. I am convinced that her demise came at the hands of that murderous jerk Van Arpel. I know the circumstances don't match his modus operandi. Are you aware of the circumstances surrounding her death?"

Aurea shakes her head. "I am not aware of it. Given how little our Orders even converse, this is actually the first time I heard anything about this. So, you think this was Arpel's doing even though it doesn't fit?"

"It was odd. The day before she was killed, Sally called me from the bookstore and told me this guy had come in asking for books that I had allegedly written. Well, I have not published anything in all my years, so I knew this was some kind of ruse. She described him as odd and hard to read. I figured it was just some run-of-the-mill hunter, so I told her that if he came back, she should tell him that she found a collector and tell him to come over to my place that evening." He pauses. "I wonder if that had anything to do with her getting killed. Perhaps he did not believe I would be there. I really did give her leave to tell him my real address. Well, last I heard from her was a text message saying he was there. About a half hour later, I sensed that something was horribly wrong, even though I had received no distress signal."

Aurea looks thoughtful. "That is a possibility. If it was him, he might have figured this was a set up for an ambush. He probably did not think you would be at that address during the day. However, if it was him, she was dead no matter what she would have told him. So what did you find when you arrived at the bookstore? Was her ring still there? Was the body identifiable?"

Tomas sighs. "I dressed accordingly and risked the daylight. By the time I arrived, the bookstore was fully engulfed in flames. It took the fire department an hour to put it out. They found her body, very badly charred. They had to use dental records to identify her, but I knew it was her. I checked the ruins carefully, and I did not find the ring. I was able to attend the autopsy, and the findings were rather telling." He pauses to regain composure. "She did not die in the fire. She was already dead. The fatal wound was that her throat had been slashed. Though fire damage to the body made some conclusions rather tentative, there were marks that were likely made from caustic acids. She clearly died horribly to protect me."

"Caustic acids are definitely a tool of the trade for Arpel. Arson isn't, but if he became exceptionally agitated, as unbalanced as he appears to be, he might well have done something like that. I do know that he has not called his sister, Abigail, at the Richmond motherhouse since he killed Dave West and his porfa." She sits in silent thought for a moment. "Might be that Mr. Arpel is an egomaniac along with being a deranged killer. I don't think he would call his sister if he failed. It would likely shock him to the core of his being to fail. Very well, Tomas. I sense that your intuition is correct and this was the work of Van Arpel. I sense though that your call has more to it than reporting this tragic event to me."

Tomas wipes a tear off his cheek. "I want to put up a million in gold toward the reward for neutralizing that guy. I can send it to you folks via special courier so that Olos Parana's goons don't find out about it. I hope someone catches that guy alive. If they do, I am asking for just one favor, just one."

Aurea nods. "We accept your contribution. What is the nature of the favor you are requesting in the very unlikely event this man is taken alive?"

He smiles thinly. "I know that this would get me declared a pariah in the Order, but it would be so worth it. I want to take part in his very public execution, a death that I want to be very slow and painful. To be sure, chances are that he will die on the spot, and if that happens, so be it. In that case, I will want to shake that person's hand and congratulate them for ridding us of that threat once and for all."

"You shall have it then, sir. I give you my word-bond on that."

"I know your word is your bond, Madam Enforcer. No one has ever accused you of being a fraud."

On Tuesday evening, Arpel is back at the bar, talking to Alfred, working at extracting more information from him about the local vampires. He is quietly listening to a story that really holds little interest to him. "Anyway, yeah, a couple weeks back, I met this Ruby fledgling going by the name of Star. She's an exotic dancer, real popular and all. She is a totally hot babe, my man. So, like, she tells me she wants to do it with me. I'm like, whoa! Not unless you have some goldenrod oil, lady! Then she started to pout and—"

Suddenly, Arpel is interested. "Hold on, my friend. Why did you decline unless she had goldenrod oil?"

Alfred gives him a mystified look. "Don't tell me you don't know, man! Don't they tell you anything there in West Virginia? Mere mortals like us don't dare get intimate with vampires unless they use some goldenrod oil, not unless you want to risk having limbs torn off if they really get into it. From what I hear, they tend to be really passionate. Something to do with the transformation I guess. Sounds wicked cool actually."

Van thinks hard. "So this goldenrod oil takes away their superhuman strength and speed?"

"Exactly, man! It makes it so they are only as strong as a normal human for a couple hours or so. Then, yeah, you can party with them and not worry about accidentally getting turned into confetti. It has no effect on their psychic powers at all. I've been with a couple of Emerald and Ruby chicks who did use the rod, as we call it on the street. They were fine. Star refused to use, so I just said later and moved on."

"I see what you mean. That is interesting that something like that would affect them. Do they have to drink it to have it affect them, or do they have to inject it like some kind of drug?"

Alfred gulps down his beer and orders another one. "Nah, they don't have to do that. The babes I made it with just sprayed some on their arms. It gets absorbed by the skin. Agreed, it is something that it affects them adversely. Goldenrod is so benign to normal folks."

Arpel smiles and lets Alfred chatter on about his exploits. He will get some goldenrod oil both for his trap and for future ambushes. He finally has learned of a weakness that he can exploit easily. It will simplify his work for the Lord in exterminating these undead fiends.

Late on Thursday afternoon, Victor checks into his hotel room after having spent the better part of the day at the United Nations. This time, Moore is having him sit in on a conference regarding desertification of sub-Saharan Africa. A real concern, granted, but the solutions that he is hearing about there are simply absurd on their face.

"There are no political solutions to a technological problem," he muttered to himself.

The room phone rang, startling him a bit. He picks up the receiver. "Victor Trent speaking."

A female voice answers him in the special Plaz Seschni tongue he is just beginning to master. "Hi. This is Paulina Wong. I'm Carol Ann Vincent's porfa. I'm down here in the lobby. Care to join me for dinner? I know a decent place a couple blocks away, unless, of course, you have other plans?"

"That sounds fine to me, Paulina. I will be right down."

He throws on a jacket and takes the elevator down to the lobby. He watches the numbers click down. He enjoys that on some level, kind of a game that he plays in his mind since he was a young child and went to the skyscrapers in Los Angeles with his father. He had truly loved his father then. He cannot stand the man his father has become, but the good memories are still there. The elevator doors open and he sees Paulina sitting patiently on one of the comfortable chairs down here. This is an ostentatious hotel, one that he would never consider staying at except for the fact that Moore has an in with the owners and gave his staff dirt cheap rates. She sees him and stands up. She is wearing a stylish black jumpsuit and comfortable, low-heeled walking shoes. As he walks over to her, he reflects on what he does know about her. He only met her in passing on that rather fateful evening. They have conversed via e-mail and on the phone a few times since then.

Once he reaches her, she gives him a hug, somewhat catching him off guard. "Welcome back to New York, Victor. Certainly much better circumstances than the last time we met. Aurea and Carol Ann are making the final arrangements for the reception tomorrow night in Brooklyn." She scowls a bit. "Sorry. Party planning is just not my thing. I had the evening off, so I figured I would check in on you and see if you wanted to grab a decent meal. I do know of some really decent very reasonable restaurants in this city."

Victor holds the door open for her, and they start walking. "Well, these are certainly less bizarre circumstances than when we last met. I understand you passing on dealing with party planning; I'd have done the same." He smiles warmly. "I'm glad you decided to check on me. I was expecting to have to eat alone there in the hotel. So, where are we going?"

"There's a little Tibetan place just a couple blocks away. It's owned by a nice family, who is actually from Tibet. They managed to get out shortly after the Chinese government trashed the place. They are very nice people and serve up excellent food. I will miss them once I become a vampire." She looks over at Victor. "So how was the UN today? As ridiculous as I have heard?"

"Nothing beats actually going there and watching these people in action if you really want to reinforce a cynical outlook on the future of the human race. I mean, their solutions are always to make states do something. They never even consider encouraging individual, private-sector initiatives, not like there really is much of a true private sector in our mercantilist world."

They walk into the Tibetan restaurant, and they are seated promptly. Victor admires the décor and appreciates the aromas. He is scanning the menu when Paulina looks over at him.

"Do you trust me, Victor? I have been here lots of times. Let me order, and I guarantee you will like it."

Victor puts down the menu. "That sounds great to me, Paulina. I have never been to a Tibetan restaurant before. I don't think there are any in the mighty OC anyway. My Uncle Reggie used to rave about a Tibetan place on Lombard Street in San Francisco, but he says it closed a long time ago."

When the waiter returns, Paulina speaks to the man in very correct Tibetan. They converse rather animatedly. When he walks off, she turns back toward Victor. "Yes, I am Chinese. My family came out of the Hunan province, and my ancestors worked on building the railroads in the West. Anyway, since I am not Han, I have gotten along well with the Tibetans here in New York. Very small community of them settled here. They are a very quiet and private people." She grimaces. "They would not take well to knowing that we associate with vampires. It would appall them to know I intend to become one. Buddhist belief systems take a very dim view of blood drinkers. They don't really understand. Then again, to be honest, I don't think any formal belief system really does understand what it is all about."

The wait staff brings over the meal, and the two of them are silent for a couple of minutes, truly savoring the food.

"I was right to trust your judgment about this meal. It is nothing short of remarkable. You will have to e-mail me exactly what it was we had so I can come back here again sometime, or at least share this with Zoe and my Uncle Reggie. He will be quite envious, I'm sure."

"I can do that for you. If you were to come back and order some of this, the waiter would likely be surprised you knew of these dishes. Half of this meal was off menu. Like I said, I know the community well. So tell me, what do you think of Aurea? How does she make you feel? Do you have any lingering resentment over how you were tested? I certainly wouldn't blame you. That test was very harsh."

Victor considers his reply. "When I think about that test, I am still more mystified than resentful. On an intellectual level, I do understand why they did it. On an emotional level, I still find it troubling at times. Not so much when I am dealing with Cassie Mae. I know full well how she felt about it. This was Aurea's doing from the beginning. So what do I think of her? I respect her certainly; however, I do not know if I will ever fully trust her. I can tell that she has plans within plans. I have heard about some blood debt that the Vitzameri owes to her for a grievous wrong. I have also heard she carries the nickname of The Enforcer in some circles. I don't really know what to think completely until such time as I have spent some time alone with her, and I am not getting the impression that such is likely to happen anytime soon."

Paulina nods. "Sounds like I have you figured out pretty well, Victor. I do like you. I actually read your master's thesis. I found the scholarship remarkable, and I even checked out some of your reference material. You are definitely an intelligent man, and I respect that. Noting that, I am also certain there are certain nuances that you might not pick up on immediately. It isn't that you aren't observant; you are, but you automatically process some things as being trivial when they really aren't." She smiles. "Trust me on this, Victor. You are learning quickly, but you can use a few words of advice, especially when it comes to the mighty Madam Aurea. Do you know why there are those who call her The Enforcer?"

"From what I have read on Ruby Net, it has to do with the Order Amethyst Eradication and was further bolstered by the more recent destruction of the Sapphire Society of Redemption. It is generally not used as a title of respect or endearment. I also know that many regard her as being very bitter over being blamed for the death of Lady Vetrina by the Vitzameri. If she is, well, I would not blame her."

"Very well put, Victor. Well, there are two reasons I wanted to see you tonight, besides wanting to have some intelligent conversation and a great meal. The first is to give you some advice about dealing with Aurea. I have known her for some time now, and you are right; she does have plans within plans. Be wary of her, even once you do become a vampire. She will always keep her word-bonds to the letter. On those you may rely. So long as she views you as being useful, you will have nothing to fear from her. However, if you truly want to be able to trust her fully, you will have to get her to become your sister in the blood, which is something that she is not likely to want to do. I have never heard of her doing that."

"I will certainly keep all of that in mind, Paulina. What was the other reason you wanted to see me?"

Paulina blushes. "I'm going to undergo the transformation on the Summer Solstice. At sunset on the twenty-first of June, I will become Ruby irrevocably. I am fine with all that. Usually, they do not want a porfi observer because of the possible danger involved. As you have learned, sometimes transformations fail. Usually, that means that the initiate simply never regains consciousness and thus dies. However, sometimes a botched transformation will create a revenant. That is why there are always three vampires at a transformation. One actually does it, usually the eldest present, and the other two are there with very large blades to decapitate the initiate, should he or she become a mindless revenant. Anyway, they tell me that mine should go very smoothly, so I asked them if I could have an observer. They said yes. I'd like you to be that observer. I think you should see how this works. Will you do this for me?"

Victor is definitely surprised. "Wow. I wonder if they would have consented if they knew it was me that you had in mind for an observer." He thinks for a moment, and then it dawns on him. "You want me to be there because it is going to be Aurea bringing you across and you want to make sure she doesn't try something? Is that it? Or is it just that you will be more comfortable with someone else there?"

"She won't try anything, Victor. You are right; she will be bringing me across. A bit unusual, but they want me to have a powerful natra. They say it will be better for me in the long run, so I defer, especially since Carol Ann is just too tenderhearted to do it. Once I have gone over, I will be working with Aurea and Carol Ann, much as I do now. It will make me feel better to have someone else there." She wipes away a tear. "Also, I want you there to be able to console Carol Ann in the unlikely event that it does get botched. To put it mildly, she won't take it very well. I can tell that by the way she looks at me sometimes. So, will you do this? It will put my mind at ease to know you are there no matter what happens."

"I will make sure that I am here in New York on that evening. I guess we need to let Aurea and Carol Ann know about that tomorrow night at the reception." He pauses and thinks for a moment. "Why are you doing this so soon? It was my understanding that you were going to wait a couple of more years, have a child, that sort of thing? What happened to change your mind?"

"You are right, Victor. I had originally planned to do all that. However, I had a premonition several weeks ago that frightened me." She smirks knowingly. "Yes, imagine, me being frightened of anything. I went to my gynecologist, and she confirmed my fears. To be blunt, I likely can't conceive, and if I did, most likely I could not carry a child to term. So you see, there is nothing to be gained by waiting any longer. Physically and mentally, I am ready. Emotionally, I will be by then."

"I am sad to hear that, but I respect your decision. I will make sure I am in New York to be there for you."

That night, Arpel makes the mistake, in his mind, of arriving at the bar before Alfred does. He has to sit through the opening act for the Czarista Cosmonuts, some band called Creepz.

How can anyone claim that this garbage is music?

When Alfred finally does show up, he is disappointed to see that he has arrived alone. "Man, you got here early! The opening bands here usually stink! Were the Creepz worth hearing at all?"

Arpel shakes his head. "No. They did totally suck."

Alfred sits down and orders a beer.

"So, when will Zack be showing up tonight? You were saying that this was his favorite band and all."

"Man, that's another thing that really sucks. Zack can't make it tonight. He got really sick, flu or something. I hear Syd has to run the nets for him. Probably true, as the service has been a bit flaky tonight. Not seriously so, but certainly not up to his standards. I hear they are calling Emille in from Boston or some such nonsense." He gulps down his beer. "This sucks, man! Guess we will just have to rock on without him. The Cosmonuts are just so wicked cool! I've been waiting to see them for weeks."

While he keeps a poker face on the outside, Arpel is fuming on the inside. He needs to think of a plan B, and fast. He does not dare stay in this city past the weekend. He has to move on. His visions have told him that. He has to be on the road to New Orleans by sundown on Saturday or he will lose the Lord's favor, something that he just cannot bear to do, not after that prideful debacle in Providence. No, sir. An idea does come to mind.

"Tell me, Alfred, if you needed to contact Madam Aurea directly, could you do it?"

A strange look crosses Alfred's face. "Actually, yeah, I could, man. Zack gave me her cell phone number. I have never used it. He said to make sure I had a really good reason to call her if I ever did."

Arpel looks Alfred straight in the eyes. "Answer me this then. If you could tell her where to find the nefarious Van Arpel, do you think that would fit the criteria of having a 'really good reason to call' her?"

"Uh…yeah, man, that would definitely be a good reason to call her." He shudders. "Well, except for the tiny little fact that I don't have the slightest idea where that murdering scumbag happens to be."

Arpel stands up. "Come with me, Alfred. I have a pretty good idea where he is. This is worth so much more than seeing this band perform. Of that you can be certain."

Alfred gets up and follows Arpel out of the club. His car is just around the corner, and they both get in.

As Arpel starts the car, Alfred looks at him quizzically.

"How would you know where Van Arpel is?"

Arpel grins. "I didn't say I knew for sure. Just that I had a pretty good idea, which was a lie actually, but this matters not when dealing with agents of the devil like you." He enjoys the sudden look of comprehension on Alfred's face. "Yes, I am Van Arpel." He then knocks Alfred out cold and speeds off into the nighttime traffic.

It is about midnight, and Aurea is alone in her house on Staten Island. Carol Ann and Paulina had gone out about a half an hour ago to go prowl Times Square. Paulina had been dressed stylishly earlier, but she left in her usual faux ninja garb. Aurea sighs, thinking that there is just no accounting for taste.

She is startled when her cell phone rings. She looks at the number. She is not familiar with it, but the name that flashes up seems to match a porfo that she vaguely knows of.

"This is Aurea."

An excited male voice comes on. "Yeah, Madam Aurea, this is Alfred. Listen, I have Van Arpel cornered here at the old Isidore's warehouse in Brooklyn. I think we can get this guy and end the menace. Yeah."

She can sense the stress in Alfred's voice, but she senses that he is sincere. He at least clearly believes he is dealing with Van Arpel. *What can it hurt to check this out? I will be a hero if I take him out.* "Listen, Alfred. You stay undercover, and do not attempt to approach this maniac until I arrive. It could take me about an hour since I am here on Staten right now. Where in Brooklyn is this warehouse?"

Alfred gives her the address. She thanks him and ends the call. She decides not to tell anyone else. She can certainly handle Arpel, especially if this porfo has the guy cornered. He will be well rewarded for his work, and she will get the accolades for taking him out without backup. She leaves in haste.

At about that time, Victor awakes from a rather fitful slumber with a sense of dread. He looks at his Ruby ring that he had set on his nightstand, and he puts it on. It does not glow, but he still cannot shake off the feeling. He gets up and splashes some water on his face and tries to concentrate. He can visualize an old, deserted warehouse down in Brooklyn. He really does not have a good working knowledge of New York City's streets away from the expressways, but he is getting the strong impression that it is just a couple of blocks off Flushing. He has driven here this time, so he does have his trusty .38 with him. He makes sure it is fully loaded, and then he gets dressed. He slips the gun into his shoulder holster. He has the strong sense that he is going to need it. He takes the elevator down to the parking garage, gets in his car, and drives off onto the streets of Manhattan, heading for Brooklyn. He will let his intuition guide him. He feels in his bones that this is not any sort of false alarm. Something very dangerous is going down.

Aurea arrives at the warehouse at about twelve forty-five in the morning. A car that she does not recognize is parked outside; otherwise, the derelict building appears very much empty. She notes with satisfaction that her ring is not glowing, which means the porfo is not in distress. She decides to risk making a phone call to Alfred.

"Madam Aurea, is that you?"

“Yes, Alfred. I’m here. Where are you? Are you still safe?”

A blood-curdling scream comes out of the cell phone. “No! He’s got me! He’s dipping my hand into a kettle filled with acid! Ah!”

Without thinking, she drops her cell phone to the ground and crashes through the door, which gives easily under her preternatural strength. She rushes in and barrels through a second door as well. She smashes through a third door and suddenly feels herself drenched in a foul smelling liquid. As she feels her strength diminishing, she mutters, “Goldenrod.” She stumbles through the last door and falls into a net, which then automatically sweeps her up, and thus she swings, trapped in the net a few feet off the dirty floor. She howls in rage. She will be as weak as a normal human for several hours, if she has several hours. She looks over and sees Arpel laughing maniacally as Alfred continues to scream in pain.

“Let him go Arpel. I know he isn’t the one you want. You caught me because I underestimated your cunning. I had no idea you knew anything about goldenrod oil. That was never part of your modus operandi.”

Arpel laughs with mirth. “This fool told me all about goldenrod oil! Of course, he was bragging about how he used it to score with undead chicks.” He looks over at the whimpering Alfred. “Well, I hope you said your prayers, Alfred, because now I will send you to eternal damnation. Say hi to Satan for me.”

Alfred looks over at Aurea and manages to mouth, “I’m sorry,” before Arpel puts a bullet into the back of his head.

Arpel then walks over to the shivering Aurea. He moves quickly and takes off her ring. “You won’t need that anymore. Besides, it would ruin my night if some of your friends were to show up before I had my fun. You are an elder, and I want you to cease to exist slowly and painfully. Once I am through with you, they will only know who you were because I am going to videotape this whole process and leave a copy here. I am sure it will be quite satisfying.” He laughs. “It will be the first undead snuff film! I love it!”

"Despite your delusions, Mr. Arpel, we vampires are not undead. We do live. It is simply that we become different when we are transformed. Surely poor Abigail, your sister, tried to explain that."

Arpel smirks. "I have heard that many times, fiend. The Lord has told me that is not so. I am his instrument. By dealing with the likes of you, I am buying my sister's way out of hell when the time comes."

"Another delusion on your part, I fear. From what I understand, by the tenets of your faith, souls are saved by the grace of God. He would not hold a soul ransom for someone else to bail out. Abigail is no more evil now than when she was a mortal. Besides, if we really were 'creatures of Satan,' as you accuse us of being, then wouldn't crosses and the like destroy us? You know full well such things are harmless to us."

"I've had enough of your lies, elder. You are all evil. I will put an end to your madness!"

Victor pulls into the derelict warehouse's parking lot right about this time. His ring had glowed briefly when he came close to the warehouse, but now, it simply looks normal. He reaches out psychically and determines that Aurea is inside and in deep trouble. He can also sense a presence that feels like some kind of psychic void.

That must be Van Arpel. I better figure out a way to get in here and put the drop on him before he manages to destroy Aurea. I wonder why she came here alone.

He draws his gun and makes his way around the back of the building. He sees the battered door that Aurea has gone through, but he does not think he can catch this guy by surprise going in that way. He also concentrates on the ring and makes it glow. He does not know if anyone will arrive in time to help him, but he figures it is worth a shot.

He finds a door in the back and opens it carefully. Thankfully, it does open with a minimum of creaking, not that Arpel will hear him since he is laughing maniacally and ranting on about Satan and eternal damnation and undead fiends. Hearing Aurea's cries, he knows that she is injured, so time is of the essence, but so is stealth. He pauses and focuses himself, clearing his mind to concentrate solely on the task at hand. If he wants to survive this night, nothing less will suffice. He then directs a thought at Aurea, managing to break through the turmoil swirling through her mind.

I'm in the building. I'm trying to be quick and quiet at the same time. It's definitely a challenge with all the junk back here. Keep him occupied, and don't give me away.

A thought comes crashing loudly into his skull.

Hurry! This maniac wants to drench me in acid and set me ablaze. He already killed Alfred, and he has been cutting out his organs and throwing them into pots of acid. Please! Let's end his reign of terror tonight! Save me, Victor!

Victor has his gun ready and makes his way to the door. He watches his footing, as there are plenty of glass shards and other types of debris strewn about. It seems like forever, but in about a minute, he has reached the door to the part of the warehouse where Aurea and Van Arpel are playing out their dialogue. Aurea is largely sobbing and pleading while Arpel laughs and makes ridiculous statements. He opens the door to this scene of horror. He lets his eyes scan the room briefly. He sees Alfred, obviously dead. He sees Aurea trapped in a net a few feet off the floor. He figures that it is standard cargo netting, so he wonders why she cannot just tear her way out of it. He then gets a good look at Arpel. He is preparing to spray Aurea with caustic acid. This he simply cannot allow.

"I hope you like intense burning pain, you undead wench!" Arpel howls with glee.

Aurea screams as Arpel starts to lift the device, finger on the trigger.

"Drop it, Arpel!" Victor shouts. "You won't leave this building alive unless you do!"

Van turns away from Aurea. A look of surprise crosses his face. His eyes are wild as he focuses on Victor. He looks down at Victor's ring, which is clearly glowing. "You've ruined my plan for giving her a slow death! No matter. I'll douse the undead fiend, and then I'll kill you before your friends arrive!"

It seems to happen in slow motion from Victor's perspective. Arpel starts to turn back toward Aurea, his laughter sounding triumphant. Aurea's eyes are filled with fright. Victor's first shot hits Arpel high on the left shoulder. The sound of his clavicle cracking from the impact seems loud. Still, Arpel tries to get the device ready to spray Aurea with acid. Victor's second shot severs Arpel's spinal cord and crashes into his heart. In a second, he falls to the floor in a heap. His acid-spraying device also falls harmlessly to the ground. It takes Victor a second to realize that Arpel is down and Aurea is trying to speak to him.

Aurea is sobbing. "Please get me out of here, Victor. I haven't been so frightened in centuries. How did you know I was even here?"

Victor kicks at the still form of Arpel, making sure he is dead. He then walks over to the pulley and pushes a button, slowly lowering Aurea to the ground. "Actually, I had no idea you were here until I arrived and sensed your presence. I also sensed a psychic null that must have been the late, unlamented Van Arpel. I came here because, essentially, my intuition insisted on it. I sensed grave danger, but I did not know to whom or for what reason. I learned long ago never to second-guess my intuition."

Once Aurea is safely lowered to the floor, she walks over to Victor and holds him tightly. She is trembling and sobbing fiercely. "Until I heard your thoughts, I was certain that the assassin would kill me." She looks over at the lifeless Alfred and scowls. "That faithless porfo told Arpel of the one substance that makes us so we are temporarily sapped of our great strength and become like a normal human. He hit me with a couple liters worth of goldenrod oil. I probably won't be back to normal before sunset." She wails in pain and fury. "I came here alone because I thought I could take that guy out by myself. I thought Alfred had the drop on him. It turned out he was a pawn in the madman's game."

At that point, Paulina Wong comes into the room through the same door Aurea had, followed by Carol Ann. Paulina looks around and swiftly assesses the situation. She looks at Victor, who is still holding the sobbing Aurea. “So he’s dead? You killed Van Arpel, and you saved Aurea? That is most impressive, sir.”

Carol Ann makes a move toward Aurea, who looks at her with tear-filled eyes. “You had best not touch me right now, dear friend. The fiend doused me with goldenrod oil. Don’t touch the bottom of your shoes.”

Carol Ann nods. “Shall I tell the others to clear off? Three others and two porfi are waiting in the parking lot to see if we need help.” She looks around and grimaces. “Maybe we need help cleaning up this mess.”

Aurea composes herself. “Yes, please do have them come in. Others should see this and hear what I have to say.” She looks at Victor with admiration. “We have a hero in our midst, and I will see to it that this is properly noted. Then, yes, we will have to have this place scoured. No trace of what happened here must remain.”

Carol Ann gestures, and the others enter. One of the vampires that enter radiates immense power. Victor notes the Emerald ring on her hand.

This one scans the room and smirks at the lifeless body of Van Arpel. “I see that you live, sister. That is well.” She looks over at Victor and nods. “I see we have you to thank for this, Victor Trent. I am Patsy Plontz, Aurea’s Emerald counterpart here in New York City. It is an honor to meet you, even in circumstances such as this.”

Aurea gives Victor a hug and steps away. She then scans the room, making eye contact with all present. “I trust someone is recording this? I will want a feed to Ruby and Emerald nets, as well as a message sent to Order Sapphire.” Paulina shows Aurea her phone with video running. “Let it be noted that the scourge that terrorized us all, Van Arpel, deranged brother of Abigail Arpel, met his end at the hands of our brother, Victor Trent. Sadly, we must mourn the loss of porfo Alfred Connelly. Though he unwittingly served the ends of this madman, I am certain it was not done in malice. As anyone can see, he died most painfully." She then fixes her gaze on Victor. "You saved my life. As per the protocols, I now owe you a blood debt. I acknowledge this in front of all assembled and all those who view this. I ended up in this predicament because I was foolish and headstrong. I would have been at least grievously burned, if not killed, before anyone else would have arrived, if, in fact, anyone would have because he took my ring. You may ask of me what you will, Victor."

Victor is dumbstruck. "I was only following my intuition getting here. I knew there was a dangerous situation, but I had no idea who it involved, only that I needed to get here." He scans the room, studying the faces of the assembled. "I acted to defend the life of a friend. I don't feel like a hero, but then I have no clue what that is supposed to feel like. I took a man's life because I had to. It was the right thing to do." He looks at Aurea. "You say you owe me a blood debt. Well, I understand the protocols well enough to know why you do. That is part of the new set of ethics I am having to learn because, frankly, I would expect nothing further than your continued friendship, were this not a matter of honor, that and your promise to not once again go into a situation similar to this without some backup."

Paulina stops the transmission as Aurea takes Victor aside. "You are a noble ancient soul, sir. That is abundantly clear. Under normal circumstances, I would offer myself to you as part of your reward, an entertaining way to work off a blood debt. However, I can tell that you would turn me down, politely, of course. You have your sights set on another, whether you know this consciously or not." Aurea laughs. "I wonder if she even knows it herself. No matter. We can discuss a proper compensation later. Best to have the others clean this place out and go about their business."

Carol Ann walks over, holding her phone out. She hands it to Victor. "It's a call from the Richmond motherhouse. Abigail Arpel, Van's sister, wishes to speak to you."

Victor puts the phone to his ear with a grimace. "I am sorry that I had to take your brother's life, Abigail."

"Don't be. He has terrorized me for the last two years. He would call me and brag every time he took out a vampire. He was insane. I will mourn him, yes, but then, I have been mourning him for some time. I hope we will be able to meet soon so that I can thank you in person. Good night."

As Victor hands the phone back to Carol Ann, Patsy comes forward. "I've made some calls. My people can get this taken care of. I see Paulina has already retrieved a bag of rings from Arpel's corpse. You take out the Ruby rings, and I will see that Sapphire gets back what is theirs. I will take care of my Order's rings personally." She looks at Aurea. "You know, except for yours, each of these rings represents a lost comrade." She then looks at Victor. "You are also entitled to a rather substantial reward. People from all three orders contributed to it. Sure, some of us would have liked to have caught that guy alive, but that was not to be. Thank you for saving my friend. I look forward to seeing you again under better circumstances."

Victor escorts Aurea out to her car and puts her into the passenger seat. Paulina gives him a hug.

"What a night it has been. Bet you never thought you would be saving an elder's hide. Maybe this will get her to calm down a little. Powerful she certainly is, but she isn't invincible. None of us are. Oh, I found her phone on the ground. I will give it back to her. Good night, Victor." She gets into the driver's side and pulls out of the lot with the still-stricken Aurea, who does manage a small wave.

Victor looks out on the lot toward the eastern horizon, the first light of false dawn showing. Carol Ann walks up to him. "Are you going to be okay? Do you need anything? That's a lot to have to endure. I am guessing you have never had to kill anyone before, at least not in this incarnation."

"No, Carol Ann. That was my first this time around. I feel numb inside. It was the right thing to do; he deserved it, but that does not make me feel better. I'm glad I drove here and had my gun with me. I don't know what I would have done without it. No, I don't need anything besides time to reflect. Thanks."

She nods. "Well, don't worry about the reception. I am canceling it. I mean, she won't be in any mood to socialize, and, frankly, I don't think any of us will be." She gives him a kiss. "Well, here's hoping your day at the UN won't be anything like this night has been."

Victor scowls at that. "Well, I'm sure it won't be. I will stay in town tonight anyway and check in with you to see how things are."

With that, they both leave the parking lot. Emerald Order people start the cleanup process inside.

Patsy looks at Arpel's body and motions to a porfo. "See that the head is kept intact. We need to examine his brain."

"As you wish it, Madam Patsy."

Victor returns to his hotel room after another mind-numbing day at the UN. He had a hard time paying attention to what was going on at the conference. He is still coming to grips with what had transpired at the warehouse in Brooklyn. He places his laptop on the desk and falls onto the bed and stares at the ceiling for a while, trying to center himself.

After a few minutes, he gets off the bed and goes over to the window. He looks outside at the traffic and the people going by. He takes his cell phone out of his pocket and dials Carol Ann as he had promised to do.

She answers on the second ring, sounding unnaturally subdued. "Hi, Victor. How has the rest of your day been? I trust it hasn't been as bizarre as how it started."

"It went precisely as I would have expected, a whole lot of people talking about things they really know very little about and proposing solutions that would be anything but. How is Aurea faring? How are you doing?"

"I'm all right. Thank you for asking. Aurea is finally resting. As you can imagine, she is still badly shaken up, more, I think, for how close she came to being destroyed. If you hadn't been in the city and been a returned elder, she likely would not have survived. Patsy told me she felt something, but it wasn't enough for her to go on, at least not until you arrived at the warehouse and sent out your distress call. Her rashness was nearly her undoing this time. She owes you a lot for this, and she knows it."

"That's probably the hardest concept for me to accept, the notion that Aurea incurred a blood debt to me because I saved her. Please don't misunderstand me. I have studied the protocols, and I know this is a matter of honor. I certainly do not and will not make light of it. I understand why the Vitzameri owes her a blood debt because he seriously wronged her. Aurea did not wrong me. Granted, what she did was foolish, but still, I am having qualms about it. Will this protocol system ever make sense to me?"

Carol Ann sighs audibly. "It will make more sense to you as you live it. After a few decades, it will become second nature. I can tell that you are exhausted, so we can talk more about this another time if you like. I hope you have an uneventful night and a safe trip back to the imperial city."

"Thanks for listening, Carol Ann."

Victor ends the call and yawns deeply. Still, he ponders the statement that Aurea made after announcing the death of Van Arpel and the existence of the blood debt. *I have my sights set on another even if I don't know it consciously? I wonder what she meant by that.*

Victor's cell phone chimes. He looks at the caller ID and smiles when he sees the name. "Hello, Cassie Mae. How are you doing?"